No Longer Strangers

— A NOVEL —

OTHER BOOKS BY
RACHEL ANN NUNES

No Longer Strangers

— A NOVEL —

Rachel Ann Nunes

DESERET
BOOK

Salt Lake City, Utah

Library of Congress Cataloging-in-Publication Data
Nunes, Rachel Ann, 1966–
    No longer strangers / Rachel Ann Nunes.
      p. cm.
    ISBN 1-59038-475-X (pbk.)
    1. Children of missionaries—Fiction. 2. Adopted children—Fiction.
3. Mormon families—Fiction. 4. Zoologists—Fiction. 5. Adoption—Fiction.
6. Orphans—Fiction. I. Title.
    PS3564.U468N6 2005
    813'.6—dc22   2005008625

Printed in the United States of America   72076
Publishers Printing, Salt Lake City, UT

10   9   8   7   6   5   4   3   2   1

To Jordan, my 4.0 high school junior,
who has suffered an allergy to cold (cold urticaria)
since he was eight years old. You are an example to me
of what can be done when you work to attain goals.
I'm so proud of you!

Acknowledgments

Thanks go to Jana, my wonderful product manager; Suzanne, my editor extraordinaire; Sheryl, the skilled and long-suffering art director; and all the many others at Deseret Book who work hard to typeset, print, market, and sell my books. I so appreciate every one of you. You're the best!

Chapter One

Mitch Huntington groaned as the sound of the doorbell sliced into his unconscious thoughts. Reluctantly, he swam through the murky waters of sleep and managed to open one eye, the other still firmly smashed into his pillow.

"Coming," he called in a croaky voice that wouldn't have made it past his bedroom door, much less carried to the porch. The brightness spilling in from his window was painful, and he blinked that single eye several times to help it adjust. Who would wake him up before eight on a Saturday morning? He hoped it wasn't one of the neighbor children, newly let out of school for the summer. They often came to see his animals.

Ding, dong!

"All right already!" He put both hands on the bed and heaved himself off his stomach, twisting his legs to the floor. Trying to stand, he tripped over the tennis shoe Muffin the Mutt had been using to sharpen his teeth. Mitch's face hit the carpet, and the top of his head slammed against the ten-gallon glass aquarium that was home to a pair of his gerbils. Or had been. The two animals were no longer alone.

Mitch opened his other eye, now pressed up close to the glass. He

1

blew his hair out of his face. "One, two, three, four, five, six . . ." That was all he could count before Hiccup covered her new babies, aided by Elvis, her faithful companion of two months.

"Well, looks like you had a productive night," Mitch muttered, more than a little irritated. He'd spent half the night waiting for the blessed event and had missed it entirely.

The doorbell rang three more times, staccato and short, like an impatient woman tapping her foot. Mitch hauled himself to his feet and hurried to the door of his room, stubbing his toes first on the edge of the gerbil cage and then on the smaller aquarium containing Lizzy Lizard, his western fence lizard, who was fighting a cold with antibiotics and two extra heating lamps.

"That's it!" Mitch yelled, grabbing his sore toes and hopping around on the other foot. "Tonight, you're all going back to your own room. I don't care how many babies you have or how many respiratory diseases you get!"

Hobbling down the hall and through his living room, he opened the front door in time to see a woman in a trim black suit moving gracefully down his steps.

She turned. "Oh, good, you're home," she drawled with a faint accent Mitch thought might be Texan. She was an attractive woman with long black hair, a full mouth, and dark eyes that were clearly annoyed. Mitch straightened his tall frame that was still too thin despite the ten pounds he'd recently gained. Belatedly, he realized he was wearing his black pajama bottoms, spotted with white soccer balls and topped by a black, short-sleeved T-shirt.

"I had a late night," he felt obliged to say. He drew a hand through his brown hair, which was barely short enough to be acceptable to his family. Parted near the middle, his hair reached to the bottom of his ears, falling forward whenever he dipped his head.

"You're Mitch Huntington?" She sounded as if she hoped he'd say no.

2

He wondered if he'd done something wrong. "Yes. Why do you ask?"

"I'm Dolores Clark, attorney for Lane and Ashley Grayson."

"Lane and Ashley?" Mitch's stomach twinged, warning that something was wrong. He and Lane had been like brothers during their missions to Brazil, sweating together over Portuguese verbs while tracting in the humid temperatures near the equator. Their friendship had continued after they left Brazil—even when Ashley Steele entered the picture. In fact, if Lane hadn't married Ashley, Mitch would have tried to marry her himself. Instead, he'd remained their best friend.

Dolores Clark shifted her slight weight to her other foot. Her high, thin-heeled shoes didn't look comfortable, and Mitch was sure they added to her impatience and irritation. "Yes," she said. "I'm their attorney and the executor of their estate."

"They're in Texas," he began. "Wait a minute, did you say executor? What do they need an executor for?" His friends and their baby daughter had moved from Utah to Texas six months earlier when Lane graduated from Brigham Young University and started a new job. Mitch had kept in touch by phone and e-mail. Only last week Ashley had e-mailed a snapshot of their family. He'd marveled at how much Emily Jane had grown. Looking like a baby doll, she was in her mother's arms, one hand caught in Ashley's long curly red hair, as it always seemed to be. They had all looked happy.

"You haven't heard?" For the first time there was an emotion other than annoyance in the lawyer's pretty face. But what? He couldn't tell.

He was beginning to feel light-headed. "Heard what?" he asked, gripping the doorway.

"Five days ago the Graysons were killed in a boating accident. I'm sorry, I thought you might have heard."

Mitch shook his head slowly, knowing there was no one to tell him anything. Lane was an only child whose parents had died when he was in high school. Ashley's mother had died when she was a child, and she hadn't talked to the rest of her family since they'd disowned her when she joined the Church four years ago. "Lane and Ashley didn't have anybody," he said for the lawyer's benefit, still reeling from shock. "Except each other . . . and me."

"I know. That's why I'm here. You're listed in their will."

Mitch stepped out onto the porch and sat down in the doorway, tears blurring his vision. He felt sick and dizzy, as he did each time his allergy to cold temperatures kicked in. But the porch had been warmed by the morning sun, and there wasn't even a whisper of a breeze in the air. Not since his brother-in-law's death a year and a half ago had Mitch felt so horrible and lost. "Oh, Lane," he murmured. He couldn't even say Ashley's name. And when he thought of the baby . . .

Tears slid down his cheeks. "She was only a year old," he murmured. "That's too young. Way too young." He tried telling himself it was better that they were all together, but he found it impossible to bear the thought of never seeing them again in this life. Why hadn't he gone to visit six weeks ago in April for Emily Jane's first birthday? They'd invited him, but instead he planned to fly out during his vacation time in August. He let his head drop to his hands and wept.

A comforting hand squeezed his shoulder. He was surprised to find the lawyer hunched down next to him. "I'm sorry," she said softly. "I did try to call repeatedly this week before the funeral, but you don't have an answering machine, and there was no time for a letter. Emily Jane needs to get on with her life. Of course, I have some papers you'll need to see." She tapped the briefcase she'd set down on the porch. Standing, she went down the stairs toward the sedan parked out in the street.

Mitch stared after her. *What did she just say?*

The car door opened before Dolores reached the sidewalk, and a short, older woman emerged with a baby in her arms and a fat diaper bag slung over her shoulder. She moved aside as Dolores brought out a car seat and a large suitcase.

Mitch stared, hope bursting to life in his heart. The baby had a mass of fine, curly hair a shade or two paler than a carrot. Just like

Ashley's. *Emily Jane,* he thought. Could it be? He urged himself to meet them halfway, but he only managed to stand, his tears abruptly halted and drying on his cheeks in the morning sun.

The short woman came up the stairs and pushed the baby in his direction. "I was the Graysons' neighbor," she said, with a Texas drawl much heavier than the lawyer's. "I run a day care. Emily Jane came over in the mornings while Ashley went to school. She's been staying with me since the accident."

Mitch's arm instinctively secured the baby to his chest. She opened her blue eyes wide at him as though unsure how to react. "Emily Jane," he breathed. He recognized her now. Would she remember him?

The baby glanced at the short woman and then back at him. Her face wrinkled as she started to cry. "It's okay," he murmured, patting her back awkwardly. He tried to return her to the woman, but she shook her head.

"Better keep her," she said, her hazel eyes kind and compassionate. "She'll stop in a minute. Usually she's good with strangers, but she's been sad and upset. Probably misses her parents. She'll get used to you. Just talk to her."

The baby's large eyes reminded him of a wounded or frightened animal. "Don't worry, sweetie," he told her. "You remember me, don't you? Okay, so maybe you don't. Anyway, I know your mom and dad." He stopped. He *had* known them. He tried to swallow a sudden lump in his throat, biting back his own tears. "It's okay. Don't cry, sweetie. You know what? I have something to show you. Come inside with me." Vaguely aware of the women following him, he walked to the large dog kennel in the kitchen where Muffin was yipping in excitement.

"This is Muffin," Mitch said to Emily Jane. "He normally sleeps in my room, but I had to put him in here last night. I promise he won't hurt you." He bent down with the baby on one knee and opened the kennel door.

Muffin shoved his wet nose into Mitch's hand before exuberantly sniffing Emily Jane. The baby's tears stopped, but she clutched at Mitch in fear, trying to climb up his chest.

"Oops. Sorry. Down, Muffin! Down boy!" Mitch stood to keep Emily Jane out of reach. At least she was no longer crying.

"I'll leave these papers," Dolores said, placing something on the table. "There's a list of finances and other items regarding custody. You'll need a lawyer here to finalize everything. As Emily Jane's lawyer, I'll be happy to help things along in Texas, although you may have to make an appearance there. I'll keep in contact with you about that and about the rest of the estate. I'll need to know what you want done with the house and car. And of course the Division of Child and Family Services here will be in contact to make sure everything's okay on this end."

"The suitcase by the door has Emily Jane's clothes," the older woman added. Mitch was too stunned to reply to either of them.

"We'll get out of your hair now." Dolores walked to the door, followed by the other woman whose name Mitch had never learned.

"Wait! What about Emily Jane?" He hefted the baby in his arms.

Dolores arched an impatient brow. "You're her godfather, aren't you? The will stated clearly that I was to bring her to you."

Mitch remembered signing something in front of a lawyer soon after Emily Jane was born. Ashley, weighed down with the responsibility of new parenthood, had planned for every possibility. "If something ever happened to us, I'd want Emily Jane to be raised in the Church," she had said. "I can't bear the thought that she'd go to my dad or my sister. It would be different if they were members. Please, Mitch. Will you do this for me?"

Mitch had agreed—anything to set Ashley's mind at ease. Besides, he'd loved Emily Jane from the minute she was born. But he'd never imagined that being named her guardian would mean anything more than pony rides on his shoulders, presents at birthdays and Christmas, and maybe an occasional day at the circus. It simply couldn't mean that Emily Jane now belonged to him.

The women descended his steps, and Mitch panicked. It was one thing to be an exceptional uncle to five nieces and nephews or to be a godfather—but to be solely responsible for a child?

"Hey, I don't know anything about babies!" he protested. "What am I going to do with her?" He felt guilty saying the words with little Emily Jane watching him so seriously, her lightly freckled face rigid with fear.

Dolores shrugged. "We just came to bring her to you. Of course, if you'd rather, Mrs. Sumner and I can turn her over to Texas state custody. I'm sure an adoptive family could be found for her. She's young enough."

Ashley's voice echoed in his head: *I'd want Emily Jane to be raised in the Church.*

"No," he said, backpedaling quickly. "We'll be okay. I have sisters with children who'll help. My mom lives only fifteen minutes from here. Less, maybe."

He was about to say more to convince them, but the women nodded and continued to their car, relief apparent on their faces. As they drove away, Mitch clung to Emily Jane as tightly as she clung to him.

Chapter Two

Cory Steele held her breath. She was in more danger right now than at any other time during this photo shoot—maybe more than she had been at any other time during the fourteen months she'd lived in the Amazon. The Brazilian jaguars, called *onças,* had so far allowed her to crouch this close to their den located under the heavy foliage, but if she made one false move, the mother might decide to retract that reluctant invitation. Of course, Cory was prepared for that, with a tranquilizer gun and her .38 special, though she wondered if she would be capable of using the handgun on one of these magnificent ebony creatures.

Sweat ran in rivulets down the back of her green tank top. The evening temperature had dropped from the high nineties of midday, but the humidity made her clothes stick to her skin. She longed to remove her green cap and free her sweaty head from its plastered layering of reddish orange ringlets. But she didn't dare. The jaguars could be startled by much less.

The calls of several macaws and a monkey or two echoed over the jungle. Cory wondered idly if Meeko, the official camp mascot, was nearby, if maybe he had followed her as he sometimes did. Even if he had, he wouldn't come to her now; she was much too close to the jaguars.

She took one hand from her digital camera and ran it across her forehead, wiping the wetness on the strong, lightweight pants that were a must for squatting in bushes. She'd removed her long-sleeved shirt, though, unable to bear the heat. The tips of her fingers grazed the long new scratch on her arm, extending from her shoulder and curving down to her elbow. That was the trouble with a tank top, but at the moment she would rather have scratches than endure long sleeves. Chewing off a piece of fingernail, she waited. She was good at waiting.

The mother jaguar had dragged home a small white-tailed deer for her twin cubs to devour. One of the cubs tugged the carcass away from his sibling. The sibling pounced, growling under his breath. The mother watched with apparent unconcern. Cory had seen this scene repeated often over the years with different animals, and she had lost her initial sense of disgust. Animals needed to eat; they were only following instinct.

She began snapping photos. Soon the cubs finished eating and started playing, jumping over their mother and wrestling each other until at last they sprawled, exhausted, their fat tummies moving in and out with their quick breaths. It was great footage.

When she had exhausted the memory card in her digital camera and taken several rolls of 35mm film in the old Nikon that had been her high school graduation present eight years ago, Cory was satisfied. More perfect shots for *Wildlife Conservation*, the magazine that paid her well to do the work she loved.

"Next it'll be *National Geographic*." The idea brought a smile.

She inched backward through the bushes that had made such a great hideout these past few days. At first her muscles rebelled from the long hours of inactivity, but gradually she made progress. Her foot stepped on a thin branch. *Snap!*

The mother jaguar's black ears shot forward, and she gave a

warning growl to her cubs. The small black shadows jumped to their feet and hid, whining, behind their mother.

Silently cursing her clumsiness, Cory froze, debating whether she should remove the tranquilizer gun from the sling around her shoulder. She broke into a cold sweat. With a loud snort, the mother jaguar prodded her cubs into their den. Before entering herself, she gave one last look around, accompanied by a low, challenging growl. Then her inky body disappeared into the bushes.

Cory moved again, still slowly, feeling unseen eyes upon her. Only when she was a hundred yards from the den did she breathe a sigh of relief. She no longer felt hot. Digging into her pack, she saw that her thermometer read eighty degrees. Practically cold by Amazon standards. At least for early June. She took a swig of warm water and pulled off her green cap, fluffing her hair from its plastered state. The orange-red locks fell in loose curls to her shoulders.

Refreshed, she clomped through the jungle in her hiking boots, following a path barely discernible to her eyes. The bamboos, trees, and creepers were so thick that at times she had to skirt around or climb over them. The great vastness and majesty of the Amazon amazed her at moments like this, and she savored the lush, unspoiled beauty. Several hundred yards from the jaguar den, she crossed under a group of dense trees, setting off a cacophony of jitters and calls from an audience of white-bellied spider monkeys. Laughing, she waved at them and continued on.

After a few more minutes, a small monkey skittered down from a low-hanging palm, landing on her pack and scrambling over to sit on her shoulder. "Hello, Meeko," she said. "Careful. You're scratching me."

The creature chattered, sounding seriously offended. Cory laughed. "I know you wanted to come with me. Good thing you were too scared. You'd hardly be a mouthful for that mother jaguar. Don't be mad. You know I have to earn a living, and as cute as you are, only so many magazines are looking for a picture of a dwarf cebus." She slipped him a piece of dried apple from her pocket, and he settled down to munch on his treat. Cory continued her way through the jungle, glad that Meeko had singled her out from the others at camp. He was more than a pet; he was a friend.

When Cory entered camp, several people looked up from the large communal table to greet her. She lifted a hand in response. The split-log table and cooking area was covered by a huge wooden canopy that shielded the cooking fires and the diners from rain during the wet season. The area was the main gathering place when work hours were over.

Many of the camp inhabitants were biologists on grants to study the Amazon, a few were photographers like herself, and several were writers. All had come to this camp off the Black River—*Rio Negro*— because of its remoteness and relative safety. The camp, built in a large, mostly natural clearing, was run by a group that sponsored the protection of the rain forest. For a nominal fee, anyone dedicated to a similar cause could pitch a tent and stay awhile. Dinner was provided by natives employed to tend the camp.

As Cory passed the table on the way to her tent, one of the men separated himself from the others and came to meet her. "Where've you been?" he asked, offering a piece of fruit to Meeko.

"Working. What else?" Cory smiled to soften the words. Evan Kammer was the talented writer who had been assigned by *Wildlife Conservation* to work with her. Standing a few inches taller than her five and a half feet, he was good-looking, though rather out of place in the Amazon. Oh, he wore the clothing and talked the talk, but she'd discovered quickly that he wasn't good for long-term hiking, lifting, or climbing. In fact, she wasn't sure she'd ever seen him break into a sweat that wasn't induced by the weather. Even so, he was witty, fun, and attractive, and she liked him a lot. They'd spent many hours together since his arrival two months ago.

"You left so early this morning." Evan fell into step beside her. "Why didn't you wait for me? It could be dangerous out there."

She rolled her eyes. "It's *always* dangerous out there. Look, I haven't answered to anyone since my father died, and I'm not about to start now. I'm a big girl. I can take care of myself." On her shoulder, Meeko chattered at him, echoing her annoyance. Swiftly touching her ear in a farewell caress, the little monkey jumped down and disappeared into the forest.

"Sorry." Evan made a face. "Must be the primitive male in me. Every time you're gone all day, I start to worry." He put his arm around her, and she had to admit it felt good having someone worry about her. There hadn't been anyone like that in a long time.

"I get better pictures when I'm alone," she said, fighting the tenderness.

"Yeah, but it'd be funner with me."

Okay, so she probably should have let someone know where she'd be and what time to expect her back. People here looked out for each other. Of course, the last time she'd told Evan where she'd be, he'd appeared with a picnic lunch and a bottle of wine. Not exactly her idea of a successful photo shoot, especially since he lacked patience when it came to waiting for just the right picture.

"Maybe next time," she said lightly.

"You took pictures with that?" He touched her Nikon hanging from its strap around her neck.

"Why not?" The camera had been top of the line when she'd graduated from high school, and it still turned out incredibly clear, brilliant photographs.

He shrugged. "Nothing. It just looks ancient."

"When you have as many writing credits as I have photo credits, *then* you can criticize my methods." Cory pushed off his arm and turned away from him. Her father and sister had given her the Nikon. Now her father was dead and AshDee out of her life as surely as if she had died. No one was separating her from this camera.

"Wait!" he said, looking contrite.

She stopped, knowing she'd overreacted. Evan had made a simple comment, and she'd jumped down his throat. He certainly hadn't meant to dredge up her past.

"I'm sorry," Evan continued. "That's the camera your father gave you, isn't it? I forgot. Forgive me? It's none of my business anyway. I don't even know how to take pictures." He sounded sincere, though Cory knew that before meeting her he'd asked the magazine to let him do both the writing and the photographs for the article. Even now he was constantly snapping pictures with a digital camera that was at least as expensive as hers, but she'd seen the resulting pictures and didn't worry about being replaced.

She blew out a sigh. "I'm sorry. It's been a long day."

"How about dinner?" He gave her a smile that melted her heart.

She laughed. "Beans and rice? Or rice and beans?" In the year she'd been in the Amazon, she had eaten her share of those two staples. Of course, the rice and beans were a far sight better than the wood worms, ants, and grasshoppers the wizened natives ate as appetizers. She usually had barbecued fish or fish stew each day as well. There was also a lot of poultry, but as a quasi-vegetarian the only meat she ate was fish. What she really craved was a large green salad. The natives served manioc, yams, palm hearts, and a variety of tasty fruits, but salad greens weren't popular.

"I was thinking we'd go into town," Evan offered.

"The boat's here?" It came once a week, bringing mail and supplies, and offering rides to anyone who wanted to return to what Cory termed semi-civilization in Novo Airão. The city was stuck in the nineteenth century, but after weeks or months in the jungle, its amenities were luxuries.

"It's been sighted downstream. Thought we'd take a ride in tonight. We'd be eating steak tomorrow." He smiled to show he was teasing about the meat.

If they went into town, Cory knew she might not make her picture deadline. In all, because of the boat schedule, the "dinner" meant a precious week lost—time she didn't know yet if she could afford. "In a few weeks, maybe," she said. "I'll be closer to finishing."

"Don't sweat it too much. If you don't get all the animals on the list, we'll go with what you have. I can write around it. They understand that you can't always find every animal exactly when you need to. Come on, let's go have a little fun. You deserve it."

For a moment, she was tempted. His words might be able to cover any deficiency on her part. Yet could she afford to let that happen? After all, her reputation was at stake. No, she wouldn't trust her career to anyone, not even Evan, who had as much on the line as she did. She'd been given a list of animals to photograph, and she would do everything in her power to find those animals and take the best pictures she possibly could. That was who she was. She sighed and shook her head. "Sorry."

He grimaced, but without rancor. "Work first, huh? Then play?"

"You got it." That was one thing she loved about him. He understood how important her work was to her. Or maybe he'd finally learned that when she dug in her heels, she wouldn't budge. "But you go ahead."

He stuck out his lower lip in a pout that reminded her of a little boy. "It wouldn't be any fun without you."

"Wait, then, and we'll go to Manaus instead. I'll need to send my agent the pictures. Since the city is so much bigger, it's bound to have better food. And I'd love to look around." She hadn't seen much of Manaus when she'd first arrived in Brazil, except the airport and the dock. Her subsequent trips to the city had been equally quick. Yes, it was high time she saw Manaus's fabled *Teatro Amazonas*, the opera house made of Italian marble and Bohemian crystal.

He grinned. "Deal."

"I'll help unload supplies from the boat," she said. "I'll need a shower first, though. I reek."

"Not to me." He tried to put his arm around her again.

"Yeah, right." She shook him off and headed for her tent.

The best thing she could say about the large, ugly, battered tent was that the heavy green canvas kept out the rain from all but the fiercest of storms. Taking a moment to download her images onto her laptop, she wished she could have afforded the equipment to give her e-mail capability in the forest. Of course, last year she'd been worried about spending too much of her dad's life insurance on the solar rechargeable laptop itself, the laptop CD burner, the new digital camera, extra memory cards, and writable CDs—not to mention her ticket to Brazil and the jungle supplies she had needed. She hadn't dared spend a penny more until the various magazines she worked for began sending their payments.

After this project, I'll buy the equipment, she promised herself. Sighing, Cory put her 35mm film in a black storage bag, locked the cameras, film, and laptop in her wooden chest and headed to the showers.

To get to the bathroom facilities at the edge of the camp, she had to pass the dozen or so tents scattered in three loose rows. Some were large and shared, while others could only hold a single person. New, elaborate versions sat feet away from older, plainer tents with large patches. Some tents had adjoining makeshift lean-tos for equipment storage. Lawn chairs, clotheslines, and small fire pits bordered all but a few of the tents. Bushes, trees, and native vegetation ringed the whole area and had to be constantly trimmed back to preserve the camp itself. The only permanent quarters were the camp leader's ramshackle cabin, the outhouse, the showers, and the log table with its wooden canopy.

Cory was glad to see the two-sided showers were empty. Though each side was separate, the inner wall didn't reach all the way to the ceiling, and seeing the top of someone's head on the other side always made her nervous—probably her strict Baptist upbringing.

Turning the knob that would send water down from the basin on the roof, she sighed with anticipation of her timed three minutes of spray. Besides capturing incredible scenes with her cameras, this was the best part of her day—when she washed away the sweat and grime that was her constant companion in the Amazon. The water was warm from a day of baking in the sun, but not too warm, and it felt good against her skin. She vigorously used a bar of strong, sweet-smelling native soap she had purchased months ago in Novo Airão.

Reluctantly, she left the shower, her time exhausted. In the small adjoining dressing room, she lathered her body with sunscreen and then sprayed herself liberally with bug repellent, wrinkling her nose at the smell. This was the worst part of living here, but worth it, especially as dusk approached. The flies and mosquitoes here made those back in her native California look miniature by comparison. After rubbing the spray from her hand onto her face, she dressed in a long-sleeved shirt and pants—all lightweight and also treated with repellent. It was still hot and humid—it was always hot and humid—but the long-sleeves were bearable at night and offered more protection from creepy crawlies. Glancing longingly back at the shower nozzle, she left the building, knowing that in fifteen minutes she'd need another shower.

Outside, Meeko swung down from a branch and landed on his customary place on her shoulder, wrapping his tail around her neck. Cory laughed. "Okay, you can come, but just so you know, Evan will be there. Don't be jealous."

Sure enough, Evan was waiting for her near the river with a small group of biologists and photographers, watching the boat glide up the river toward them. Several of the men were swimming in the water, and Cory briefly wished she'd delayed her shower. This part of the river was clean and perfect for swimming almost any time of day.

They helped unload the boat: rice and beans, specially ordered clothing, fruit, and soap. Her extra laptop battery had finally arrived, along with the engagement band the French male biologist had promised to a female American biologist. No doubt, there would be a wedding the next time the traveling minister came to camp.

"Letters," called a worker, slinging a small canvas bag over his shoulder. Marcia, an American who'd made no secret that she was in the Amazon only because of her biologist husband, held out her hands for the bag. Cory felt a twinge of remorse. If she'd been better at writing to her friends back in California, maybe she would receive more letters. Shouldering a large bag of rice, she headed back to camp.

Tonight would be a good time to write letters; maybe she'd even send one to AshDee. Her sister had written three times since the birth of her baby last year. The first time she'd sent a card for Cory's birthday. The second time she'd sent pictures of Emily Jane, or EmJay, as Cory thought of her. The infant was adorable, reminding Cory of AshDee when she was little. The images had softened Cory's heart as her sister's words hadn't, and Cory had sent her a single postcard in return. Perhaps AshDee was right. Perhaps it was time to look beyond their differences. Their father was dead now, and his severe Baptist, Mormon-hating upbringing no longer needed to come between sisters who had once meant everything to each other. Maybe someday Cory would even be able to forgive her sister for leaving.

Yet as she had the thought, the old bitterness rose in her throat. AshDee's betrayal of the family had caused their father much suffering, and, as Cory believed, had driven him to an early grave. He'd been hateful and bitter in the end. He hadn't allowed her to call her sister and tell her he was dying; not even with his last breath had he forgiven AshDee. Three years had passed, and Cory still hadn't told her sister he was gone. How could you give even a betrayer such as AshDee news like that in a postcard?

Unloading the boat didn't take long. Soon Cory let the last bag of rice plop onto the table and sat down to open her new battery. If she let the solar attachment on her laptop charge both her batteries, she would have a spare for important jobs, allowing her to crop and arrange her photos to perfection before burning CDs to send to her agent.

For what amounted to a few bucks, one of the natives would look out for her equipment while the batteries charged. The camp folk were an honest bunch, but one couldn't vouch for the neighbors that ran on four legs or swung in from the trees. There were also natives not attached to their camp who wandered in occasionally and who were prone to take anything that did not appear to have an owner. Their "findings" would eventually make their way to the black market, the proceeds going to feed their large families for another week.

Cory never understood how there could be people who lacked food here in the rain forest, where practically anything planted in the fertile soil would sprout roots and bear fruit, but there were many who seemed to go hungry. Then again, perhaps it was only the variety they craved. Variety from the endless beans and rice and grasshoppers.

"Cory! Are you listening?"

Cory blinked at Marcia, who hovered over her. "Did you say something?"

"You have an express letter from the States. Only sat in Manaus a few days."

Cory grabbed at the cardboard envelope, her surprise giving way to excitement. Meeko, sitting next to her on the table, tried to steal her prize, but she pushed him away. She wondered if the letter had anything to do with her twenty-sixth birthday tomorrow. But who could it be from? No one except Vikki Moline, her agent, had written her for months. The letter had to be from Vikki.

Unless it was from AshDee.

Cory's heart thumped painfully. She'd kept the card AshDee sent last year, and it now held the photographs of baby EmJay. Painful, precious reminders.

Swallowing hard, Cory examined the envelope. The return address wasn't from Texas where AshDee had moved or California where Vikki lived, but from Ohio, of all places. Who could have sent it?

She was disappointed to find the letter was indeed from Vikki, who was visiting her elderly parents in Ohio, touring Amish villages and buying Longaberger baskets. But scanning the letter, Cory's heartbeat quickened. She jumped from the bench and gave a loud "Whoop!" This was the best birthday present ever!

"What is it?" Evan looked up from the magazine he'd received.

"My agent says I'm in the final running for *National Geographic's* next spread on the Amazon!"

"Congratulations!" Everyone gathered around, pounding her back.

"Hey, I wonder if they need a writer," Evan said. "I don't suppose you could put in a good word for me."

Cory shook her head. "If you want it, have your agent talk to them. I don't even know if I have the job."

"You will." He winked at her, and Cory's insides turned warm. "And I will talk to my agent. Who knows? We might be working together again."

Cory smiled. Working with Evan on another project wouldn't be bad at all. What's more, getting the *National Geographic* job meant she could stay in the Amazon longer. The exposure she'd receive would build her reputation and possibly make her career. Others would line up to hire her. If she decided to work only for magazines wanting pictures of the Amazon, she might be able to stay in the country for several more years. She was happy with that idea. Here, she'd found meaning to her life, a reason for why she had been put upon the earth.

After a dinner of fish stew and tiny sun-dried cakes made of manioc root, Cory whistled as she strolled to her tent. Meeko trailed along in the trees, and Evan walked by her side. She felt content with the world. At the zippered canvas flap that served as her door, Evan put his arms around her, pulling her close for a kiss. Cory sensed by his touch that he would like to further their relationship, but as their kiss deepened, her father's face swam before her eyes. She broke away.

"What is it?" Evan said, his voice low and husky.

How to explain? All Cory's life, her father had taught her that God would not condone a physical relationship between a man and a woman, except in marriage, and while she told herself she no longer believed in God, her father's seeming presence in her mind wouldn't allow her to completely shake off his warnings. Her Baptist upbringing was too ingrained.

She wasn't sure that was such a bad thing. Though Evan was a nice guy, she had serious reservations about their involvement. Could their relationship endure beyond an assignment? Did she want it to? He was a talented, rising star, but she knew his attraction for her beloved Amazon didn't run deep. What else did they have between them besides the jungle and attraction? Only time would tell. One thing for sure, she didn't want to get stuck in a relationship that would imprison her. Living with her father had taught her that much. A part of her wished she could take Evan's attention a day at a time, that she could live for the moment, but she simply couldn't. Not yet. *There's time,* she told herself.

"Nothing's wrong," she said aloud. "I'm just exhausted."

He searched her face for a long, silent moment. "Okay, then. G'night, Sleeping Beauty." He kissed her again briefly on the lips.

She had a sudden urge to grab him and ask if he really thought she was beautiful, if she was a woman he might want to build a future with. *Ridiculous.* What was she thinking? She wasn't ready to be tied down. She was only now beginning to soar.

"Good night, Evan," she said softly.

Meeko swung down from the trees as Evan left, chittering at full volume and dispelling the sudden melancholy that overcame her. "Come on in, Your Highness," Cory said with a smile.

As she lay down on her cot, with Meeko snuggled up to her legs, Cory thought about what she might do for her birthday tomorrow. She hadn't told anyone in the camp, so she didn't expect a fuss, but she was beginning to regret that decision. She should at least have some sort of cake, even if it was made of manioc root. If he'd known, surely Evan would have arranged something.

Will AshDee send another card? The thought came unexpectedly but not surprisingly since she'd been thinking so much about her sister.

Pushing the unwanted question aside, Cory arranged her mosquito netting around her bed more securely. Satisfied, she clicked off her flashlight. Except for the critters attached to Meeko, she should be safe.

Some time later, a high-pitched wail pierced Cory's awareness. She jerked from a troubled sleep and stared into the darkness. Meeko was curled into an oblivious ball, sleeping peacefully. But something was wrong. Dreadfully wrong. The cry was different from the continuous chirping, buzzing, chittering, squawking, and growling that usually punctuated the Amazon. It was human.

She'd heard the same haunting cry before; AshDee had sobbed like this when their mother died. Closing her eyes, Cory could almost see two young girls clinging to each other in the night, crying softly so their father wouldn't hear.

A dream. Texas was thousands of miles away. AshDee wasn't alone. She had a husband and EmJay, the niece Cory had never met—might never meet.

The wail came again, this time accompanied by a soft Portuguese lullaby. Cory clutched at her blanket and listened. *Just a baby,* she told herself. Probably little Yedo, the black-eyed native child who stared at her from the sling on his mother's back.

When sleep finally came again, Cory's dreams were haunted. On and on went the lullaby whose meaning she could not discern.

Chapter Three

How hard can this be? Mitch stood on the porch in utter disbelief at the sudden change in his circumstances. He had raised ten dogs, fifty-four gerbils—more now that Hiccup's babies were here—eight hamsters, three guinea pigs, four parakeets, two lizards, a dozen rabbits, and singles of almost every variety of pet known to the general populace and many more that most people only read about in books. He *knew* about taking care of living creatures. He'd studied years of wildlife biology and now worked for a wildlife research company as a zoologist. True, his actual work rarely had anything to do with live animals, but he made up for that with his own pets. Given his experience, one small child shouldn't be much trouble.

Should she?

That was when Emily Jane started to cry. She didn't scream and pound her fists, or even struggle to get down but simply laid her head on his shoulder and cried. Tears leaked from her wide, frightened eyes, and her tiny shoulders shook with sobs. "Momma," he thought he heard her say but couldn't be sure. Emily Jane was thirteen months old—at what age did babies begin talking?

"Momma," Emily Jane repeated, this time unmistakably. She held out her small hand in the direction of the street, opening and closing the fingers as though trying to motion someone closer.

Mitch's heart ached. "Oh, sweetie. Your mommy would be here if she could. Your daddy, too. They love you so much." He rocked her as his own tears fell into her hair.

Muffin sat on the porch staring up at them, as confused as Mitch himself. Slowly, Mitch entered his house and shut the door. As Emily Jane's sobs grew weaker, he sat on the brown couch that had once graced the family room at his parents' house. The baby lifted her head and stared at him with watery blue eyes.

"I'm here," Mitch told her. "I know that's not good enough, but I'll do my best. Everything will be okay. I promise." Yet how could he ever do enough for this child who had lost everything?

Emily Jane must have found what she needed in his face because she laid her head back on his shoulder, gave a shuddering sigh, and closed her eyes. His arms tightened instinctively. Every now and then her body shook with a stray sigh. After long moments, her regular breathing told him she was asleep. Mitch found his own eyes growing heavy.

His stomach woke him shortly before noon, his neck and back aching from the unaccustomed position. Emily Jane still slept on his chest. The heat of tears had left her face, and she looked peaceful now. His heart swelled with the grim reality that awaited her upon waking, followed by an amazingly strong protective urge that left him both determined and breathless.

He decided the first order of business was to get himself something to eat. Afterward, he'd call his family for backup. Or at least his sisters. Only now did he remember his parents were visiting friends in Arizona.

Gently, he lowered the baby to the couch until she nestled with her back against the cushions. Then he sprinted to his room to find a pillow in case she rolled off. Thinking of his experiences with his nieces and nephews, he tried to remember what babies of her age could do, but his memories failed him. One of his sisters would know best—probably the oldest, Kerrianne, since she had three children, one a boy some months older than Emily Jane.

"Come on, Muffin," he called to the dog, sleeping in the middle of the carpet. He let Muffin out the back door, grabbed a blueberry bagel from the fridge, and went to find his cordless phone—which he eventually discovered in the garage next to the ferret cage. No wonder the lawyer hadn't been able to reach him. He was lucky the phone had any charge left. He really needed to invest in a good cell phone to replace the one he'd lost.

Sighing, he pushed Kerrianne's number. She didn't answer until the fifth ring, but he was used to that. Since her husband's death a year and a half ago, life was a struggle for her every day. "Hello?"

"Hi, it's Mitch. I need help. I have a baby here." A fresh wave of sorrow shook him as he thought of Lane and Ashley and the orphan now in his charge.

"A baby? Why do you have a baby?"

"Do you remember Lane, my first mission companion? And his wife, Ashley?"

"Of course I remember them. You were all inseparable for a while."

"Well, they moved to Texas and now"—Mitch took a deep breath for what he had to say next—"they're dead. A boating accident. Their lawyer brought their baby to me." His voice choked, despite his resolve to be strong so he wouldn't add to her already heavy burden. "But I don't know what to feed her—or anything."

"Okay," came Kerrianne's soothing voice. "First, take a deep breath."

Mitch obeyed, glad she believed him. His other sister, Amanda, would have asked if he were pulling her leg.

"Good. Now where's the baby?"

"Sleeping on the couch."

"How old did you say she is?"

"Thirteen months."

"Well, she should be in a crib or a toddler bed with a railing. I have either of those you can use. Caleb doesn't need them since he sleeps with me." Kerrianne paused briefly, as though remembering that her husband's death was the reason she had plenty of room in her own bed for little Caleb. "But we'll worry about that later. Can you see her?"

"Uh, no, I'm in the garage by the ferrets' cage."

"Well, go make sure she's okay. At this age you can't leave them alone for a minute. She might fall or wander off."

Mitch stumbled over his own feet as he ran through the kitchen and into the living room. The couch was empty, the pillow tossed onto the floor. "Uh, Kerrianne, she's gone."

"Is there an outside door open?"

"No."

"She can't be far. Do you have anything dangerous lying around?"

"How should I know?" His voice rose a notch. "What's dangerous to a one-year-old?"

"Everything." Her answer was far from reassuring.

Mitch first checked the spare room where he kept most of his animals. If Emily Jane climbed onto one of the cages, there could be a problem. But she wasn't there, so he headed for the bathroom.

"Oh," he groaned into the phone.

"What's wrong?"

"She's in the bathroom."

Kerrianne gave a little laugh. "I should have guessed. You'll have to keep the door shut or you'll—"

"Have toilet paper everywhere." Mitch surveyed the mess with dismay. Emily Jane was surrounded by unrolled paper. The cabinet under the sink was open as well, and a new roll was clutched in her tiny hands. Several chunks were missing.

"Uh, Kerrianne, she's eating the tissue." Sure enough, as she stared up at him with wide eyes, she brought the roll to her mouth and tore out another chunk. He reached out. "No, don't do that!" Her face scrunched, eyes filling with tears. He retracted his hand instantly.

"That's okay," Kerrianne said. "At least she's not playing in the toilet. A little paper won't hurt her. Just take the rest away."

"She doesn't want me to take it."

"Then get her something to eat in exchange."

"Like what?"

"Cereal, uh, anything small. Yogurt. Look, I'm coming right over. Stay put!"

Mitch hung up the phone. Kerianne lived in Pleasant Grove, about twenty minutes south of his place in Sandy. He would have to survive until she arrived. He knelt on the floor by Emily Jane.

"Here, sweetie, can you give me that?" He held out his hand. "I know you're hungry, and I admire you for trying to find something to eat, but I have much better stuff in the kitchen. Come on, give it to me."

Emily Jane smiled through her tears, a hesitant, toothy smile that brought a ray of light into his heart. She held out the roll. Just as his fingers touched it, she pulled it back . . . and laughed. Mitch laughed, too, but softly, so as not to startle her. He laughed until the laughter threatened to turn to tears.

"Why don't you keep it, sweetie? Give me your hand, and we'll walk to the kitchen. You can walk, can't you? I thought so." Emily Jane let him take her hand, and she walked beside him, still hugging the roll of tissue to her chest.

After rejecting the kitchen chairs as a possibility, he settled her on the linoleum floor. "Let's look in your bag and see what's there," he said. "Maybe that lawyer left something to eat." Thankfully, he found several jars of baby food, a baby spoon, a bottle, and a can of formula.

Emily Jane picked up the spoon, so Mitch opened a jar that contained broccoli. He scooped some out and gave it to her. She opened her mouth obediently but made a sour face as she ate.

"That bad, huh?" Mitch dipped his finger in the green mound clinging to the lid and tasted it. "Yuck. Don't they put any salt in this stuff?"

Emily Jane brought the roll of toilet paper up for another bite, but Mitch beat it to her mouth with the broccoli. She swallowed, but she definitely wasn't impressed. Vowing to find something more appetizing, Mitch sprang to his feet and rifled in the cupboard, his hands closing on a box of cornflakes. Between feeding Emily Jane bites of green gunk, he mixed her formula in a bowl and tossed in the cornflakes. When they had softened a bit, he gave her those. She let the roll of paper drop to the side and stuck her hand in the cereal.

"No," he began, but she was too fast. "Well, okay. Go ahead, help yourself. Why not?"

They sat on the floor for what seemed an eternity to Mitch. He was sure more food made it onto Emily Jane's face and clothes and the floor than into her stomach. After a while, she stopped eating and looked around the kitchen. He tried to feed her more, but she turned her head and grunted, pointing at the cupboard.

"What do you want?" Mitch stood, opened the cupboard, and peered inside. Nothing but more cereal boxes and a few dinner mixes. She grunted again, accompanied with a little whine.

He was relieved to hear the doorbell. "Come in," he yelled, but the door was already opening, revealing Kerrianne. She was average height but too thin at the moment. Her long dark blonde hair was pulled back in a ponytail, and she wasn't wearing makeup—he wasn't sure he'd seen her wearing makeup since Adam died. She had expressive blue eyes, high cheekbones, and fine pale skin.

Behind Kerrianne came his other sister, Amanda. "You should lock your doors," she said. Amanda was taller than Kerrianne, her hair shorter and blonder. Her eyes were like their father's—a bright emerald green. She wore dark eyeliner and mauve lipstick that emphasized her already striking features.

"You?" he asked Amanda, rising to meet them.

"What? Don't you recognize me with this big belly?" She was six months pregnant with her first child and rather sensitive about her size.

"I just didn't realize you were coming," he assured her.

27

"Kerrianne stopped to get me. Don't worry, we didn't bring the kids. They're all with Blake. Thank heaven it's Saturday."

Mitch was grateful. Amanda and her husband, Blake, had guardianship of Blake's cousin's two children. They were awesome, but with Kerrianne's three, the resulting noise was more than he could handle at the moment. This *one* child was already causing him plenty of stress.

"I fed her cornflakes and this broccoli—nasty-tasting stuff, if you ask me." He wrinkled his face in disgust.

Amanda shrugged. "Most babies don't seem to mind it."

"Mine did," Kerrianne said. "They would never eat anything from a jar."

"Mara didn't like the green ones either. But she gobbled up everything else." Amanda knelt on the floor by Emily Jane. The baby gazed at her warily, her eyes large and sad. At least she wasn't whining anymore.

Kerrianne squatted down next to Amanda. "What a pretty child! Look at those curls! I bet it'll stay curly, too."

Amanda reached out to touch a lock of Emily Jane's hair. "She's adorable. Even her little freckles are perfect." Emily Jane pulled away from Amanda's touch, a frown tugging at the corners of her mouth. Making a sympathetic noise in her throat, Amanda let her hand drop.

"She is cute," Mitch agreed. He felt more pleased than he had any right to at his sisters' praise, seeing that he had nothing whatsoever to do with Emily Jane's looks. "Before you came, she kept grunting and pointing," he added. "But I can't figure out what she wants."

"Maybe a diaper change?" Amanda suggested.

Kerrianne snapped her fingers. "A drink. I'll bet she wants water. It's taken months for Caleb to say water instead of pointing or grunting."

Mitch found the smallest plastic cup he owned, filling it halfway. "Do I just give it to her?"

"Sure." Amanda's green eyes twinkled with mischief.

Kerrianne snorted. "Only if you want her to dump it. Let me show you." Taking the cup, she held it to Emily Jane's mouth. The baby slurped eagerly. "You'll need a sippy cup. That way she can do it herself."

"Aw, but the regular cup is more fun," Amanda said with a laugh. "But you should always use a bib. Saves on cleaning."

"Yeah, she got broccoli everywhere. Cornflakes, too." Mitch wondered if he was supposed to wipe her mouth with a regular rag or something special. Amanda solved the problem by getting out a fresh cloth.

"Good thing about babies," she said, rubbing Emily Jane's face and hands. "They wash up nicely."

The baby started to cry at Amanda's ministrations, but Mitch picked her up, and her tears stopped almost immediately. His sisters were at once serious and thoughtful.

"Aw, the poor thing." Amanda arose from the hard floor and sat on a chair. "Too many strangers all at once."

Kerrianne nodded. "You have to take time off from work, if you can. She'll need someone steady—especially in the beginning."

"I've only been there ten months. My vacation isn't scheduled until August." He sighed. "Maybe I can work something out with my boss."

Amanda rubbed a hand over her swollen stomach. "I can't believe you're keeping her."

Mitch glared at his sister. He and Amanda had always been close, but this comment made him want to strangle her. "What else can I do? Her parents wanted me to raise her. How can I say no? It's not as if she can be adopted and sealed to another family—she has a mom and a dad already."

"Relax." Amanda lifted herself from the chair and put a hand on his shoulder. "I didn't mean anything by it. Honestly, you'll do great. And I'm behind you one hundred percent."

Kerrianne nodded agreement. "Call, if you ever need any help."

"How hard can it be?" Mitch asked. What was *wrong* with them? Sure, he'd had a challenging few hours with Emily Jane that morning, but his sisters seemed to think raising a child was the most difficult thing on the face of the planet. Did they forget that he'd raised baby birds from eggs? Now *that* was hard.

Amanda and Kerrianne grinned, sharing some secret he couldn't begin to fathom. "What?" he said, annoyed. "Look, just show me the ropes. I'll take it from there."

Amanda gave his shoulder another pat. "You'll do fine. You're a wonderful uncle, and I don't know what I would have done without you in the past year and a half. Gaining a husband and two children at the same time was a big adjustment for me. You've been a great support."

"For me, too," Kerrianne added. "You've been there for me every step of the way since Adam passed away, and we'll be here for you now." She started for the front door. "We threw some things in the van that you might be able to use. While we bring them in, you should run a few inches of water in the bathtub to clean her up. Remember to check the temperature before you put her in."

"Okay." Mitch had been silently debating whether he should use the kitchen sink but decided the risk of dropping her was too great.

While the water ran, he washed the food from the floor. By the time the bath was ready, his sisters were back inside giving orders on the proper way to bathe a child. Emily Jane was thrilled to be in the water, and her smiles were frequent. After a rather long time in the tub, she was sleepy again.

"It's been a big day for her." Kerrianne handed him a towel.

"I'll make her a bottle," Amanda said. "Babies this age still like to drink one before they sleep." She left the bathroom.

"Does she have any clothes?" Kerrianne asked.

"Yeah, in a suitcase somewhere. The lawyer left it with a car seat."

"Better put a diaper on first."

Emily Jane "helped" them go through the contents of her suitcase—mainly by spreading items around the living room. Mitch was pleased to see she had what looked like sufficient clothing, and even Kerrianne was impressed. "Someone really loved to dress up this little girl," she said, blinking her eyes as she always did when feeling emotional. Mitch didn't blame her. His heart ached at the idea of Ashley shopping for all these clothes.

"This looks comfortable." Kerrianne handed him a short-sleeved cotton shirt with matching capri pants. With an amused smile, she watched as he struggled to dress the baby.

Amanda returned with the bottle, tossing it to him, and he sat on the couch with Emily Jane. This he was good at, having helped Amanda many times with little Mara, who was now two. He was glad Amanda had come today with Kerrianne, who to his knowledge had never once used a bottle with any of her three children.

As he held the baby, his sisters went about childproofing his house, placing anything they considered dangerous out of reach—including a plant, a stepping stool, a porcelain vase, dangling cords, and his model rocket collection. Together they set up a small portable crib in Mitch's bedroom. Then, while Amanda ran to the store for diapers, wipes, and more baby food, Kerrianne organized Emily Jane's clothes in his closet and in his top dresser drawer.

By the time his sisters left, Mitch felt more in control. Emily Jane was asleep in the crib, covered with a quilt Kerrianne had made for one of her children. He also had a high chair, baby toys, and a book on childrearing. As a schoolteacher, Amanda thought of books before anything else.

He thumbed through the book and after a few minutes was feeling overwhelmed again. What was he thinking? A child wasn't like a bird or a gerbil. Or even a dog. A child was a human creature he could possibly damage for life. Who knew what emotional trials she would face from losing her parents so young? How could he possibly make up for their loss?

Clenching his jaw, Mitch stilled the inner voices. Emily Jane had been left to him, and he would do everything in his power to give her everything she needed. With this in mind, he called his boss's emergency cell phone number. "I need to take a few weeks off," he said after explaining the circumstances. Belatedly, he added, "Please."

His boss was silent for a few minutes. "I'm sorry about your situation," he said, "but we can't wait two weeks for your report. Our grants depend on your research. And don't forget the new wolves at the zoo. They'll be arriving next week, and I've told our boys you're going there to observe."

A shiver of anticipation ran up Mitch's spine. He'd been excited to learn about the new wolves and at the idea of working, however briefly, with live animals instead of researching documents written by others who studied in the field. Lately he'd begun to regret his choice of careers. Maybe he should have been a vet—except then he would have worked with ordinary animals instead of the wild variety, and that didn't thrill or excite him as it had when he'd been a child. Maybe he should consider teaching, but going back for a teaching certificate meant more classroom study, which would further remove him from the animals he loved.

"What if I work from home?" he suggested. "I can research anywhere. She sleeps a lot, and I'll get a sitter when I go to the zoo. I wouldn't ask if I didn't have to, but this little girl has just lost both parents. I'm all she has." The lump was back in Mitch's throat, impossibly large and painful.

"Okay. We can try that for a few days. But keep me informed."

"Thank you. I will. And I'll get it finished."

"I know you will. And Mitch?"

"Yes?"

"Good luck. It's a good thing you're doing."

"Thank you." Mitch hung up, feeling happy. He *could* do this! Somehow the Lord would help him take care of Emily Jane.

The phone rang, and Mitch was grateful to hear his mother, Jessica Huntington, on the line, calling from Arizona where she and his father were vacationing. "I heard what happened," she said. "How are you holding up?"

"We're doing fine." He hoped his confidence showed in the words. His mother wasn't fooled. "Raising a child isn't like raising a pet."

"I know. I can do this, Mom."

"Of course you can. And we'll all help. Poor little girl—she must really be confused right now. A baby deserves to have both parents."

"What do you want me to do? Give her up for adoption?" Mitch *couldn't* do that without betraying Lane and Ashley's trust. Except maybe to Amanda or Kerrianne, where he could keep a close eye on her. But Amanda had been so sick with her pregnancy that she had barely managed to teach until the end of the school year, not to mention her challenges in dealing with the two children she was responsible for. As for Kerrianne, now that Adam was gone, she was already raising three children alone.

"What I meant was that maybe it's time you thought seriously about finding a wife." His mother's tone rebuked him.

"Oh, that." His mother was always stomping up that trail. Since Amanda was safely married, Mitch was next in his mother's mind, especially since he would soon be twenty-five. "I thought you were suggesting that I give her away—maybe to Manda and Blake."

"I think Amanda has her plate full right now."

"The point is that Lane and Ashley wanted *me* to raise her."

"Yes, but it'd be easier if you were married. I'm sure Lane thought you would be by now."

"So did I." There, it was out. Now his mother would close in for the kill. "What does everyone expect?" he added before she could respond. "That I drive down to the wife dealership and pick out my favorite model?"

She chuckled softly. "Well, maybe not that. But I have faith the Lord knows what He's doing." Mitch hoped so, too.

"We're coming home early," she said. "We'll be there tomorrow."

"You don't have to do that."

"We're doing it anyway. We want to see this freckled cutie, as Amanda calls her. She's our grandchild now, you know."

Mitch's heart filled with warmth. "Thanks, Mom."

A short time after the call, Emily Jane awoke, struggling to get down when Mitch lifted her from the crib. She wandered around the small house, checking out each room. "Looking for paper to eat?" Mitch teased.

Ignoring him, she searched the rooms again, this time uttering a pitiful "Momma?" as Mitch followed her helplessly. She pushed him away each time he tried to hold her. At last in desperation, he pulled his chinchilla from her cage. Emily Jane stopped sniffling and stuck a hand in the long white fur.

"Softly," Mitch said, taking her hand and showing her how. "I bet Lady's hungry. Wanna help me feed her?"

Emily Jane enjoyed helping him pour food into the containers so much that he let her help him with Hiccup and Elvis (whose pink, hairless babies numbered nine), Lizzy Lizzard, Muffin the Mutt, and Dizzy, his other gerbil, who now seemed quite lonely in her small cage. More food ended up on the carpet than in the feeders, but Mitch didn't care. By the time he took Emily Jane to the garage to meet the ferrets and out back where he'd stuck the rabbits, she was smiling again.

Inside once more, she discovered a piece of paper with his home teaching assignments that had fallen from the countertop. She promptly began to tear off little bits with her teeth and swallow them.

Mitch didn't dare protest too much or take it away. Instead, he placed her in the high chair his sisters had brought and gave her tiny pieces of microwaved pizza. "You love that, don't you?" he said. "Much better than tasteless broccoli."

Emily Jane jabbered something unintelligible and shoved another piece into her mouth. She was eating the pizza so well that he was sure it was very last on the list of things to feed a baby—if it had made the list at all. Didn't children always like things they shouldn't eat?

Guiltily, Mitch cut up a fresh pear and set the bits on her tray. Then he opened a baby food jar of peas, but she spat them out repeatedly. "At least you like the pears. Hmm, I'll have to remember that."

After dinner he played with Emily Jane until she was tired. Then he changed her into pink pajamas and gave her another bottle. She fell asleep easily. He had put her in the crib and was congratulating himself on a job well done when she awoke and started to sob heartbrokenly for her mother. Mitch paced the floor with her in his arms until she drifted off again.

She woke up five more times that night, calling for a mother who could not answer. Each time Mitch held and rocked her, his own tears slipping down his cheeks.

It was a long, long night.

Chapter Four

Emily Jane grabbed Mitch's hand from the computer keyboard, babbling something that made perfect sense to her but that he couldn't begin to understand. It sounded something like, "Mitch, buddy boy, you've been at this computer too long—at least five minutes—and I'm bored. You should come play with me because I'm ever so much cuter than those wolves you're writing about. Besides, I've run out of typing paper to snack on, and if you don't get me some more, I'm going to raid the bathroom for more tissue."

When Mitch put his hands back on the keyboard, Emily Jane slapped his jean-covered leg. "Babjan ba-ba-da, juba-ching dup, dup, lo!"

He didn't know what to do. This sweet, demanding, energetic, emotional little creature had been with him only five days, but it felt like much, much longer.

Sunday had been good. He was the focus of attention at his singles ward, and afterward his family had rallied around him—even his brother Tyler, who was scarce these days while working on his journalism degree at BYU. That night was rough again, but since Mitch didn't need to get up early for work on Monday, he didn't mind.

After he'd stopped at work to get a few files, he'd spent some of Monday buying baby items and introducing Emily Jane to the neighbors. The afternoon and evening went well. But Monday night was the worst yet, bringing back the stark reality of his new existence. Neither he nor Emily Jane slept for longer than fifteen minutes at a stretch.

On Tuesday he'd managed to get in an hour of work but was positive that whatever he'd written about those darn wolves would have a million holes in it. How could his employer get grant money that way? Again the night passed slowly, with Mitch dozing between Emily Jane's screaming fits. He discovered that she slept longer if he held her on the couch, but the position afforded him little rest.

That brought him to Wednesday—today—with little sleep and next to no work completed. He'd tried to take her to his neighbors' that morning, but she had cried and clung to him with such fervency that he hadn't the heart to leave her. The woman with the lawyer had said Emily Jane was good with strangers, but apparently she'd changed her mind. She was more needy than any little animal he'd ever rescued. He only hoped that rescuing her wouldn't put him in an early grave.

Emily Jane took his hands from the computer again and tried pulling herself onto his lap. He lifted her up, and she banged on the keyboard. Then she grinned at him for approval.

"You are a lot cuter than the wolves," he said softly, tiredly. "But I'll lose my job if you don't let me work, and then we'll be living under a bridge somewhere, sipping rancid milk heated in a dirty tin pan."

Emily Jane smiled, but when he didn't respond, her smile vanished, and she stared at him with wide blue eyes. Her lower lip quivered. That galvanized him into action. He hurried from the living room where he'd moved his computer so that he could watch her play as he worked and went to the kitchen for the phone.

When his sister picked up, he began talking immediately. "Manda, I don't know how I can do this. You and Kerrianne were right. No, don't say you didn't think I'd bit off more than I could chew. I saw those looks you exchanged. And you were right. Are you happy? I've learned now. Emily Jane isn't like a bird or any other kind of animal. She is way harder to take care of. I don't know whatever possessed me to think I could do something so hard. I'm just too young—or something. I swear I'm going crazy! And we both know that can't be good for her or me. What should I do? Don't say call that Texas lawyer because—"

"Hold it!" For some time Amanda had been trying to talk over his torrent of words. "Everybody has days like this. How much sleep have you had?"

"Last night or since Saturday?" he asked. "Not that it matters. Either way I can count the hours on one hand."

"Ah, that explains it."

"That explains nothing! Who cares about sleep? If I don't get my work finished, I'll be moving in with you and Blake."

"I can't come over right now because Kerrianne's having a bad day," Amanda said, "and I promised I'd go to her house for a while." Mitch began to feel guilty. Here he was whining about taking care of one child when Kerrianne was taking care of *three*. "But don't worry," Amanda continued. "Reinforcements are on their way."

"Blake?" he asked doubtfully.

"No, he's at work. But that reminds me. He first got Kevin when he was years younger than you are. He muddled through and so will you. And look how good Kevin's turning out."

Mitch laughed despite his exhaustion. "I don't know why, but that makes me feel better somehow. Either that or it made me feel worse, and I'm so numb that I can't feel anything."

"Hang up," Amanda ordered. "Take a break until your reinforcements arrive."

"They won't be able to take her from the house. She'll cry. I can't let—"

"Don't worry. Now hang up."

Mitch obeyed, already feeling more positive. He wondered briefly who Amanda would call. Probably his mother. That meant he'd have to endure another speech on finding a bride, but any help was worth at least three lectures. Maybe she'd even put in a load of laundry or two while she was here. Emily Jane would love that. Last night she'd become so eager to help push the wet clothes inside the dryer that he'd had to stop her from climbing right in after them.

A ghastly smell and the intense expression on Emily Jane's face signaled time for a diaper change. He set to work, marveling at how his life had changed in so few days.

"Say *Mitch*," he told Emily Jane in singsong as he finished. "*Mitch, Mitch.* Come on, you can do it." He should probably teach her to say Daddy instead, but he couldn't—not yet. The memory of Lane was still too fresh. Yet a child deserved to call someone Daddy. *And Mommy, too,* he thought. *But I don't have a mommy for her.* Earlier that year he'd dated a girl from work, but they'd drifted apart when she got a new job. Now he had only the occasional date with someone from his singles ward.

"Jajahda," Emily Jane said. Mitch wasn't sure what that meant, if anything. So far her repertoire of comprehensible words consisted of Momma, Da, here, no, and ow. She used *ow* as a universal word when she didn't want to do something—particularly cleaning her face or hands. Quite a good start, in his opinion.

When the doorbell finally rang, it wasn't his mother but his younger brother, Tyler, and their friend Savvy Hergarter. Mitch's despair returned until he remembered that as the sister to four younger siblings, Savvy must know something about children.

"Come in," he said. "Did Manda call you?"

Tyler nodded. He was shorter than Mitch by a head but still taller than Savvy. He had close-cropped sandy blond hair, a nice build, and green eyes topped with stylish black-framed glasses. He was gregarious and popular with the ladies. "We're yours all afternoon and evening. Savvy and I were going to a foreign film down at the Y later, but it wasn't something we *had* to do." Tyler frowned and added, "Besides, a person I was hoping would be there isn't going after all."

Mitch knew that meant Tyler was hung up on another woman. Last time it was a too-skinny girl in his journalism class and before that a tall girl from ballroom dance.

Savvy's jaw tightened almost imperceptibly at Tyler's statement, but to Mitch, with everything minutely focused due to his lack of sleep, it was as though she screamed her irritation. That confused him. Yes, Amanda had set Savvy up with Tyler when he arrived home from his mission to Bolivia, but if anything had been going to develop between them, it should have happened by now. Besides, Tyler had assured Mitch that he and Savvy were just friends.

Savvy held her arms out to Emily Jane. "Hey, cutie. Want to come to me? Huh?" Savvy was Mitch's idea of a beautiful girl. Her blonde hair was cut to one length, reaching halfway down her back. She had clear smooth skin and blue eyes the color of a bright sky. He knew she bemoaned her curvaceous figure, as it didn't match the anorexic look that seemed to be popular these days, but he thought she was one attractive woman.

"How about it, sweetie?" Mitch asked the baby. "Want to go see Savvy?" For an answer, Emily Jane buried her face in his shoulder. "Don't worry. She'll warm up to you. She seems to like strangers as long as they don't pick her up. Look, I'll put her down and get her playing. Then I'll slip over to the computer. She's tired, so she might fall asleep if we give her a bottle."

"I don't get it." Tyler wrinkled his brow as Mitch set Emily Jane among the toys. "Aren't you supposed to put kids in their cribs and let them cry themselves to sleep? From what I heard, they get used to it quickly and then everybody sleeps."

An unexpected rage built inside Mitch. "Not this baby," he snarled. "She's just lost her mother and father, and I'll go without sleep for the rest of my life if I can begin to make that up to her. I only hope I can make her happy again."

Tyler stared at his vehemence, lifting his hands in surrender. "Okay, just asking. I'm sure you're right. I don't know anything about kids."

Savvy gave a disgusted sigh and settled down next to the growing mound of toys people had given Emily Jane. The baby suspiciously eyed the newcomers for several minutes but eventually crawled over to Savvy and began going through her purse. Mitch returned to his computer, stuffing cotton in his ears. Emily Jane studied him briefly, as though making sure he wasn't deserting her, before reaching for Tyler's glasses.

Mitch soon became involved in his work. True, it wasn't as fascinating as Emily Jane or working with live creatures, but the wolves and their curious habits pulled him in. Before long, Savvy was tapping his shoulder and pointing to the door.

"Co ee rake er or uh ak?" she asked.

Mitch removed the cotton from his ears. "What?"

"A walk. Can we take her for a walk?"

"Sure, if she'll go with you. But I don't have a stroller or anything."

"At this age, she'd probably rather walk."

Emily Jane grinned when the door opened. She stepped outside, one hand clinging tightly to Savvy's. As she crossed over the threshold, she glanced back at Mitch and waved. "Bye-bye," he called, feeling an odd pang when she disappeared from sight. For five days she'd been his constant companion, and suddenly he was alone. Almost, it was as if a part of him had walked out the door.

"Don't worry," Tyler assured Mitch. "Savvy's good with kids."

Pocketing the cotton, Mitch opened the window—just in case something happened outside to Emily Jane that he should hear.

The rest of the afternoon went smoothly. Emily Jane fell asleep on Savvy's shoulder during their walk and slept on the couch for another hour. Savvy and Tyler made dinner while Mitch kept working. His words came faster now that Emily Jane was near and he could be sure she wasn't crying or unhappy.

He'd made great progress by the time Savvy called him to eat spaghetti—Tyler's favorite food. The timing was good, since Emily Jane yawned and sat up. The baby loved the spaghetti and took a particular joy in smearing it around her face and on her head. "She'll need a bath," Savvy said, grinning.

Tyler rinsed his plate and set it in the sink. "I'll run the water."

"Yeah, anything to get out of cleaning up," Savvy teased.

Tyler grinned. "Hey, this little baby *is* the messiest thing I see here."

"Whatever." Savvy rolled her eyes as he left the room.

"Only a few inches," Mitch called. "Not too hot or too cold!"

Savvy laughed and began dumping the leftover spaghetti into a plastic storage bowl. "He'll do okay, I think. He's not as inept as he likes to pretend."

Mitch finished his spaghetti, watching her work, and for a moment wished things were different between them. Amanda had tried to set them up long before Tyler had come home from his mission, but it hadn't worked, either. Of course, that might have had something to do with how he'd brought Lizzy Lizard along to the dance club. Lizzy had crawled out of his pocket and lodged in Savvy's hair. She'd laughed good-naturedly but wasn't impressed. Mitch hadn't apologized—not because he was discourteous but because he was so disappointed. The woman he married would love his animals as much as he did.

At the sink, Savvy stopped moving, staring out his window, looking lost and sad. In a heartbeat, Mitch was at her side. "What's wrong?"

Impatiently, she clenched her lips and shook her head. "Nothing."

"We've been friends too long. I can tell something's wrong. Maybe I can help." He touched her shoulder gingerly; if she'd been one of his sisters, he would have hugged her.

She let her plate clank into the sink and met his gaze. "It's your brother."

"What did he do?" Mitch growled. "I'll kill him."

"He's done nothing. That's the whole point." She sighed loudly before continuing. "Do you know how many proposals I've had in three years at BYU? Eight. Nine, if you count that student from Africa who was trying to extend his visa. Anyway, I've had eight serious proposals from nice guys who wanted to marry me and make a good life together. But there wasn't even one I felt it could work with, not one who was more interesting to me than astronomy. Not one that I could imagine promising to love for eternity."

"Well, that's okay." Mitch was unsure where she was heading. "You have the right to be in love. You didn't have to accept their proposals."

She glanced toward the doorway where Tyler had gone. "I know. But I also know that I'm a little hardheaded when it comes to romance. Cynical, you might say."

"Aren't we all?" Mitch had a good share of that himself. For all the women he'd dated over the years, none had clicked with his heart. Lately he had begun wondering if such a thing as falling in love even existed.

"Well, now that's all changed. I don't care about school anymore. I'm only taking one class this summer, and I can't seem to concentrate."

Mitch anticipated what was coming next. "You're in love."

"Yes." She shook her head and snorted delicately. "With your brother. But he's always chasing after someone else. Usually a skinny, popular someone else. In fact, I'd say he's rather fixed on the worldly things right now. Basically, he's a big jerk." This last came with undis guised forcefulness.

A smile tugged on Mitch's lips, but he didn't let it show. "You have awfully clear vision for someone in love."

She shrugged. "Just because I say he's acting like a jerk doesn't mean I don't care about him. I do. At first when he came home and we started dating, it seemed we were headed the right direction. Then after six months, we suddenly became only friends." She bit her bottom lip. "I really should tell him to get lost."

"You should." Mitch shook his head at his brother's stupidity. He had seen how well Tyler and Savvy got along, though admittedly, Tyler was a little on the immature side. Couldn't he see a good future when it stared him in the face?

"Look, I'll talk to him," he said.

"No, no." She shook her head. "I'm working on a plan right now to cure myself of this stupidity. I'd rather you forget I said anything."

"I can't, Savvy. We're friends." He squeezed her shoulder awkwardly.

She smiled at him, her wide eyes filling with tears. "Oh, why couldn't *we* have hit it off? Everything would be much easier."

"Funny, I just had the same thought. My mom says that I should hurry and get married. You know, for Emily Jane's sake. And you're someone I really admire."

Savvy sighed. "Do you still have your lizard?"

"Sure. You want to see her? She got out the other day and caught a cold while she was away from her heating lamps, but you can take a peek—"

"No, I don't want to see it. Sorry, Mitch." She hugged him tightly as she glanced over at Emily Jane, who sat in her high chair playing with her food. "But I'll help you with the baby any time you want."

"Ahem," came a voice behind them. The two parted quickly as Tyler reentered the room. "Look at that baby," Tyler said into the awkwardness. "With all that spaghetti sauce, she looks like an accident victim."

Mitch didn't find his brother's choice of words amusing, but Emily Jane grinned, happy to be noticed. "Come on." Mitch unlocked her high chair tray.

"Let me bathe her," Savvy said. "Then you can get back to work."

Happy to be released, Emily Jane didn't mind who carried her. Mitch knew she'd be happy in the bath as well, so he went back to the computer. Thinking of Savvy's confession and his brother's apparently obliviousness, he sighed.

After Tyler and Savvy left, Mitch put Emily Jane and himself to bed early. Emily Jane seemed to sleep better. Several times he awoke to find her in his arms, though he couldn't remember getting up and taking her from the crib. He decided then and there to figure out a better sleeping arrangement.

The next day he went early to Kerrianne's to borrow her toddler bed. He found his sister dressed and alone on her front porch, holding her mail in her hands as she stared off into the distance. "You're up," he said, shifting Emily Jane to one hip. "I was worried I'd get you out of bed."

Kerrianne started, and she then turned toward him, smiling. "My mail comes early. I think this street must be the first on the mailman's route. I don't like the idea of it sitting out too long these days, what with mail thieves around and all."

Mitch scratched an itch on his neck. He had never thought about mail thieves before, but if they got his sister dressed and out of bed to bask in the morning sun, he was glad they existed.

"How are you, Emily Jane?" Kerrianne asked the baby. Emily Jane babbled nonsense that made Kerrianne laugh. Turning her attention to Mitch, she asked, "Are you sure it's not too cold out here for you? You're scratching and your neck is red. You should have worn a jacket."

Now that she mentioned it, he felt cold, and hives were already forming on his arms. He should have worn something more than a T-shirt and long denim shorts. He almost never wore shorts, unless it was baking outside, and he often wore a light jacket in the mornings during the early weeks of summer. But he'd been in a hurry when he'd left the house this morning and had put on the first thing that came to hand. *Sheesh!* he thought. *A guy shouldn't have to worry about a stupid allergy to cold in the summer.*

"I'm okay," he told his sister. "It'll pass when the sun warms things up."

She frowned. "Not for an hour. I know how your hives get." She took him inside and gave him a jacket he recognized as having belonged to Adam. "Wear it while we get the bed into your car," she said. Not wanting to offend her, he agreed.

She helped him carry the small bed out to his orange-red Mustang that had garnered him more than his share of odd looks. His family called it ugly, but Mitch told anyone who would listen that it was exotic. Emily Jane watched with interest as Mitch dismantled the boards of the bed so most of it would fit in the trunk. The rest went on the floor of the backseat.

"Are you still heading for the zoo today?" Kerrianne asked.

"Yeah. I just hope it doesn't rain." His allergy really acted up when he was out in the rain—no matter how warm the weather. Only on his mission in northern Brazil had he been able to enjoy a warm summer rain.

"Do you want me to watch Emily Jane?"

He shook his head. "I don't want to leave her yet. She gets too upset. Manda and her kids are coming with me to watch her. We're taking their van."

"You'll need my double jogging stroller then, for the babies. Manda only has a single. I'll call and have her pick it up on her way over."

"Thanks." Mitch gave her a hug, not liking the dark circles under her eyes that hinted of lost sleep. Remembering that Amanda had said Kerrianne was having a rough day yesterday, he asked in a low voice, "Are you okay?"

She smiled. "The nights are still hard, that's all. But I know Adam's near. I feel him."

"Thank heaven for temple sealings." Mitch gave her another hug, put Emily Jane in her car seat, and drove back to Sandy.

He thought about his sister as he unloaded the bed. Kerrianne was sealed to her husband, and they would be reunited. Emily Jane's parents would also be together and would one day have Emily Jane with them. More than anything Mitch also wanted an eternal relationship, but now with his new responsibilities, he didn't see how he'd have time to meet anyone. He wondered if the single father Internet group he'd heard about would know where he could find a good wife. Or maybe he could take out an ad in the newspaper: Temple-Worthy Bachelor Seeks Single Woman Who Likes Children/Animals.

Maybe not.

He set up the toddler bed next to his own. With this arrangement, he figured he could get Emily Jane to sleep with him and then roll her into her own bed. If he was careful, she might not wake. Later, when she began to stir during the night, he could pat her back without getting out of bed. If he timed it right, they both might be able to sleep for longer periods of time. He suspected that Emily Jane had slept with her parents and that she missed having someone close.

The toddler bed had a safety rail, and after securing it in place, he felt satisfied the arrangement was as safe as the crib. There was an open space near the end of the bed that wasn't covered by the rail, and he worked with Emily Jane until she could get in and out of the bed by herself. She giggled as they practiced.

"Nothing like a little independence," he said.

She picked up an empty cardboard cracker box from his bedside table and began to chew on the edges. "You like cardboard, too?" he asked. Her response was to bite off a small, soggy section, swallowing quickly before he could fish it out. Sighing, Mitch picked her up and went to find her a snack.

Amanda arrived in her new van a short time later. "Are you sure you don't mind doing this?" he asked, as he loaded Emily Jane's car seat. "I could have asked Mom."

"I don't mind," she said. "The kids need to get out, and they'll be good company for Emily Jane." Sure enough, blond little Kevin, soon to be six and self-appointed baby tender, was already making both Emily Jane and his two-year-old sister, Mara, laugh like crazy.

"We'll have time to walk around a bit." Mitch slipped into the passenger seat. "Then I'll go alone to the wolf habitat with the zoo employees."

"I'll show the kids the monkeys," Amanda replied. "Emily Jane'll be fine."

Mitch hoped so. He couldn't stand the thought of her crying any more than necessary. He knew he'd have to stop being so paranoid about her tears and about the permanent effect her parents' death would have on her, but now was not the time. When would he quit worrying? When he found her a mother? Or maybe when she called him Dad.

As though reading his mind, Amanda said in a low voice. "Kevin asked us last night if he could call us Mom and Dad." She checked her rearview mirror to be sure the children were watching the animated DVD she'd put in.

"Well, that's great, isn't it? You sound a little uncertain."

"Well, Blake's been the only father Kevin and Mara have ever known, so that's great where he's concerned, but it becomes a bit sticky calling me Mom since they have a mother in California."

"One who hasn't seen them in eighteen months."

"She calls and sends cards and presents . . . sometimes."

"It's not the same."

Amanda sighed. "If they keep calling me Amanda, my own baby will probably do the same, and I definitely don't want that. Truthfully, I feel Kevin and Mara *are* mine. I've been with Mara for all but eight months of her life. And Kevin was only four when we met. Every day I thank the Lord I can be a part of their lives. Nothing would make me happier than to have them call me Mom. I'm just worried that Paula will come back and be furious when she finds out."

"Hey, she's the one who gave up custody."

"Because she loves the children."

Mitch shook his head. "If Kevin asked, I think he's needing a change."

"He may have overheard me talk to Blake about it."

"So you think he's just trying to please you?"

Amanda frowned at the freeway in concentration. "No, I think what I said made him speak up, but I suspect he's been wondering about it for a long time. He said he wanted to be like other boys and girls at school."

"Then you should definitely let him call you that. He deserves to have both a mom and a dad." Mitch felt a little guilty as he said this. Emily Jane deserved two parents, too, and likewise Kerrianne's children deserved to have their father.

I guess we do what we can, he decided. *Beginning with Kevin and Mara calling Manda Mom.*

He looked back at Mara in her car seat next to Emily Jane. Mara's head was framed by dark waves that exactly matched her brown eyes. Her bright grin was contagious. Obviously, Mara had survived losing her mother. Though the way she had lost her mother was far removed from what had happened to Emily Jane's, her apparent contentment gave him hope. She was doing well with the replacement of what she had lost.

Mitch wished he could find a way to replace what Emily Jane was missing. But was there any woman in the world who would put up with Lizzy Lizzard and company?

Somehow he didn't think so.

Chapter Five

Two weeks after Emily Jane's arrival, Mitch went to his parents' house in Alpine for Sunday dinner with all his siblings. Mitch was glad to have Emily Jane distracted by the other children, though she still seemed leery of the adults. He himself was having trouble concentrating on the conversation.

"Mitchell, what's wrong?" asked his mother. "You've hardly touched a thing." Jessica Huntington was a beautiful woman who had aged gracefully. Blonde hair, gently teased in the latest style, bordered her slim face, and her artfully applied makeup made her appear younger than the fifty-odd years she claimed.

Mitch dragged his eyes from his plate. Normally meatloaf was his favorite, but today he didn't feel like eating.

"And you haven't said more than two words," Amanda put in.

Mitch looked at Emily Jane, who sat in a high chair next to him. "I'm not sure," he said. "I feel depressed."

"Are you sleeping?" Kerrianne asked.

"Yeah. But I keep thinking about Lane and Ashley. In fact, I think about them all the time. I know it sounds weird, but it's almost like I

50

expect them to show up any minute." There, it was out in the open. Would his family think he was crazy?

"That's because you need to say good-bye," Kerrianne said with a surety that came from personal experience. "That's what funerals are for."

Mitch sighed. "I would have been at their funeral if I'd known about it. Believe it or not, I did finally get a notice in the mail, but it was delayed because of a wrong zip code. Two of the numbers were off."

"That's too bad," Amanda consoled.

"We need to have a memorial service." Kerrianne passed him the applesauce for Emily Jane. "It hasn't been all that long since Lane and Ashley lived here. I bet a lot of people would love to come."

"How would I tell them about it?"

"Easy." Tyler pulled out his cell phone. "I can get a friend to do an article."

"Plus the paper has funeral announcements," Amanda added. "You could call their old bishop to spread the word. I bet he'd speak, too."

"I'll take care of the food," their mother volunteered. "Your father can find a place to hold it."

The ball began rolling. With all the help from his family, the only thing Mitch had to do was dig out one of Lane and Ashley's wedding portraits from the numerous boxes the Texas lawyer had shipped to his house a few days ago—most of which now sat in his garage. He'd decided to wait to go through them until Emily Jane was older and could share in the experience. For the time being, he contented himself with taking the boxes containing photo albums and framed pictures inside the house where the moisture wouldn't damage them.

On Monday morning, Mitch called Dolores Clark, the Texas lawyer, to tell her about the service. "I thought you might know of others we could invite."

"We have discovered a list of e-mail addresses," Dolores said. "We couldn't find an address book at their house, but when my assistant was boxing up their possessions to send to you, she checked their computer for information we might need and printed the list. Many of the contacts may not have heard of the accident." She paused before adding. "Your e-mail address was on that list. I'm sorry we didn't find it before, or I would have e-mailed you. The only information I had on the official custody documents was your name, phone, number, and address—with the wrong zip, as you already pointed out to me last week."

"I know you did your best. And you brought me Emily Jane."

"How's it going with her?"

Mitch gave a low chuckle. "It was rough at first, but she's settled in. Won't let me out of her sight, though. And she doesn't like strangers anymore."

"Sounds like she's doing what she must do to cope."

"That's what I think." He didn't add how hard it still was for him or how many changes he'd made in his life. Lane and Ashley would have done the same thing for him. Besides, there were rewards. Each time Emily Jane put her little arms around his neck, Mitch marveled at how much love he felt for her.

"Why don't I e-mail you the list?" Dolores said.

"Thanks, I'd appreciate it."

"I do have some good news."

"Oh?" He could use it right now.

"I think we have a buyer for the house. Because the Graysons weren't there long, I don't expect there'll be much profit, but with the proceeds from the estate sale, Emily Jane should receive a few thousand dollars. I know it's not a lot, but they had little savings and Lane wasn't yet eligible for his company's life insurance policy."

"It's better than owing money," Mitch said. "I'll put it away for college. For now, I can pay her expenses." That was true, though he'd have to earn a few raises before he'd feel comfortable again.

"You did apply for Social Security for her, didn't you?"

"Yeah, but it hasn't kicked in yet. They want me to save receipts to show I'm spending the money on her. Won't be a problem—I never knew babies cost so much. Anyway, I hope that will help me pay a sitter when I go back to work." *If Emily Jane ever lets me,* he amended silently.

"That's good, then," she said. "I'll e-mail you that list right now. I'll let you know later about the house."

"Thanks." Mitch hung up the phone, feeling grateful. When Dolores's e-mail came in, he sent out an announcement. By the end of the day, he'd received eleven responses from people who lived in Utah and planned to attend the service. He hoped there would be more coming who hadn't replied.

Several people said they couldn't attend but would like to donate money for Emily Jane. Mitch was surprised, and his first thought was to refuse, but after talking to his father, he agreed to set up an account for Emily Jane at the local bank. At the very least, the funds would help pay the legal expenses he was incurring as he completed custody documents. Besides, if Emily Jane had gone to someone else, he would have wanted to help in the same way. It would have given him a measure of peace that seemingly escaped him now.

Cory enjoyed sailing down the Black River on the supply vessel with the others who were hitching a ride to Manaus. On the river, the lushness, the vastness, the primitiveness of the Amazon came clearly into focus for her. Every bend seemed to hold a new treasure, a hidden surprise. Over the course of two days, they observed a host of different animals from the deck, went ashore to see several small villages, and stopped at great waterfalls where they swam in clear, clean water. Everywhere they went, Cory snapped photographs.

The most impressive sight for her was one she had seen before but never tired of—the white herons standing in groups on one leg in the shallows. Toward sunset, the birds would fly together and settle in the same tree until it appeared each branch had sprouted large white blossoms. Not even her pictures could do justice to the glorious sight.

There was a joy in moving along the river that she didn't feel in the jungle camp. A freedom that was as sweet in its temporary nature as in its unexpectedness. She knew from experience that she would feel a similar freedom when she returned to the jungle and her work. The jungle would welcome her back, especially tiny Meeko, whom she'd made stay behind but who had followed the boat along the river in the treetops for what seemed like miles.

She wasn't finished photographing all the animals, as she had hoped to be when she suggested this trip. In particular, she needed a good shot of the gigantic jungle pig, a supposedly new species recently discovered in the Amazon. The creature resembled a boar without the fat, hairy neck ring, and goatee—or the smell. One of the biologists at the camp was studying them, so Cory didn't anticipate a difficult time capturing one on film as soon as she returned from her week-long jaunt. There was still plenty of time to meet her deadline.

Meanwhile, a little trip to Manaus was certainly in order. Both she and Evan had worked hard. He'd read bits and pieces of his article to her and the others in the evenings as they sat around the big table, and she thought it was shaping up well. She'd made a point of not digging into the whole article, however, despite an offer from Evan to do so— and not only because she'd been working so hard. Usually, when she read what a writer put down about her photos, she had a million suggestions to emphasize the life she portrayed in her pictures. But writers in general hated her advice, and because she couldn't seem to write a decent article herself, she was left to their mercy. Not delving into Evan's article was her way of avoiding potential trouble between them, especially when she certainly didn't plan on accepting any picture-taking advice from him.

Even before they reached Manaus, they began seeing wooden, box-like houses along the river. Children in small canoes came out behind their boat and played in its wake, laughing with glee as their canoes rocked in the water.

Evan shook his head. "I guess they never heard of video games."

"A good thing," she retorted, snapping photographs.

The first order of business after they pulled ashore was to find a couple of hotel rooms and drop their duffel bags. Then they walked around until they found a nice place to eat. Cory had a big salad with several mixed vegetables—some native and some she knew from home. To her surprise, the unfamiliar dressing was remarkably good. *Either that or I've been deprived too long,* she thought with a smile.

"What are you thinking?" Evan's fork poised above a slab of grilled steak.

"That I've been so long away from regular salad dressing that I wouldn't know if they gave me a terrible-tasting substitute."

He chuckled. "Well, it'll be over soon."

She sobered. "For you. I'd like to go home and visit after our project is finished, but I plan to come back. I love it here."

"You want to stay forever?" His eyebrows rose in surprise.

"No. Not forever. But right now it's where I want to be."

She could tell he was disappointed but not yet giving up on their relationship. "I can write here," he said, letting the sentence hang.

A sudden shyness overcame her. "I'd like that," she replied. His hand covered hers, feeling warm and comforting.

When they left the restaurant, gray clouds billowed in the sky. Rain was coming. Despite this, they walked to the Internet café so Cory could e-mail low resolution copies of her work to her agent. The high resolutions would be needed for the final layout but were simply too numerous and too large to send in bulk through her e-mail provider; these would have to be mailed on CDs.

They purposely chose a route that passed close to the famed Manaus opera house. The pink and white, three-story building was an amazing, elegant work of art, both inside and out—all but its blazing gold, blue, and green dome that had always appeared so contrastingly

loud and bright. Only when Cory had learned that the colors repre-
sented the Brazilian flag did she understand and appreciate their
inclusion on the structure.

"Maybe we can come back here tomorrow," Evan suggested,
motioning to the opera house. "Since we'll be here for three days."

"Good idea. I'd like to get some photos, if they'll let me."

They walked the streets together, enjoying the sounds and the life
of the city, foreign to them after so long in the primitive jungle. When
they arrived at the Internet café, they unzipped their laptops from their
carrying cases. Cory laughed as she began to download her e-mail
through a wireless connection. "It's just so weird," she said. "Can you
imagine what the natives in one of those tiny villages we passed would
think about sending and receiving messages in nothing but air?"

Evan looked up from his laptop. He had text messaging on his
phone and could also send small files from just about anywhere in the
Amazon, but he was taking the opportunity to do research on the
animals she'd photographed. "We would have a hard time explaining,"
he agreed, "even if we spoke Portuguese."

"I'm getting better at communicating. Well, not really." She grinned.
"But hey, I have a brother-in-law who knows Portuguese."

"A brother-in-law? I didn't even know you had a sister."

Cory had surprised herself. It was the first time she had thought of
AshDee's husband as her brother-in-law. Oddly, doing so now gave her
a feeling of connection.

"First you don't tell me about your birthday, and now your family?
What else are you keeping from me?" He laughed, but his eyes were
clearly hurt.

"My sister and I are estranged," she explained. "Apparently her husband came here on a religious mission of sorts. Well, not here exactly. I
think he was mostly in the cities farther south."

"A missionary?" Evan grimaced. "Must be an older sister."

"No, younger by two years. He was a missionary before they met."

"Probably one of those Mormon boys."

She raised a brow. "How did you know?"

He shrugged. "Believe it or not, I have a cousin who's a Mormon. He went on a mission, too. I think it was to England. Lives in Utah now. I'd like to say the guy's a jerk, but he's not. He works in insurance. Quite successful, I hear." He shook his head. "What a small world."

"Isn't it?" Cory turned back to her screen and clicked on an e-mail from a friend she'd gone to high school and college with but hadn't seen in a long time.

Hi, Cory,

I hope this is still your e-mail addy. I really should have kept in better touch. Sorry about that. Last I heard you were planning to move to Brazil.

I just had to write when I read about what had happened in the newspaper. I couldn't believe it! I'm so sorry about Ashley. Despite your disagreements, I know how much you cared for her. I wanted to attend the funeral, but I didn't know where it was being held (the article didn't say). I've probably missed it by now.

Please know that my thoughts are with you. If you need anything— ANYTHING—please don't hesitate to e-mail me. I have vacation time coming if you want me to visit (if you're back in the States) or if you'd like to come here. My door is always open.

Love,
Pam

P.S. What's going to happen to your niece? Did your brother-in-law have family?

Cory gave a small cry. *Funeral? AshDee? No!* Her heart began a painful pounding in her ears. Her breath rasped through clenched teeth. *No!* Pam must be mistaken. She *had* to be mistaken.

Searching the e-mail, Cory found a link and clicked on it. A newspaper article came up, dated on a Tuesday more than three weeks earlier. The headline read *Boating Accident Claims Five Lives.* AshDee's name popped out at her from the text below. Cory felt ill. A dozen thoughts careened in her head.

What on earth was AshDee doing on a boat on a weekday? What had she been thinking? Had AshDee perhaps suspected when she stepped on the boat that her life would be forfeit? Had there been time for her to consider how her death would change the lives of those she left behind?

Except that Cory's life wouldn't change, not really. Her sister hadn't been an active part of her life for four years. Like her father, she had written AshDee off as dead. And now she was.

Dead.

Oh, dear God, Cory prayed, falling back on her Baptist upbringing, though she was no longer a believer. *Oh, AshDee!* Other thoughts followed the first wave but nothing coherent. Just a jumble of pain and loss. Of terrible, bitter regret.

"Is something wrong?"

Cory couldn't tell—didn't care—who spoke. Her eyes riveted on the screen as she struggled to read the rest. Words swam across the page. Why wouldn't they hold still? *Husband and wife . . . boat . . . three others . . . capsized . . . drowned . . . survived by . . . Emily Jane . . .*

Cory looked away. AshDee was gone. Like her mother. Like her father. The regret burned deeper into her heart. Just when she believed she could no longer endure the pain, another thought worked itself into her pounding head.

EmJay was alive! Her *niece* was alive!

"Cory?" Evan was at her side, staring at her anxiously. Cory saw him through a haze. She stood and stumbled away—away from him and from the laptop that had transmitted the terrible news.

"Everything okay?" asked an employee in accented English.

"She's had some bad news, I think." Evan shoved money at the employee and scrambled to pick up both their laptops.

"Cory!" Evan caught up to her on the street. "What's wrong? Talk to me!"

She saw him then and reached for her laptop. "Thank you."

"Cory, what happened?"

"My sister's dead. She and her husband drowned."

His face paled. "I'm so sorry. Come, I'll help you back to the hotel."

Cory didn't remember the return journey at all. She did remember insisting on being left alone. In her room, she fumbled through her duffel bag, searching for the pictures of her niece. She found them and AshDee's two other letters inside the worn birthday card that she'd stuffed between the folds of her second-best pair of jeans. The baby grinned out at the world, her blue eyes laughing. In one picture, her hands were raised to her head, a sparse lock of curly reddish orange hair twisted around a chubby finger. A tear slipped from Cory's left eye.

"I'm coming, EmJay," she whispered. Never mind that no one had contacted her about the baby. She had the responsibility to make sure EmJay was safe and happy. She had left her relationship with her sister until too late, but she refused to do the same with EmJay.

Outside, it began to rain.

Chapter Six

R ain had poured steadily since Cory found out about AshDee, the sky weeping tears that Cory wouldn't shed.

She'd become a machine, thinking only of leaving. Like it or not, Evan was a big part of those plans. He would have to make arrangements with the conservationists to allow her tent to remain until she returned. He would also have to finish the article without her picture of the gigantic jungle pig. Or take the photograph himself.

Cory gave Evan a CD copy of her favorite photographs, as there wasn't time to make hard copies that he could study for his article. She hadn't even e-mailed Vikki the low resolution versions or mailed the CDs she'd burned for her. All that would have to wait until she arrived in Texas. Cory was glad now that she'd brought all her 35mm film with her for developing in Manaus. She'd get it done in the States as well.

"You *are* coming back, aren't you?" Evan asked at the airport the next morning. Four o'clock was too early for either to be in a good mood.

"Of course I am." For a long moment she let him hold her, feeling safe and protected. At last she disengaged his arms and pulled away.

On the four-hour flight to São Paulo, she puzzled over Evan's question. She wanted to return soon, but how could she make plans until she met EmJay? Cory was AshDee's only other living relative, and despite their estrangement, she had a duty to AshDee's daughter. Late last night the thought had come to her that EmJay might need her as much as AshDee had once needed her after their own mother's death.

She wondered what EmJay was like and how she would feel about Cory. *And how do I feel about her?* She couldn't answer that exactly, but thoughts of her niece had never brought bitterness to her heart, only a sense of sadness that Cory was not a part of her young life.

Beyond the windows of the plane, the gray clouds made a soft, marshmallowy carpet that blocked all but the occasional glimpse of the country below. Cory didn't care. She clutched her laptop and tried to stem the pain and guilt that ate at her heart.

In São Paulo she had a tedious, twelve-hour layover that only added to her anxiety. When she finally boarded the plane to Atlanta, she was a nervous wreck. The overnight flight was supposed to last more than nine hours, but they landed early for once, due to good air currents. It was four-thirty in the morning, the same time as in Manaus, more than twenty-four hours since Cory had said good-bye to Evan. She hadn't slept well on the plane, and she felt exhausted. After another three-hour layover at Atlanta, she finally boarded her last flight to Dallas.

The trip took nearly four hours, and at last Cory slept. As the plane circled over the airport in Dallas at fifteen minutes to ten on Thursday morning, she awoke with her neck aching and her seat partners—a young college-aged boy and an older, distinguished-looking gentleman—giving her such odd stares that she was sure she'd been snoring. Flushing, she collected her duffel, stuffing her laptop, case and all, inside.

Outside the airport, she became immediately aware that the air was different. The heavy blanketlike humidity of the Amazon was gone. Though the heat of midday might actually be higher, the lower humidity made her feel more comfortable than she'd been in over a year.

Cory stopped abruptly. What next? Where to start? She'd made no plans other than to get to Texas and find EmJay. *I can do this,* she thought.

First, she took a large withdrawal from an ATM, then she drew out AshDee's last letter with the return address in the corner, the one she'd received after her sister's move to Texas. Next, she hailed a taxi and jumped inside. The thin, balding taxi driver tried to start a conversation in his warm Texas drawl, but when Cory replied perfunctorily, he left her to wallow in her misery.

How different this trip would have been if she and AshDee had made up. Or if AshDee hadn't drowned. Cory's excitement might have overshadowed the hurt of four years apart—of four years of betrayal. But now she was too late. Bitter thoughts burrowed into the center of her soul. *Now I can never tell her how much she hurt me by leaving. I am truly alone in the world.*

As for AshDee's feelings in the matter, she simply couldn't go there. AshDee would never have feelings again. Yet in the depths of Cory's despair, there was always one bright hope: EmJay. Part of her sister lived on.

"We're here, miss." The taxi driver watched her curiously.

Checking her watch, she saw the drive had taken fifty minutes. She handed him a wad of cash. "Thank you."

"You want me to wait?"

She hesitated, not sure how he could possibly guess that she had no idea what she would find here. "Thanks. I'd like that."

"I'll wait then." Leaving his engine running, he picked up a Dean Koontz paperback from between the seats.

Cory surveyed the area. She was in a subdivision of modest, two-story homes. Children played on tiny front lawns or driveways. Some were on bikes in the deserted street. *Modern America,* thought Cory. *A concrete jungle.* She felt a pang of longing for the green denseness of the Amazon. For the smell and feel of the trees and earth. For the growl of the jaguar, calls of the parrot, and scolding of the monkeys. Would Meeko forget her and leave before she returned?

Taking a determined breath, she sauntered up to the door where Ashley had lived. No one responded to her ring. Too late she noticed the For Sale sign in the yard. She went next door, where a thin, blonde woman about her own age answered. Her eyes ran over Cory's disheveled hair, white cotton T-shirt, green shorts, and sturdy Brazilian leather sandals. Cory knew she was a mess, but there was nothing she could do about it now. She had to get to EmJay.

"My sister used to live next door," she began.

The woman nodded. "You look like her. I was thinking you might be related. I'm sorry about what happened."

Cory breathed a sigh of relief. She'd been afraid AshDee might have moved again and that no one would know where EmJay was now.

"I'm Tamra." The woman's soft drawl was not as noticeable as the taxi driver's but still present nonetheless. Cory wondered if her sister had picked up the accent.

"I'm Cory. Cory Steele."

"Would you like to sit down?" Tamra asked. "You're a little pale."

"I haven't eaten," Cory admitted. "I just flew in from Brazil. They served something on the plane. I don't remember what." *Or if I even ate,* she added silently. She followed the woman to a room where a TV was blaring.

"We weren't sure how to reach any family," Tamra said, flicking off the TV with the remote. "She must have kept her address book in her purse because it wasn't in the house. Her purse was never recovered."

Cory fought to keep the tears from falling. "I've come for EmJay. Do you know where she is?"

Tamra looked surprised. "You mean Emily Jane? She's gone. The lady across the street used to baby-sit her while Ashley went to class down at the college. When it . . . uh, happened, Emily was here playing with my daughter, but Jodi came and got her because she knew I had to work evenings. She stayed there for four, maybe five days, and then Jodi went with Ashley and Lane's lawyer to take her someplace—Utah,

I think. Apparently Ashley and Lane had arranged for someone there to take care of Emily Jane if something happened to them."

Shocked disappointment filled Cory's heart. The idea that everything would be settled without so much as a nod in her direction had never crossed her mind. "This attorney should be in her office on a Thursday, shouldn't she? Do you have her name and address?"

"I bet Jodi does. I'll give her a call. She'll be baby-sitting, though, and won't be able to come over."

Cory felt dizzy, and she put her head between her knees. The next thing she knew Tamra was pushing a plate of banana bread and sliced apples into her hands. "Here's some juice. Hope you like orange—it's all I have."

"Thank you." Cory drank gratefully and felt the dizziness pass.

"Jodi gave me the address. She said not to worry, though, that the man they gave Emily Jane to must have been a good friend because when the lawyer told him about the accident, he sat down on his porch and cried."

"They gave my niece to a man?" Surely they didn't have all the facts.

"Yeah, Jodi wondered about that, too, but the lawyer told her he was the same religion they were and that was part of why they chose him."

Cory nearly choked on a piece of banana bread. "He's not even family?" She had thought perhaps the man was related to Lane.

Tamra gave her a consoling look. "Jodi says he has sisters with children and parents who live nearby. I'm sure Emily Jane is fine."

"He probably has a wife," Cory said.

Tamra shrugged. "If there is a wife, Jodi didn't see her."

Cory gulped down the rest of her food, barely chewing. "I should get going. I have a taxi waiting." Or she hoped she still did.

She thanked Tamra for her helpfulness and left the house clutching the attorney's address, vowing to find out firsthand exactly where they had taken her niece.

On Friday morning, Mitch was feeding Emily Jane oatmeal in the high chair when the phone rang. Or he was *trying* to feed her. She was having too much fun tipping her sippy cup upside down and shaking it to pay him much heed.

Mitch answered on the second ring. "Hello?"

"Hi. Dolores Clark, here."

"Oh, hi. What's up?"

"I called to let you know that an offer was made on the house. A bit less than I'd hoped for, but we can wait for another offer if you'd like."

"No. I say take it. We might not have another chance."

"That's my feeling. The market isn't strong right now. At least this way we won't have to use any additional funds to make house payments."

"Let's sell, then."

"There is one other thing." Dolores paused, as if unsure how to continue. "A man named Cory Steele was here yesterday demanding to see me about Ashley. I was in an important meeting and couldn't see him, but the receptionist noted that he stayed all afternoon. Said he'd be back this morning. Now, I don't know who this person is, but given the name, it could be a relative."

Mitch's stomach twisted in knots. For weeks he'd wished that Emily Jane had relatives who could help him care for her, but now he'd accepted his role as sole guardian. What's more, he had developed a deep attachment to Emily Jane. He loved her.

Stifling his worry, Mitch asked, "What do you think he wants?"

"Money, probably. You'd be surprised at how many people believe they're entitled to receive something when a relative dies."

Mitch snorted. *Cory Steele,* he thought. *Cory Steele. What kind of a name is that?* It sounded hard and stiff. Probably belonging to a little weasel of a guy, some remote relative out to steal what he could—even if it was Mormon money. Ashley's family had disowned her, but now it seemed they would appear out of the woodwork. Well, Mitch didn't care about the money—the lawyers could deal with that—he only cared about Emily Jane and fulfilling his friends' last wishes.

"However," Dolores continued, "there's always a slight chance that he's not here for money."

"You mean he might want Emily Jane?" Mitch's stomach turned at the thought. The baby was staring at him now from the high chair, her sippy cup on the floor. He gathered his wits enough to give her a bit of cereal, and she rewarded him with a grin.

"It's an unlikely possibility."

"But if he does?"

"Lane and Ashley gave you custody. The papers will stand up in any court. I mean, there's always a chance of finding a loophole, but their first lawyer was thorough. When they moved here, I rechecked all the paperwork."

Mitch blew out a sigh. "Good."

"So how're the plans for tomorrow's service coming along?"

"Everything's set. I've had fifteen responses from the e-mails you gave me and a lot of calls from a story in the newspaper. Should be a good-sized crowd."

"A few people have contacted me about it. I'm not sure how they heard or how they found my address. Something related to the Graysons' church, I believe. I've passed on the service information."

"I appreciate that. Let me know what happens with this guy, okay?"

"I will. I have a meeting this morning, but I've left a small window before lunch if he shows up again. Meanwhile, don't worry about it, okay? You've got enough on your plate."

Mitch thanked Dolores and hung up the phone, feeling a little unnerved but determined not to worry. He fed Emily Jane another bite of cereal, marveling at the miracle of the little mouth opening and chewing. Her blue eyes sparkled. For the moment, at least, she was content. And so was he.

Cory was furious. She'd been kept waiting far too long in the attorney's office—first yesterday and now today. What right did this lawyer have to keep her waiting? Her sister was dead, and someone had to tell her what happened to EmJay.

Sometime during the night, Cory had realized that she would have to step forward and take full custody of her niece. She had several reasons for reaching this conclusion. The first was that AshDee couldn't seriously want someone who wasn't family rasing her child. Blood was blood. Period.

Yes, she and AshDee had been at odds, but she had always known that someday, somewhere, they would put their differences aside. Cory had dreamed about it happening several times: AshDee divorcing her husband and turning to Cory for forgiveness; AshDee coming to Cory's wedding, though Cory hadn't gone to hers; AshDee in the audience when Cory was receiving a Pulitzer. She'd always liked this last scenario the best, but now all their chances were over.

Not so with EmJay. Cory would accept the responsibility. She would raise EmJay as her own, fulfilling her duty as she had with her father. Only this time it would be different. She had only to look at the little face in the photograph and know that she would love EmJay in a way no one else in the world could. In return, EmJay would love Cory more than AshDee ever had. For Cory it would almost be like turning back the clock to the time before their estrangement.

There was another, powerful reason for her decision. In accepting custody of EmJay, she would be true to her father's memory. He wouldn't have been at all pleased to have his granddaughter raised as a Mormon.

When at last Cory was allowed to see Dolores Clark, she strode into the office, keeping her body rigid and her face stern. "Thank you for seeing me," she said between clenched teeth.

Dolores stood, one hand pushing her long black hair over her shoulder, her eyes puzzled. "And you are?"

"Cory Steele. Didn't your receptionist tell you? I've been waiting for two days!"

"She gave me a memo." Dolores passed Cory a yellow square of paper, and Cory's eyes riveted on the words: *Cory Steele waiting urgently to see you. Will return tomorrow if you don't make it out of your meeting by closing time.*

"I had the impression you were a man," explained Dolores, seating herself once more. "Sorry about the wait. It couldn't be helped. Please, have a seat."

Cory perched on the edge of a leather chair in front of the desk. She wet her lips with the tip of her tongue before saying, "I've come about my sister."

"Your sister?" The attorney shook her head. "I'm not sure what you're referring to. With your last name, I thought you might be here because of Ashley Steele Grayson, but perhaps you—"

"Ashley was my sister." Cory gripped the armrests of her chair. "I've come about my niece. They told me you gave her to a man in Utah?"

"He was named in the will. We followed the Graysons' instructions."

Cory listened as the attorney outlined the details. "I didn't realize Ashley even had a sister," Dolores concluded. "I remember a mention of her family in the custody documents but no specific mention of a sister. I can only assume you weren't close?"

Cory's mouth tightened, but she refused to give Dolores the satisfaction of an answer. "I understand that my sister's husband had no family. As AshDee's only relative, I should be responsible for their daughter."

"It doesn't quite work that way." There was no emotion on the attorney's face, and Cory wondered if she practiced the facade in the mirror.

"I'm her only relative! There's no one else." Tension built in Cory's head.

"I'm sorry, but you were not named as guardian."

"Where is she?" Cory hated that her voice sounded shrill, out of control.

Dolores shook her head. "I'm going to have to talk to her guardian."

Cory leapt to her feet, seething with the frustration of her two-day wait. "I want to know where she is now!" Her purse banged against the edge of the desk, scattering a few papers. "If you don't tell me, I'll get a court order. And if that doesn't work, I swear, I'll take this place apart!"

Dolores stood. "Ms. Steele, I think we can handle this without becoming violent. Sit down or I'll call someone to escort you out."

Taking a deep breath, Cory sat. "Sorry," she said, trying to remain calm but not feeling a bit repentant. "I just want to make sure she's okay. And I need to talk with her present guardian. I believe I'll be able to work things out to everyone's satisfaction. Will you tell me where she is?"

Dolores studied her in silence awhile before pressing a button on her intercom. "June, can you bring me the Grayson file I asked you to pull this morning? Thank you."

Cory felt a little thrill of victory. She was going to get the address in Utah.

A young woman came into the room carrying a thin green folder. *My sister's life reduced to this folder,* Cory thought, and almost wept.

"Ms. Steele, this is my assistant, June Clancy. June, this is Ashley Grayson's sister, Cory Steele."

"Steele?" June looked puzzled as she studied Cory. "But she didn't have . . . wait a moment." She opened the file. "I think I remember seeing . . . here it is, in the middle of these names."

Dolores glanced at the line in question. Cory wished she dared jump to her feet and push them aside to see what was so compelling.

"Are you Corrine?" Dolores asked after a few interminable seconds.

"Yes, but AshDee never called me that."

Dolores's mouth turned upward in a slight smile. "People have a tendency to use given names in legal documents. Apparently there is a mention of you in the will. A small bequest of a photograph. I believe it's of your mother."

Cory instantly remembered the photograph. She'd taken it herself with her first camera all those years ago. She couldn't have been more than eleven years old. After their mother's death a year later, she'd asked a neighbor to have it enlarged for AshDee's birthday. Before wrapping the picture, Cory had placed it in a pewter frame that had belonged to their grandmother.

"Do you have it?" Cory asked quickly.

"Yes. We were about to send it along to her daughter, with several other unclaimed items. But June will get it for you on your way out."

June started for the door, motioning for Cory to follow her.

"What about the address? I need to be able to contact my niece."

Dolores sighed and jotted something on a pad of paper before ripping off the sheet and handing it to Cory. "As I said before, I can't give you that information until I talk to her guardian, but this is the address of a memorial service they're holding in Utah tomorrow morning. Both your niece and her guardian will be in attendance. If you hurry, you can make the service. I'll try to call to let them know you're coming."

Cory took the paper, knowing she wouldn't get anything further from the woman. "Thank you," she forced herself to say. Dolores inclined her head gracefully.

"Come with me," said the assistant, "and I'll get your picture."

Cory followed her out the door. Yes, she would collect her picture, catch a taxi to the airport, and then, so help her, she was flying to Utah to take EmJay away from that interloping cultist or die trying.

Chapter Seven

Mitch took his time dressing Emily Jane on Saturday morning, exactly three weeks after she'd been put in his arms. Today was special—and not only because it marked the first three difficult, life-changing weeks they had spent together. Today they would attend the memorial service for Emily Jane's parents.

The baby grinned at him as he finished buttoning her red blouse and started on her hair. When he was finished, she promptly pulled out the bow. Sighing, he gave her some paper to play with until he had the hair ready again. Then he rescued the paper before it became her second breakfast. Her shoes and socks were a breeze. Shoes meant going "bye-bye," and Emily Jane loved leaving the house with him. "All ready," he said at last.

Mitch picked up Emily Jane and swung her onto his shoulders. Giggling, she thrust her hands into his hair and hung on tight. She was almost sleeping through the night now. When she did wake, he only had to reach down into her bed and hold her little hand or pat her stomach until she went back to sleep. It wasn't a perfect system, but it was working. His research, however, still suffered. Emily Jane didn't like to share his attention during the day, and the truth was, he had a hard time pulling himself away from her. She had rapidly become more important than wolves to him.

At the church near his parents' house in Alpine, people were already arriving. As he walked in the foyer, he immediately spied a guy he knew from his mission to Brazil.

"Elder Lundgren!" he said, shifting Emily Jane to his left hip.

"Elder Huntington!" They shook hands firmly.

"Only it's Mitch now. And you're . . . Roger?"

"Yep, that's me. I grew a little." Roger patted his stomach. "Now my wife's complaining that I'm starting to lose my hair. But you've gained weight, too, Mitch. Not enough, but it looks good on you."

Mitch grinned. "I ate eggs every day for three months to gain weight."

"Did you? That reminds me of the time Lane snuck into that old hen house and stole those eggs. Remember?"

Mitch hadn't until now. He laughed. "Can you believe he tried to juggle them?"

Roger let out a loud guffaw. "Ha! I'll never get over the sight of him wiping raw egg out of his eyes."

It was just these memories that Mitch craved. Biting back tears, he bounced the baby in his arms. "This is Emily Jane."

"She looks like Lane's wife, doesn't she? I saw the picture you have set up here. Beautiful child."

Mitch nodded his agreement. "It's good to see you, Roger. Glad you came."

There were many more guests—some he knew from Brazil, others from Lane's old ward, and even five college friends of Ashley's. Some had come alone, while others had brought their families. In all, they filled up nearly half the chapel.

Lane and Ashley's former bishop spoke first, and afterward he invited any who wanted to speak to come up to the pulpit. As Mitch listened to stories of Lane and Ashley, he felt that his friends weren't far away. He was glad he'd asked Tyler to videotape the event for Emily Jane.

When everyone had finished, Mitch's father, Cameron Huntington, sang "O My Father," Ashley's favorite hymn. As his rich voice filled the chapel, Mitch recalled the day Ashley told him this song had been instrumental in her conversion. "When I sang the part about having a Heavenly Mother," she'd said, "I knew the gospel was true."

His father returned to the bench, and Mitch handed a sleeping Emily Jane to him before going to the pulpit. "Thanks for coming," he said. "I've been feeling disoriented these past weeks, especially with the change at my house." A few chuckled at this. "It's really helped me to have this memorial service since I didn't have the chance to be at the funeral. I know that when she's older, Emily Jane will appreciate all the stories you have shared today. As for me, I met Lane in the mission field. He was my trainer when I first arrived in Brazil, and we spent six crazy, marvelous months together. The last month he was there, we were together again, opening a new area. He was as close as a brother to me. And Ashley, well, if he hadn't been in the way, I would have married her myself." More laughter. Mitch's emotions rose in his throat, making it difficult to speak. "Lane and Ashley were the best kind of people, and I know they've gone on to better things. I promise I'm going to do the best I can to raise Emily Jane the way they would have—in the gospel, with love, and a lot of support from my family. Thanks again. Remember, we have lunch here for anyone who'd like to stay."

At that moment he noticed the woman sitting alone on the back row. She wore a sleeveless, flowing dress that reminded him of a finger painting he'd made in kindergarten. Blues, mauves, yellows, and greens blurred together in a jumble of wild celebration. Yet it wasn't the dress or its conspicuous lack of sleeves in an LDS chapel that arrested him, but rather her face. She looked like Ashley.

Yet Ashley was dead.

"Are you all right?" asked the Graysons' former bishop, touching his shoulder.

Mitch blinked, but the woman was too far away for him to see clearly. Goose bumps broke out on his arms, though the chapel was comfortably warm.

"I'm fine," he whispered. Another part of his mind registered that Emily Jane had awakened in his father's arms and was beginning to cry. He hurried toward her.

"Come to Mitch," he whispered. Emily Jane smiled and held out her arms, arching her body toward him. She might not be able to say his name yet, but she could certainly let him know how happy she was to have him back. Rubbing her sleepy eyes, she snuggled her head in the space between his neck and shoulder. Mitch turned to see the woman who looked like Ashley, but his view was blocked by Roger's head two rows back.

He faced the front and sang the closing hymn with the others. After the prayer, he stood and looked for the woman. Would she be there? Or had it been some type of vision?

No vision. She was still in the back, standing now. Alone as before.

"Mitch," Amanda hissed. "Is something wrong? You look pale."

Like I've seen a ghost, he agreed silently. "Do you see that woman in the back?"

"Yes. Who is she?"

"I don't know." As his initial shock faded, curiosity was quickly taking its place.

"Well, go and see. I'll help Mom direct the others to the food."

Mitch had the odd urge to give Emily Jane to his sister so the woman wouldn't see her up close, but that seemed paranoid and would only make Emily Jane cry.

He shuffled sideways to the aisle and began walking toward the woman. Though her curly hair was the same bright reddish orange as Ashley's, he saw now that it barely brushed the top of her shoulders. Ashley's had gone halfway down her back. This woman definitely had more freckles, which he suspected had been enhanced by repeated exposure to the sun. Her slender arms looked much more defined, and her face was more oval than Ashley's.

Mitch gave an inaudible sigh. She definitely wasn't Ashley. This close up, he wasn't even sure they looked that much alike—aside from the hair. He was not seeing a spirit but a live woman. He almost laughed.

Shifting Emily Jane to his left arm and hip, he held out his right hand. "Hello, I'm Mitch Huntington." Her hand felt small in his, but she returned the handshake with a strong grip. "This is Emily Jane," he added, tilting his head toward the baby. "Who are you? How did you know Lane and Ashley?"

There was a shimmer in the woman's blue eyes, as though she might have recently been close to tears. She was attractive—beautiful, even, he would say. Not in the frilly way of Ashley, but in an active, energetic way. He bet she could beat him to the top of Mount Timpanogos, all the time looking as pretty as she did at that moment. He liked the idea, though he wasn't sure at all if he appreciated the way his heart was racing.

She blinked several times before replying in an icy, unfeeling voice. "I'm Cory Steele. I'm AshDee's—Ashley's—sister."

Mitch sucked in a breath, feeling as though someone had punched him in the gut. Was this the greedy, weasel-faced Cory Steele, who was trying to put his nose in where it didn't belong? This was the guy Mitch had secretly envisioned punching in the face if he so much as dared question Mitch's guardianship? He struggled to make sense of the change. She definitely wasn't a man, and her face didn't begin to resemble that of any weasel on earth.

"Ashley's sister?" he croaked, willing himself not to be fooled by her attractiveness. She nodded.

Definitely trouble. "Why are you here?" he asked. Since Ashley's family had disowned her for following her heart, he felt it was a valid question.

Cory's eyes went to Emily Jane and then back to him. "That should be perfectly clear. I'm here to take custody of my niece."

Chapter Eight

Cory hadn't believed her claim on EmJay would go over without opposition, but she hadn't expected the sudden, violent anger burning on Mitch Huntington's face. His jaw clenched, and his posture became instantly defensive. The immediate and powerful reaction destroyed her preconceived notions of him as a weak competitor. Sure, he was attractive enough in a casual way, with his bright blue eyes and the longish hair that framed his angular forehead, and his handshake had been surprisingly firm and confident. But his stylish suit didn't hide the fact that he was a bit too thin for his height, and the way he held the baby made him seem, well, rather domesticated. Nothing to really challenge her—or so she'd thought.

What disturbed her most was his control. He didn't allow his feelings to burst out of him as she had in the attorney's office yesterday. In fact, he studied her a full fifteen seconds without speaking. Cory counted it out, each second building the pressure inside her chest.

Then he said quite calmly, "I'm Emily Jane's legal guardian, and she stays with me. However, you're welcome to hold her, though I must warn you, she doesn't take kindly to *strangers*."

The emphasis caused Cory a fresh wave of guilt. All at once, she knew she deserved every bit of his scorn. Here she was looking at her very own niece—her only niece—for the first time. There was no excuse under heaven for that.

It's AshDee's fault, her mind cried in response. *She's the one who walked out!*

Cory glared at Mitch, but he met her gaze with equal intensity. Some part of her mind noticed the music that ebbed and swelled around them as the last few people filtered from the chapel. The melody somehow reminded her of the jungle, where she had felt, albeit for only brief instances, a connection with something otherworldly. Something her father might have termed godly.

Swallowing with difficulty, she looked away from Mitch's angry, challenging eyes, focusing instead on her niece. EmJay stared at her with enormous eyes, neither smiling nor frowning. She was more adorable than in her pictures. Her skin was white and smooth, marred only by a few freckles. Her bright hair poked out in curls everywhere except on top where a red bow secured them in place. She wore a red blouse, a brown-and-red plaid skirt, off-white tights, and brown suede dress shoes with straps that emphasized her chubby feet. Cory fought tears—fought any weakness within herself. She reached for the baby.

Still staring at her, EmJay lifted her arms toward Cory. This time Cory's tears came with no way to stop them. All the reasons she had come to Utah in search of EmJay melted away—all but one. The love she'd hoped to feel for her sister's baby surrounded her in huge undulating waves, blotting out everything else. *I never knew,* she thought wonderingly. *I never knew.*

Triumphantly, she glanced at Mitch and saw with satisfaction that his mouth was silently ajar, his anger apparently given way to surprise. But was it surprise at the baby's desertion, or at Cory's tears?

"Hi, EmJay," she crooned in a high voice. She'd often played with the native children at the camp in Brazil, and the babies liked it when she talked this way. "I'm your Aunt Cory. Yes, I am. And you're so much prettier than in your pictures." She found herself swaying back and forth to the rhythm of the postlude music.

The baby's solemn eyes didn't leave Cory's face.

"I'm sorry I didn't come sooner. I know I should have."

EmJay finally spoke in a soft, tentative voice, "Momma."

The man beside her gave a little groan. "She sees the resemblance," he said half under his breath. The surprise in his eyes was now muted by sadness.

Shaking her head, EmJay strained away from Cory in a valiant effort to return to Mitch. Cory resisted the urge to hold onto her niece and run. EmJay buried her face in Mitch's chest, yet almost immediately turned her head to peek at Cory.

"Would you like to eat lunch?" Mitch asked. "They have it set up in the next room." To his credit, though she hated giving him any, he didn't appear to be gloating but seemed as shaken as she was at the baby's response.

"I am hungry," she admitted. She had to eat and could use the time to regroup. Somehow she had to convince this man that EmJay belonged with her.

"Mitch!" a pregnant woman Cory assumed was his wife appeared behind them. "Come on. Hurry, everyone's waiting."

EmJay lifted her head and smiled at the woman before darting another shy glance toward Cory.

"Manda, this is Cory Steele," Mitch said. "She claims she's Ashley's sister."

"I *am* her sister." Cory didn't like his implication.

"You look like her. Nice to meet you." The woman held out a hand. "I'm Amanda. I knew Ashley and Lane for only a few months, but I really liked them." Cory mumbled a greeting, not daring to take her eyes off Mitch for long.

"Funny," he said slowly. "Ashley never mentioned she had a sister."

"That just goes to show that you weren't as close as you thought,"

Cory retorted, goaded beyond politeness. "And you think you should be raising my niece?"

His eyebrows rose. "Did you know about me?" he countered.

Reluctantly, she shook her head.

"I was in their ward at BYU before they were married, and even after they went to a different ward, I saw them practically every day. I was the best man at their wedding. I helped Lane with his car when it broke down. I was at the hospital the night Emily Jane was born. I helped move them to Texas last December. I answered e-mails from one or the other of them every week. I'm the one they chose to raise their daughter. In all that time, Ashley never mentioned she had a sister."

Cory didn't know what a "ward" was, or "BYU," but the meaning of his words were clear. Her sister had found a new life, a good life, apparently, and hadn't been inclined to talk about the rift in their family. AshDee had gone on without her. Hurt sliced deep into Cory's heart.

"We were like family," Mitch added.

Cory glared at him. "I'm AshDee's *only* family."

"Uh, can we talk about this later?" Amanda pulled Mitch toward the door. "Another ward has the church at one. We've got to be out of here by then."

"Okay." Mitch's face relaxed. "But I hope Mom didn't make potatoes and green Jell-O."

Amanda grinned at the apparent joke Cory didn't get. Cory watched them leave the chapel, feeling almost as bereft as she had the day AshDee had packed her suitcase and left home for good, their father shaking his fist after her. "And don't ever come back," he'd yelled, "unless you give up that cult you've joined!"

The music suddenly stopped, and Cory's eyes caught a movement on the stand. A lady was there, gathering piano books into a small canvas bag. She walked down the aisle, smiling and nodding as she passed. Cory was alone.

She hadn't been in a church since her father's funeral. This didn't look like the churches in the poor neighborhood where she'd grown up. The room was wider and there were no pictures nearby, though she'd seen one of Christ in the foyer. Everything was well built and in excellent repair.

Without the music, the silence was deafening. Not like the pregnant silence in the jungle before a storm, or the hush of the animals when a large predator was near, but rather a spiritual silence that reached into Cory's soul. She felt an unexplained urge to run to the front, to throw herself on her knees, and beg for . . . for what? And to whom? There was nothing here. Nothing but the large photograph of her sister and her husband at the wedding Cory had missed.

Then why did she feel something or someone was there? An eeriness shuddered up her spine. "AshDee," she whispered, staring at the photograph that somehow she'd approached without realizing. But, no, the presence she sensed wasn't her sister, and she wasn't about to consider that it might be God.

Scoffing at her own thoughts, Cory backtracked to her bench and pulled out her duffel bag from where she had stowed it at the beginning of the service. Afraid she might be late or lose herself along the way, she had taken a taxi to Alpine and been forced to carry her belongings with her. After lunch she'd have to rent a car and find a motel. Apparently she would also need a good attorney.

In the hallway, she followed the sound of voices. A door opened onto a spacious room with a glossy wooden floor. *They play basketball,* she thought, noting the lines painted permanently on the floor. She hadn't thought of Mormons playing ball.

Tables were laid end to end, forming two long lines. People sat at them, eating and talking. *They knew my sister,* Cory thought. *They loved her enough to attend this service.* A warmth filled her heart, and for what seemed like the hundreth time that day, she fought tears. Another thought followed, one not as welcomed. *I don't know any of them.* Once, she had known everything about AshDee.

"Cory, over here!" Amanda was waving her to an empty place next to where Mitch was seated, holding EmJay on his lap. Cory sauntered over, trying her best to look confident.

Amanda touched her arm. "Gang, meet Cory. She's Ashley's sister. I'll let you do the introductions, because I've got a runaway. Don't worry, I'll let the ladies in the kitchen know we need another plate." This last she said over her shoulder as she rushed across the room after a dark-haired toddler who was doing her best to escape past a blond boy through a side door.

Cory sat by Mitch, letting her duffel slide gently to the floor. From his lap, the baby peered out at her, offering the tiniest of smiles. Before she could stop herself, Cory reached out and smoothed the wild hair that reminded her so much of her sister's. She saw Mitch stiffen.

"Aren't you going to introduce us, Mitchell?" asked an elegant older woman across from Mitch. She wore a flowing blue dress that matched her eyes, and her blonde hair was styled becomingly. Cory guessed this was Mitch's mother, though she seemed to resemble the pregnant Amanda as well, so maybe she was wrong. At the elegant woman's right was a tall, balding, rotund man with glasses. She recognized him as the man who had sung the lovely hymn during the service. He didn't look anything like those around him, except for the green eyes, which Amanda shared. *Maybe these are her parents, not his,* Cory thought. Not that it really mattered. They were all the enemy.

"I met her myself only two minutes ago," Mitch said in a cold voice.

The older woman stared hard at him for a long, pointed moment. When Mitch didn't respond, she said, "Then I'll do it." Her gracious smile returned. "I'm Jessica Huntington, and this is my husband, Cameron." She touched the balding man's arm. "Next to him is our daughter Kerrianne and her three children, Misty, Benjamin, and Caleb."

"Nice to meet you," Kerrianne said. She resembled Amanda, in a thin, washed-out, less vibrant sort of way, though her eyes were blue like her mother's. Cory thought she seemed sad and tired.

No wonder, with three children. Cory wondered which man was her husband.

"Tyler's our youngest," Jessica nodded to the man sitting on the other side of Mitch. The young man's smile was contagious, his green eyes sparkling beneath his black-framed glasses. "Next to him with all that beautiful blonde hair is Savvy Hergarter, a family friend."

"Then there's Blake Simmons, our son-in-law," Jessica continued. Cory inclined her head toward the attractive, dark-haired man who gave her a friendly smile. "And you've already met Amanda. The children she's chasing are Kevin and Mara. The rest of the people here aren't related, but they knew your sister in some way."

Cory nodded, still unsure at even the family relationships. Was Blake married to Kerrianne?

"Did you come from California?" Jessica asked, picking up her fork.

"No, from Texas," Mitch said before Cory could reply. "She was visiting Ashley's lawyer. She wants custody of Emily Jane."

A frown creased Jessica's face, and deep lines appeared on her brow. "Oh, so that's how it is."

Cory squirmed under her intent stare, stifling a desire to bite her nails. For some reason she wished desperately that she didn't have to disappoint this woman. "Before that I was working in the Amazon," she said quickly.

The lines on Jessica's brow smoothed. "What do you do?"

"I'm a photojournalist, with a particular interest in wildlife photography."

Mitch, who'd been concentrating on getting potatoes into EmJay's mouth, turned toward her, obviously interested. "You take pictures of animals?"

She nodded. "My favorites this time were three black Brazilian jaguars. For days I watched a mother and her cubs. At times I was so close I could hear them breathing."

Everyone began asking questions, which Cory fielded easily. She was in her element, confident now, not a stranger trying to steal a baby.

At one point, Amanda brought her a plate of food, and Cory began eating. With Amanda were the dark-haired toddler and the blond boy, who seemed to be her children. *That means she and Mitch will have three when her baby comes,* Cory thought. *Why do they want EmJay as well?*

During a lull in the conversation, Kerrianne's daughter, whose name Cory couldn't remember but who reminded her of a blonde porcelain doll, spoke. "Uncle Mitch has a lot of animals. He carries them around and lets us play with them."

"He does," confirmed Amanda's son, Kevin. He was seated next to the man named Blake, who now had the dark-haired escape artist on his lap. "Did you bring one today, Uncle Mitch? I hope you brought Hiccup."

Mitch grinned, and Cory was shocked at the change in his brooding features. He really was quite handsome when he wasn't trying to kill her with evil stares. "Well," he said, "Hiccup's busy with her babies, so she couldn't come. But Dizzy wasn't doing anything, so I brought her."

"Mitchell," his mother warned in a low voice. "We're eating."

"Dizzy has to eat, too." To the children's delight, Mitch shifted EmJay to his other leg, reached into the pocket of a jacket that hung over his chair, and pulled out a small plastic ball. A little brown creature with a white stripe down the center of its face scurried around inside.

"Mitchell!" Jessica Huntington's voice rose to a high pitch.

Amanda popped up from her seat next to Jessica. "She's right, Mitch. We're eating. Put it away now."

"But everyone's almost through."

"Don't mess with me, I'm pregnant."

Sighing, Mitch put the animal back, and the children groaned with disappointment. "In a minute," he promised.

Cory chuckled to herself. This was quite a family!

Emily Jane began wriggling to get down. "Okay," Mitch said, watching her toddle a few steps away. "But don't go far."

"Right. Like she ever gets out of your sight," Amanda said with a snort.

Mitch's grin wavered. "She just wants to make sure I don't leave." He sent an unreadable glance at Cory.

"You know what he did?" Amanda continued in a conspiratorial voice. Cory leaned toward her over the table to catch every word. "He borrowed Kerrianne's toddler bed." Amanda glanced at her mother to include her in the conversation. "You know, the one she made for Misty before Benjamin was born, and he set it right next to his bed."

"Hey, it's low enough to the ground that she can get in and out when she wants," Mitch said. "The portable crib was like a prison for the kid."

Amanda giggled. "Don't let him fool you, Cory. He did it so he could hold her hand at night if she wakes up. Isn't that sweet?"

"It's so I can get some sleep," he growled. "So we can *both* get some sleep."

"I still say it's sweet," Amanda said. "Sounds like something Kerrianne or I would do."

Cory thought it was sweet, too. She tried to picture the tall man lying on a bed with his hand extended to comfort EmJay in the night. Did he really do that? By the embarrassed flush on his face, he did.

Cameron had listened with interest to the conversation. Now he said, "He gets it from me. I can't tell you how many times I used to sneak into your rooms to sing to you after your mother put you down for the night."

"I remember that," Mitch said.

Jessica shook her head. "Sorry, dear, but you didn't fool anyone by all that tiptoeing. I heard you every time."

"Did you?" His surprise caused a flurry of chuckles.

Cory was glad for the happiness she saw here. She hadn't known what to expect at this memorial service but had worried about keeping her composure. With this family, it was hard to believe that AshDee wasn't simply waiting for her in the next room.

"Oh, I meant to tell you," Cory said to Cameron as the laughter subsided. "I really enjoyed your song during the service. Thank you." Again the attention shifted to her, and Cory wished she'd kept silent.

Cameron beamed. "You're very welcome."

"You have a wonderful voice," she added. "I'm glad you chose that song."

"I didn't."

Mitch cleared his throat. "It was Ashley's favorite hymn. She sang it herself on the day she was baptized." His words firmly reminded her that no matter how friendly these people seemed, or how deeply they had awakened her sense of family, she was not one of them.

"I didn't know." Indeed, there was too much about her sister that she didn't know.

An awkward silence fell over their end of the table. Melancholy gripped Cory's heart. She had the crazy desire to be here with this family and at the same time run as fast and far away from them as she could. What was it about them that was so attractive to her? Was it the same thing Ashley had felt?

It's just a family, she told herself.

The room was quickly thinning of people, and a few came by to offer condolences to Mitch—and to Cory when they learned who she was. Cory thanked them for their stories. She knew she should call a taxi and find a motel, though she didn't want to desert her niece. She was about to ask Mitch for his address, when Kerrianne sighed loudly.

"What's wrong, dear?" Cameron put his arm around his daughter.

"I was thinking of Adam," she said, "and how he'd be pulling out that stupid old guitar right now and playing songs."

"Who's to say he's not doing it?" Cameron asked, his voice gentle. "Maybe that's the music I'm hearing in my heart." Kerrianne smiled through her tears and leaned into her father's embrace.

Cory blinked in confusion, but Jessica explained. "Kerrianne's husband was killed in a car accident a year and a half ago. Right before Christmas. Little Caleb was barely three months old. He was a wonderful man, and, as I'm sure you can imagine, it's been difficult for her. Even knowing they'll be together again someday."

"I'm sorry," Cory choked out in a barely audible voice. "I didn't realize. I guess I'm a little mixed up. I thought Blake was her husband."

Amanda laughed. "Oh, no. Blake's *my* husband."

"I thought you were—" Cory glanced at Mitch, who was watching EmJay as she wandered around the tables, dodging any hands that reached toward her.

Amanda laughed. "Mitch? You got to be kidding. He's my brother!"

Now everything fell into place—the way Amanda kept running over to deal with the children near Blake and why Kerrianne was so quiet. And most of all why Mitch wasn't willing to consider the possibility of her taking EmJay.

Cory turned to him. "You want to raise a baby alone?"

The anger flared again in his eyes, but his voice didn't grow louder. "I'm not alone." He indicated the others. "I have all the support I need. What about you? I don't see your family here."

"I don't have any family left!" she snapped. "But that's not what I meant. You're a man."

"Men can't raise babies?" Mitch pointed to Blake. "He did. See that little boy, Kevin? Well, Kevin is his cousin's son, but Blake raised him from the time he was a baby. Alone. That was long before he and Manda met. He had Mara a few months by himself as well before they were married. He's done wonders with those children, and I can do the same. When I get married, it'll be to a woman like my sister who will love Emily Jane as much as I do. I admit when Emily Jane first came to me, I was scared and worried that I couldn't do it. Wasn't even sure if I wanted to. But I've learned an awful lot these past three weeks, and I know this is something I can do!"

"Three weeks," she spat. "Three weeks! That's nothing. This is a lifetime commitment! And when it boils down to it, blood is always thicker than friendship. AshDee was *my* sister, not yours."

Mitch shook his head. "You haven't got a clue what you're saying.

86

Lane and Ashley were not only my best friends. They were my sister and brother in the gospel, and I would give up my life for their child. Can you say the same?"

"Of—of course I would!" But despite the new love blossoming in her heart, Cory realized that she didn't know EmJay enough to feel anything for her that wasn't mixed up in her tumultuous emotions for AshDee. Logically, she knew it should be worth anything to have EmJay with her, but knowing wasn't the same as *feeling*.

Cory knew she'd lost that round. "I'd better go," she said, standing. "If you won't listen to reason, then I guess my attorney will have to contact you."

"Tell him to contact my lawyer." Mitch came to his feet also, staring down at her with angry eyes.

"Look, EmJay is my niece," Cory said, trying one last time. "My sister would have wanted me to raise her."

He shook his head, which caused his hair to fall into his face. He raked it back impatiently. "That's where you're wrong. Lane and Ashley wanted more than anything for their daughter to know her Savior. To them that meant being raised a believer. They knew I would do that for them. And even if I somehow failed to teach her the gospel, Ashley still wanted me to have Emily Jane because she wanted to be sure her daughter would be loved no matter what choices she made down the road."

"I loved my sister," Cory retorted. "I always loved her! I know we both made mistakes in the past, but I'm here for EmJay now."

"Now? Now?" Mitch threw up his hands, and for the first time his anger spilled from his voice like acid. "*I'm* the one who was with her when she was mourning her mother, when she wandered around my house searching each room sobbing 'Momma, Momma.' *I'm* the one who paced the floor with her as she cried every night for a week. Where were you then, huh? I'll tell you—gallivanting after a Brazilian Jaguar!"

"How dare you!" Cory clenched her fists. "I came as soon as I found out my sister was dead!"

Her last word reverberated loudly in the sudden quiet of the room. Cory became aware of everyone staring at her, various shocked expressions on their faces. She blushed furiously as she fought to hold back tears. Maybe she should be content that she had broken through the unnerving control Mitch seemed to have on his emotions, but she knew her own control had fared worse.

"I never should have come here today," she muttered.

"Maybe you shouldn't have," Mitch agreed.

Wishing she dared slap his face, Cory seized her duffel bag and started for the door.

Chapter Nine

"Go after her!" Amanda hissed as Cory strode across the cultural hall.

Mitch's gaze shifted to his family, all of whom were on their feet now, staring at him. His mother had her hands on her hips, lips pursed. His father was shaking his head. Mitch's first urge was to defend his actions, but the sinking feeling in his gut told him he was in the wrong. Yes, Cory was wrong, too, but she hadn't been taught better. On the other hand, he was an elder, a representative of the Lord in all times and in all places. Yet he'd let his anger control him.

"I know that right now you're defending your rights to Emily Jane," his father said, "but this isn't about you—or that young woman." He nodded at Cory's retreating back.

Mitch blew out a long sigh. "It's about Emily Jane." He knew that intellectually, but that red-haired *creature* provoked more anger than any man could sanely endure.

"Your father's right," said his mother. "You have custody and should keep it, but there's no sense in starting a war. It'll only make things worse."

Blake cleared his throat to attract their attention. "Take a gander at that."

Mitch's heart jumped as he glanced in the direction his brother-in-law was pointing. Between the door and the far table, Cory was kneeling down next to Emily Jane. Was she going to grab her and run? Mitch berated himself for taking his eyes from Emily Jane. His muscles poised to spring in their direction, silently signaling Blake and Tyler to follow.

Amanda read the communication. "Wait."

Mitch waited, trusting his sister's opinion. She was right. Cory wasn't kidnapping the baby but only talking to her. The two heads, so different in size, had nearly the same odd, reddish orange hair. Their evident blood relationship caused a wave of guilt to surge in his chest.

"Go defuse the situation," Blake advised. His voice, which many had said belonged on the radio, was warm and slightly amused.

Mitch didn't need the urging. He was already wondering how Ashley would feel about the way he'd treated her sister. Granted, the woman was a royal pain in the neck, but he'd dealt with tough situations before. He should have controlled himself better.

Almost hesitantly, he traced Cory's steps. Soon her words became audible. "Yep, and I'm going to tell you all about her. I have a hundred stories, you know. Some of them are quite funny. Your mom had a wonderful sense of humor. She was cute, too. Looked just like you. In fact, seeing you is like . . ." Her voice cracked and faded. Mitch could see she was crying. The freckles on her face stood out more clearly, and the tip of her nose was turning red. For some unidentifiable reason, his heart hurt.

Sensing his presence, she stared up at him, her blue eyes glistening with tears. Uncomfortable, Mitch avoided her gaze by looking at Emily Jane. The baby glanced at him and then took a step toward Cory, making a slight upward movement that signaled her desire to be carried. Cory sucked in a breath. She reached for Emily Jane and held her close. Leaving her duffel bag at her feet, she stood and gazed at Mitch uncertainly, wiping at a tear with her fingertips.

Mitch saw the way Emily Jane's hand caught up in Cory's hair, gently toying with the curls, and reminded him of how she'd done that with Ashley. For a long moment, he couldn't speak or even breathe past the longing in his heart—longing for Emily Jane to have her mother alive and well.

"I'm sorry," he said finally, fumbling in his pocket for the package of tissue he had learned to carry in case Emily Jane needing wiping. "Look, this isn't about us, is it? It's about Emily Jane. I want to fulfill Lane and Ashley's wishes, but that doesn't mean I want to exclude you from Emily Jane's life. We'll find a way to work something out. Please, let's put all this behind us and think of Emily Jane."

Cory accepted the tissue, a hint of a smile coming to her reddened lips. "You mean start over?"

He nodded and extended his hand. "Hi, I'm Mitch Huntington, and I have to admit that I'm really jealous you got to see Brazilian jaguars in the jungle."

Now her smile became real. "Ah, I see. You're jealous. That explains a lot."

"Yes, I'm especially jealous of that dress. It reminds me of a finger painting I did in grade school, but unfortunately it didn't look nearly as good as that dress does on you." He blinked. "Oops, I probably shouldn't have said that, should I? Sort of like giving ammunition to the enemy."

Her smile faded. "I thought we were starting over."

"We are," he sighed, "but it's going to be tough."

She shrugged. "For now we'll agree to disagree on the custody issue. Deal?"

He didn't answer because something else demanded his attention. "Do you think tissue has any nutritional value?"

"Why?" She stared at him as though he'd gone crazy.

"Emily Jane likes to eat tissue—any kind of paper, really. Cardboard, too. Be warned." He pointed to the unused tissue in her hand. Emily Jane had been pulling on it and had succeeded in breaking off a large piece that was quickly heading to her mouth.

"She must be starving! Babies don't *eat* paper."

"Oh, yeah?" Mitch flashed his best all-knowing smile. "Emily Jane does—and she likes it, too."

Cory pulled the tissue away, and Emily Jane's face crumpled. She abruptly propelled herself in Mitch's direction, sending Cory temporarily off balance. Mitch was grateful to have the baby back in his arms. What would he have done if she'd wanted to leave with Cory?

"So where do we go from here?" Cory's blue eyes held his. He noticed that she had somehow managed to get a tan between all those freckles. Ashley had always tried to stay out of the sun.

"I'm not sure. Maybe we can sit down and talk about it. Get to know each other and see what our plans for the future might be. Then go from there. How long are you staying in Utah?"

"As long as it takes." Once again her voice was hard.

"I thought we had a truce."

She gave him a sardonic grin. "A few weeks at least," she amended. "I actually left my last assignment not quite finished, but they're going to work around me. I'm not sure when my next one will begin. I'll have to talk to my agent."

"You're going back to the Amazon?" He felt a surge of excitement as he said the words. How he would love to visit the jungle!

"Yes. I'll be there for an indefinite period of time."

That brought Mitch forcefully back to reality. Was the jungle any place for a baby? What did she plan to do with Emily Jane while she was out chasing jaguars?

Biting his tongue, he didn't allow himself the satisfaction of voicing these thoughts. He had offered a truce, however temporary, so for now he'd let it go. Maybe she'd come to realize the absurdity on her own as she came to know Emily Jane's needs. Perhaps it would suffice to know that she could see Emily Jane whenever she was in the States. If not, there would be plenty of time for arguing later.

"Where are you staying?" he asked.

She shrugged. "I don't know yet. I was going to call a car rental place and then find a motel." Bending her knees, she reached down for her duffel with her left hand.

"I could drive you. I know a motel in Sandy that has good weekly rates."

"Sandy?"

"That's where I live. Just around the mountain."

"You could give me directions. I'm going to need a car anyway."

"I could," he said, "but I thought I'd show you where I live so you could visit Emily Jane."

He had her then. If she didn't come with him, she'd lose valuable time searching for his address, but she clearly wasn't happy about accepting help from him. Hey, maybe that was a good course for him to pursue. He'd conquer her with kindness, all the while showing her how well he could take care of Emily Jane.

"Okay," she said at last. "Thank you."

He thumbed over his shoulder. "I'm going to check with my family to make sure they don't need me to clean up or anything."

"I'll wait in the foyer," she said, pronouncing it foi-yay.

Boy, does she have a lot to learn about Mormons, he thought, grinning.

Amanda, Kerrianne, and his mother had everything well under control. They had already cleared the plates and were supervising as the men folded the tables. "You go on, Mitch," his mother said when he told her what had happened. "We have things taken care of here." She held up a hand. "But remember, you need to be an example. The best way to share the gospel with someone is to live it."

"Uh . . . okay, Mom." He wondered where she'd gotten the idea that he was trying to teach Cory the gospel.

He snapped his fingers. That was it! If Cory were a believer, he'd feel a lot better about sharing custody. He wouldn't worry about her teaching Emily Jane poor habits that might damage her testimony later. In time, if Cory proved to be really dedicated, he might actually feel good about allowing Emily Jane to stay with her for part of the week.

The thought of not having Emily Jane with him every instant was at once a relief and an awful, fearsome thing. While it would be wonderful to have someone to share decisions and responsibility with, what would he do on the days that he couldn't have her trusting little arms around his neck?

Well, Cory's not a member and not likely to become one, he reasoned. *The best I can hope for is to teach her not to disdain our ways.* Maybe that would be enough for her to still have a relationship with Emily Jane. Besides, being a member didn't automatically make someone fit to be a parent. The ill feeling in his stomach subsided.

He retrieved his jacket as his nieces and nephews gathered around him. "Uncle Mitch, aren't you going to show us your gerbil?"

"Oh, sure." Emily Jane was growing sleepy, but he squatted anyway, cradling the baby along the curve of his left arm. One by one, he allowed the children to hold or pet Dizzy, who was ecstatic to be released from her plastic ball. "Okay, that's enough, guys," he said after only a few minutes. "I have to take Emily Jane's aunt home."

"Awww," came the disappointed cries.

"Hey, don't worry. I bet your moms will bring you over to my house today if you ask. Come on now, give me a kiss so I can get going."

They showered him with wet, affectionate kisses until he laughingly begged for relief. Standing, Mitch tucked the ball with Dizzy into his pocket, turned Emily Jane so that her cheek lay on his shoulder, and sprinted for the door.

As promised, Cory was waiting for him in the foyer. She stood by the double glass doors, staring out at the church lawn. Her bright dress hung down to her sandaled feet, emphasizing her femininity. Mitch couldn't help noticing again how attractive she was, though at the moment her face was forlorn. Was she thinking of her sister? It comforted him to know that she had loved Ashley.

She gave a little start when he touched her arm. "Is everything okay?" he asked. "You look about a hundred miles away."

"Just thinking." Her eyes went to Emily Jane. "Ah, she's almost out. Must be nap time."

Mitch didn't reply. Emily Jane didn't exactly have a nap time. Instead, she fell asleep wherever she was—usually in his arms—at any time she felt like it. He wondered now if it would work better to schedule a regular nap time. He'd read something about it in one of the childcare books he'd been reading, but it seemed rather senseless to him. If a child was tired, she would sleep, right? Sometimes the experts fussed way too much about details. But maybe he was wrong.

He certainly wasn't going to admit that to Cory. "So, aren't you going to guess which car is mine?" he asked as they went out of the building and down the sidewalk to the parking lot.

"Okay." She brought her left forefinger to her chin. Mitch noticed that the nails were extremely short—probably bitten. "Let's see," she said. "Not either of the minivans—I'd say those belong to your sisters—nor that sleek-looking car there. I bet that's your parents'. That old green truck is probably your little brother's, and that tiny red Subaru there must belong to his girlfriend."

"Savvy's not actually his girlfriend," Mitch interrupted.

"They act like they belong together."

Mitch frowned. "He's the only one who doesn't think so."

"Isn't that the way it always is?" Cory pointed at his Mustang. "That must be yours. Those others are just too blah. Nice car, but that color is really atrocious."

Mitch didn't know whether he should be pleased or offended. "Yeah, maybe so." He feigned deep contemplation. "You know, I think my car is the exact same color as your hair."

She blinked. "My hair is *not* that color!"

His gaze swung between her and the Mustang. "You're right," he said gravely. "Your hair is definitely more orange."

She glared at him—or tried to. A smile kept trying to creep its way onto her face. He laughed, and she allowed her smile to emerge fully until she was laughing with him.

At the car, he unlocked the trunk for her large duffel bag. He could tell by the way her arm muscles flexed that it was heavy to lift, but while carrying the sleeping baby, he wasn't in a position to help. He walked around to the passenger side door and awkwardly unlocked it for her.

"Can I help you with anything?" she asked.

"It's okay. I'm used to doing things with her sleeping in my arms."

"Let me at least hold your jacket." She took it from his arm. "Though why you have a jacket with you in the summer is beyond me, especially when you're wearing that suit."

"You never know," Mitch said, unwilling to tell her of his allergy to cold. "I like to be prepared."

"A Boy Scout, huh?"

"Yep. That's me, a Boy Scout through and through." Mitch placed Emily Jane in her car seat and clipped the fasteners shut. She didn't even stir. "Besides, that jacket has the perfect pocket for my especially designed gerbil ball."

"Oh, the ball that holds the famous Dizzy."

He was surprised she remembered the name. "Infamous, you mean," he corrected. When he came around to his seat, she'd already extracted the ball from his pocket.

"May I?"

He shrugged. "Sure, just don't forget that I gave her the name for a reason. I normally bring Hiccup, but she and Elvis had babies, and she would hate me to take her away from them."

"Elvis?" Cory gave a little chuckle.

"Yeah. Hiccup and Dizzy used to be cage mates until I decided it was time for them to have babies. If you know anything about gerbils, you'll know that they're very territorial and don't take to new gerbils easily. So I had to go through the whole routine of putting a metal screen between Hiccup and Elvis until she wouldn't attack him. He didn't have a problem because he was so young and just wanted to snuggle. She was older, though, and didn't like him at all. Anyway, Elvis would go up to the screen and stroke his paw against it like a guitar. It was hilarious. Must have worked because after only a week, she was ready to be friends. Now they have nine children."

"Nine?" Cory looked up from the gerbil in her hands.

"Yep. Nine. That's a problem, too, because Hiccup can only feed eight babies at a time."

"Aaaa!" Cory reacted as Dizzy took a flying leap from her hands in a valiant effort to escape. Once on the floor, the gerbil scurried under the seat. "I'm sorry," Cory said, making a face.

"Don't worry about it. She's always been a live wire." He reached near her sandaled feet, making a clicking sound with his tongue. After a few seconds, Dizzy ran from under the seat and climbed onto his hand. Mitch gave her a sunflower seed from the cup holder in the dash and then stroked the white stripe between her eyes. "Give her some seeds," he advised, "and she'll be all right. She'll do anything for sunflower seeds."

When Cory had a few seeds in her hand, Mitch passed the gerbil to her. Satisfied that Dizzy would behave, he started the engine and put the Mustang into gear.

"So how is Hiccup doing with her nine babies?" Cory asked after a few moments of comfortable silence.

Mitch grinned. "Well, there was a runt. Tiny little fellow that I was sure was going to die. Elvis kept taking the baby off by itself, and I worried that it would starve or that Elvis might hurt the little guy. It's rare, but sometimes the fathers do that. But Elvis would only cuddle up with the baby. I tried to give it some of Emily Jane's formula in an eye dropper. Didn't get much down. Then a while later when I came back to give it some more, I saw that Elvis and Hiccup had changed places. Now he was with the other babies and she was curled up nursing that little runt all by himself."

"That's incredible!" Cory shook her head.

"Yeah, it's been three weeks. He's still small, but he's as active and as strong as the others. They don't need to keep him separate anymore."

Cory held Dizzy closer to her face. "So what about you, Dizzy? Are you all alone now?"

"Oh, she has the others for company."

"Others?" Cory looked at him with one eyebrow arched. Mitch noticed that her eyebrows were a darker orange-red than her hair and thick above the beautiful blue eyes.

"Excuse me?" he asked, momentarily losing the thread of their conversation.

"You said others. How many gerbils do you have?"

He shrugged. "Just the three—plus the nine babies. By others I meant my other pets."

"You have more?"

"A few." No use in overwhelming her all at once. "Look, here's my street. I live on the left, second to the end." Ordinarily, he was proud of his house, but now as he imagined how it must look through her eyes, the brick rambler looked rather small and outdated. He'd bought the house in January when the owner of the apartment he'd lived in before complained about the smell of his outdoor rabbit cages. Then there was the time a ferret got loose, but Mitch didn't like to dwell on that memory.

He and his animal friends were much happier here. The house was in an older area, surrounded by newer construction. It was small, with two tiny bedrooms, a living room, a bathroom, a kitchen, a mini cement storage room in the basement, and a garage barely large enough for his ferrets and his sports equipment. The yard was another story. Mature trees bordered the property line, and the spacious, fenced back-yard was perfect for his lifestyle.

"You ought to see the backyard," he said, as the car rolled to a stop. "In fact, would you like the grand tour?"

She was quiet for a moment as she returned Dizzy to her plastic ball. Mitch began to feel uncomfortable during the silence. Why had he made the offer? After all, she was the enemy. He knew, though, that he had asked because despite everything, he was enjoying her company.

"Perhaps another time," Cory said, not quite meeting his eyes. "I'd better go to the motel. I need to call my agent—among other things."

"You want to call a lawyer."

She didn't respond, so he knew he'd guessed correctly.

"Might as well wait until Monday. I can't imagine many lawyers working on the weekend."

"The best ones do," she countered.

Mitch was suddenly irritated with her. He'd done nothing this past half hour but try to maintain their truce. However, he had the sneaking suspicion that she was only biding her time to shove his tolerance in his face. "Okay," he said tightly. He put the car into gear and stepped on the gas.

At the motel he made sure there was a vacancy before he hopped out to get her duffel. She was nearly as quick, racing around before he could pull it completely out. "Be careful," she warned. "My laptop and cameras are in there."

Now he understood why it was so heavy and awkwardly shaped on top. Resisting the urge to toss it onto the ground, he set it in her arms with slightly more force than necessary. She didn't seem to notice.

"Let me say good-bye to EmJay." She opened the back door and leaned in to kiss the sleeping baby, whispering something Mitch didn't catch. Straightening, she faced him. "I'll be in touch."

"I'm sure you will," he said with more than a little bitterness.

She eyed him silently.

At that moment, he remembered his mother's comment at the church about introducing her to the gospel. He felt reluctant, knowing that she was entirely capable of shooting down his offer. Maybe he could phrase it in a way she couldn't refuse.

"Look," he said, keeping his voice even. "You told me you loved Ashley, and now you want to raise Emily Jane. If that's true, then you should find out what it was your sister believed. Why don't you come to church tomorrow and see for yourself?"

"My father was a Baptist, and he knew plenty about Mormons."

Mitch shook his head. "Apparently he knew how to hate them. Even his own daughter."

"She's the one who left us!"

"She followed her heart."

A shadow crossed her face. "He told me not to see her," she admitted.

"And you just went along with it?" Mitch strode around the car to his door, once more letting his emotions show. "Forget I asked. You don't really care to know how Ashley felt at all. You're too blinded by your father's beliefs to see anything else. Beliefs, I might add, that aren't exactly shared by all Baptists. My parents have good friends in Arizona who are Baptists, and they don't hate us."

He jumped in the car and was about to slam the door when he heard her say, "Wait!" Standing again, he looked at her over the top of the car. "I'll go," she said. "What time?"

Her abrupt about-face was so unexpected that he stopped for a moment to take it in. "Nine," he recovered enough to say. "I'll have to pick you up about eight forty-five."

"Okay."

He continued staring at her, and she stared right back. Finally, he folded his tall frame back into the car and sped away. *She's crazy,* he thought. *One minute she's defensive and angry and the next she's agreeing to go to church with me.*

One thing for sure, he couldn't allow her to take Emily Jane away from him. He only hoped the courts would support his claim of guardianship.

When he arrived home, he discovered a message on his new answering machine. It was from the lawyer in Texas, warning him that a woman claiming to be Ashley's sister might be at the memorial service. He shook his head and sighed.

Chapter Ten

C ory watched Mitch drive away, wishing she had something to
throw at that stupid orange Mustang. He was infuriating, con-
descending, and annoyingly devoted to EmJay. Of course, Cory
wouldn't allow that last character trait to affect what she had to do.
EmJay needed a mother figure. Cory knew what it was like to grow up
without a mother; she wouldn't let that happen to EmJay—especially
after feeling such a strong connection to her.

Hefting her duffel, she stomped over to the motel office and
checked in. The place was nicer than expected, though they didn't have
high speed Internet. Cory would have to use the regular phone line and
her laptop modem to send her photographs to her agent because she
hadn't mailed the CDs yet. While she e-mailed the pictures, she'd use
her new cell phone to let Vikki know she was back in the States.
Afterward, she'd find an attorney.

Vikki picked up her cell phone on the second ring. "Good, it's
you!" she exclaimed. "I've sent you e-mails and even a letter, but I had
no idea how long it would be before you got them. You know, if you're
going to work halfway around the world, you really need a continuous
connection, dear. At the very least a satellite phone."

"It was a little expensive at the time." Cory sat on the bed and kicked off her sandals.

"When you hear what's happened, dear, you won't care about the expense."

The skin on the back of Cory's neck prickled. "What do you mean?"

"I mean that idiot writer. Yesterday he sent in his article early—along with a bunch of pictures that *he* took."

"He sent a CD?" Cory couldn't imagine how he'd had the time. She'd only left on Wednesday.

"No, the pictures came through e-mail. Low resolution. Said he'd send a CD if they were interested. Of course, the magazine called me because they didn't understand what was going on. They e-mailed me the pictures, and it took me only one minute to realize they weren't yours. All of them were poor quality. Well, I shouldn't say all of them. There were two that I'd lay bets were yours. One was a fabulous closeup of a mother jaguar and cubs. Anyway, the writer said you'd been called away and asked him to finish."

"That worm!" Cory experienced a sickening sense of betrayal. "He knows those pictures are the last thing on my mind right now. He's just trying to get paid double."

"I thought as much. Fortunately, the editor contacted me, and I assured him you would send in your work by the deadline. You do have it, don't you, dear?"

"I'm sending the low resolutions now." As she spoke, Cory was setting up her laptop and plugging it into the waiting phone jack. "The connection's slow, but you'll soon see the best of what I've got. I'll overnight you the CDs with the high resolutions."

"Overnight? Are you back in the States?"

"Yeah, I'll you about it in a while. Anyway, I also have rolls and rolls of film I need to develop. Might have better shots there."

"The digital will be enough for now. I'll mark the best images and submit them as soon as the CDs arrive."

"What about Evan?" Cory asked.

"The writer? You let me deal with him. Nobody tries to preempt one of my photographers without paying for it—nobody."

"Was the editor tempted to go with his photographs, do you think? I bet he'd sell them a lot cheaper."

"Honey, cheaper is exactly what those photos are. Don't worry about any of it. You leave it to me."

Cory was glad to do so, though her heart hurt much more than she would admit. How could Evan do this to her? She'd really thought they had a chance at something special. Now he'd tried to steal her job.

This was working up to being a terrible day.

"So what is going on with you, dear?" Vikki asked. "Why are you in the States? I didn't think you planned to come back so soon."

Cory found her need to talk overshadowed her desire for privacy. "It's my sister," she said. "She and her husband drowned in a boating accident almost four weeks ago now. She left behind a daughter. The minute I found out, I hopped on a plane."

"Oh, how awful! I'm so sorry. How's your niece?"

"She seems to be doing well. But there's a problem with custody. Apparently my sister left her to a single guy."

"A man? Was she crazy?"

"Must have been."

"Are you going to fight it?"

"I plan to. That's why I'm staying in Utah for a while. I have to find a good attorney."

"I'll make a few calls." Vikki's voice became businesslike again. "I had a killer attorney during my divorce, and I'll bet he'll know someone. You just sit tight."

Cory breathed a sigh of relief. "Thanks, Vikki," she said softly. "I was feeling very alone."

"Well, dear, you're not. I'm here. After two years of working together, you should know that. Now I'll get back with you by Monday, okay? Meanwhile, rest up. Shoot off a few fireworks next week for the

Fourth. Get your fill of patriotism because it's back to the Amazon for you before too long. Remember we have *National Geographic* to do."

Joy swept through Cory. "You mean . . . ?"

"Yes, dear, you got the job."

"Whoo-hoo!" Cory bounced on the bed, punching her fist in the air.

"You have a month until you start, so we should be able to get your problems cleared up by then. Or at least on their way. Just don't forget me when they decide to hire you full time and send you to exotic places all over the world."

"Believe me, I won't!"

"Do you need funds? We're due a payment as soon as I get some of the pictures to the editor."

"Well, I have some savings left over from my dad's life insurance, but I have no idea how much I'll need for the attorney."

"I'll get money into your account by Monday."

"I appreciate it. I'll also need to arrange some darkroom equipment or send the undeveloped film to you." But now that she was Stateside, Cory didn't want to send the film to Vikki. Though she trusted her agent, developing the film, playing with the colors, was part of what she loved about her job.

"Keep the film for now until I see what you've sent me. Then we'll decide what to do. I did bring some equipment to my parents' house, since I knew I'd be here a month for my mother's hip replacement, but doing it here and then sending the photographs for your input might be cutting things a little short for our deadline. We've only got, what, eight days, not counting today? Let's play it by ear."

Cory thanked her again and hung up the phone. For a moment, she chewed on her nails while she watched her e-mail sending, wishing she had a faster connection. Spitting out a piece of fingernail, she left the laptop working and began unpacking her meager belongings. If she ended up staying an entire month, she'd need to find a cheaper place to stay. Preferably one closer to EmJay.

Thinking of the baby, she pondered over Mitch and EmJay. He really was good with her, and EmJay seemed content. *Maybe AshDee knew what she was doing.*

Cory immediately pushed the unwanted thought aside. Leaving EmJay with a man who wasn't even related—a single, Mormon man, for that matter—simply wasn't an option. Her sister had never expected to die, that was all.

Anger and helplessness filled Cory's heart, but she wasn't sure where to direct her feelings. So many had betrayed her: AshDee, her father, and even her mother, who had deserted them by dying so young. And now Evan. She'd hoped Evan was different. "Stupid man," she muttered. "I'm better off without him."

When she met up with Evan again, she'd have a thing or two to say. Better yet, she'd invite him into the jungle for a romantic picnic and lose him near a den of jaguars. She snorted at this fantasy. Evan would likely be long gone from the Amazon by the time she returned. She would have to settle for writing him a scathing e-mail. Tearing off another bit of nail with her teeth, she grabbed her purse and left the room to find a place to mail her CDs.

On Sunday morning Cory put on the same dress she'd worn the day before, not possessing another suitable choice. She was lucky to have this one summer dress that she'd planned to wear dancing with Evan. Maybe she should invest in another dress.

"What am I thinking?" she said aloud to her reflection in the mirror. "It's not as if I'm planning to go to church more than once." She frowned at herself, noting how her freckles had darkened and made her look quite tan if she stood back from the mirror. AshDee had always been so careful of her skin, either avoiding the sun or wearing a hat.

At the last moment, she pulled out her makeup and lined her eyes with dark brown pencil. A little mascara and lipstick helped her feel immensely more alive. *Ready to do battle,* she thought. Sweeping up her purse, she checked to make sure she had her wallet, credit card, and trusty Nikon.

Outside, the weather was slightly chilly, but the clear blue sky promised heat later in the day. To the east, the mountains were dressed in brilliant green, as though they too had somewhere important to go.

Mitch pulled up as she walked around to the front of the motel. He jumped out and opened her door, making her feeling ridiculously feminine. "You look nice," he commented.

"You'll get sick of this dress, believe me. When I heard about AshDee, I was in Manaus, a few days downriver from my camp. I'd only packed enough for a week."

"I could never get sick of that dress." He grinned and shut her door.

As he walked around the car, she noticed that he was basically wearing the same clothes he'd worn yesterday as well, only this time instead of a suit jacket, he had donned the more casual one he'd been carrying over his arm.

Cory turned and smiled at EmJay, who was in the car seat, decked out in a blue dress, white tights, and blue shoes. A matching blue ribbon circled her head. "Jay daggona much-da," she said.

"Good morning," Cory replied. "I missed you, too."

EmJay giggled and turned to watch Mitch slide into the car.

Putting the car in gear, he asked, "Why do you call your sister AshDee? Even Lane called her Ashley."

Cory smiled. "Her full name was Ashley Dawn."

"Oh, I guess that makes sense then."

"Only if you know that when she was born I was two and couldn't say Ashley Dawn. That's what my mother called her." Cory looked out the window, quiet for a moment as she remembered her mother's soft voice, a ghost whisper from a long-forgotten childhood.

"Is that why Ashley called Emily Jane by her full name—because her mother called her by two names?"

"Yes." Cory focused her attention back to him. "Our mother grew up watching reruns of a show called *The Waltons* where all the children had two names. She loved it. My father didn't let her do that with me, but Mom put her foot down when my sister was born. AshDee wanted to carry on the tradition with her daughter."

"But you called her AshDee." Mitch glanced at her. "Did she like it?"

"I wouldn't have used it if she didn't. We were close growing up. Our mother died when AshDee was ten, so we were closer than most sisters. We did everything together. We even planned our children's names."

"She'd already picked out Emily Jane?" Mitch glanced in the rearview mirror at the baby.

"Yep, and I joked that I'd call her EmJay."

"Ah, I see."

Cory took a deep breath. "Now you know why *I* should raise EmJay. She'll want to know about her mother. You can't possibly know as much about my sister as I do."

He didn't reply, and Cory was sure she'd scored a serious blow.

A short time later, they pulled into a church parking lot. Cory jumped out and beat him to the backseat to release EmJay. "This isn't the same church as yesterday," she said, holding EmJay close and breathing in the scent of what she assumed was baby shampoo.

"Same church, a different location."

"There seem to be a lot of them. Didn't we pass a few on our way here?"

"This is Utah. We have a lot of members."

"Oh, right." Despite herself, Cory was curious about his religion. She'd heard a lot of crazy things from her father, most of which she no longer believed, but it would be interesting to see for herself exactly why her father had protested Ashley's involvement with the Mormons so vehemently.

"I could find you a Baptist church, if you'd like," Mitch told her as they stepped onto the sidewalk.

"No, thanks."

"I thought you were a Baptist. Or don't you plan to be here that long?"

She planned to stay only as long as it took to get EmJay, but that was beside the point. "I *was* a Baptist. I think I might be an atheist now." Her parents would be horrified at the revelation, but she didn't believe they could know anything now that they were dead. As for her lost faith—well, her father was to thank for that. Or at least he had been in the beginning.

"I don't believe it." Mitch was shaking his head. "Ashley said her religious upbringing was why she was able to recognize the truth when she found it."

Cory stopped walking and clutched EmJay a little tighter. "Truth? I'm supposed to accept that? You Mormons are so egocentric. You alone have the truth. Everyone else is wrong and therefore going to the devil." She fell silent as a couple passed them on the sidewalk. As soon as they were out of hearing range, Mitch picked up where she'd left off.

"Well, at least we're nonpartisan about our egotism. From what I gather, your father hated only Mormons."

"That's because you're not Christian."

"That's funny. I thought the name of my church was The Church of Jesus Christ of Latter-day Saints."

Cory hadn't known that. Turning away so he wouldn't see her confusion, she started down the sidewalk again.

"Look," he said, following her, "all I'm asking is for you to listen."

Her emotions were under control enough for her to say, "I'm here, aren't I? Not that it'll make a difference."

"It would to Ashley. But, hey, I don't care what you do."

Cory stopped before the double glass doors, trying to control her rising irritation as he seemed to do so easily. "I want a copy of Ashley's will and any guardianship papers. I'll need to go over them with my attorney." She should have requested a copy in Texas, but in her haste to get to Utah, she'd forgotten.

"Fair enough." He opened a door for her. "Come on, it's about to begin."

Mitch took a seat toward the back near the aisle in case he had to leave with EmJay. The chapel was nearly full, but there didn't seem to be any families. In fact, there was only one other child. That didn't make sense. The one thing Cory remembered Ashley saying before she'd left California was that she'd found a church where families could be together forever. Apparently not in church. Had they left their children home? She watched carefully, noticing that while there were a few young couples, most people sat with friends. There were no older people at all except a man on the stand behind the pulpit.

Cory's interest was returned. There were admiring glances from the men—all dressed in white shirts and dress pants—and curious ones from the women. No one present looked cultish or odd in any way.

Then again, neither had her sister. Cory felt irritated.

The opening hymn was followed by a prayer, and then the older man made several announcements that made no sense to Cory. After he sat down, there was another hymn, followed by what Mitch termed the passing of the sacrament. She remembered taking a sacrament in her own church, and this wasn't all that different. Cory passed the trays of water and bread to Mitch without taking any.

When that awkwardness was finished, a man gave a talk about tithing, quoting several Old Testament scriptures and stories as examples. Cory was familiar with much of it; tithing had been one of her father's favorite subjects. He'd been openly disgruntled at how few people in their church had actually complied with the law, robbing themselves, he told her, of blessings. She'd always thought it odd that her father hadn't paid the church, either, but instead kept scrupulous records to make sure he used ten percent of his income on charitable purposes. Even the cost of an egg the neighbors borrowed was deducted from his total. He told her that because he was in tune with the Lord, he knew better where to use the money than their pastor.

Mitch appeared uncomfortable during the tithing discourse and kept darting unnerving glances at her. EmJay had fallen asleep on his lap, and Cory wondered if his leg was cramped.

After that meeting, they went to a smaller room identified as the new member class. "Just in case you have questions," Mitch said. Cory was glad, because she had a lot of questions. Mitch introduced her as EmJay's aunt, who'd come to visit. She wasn't sure why it irritated her that he made it so clear they weren't a couple.

The prayer was scarcely offered when she began by asking why all the men wore white shirts. Was there some significance that all the women wore dresses with sleeves? What exactly was a *ward*? And didn't they believe in marriage and children?

"Oh, this is a singles ward," explained the man who was teaching the class. "Mitch, didn't you tell her that?"

"Uh, no." He hung his head. "I guess I figured she'd know."

A singles group! Finally, some sense. But it still didn't explain why those two young men in the second row had the same first name and were wearing black name tags with white lettering.

After learning about the missionaries, she wanted to know about plural wives and temples. Her father had said something negative about Mormon temples, but she couldn't remember what. Cory enjoyed herself immensely during that hour. She especially liked the way the teacher flushed when she challenged him and how Mitch and the two men with name tags kept jumping to the rescue.

The best thing happened near the end, when the woman on the other side of Mitch screamed and jumped from her chair, staring at Mitch as if he'd suddenly turned into a monster. The instructor dropped his lesson manual with a loud *thump!*

"What?" everyone asked at once.

"There—there's something crawling inside his jacket! Quick—get it out! Be careful of the baby." The woman pointed to EmJay, who was sitting on Mitch's lap.

A dull green creature was crawling across Mitch's white shirt—

apparently on its way to a warm spot on his shoulder. He didn't seem concerned, though his face flushed slightly.

One of the men glared at Mitch. Cory thought they'd introduced him as a counselor of some sort, and she'd wondered if he was there to make sure they behaved. "I asked you to leave them home," he said in a pained voice.

"It's not the gerbils," Mitch explained. "It's my lizard."

"Your lizard?" squeaked the woman.

"She won't hurt anyone. She's been sick, you see, but she's better now and anxious to get out after being cooped up so much. Usually she just dozes. Something must have woken her up. Honestly, I won't let her get loose."

The woman made a face but didn't speak further. She moved to another chair, leaving a space between her and Mitch. The counselor heaved a sigh, and the missionaries rolled their eyes.

Cory did her best to hold in the laughter, but it was just too tempting. "Can I see her?" she asked between giggles.

Mitch reached inside his jacket and pulled out the creature. Everyone leaned in to take a peek, fascinated despite their disapproval. EmJay's little hand stroked the five-inch lizard's back as though she'd done it many times before. Cory followed her lead. "What's her name?" After Elvis, Dizzy, and Hiccup, she couldn't wait for this.

"Lizzy Lizard," he said with a grimace. "Not very original, but I was tired when I found her in the desert."

"You found her?"

"Yeah, by the side of the road in southern Utah. She was hurt, and I took her home to help her heal."

"Mitch is always finding things to heal," said the woman next to him. "If he spent half as much time trying to find a wife, he wouldn't be one of the oldest men in our ward."

Cory studied her for a moment. She was pretty and well-spoken, but Cory sensed a frustrated undercurrent.

"Janie doesn't like my animals," Mitch explained.

"I just don't think they have any place on a date," Janie retorted.

Oh, so that's the way it is. Janie liked Mitch but wanted to change him. Cory felt sorry for Mitch. "I think Lizzy's adorable," she said. "I'm glad you brought her." It certainly livened the class up a bit—not that it needed livening with all her questions.

As they left the classroom a short time later, Mitch informed her there was one more meeting to go. Cory balked. "I think I've had enough for one day."

"But the best is yet to come. We separate into different classes. Men into one, women into another."

"I'm not going anywhere without you."

"Well, okay, but I don't see how you can get the full effect your sister did, if you don't go to all the meetings."

Cory gave an exaggerated sigh. "Okay, I'll endure one more meeting. But only if I get to take EmJay."

A look of consternation passed over his face. "Uh . . . well."

"Come on. She'll be all right. She likes me."

"I know she does. But she's not the only one I'm worried about."

His comment took a minute to sink in. "Me? You're afraid of what—that I'll steal her?"

"I guess I am."

"I don't have a car."

"You have a cell phone."

She pulled it from her purse and gave it to him. "There. Now I don't. Look. I give you my word. Isn't that enough?"

"I don't know. Is it?"

She nodded.

"Okay, but only if she'll go with you willingly."

Cory focused on EmJay. "Come on, darling. Come to Aunt Cory." EmJay giggled but made no attempt to reach for her. Cory dug in her purse and held up a granola bar like the one she'd had for breakfast. EmJay wiggled her hands for it. "Nope, come to me first." Cory took her as EmJay reached happily for the treat.

"You'll come find me if she cries?" Mitch asked.

The concern in his eyes touched her. "Promise."

"Okay, then. Here's her diaper bag. I'll meet you here after the meeting."

Cory went into the room where the women were gathering. A woman wearing a navy suit dress introduced herself as the president of the class, but Cory didn't remember her name.

The lesson was on patriotism, and Cory found herself interested. The women seemed to share a great love for their country, and she admired their zeal. EmJay was happy sorting through the contents of her purse until her eyes glazed over and she slumped suddenly against Cory's shoulder. Cory cradled the sleeping baby, her heart filling with an emotion that seemed much stronger than mere love.

The teacher ended the lesson ten minutes to the hour, and then the president stood. "As you know, we usually have our practice hymn before the lesson," she said. "But this week Janie had to go in and help the elders learn a song. So we'll turn these last few minutes over to her."

The woman from the new member class stood up in front. "Please turn to 'O My Father' in your hymnbooks," she said. "This is the song we sisters will be singing in ward conference."

Cory's heart jumped when the music started. She knew this hymn; Cameron Huntington had sung it yesterday at AshDee's memorial. Cory hadn't planned on singing, but now she grabbed the book from the chair next to her and quickly found the place. According to Mitch, this was AshDee's favorite hymn. She read the words as the women sang, sounding awkward compared to Mitch's father but somehow bringing AshDee vividly to mind. Many emotions battered at Cory's heart. A tear trickled from the corner of her eye.

The song told a story of loving parents, both a mother and father, waiting for her in a royal heavenly court. One phrase stood out: "Yet ofttimes a secret something / Whispered, 'You're a stranger here.'" A stranger. That was exactly how Cory had felt so many times—that she was a stranger lost on earth. That she had stumbled upon this life by accident and didn't really belong anywhere. Always before this feeling had been negative, but this song implied that being a stranger here was a natural occurrence because she had originally come from some other glorious place and was only biding time until she returned home.

Was this why AshDee had loved this song? Cory wasn't sure, but she didn't think so. She would bet that AshDee had loved this song because it mentioned both a mother and a father. Growing up, her little sister had so longed for a mother.

The meeting ended, and Cory stared down at the sleeping baby, hoping no one would talk to her. Gradually, everyone left except the president and another woman, both of whom kept glancing in her direction, as if wondering how to approach her. They were saved the decision when Mitch barreled into the room.

"Oh, there you are." Relief tinged his voice.

Cory looked up, forgetting for a moment her tears. "Of course I'm here."

Mitch sat down beside her. "Are you all right?" He darted a frown at the two remaining women who were now drifting toward the door.

"I'm fine." Cory blinked, and another tear inched down her cheek.

"Then why are you crying?"

"I'm not crying."

"Yes, you are. Did someone say something?" He looked ready to chase down all the women in his ward to find out what had happened.

"No, I—" She took a deep breath, knowing she would have to give him some explanation. "Look, it was that stupid song. The one you said was AshDee's favorite. I—I just miss her." Her voice rose to a squeak, and Cory despised herself for being so weak.

I swear, she thought, *if he says one more word, I'm going to hit him. I'm going to hit him, and then I am going to take EmJay and run off to Brazil.*

Mitch didn't speak. He sat there mutely while she sniffed and tried to compose herself. After a few moments, he reached out to take the hymnal from her fingers that had turned white with the force of her grip. Then he did a surprising thing. He put his hand over hers and squeezed.

Warmth shot through Cory's hand and rippled up her arm. Until that moment, she hadn't realized how cold and numb she felt. Mitch's touch traveled through her like fire. Her tears ceased.

Without meeting his gaze, she removed her hand from his. After smoothing EmJay's hair, she handed her to Mitch and began gathering the items the baby had tossed from her purse. Cradling EmJay in one arm, Mitch watched her silently.

Why would she feel such warmth at his touch? Mitch was nothing but an adversary she would have to face in court to win custody of her niece. He was nothing more than an interloper who compounded the indignity AshDee had committed when she chose to discard her family. Cory wished she never had to see him again.

When her belongings were in place, she stood, shouldered both the purse and the diaper bag, and moved toward the door. She could sense Mitch following her, and another infusion of inexplicable warmth spread through her heart.

Maybe, Cory thought, *maybe there really is a God. If Mitch could sit by me and not speak, maybe God made him stay silent.*

Chapter Eleven

Mitch didn't know what to say as he followed Cory to his Mustang. Seeing Cory cradling Emily Jane in her arms with tears on her cheeks had moved him deeply. Moreover, he was beginning to doubt his own role as Emily Jane's sole guardian.

Obviously, Cory loved her niece, and he had to admit that the baby was taking much more quickly to her than she had to him. Given a few days alone with Cory, he doubted he would still be Emily Jane's favorite. At least if Cory were to help raise Emily Jane, that would solve his problem of finding a mother for her.

Yet what about Lane and Ashley's wish to raise their daughter in the gospel?

Immediately, Mitch's confusion cleared. Teaching Emily Jane the precepts of the true gospel was more important than anything else. Her eternal salvation was on the line here, not just a mother figure. He couldn't let Cory soften his resolve. With him, Emily Jane had not only the gospel but a large and loving extended family. And eventually he would find the woman he was supposed to marry, a woman who would love Emily Jane as her own. That meant he must fight Cory with everything in his soul. Yes, she could have time with her niece, but he wouldn't give up custody.

He waited until they were settled in the car before going on the attack. "Now you know why AshDee joined the Church," he said. "Because the gospel is true."

Cory's blue eyes opened wide. "All that because of a song? Don't be ridiculous! AshDee was missing our mother, that's all. And that certainly doesn't mean it's true."

"Maybe not," he conceded. "But you felt something just now—didn't you?"

She folded her arms. "I was missing my sister."

He didn't reply. So much time had passed since his missionary days, and he wasn't sure how to deal with her. She was both the most attractive and the angriest investigator he'd ever met.

They were quiet for several long moments before Cory asked, "Do you really think AshDee believed in your church? Or was it just to punish my father for not . . . well, for not being the kind of father she wanted?" The question was clearly difficult for her to ask, and Mitch wondered what kind of childhood the sisters had endured.

"She believed," Mitch said quietly. "She believed with her whole heart. Ashley cared more about the gospel than anything besides her family, and that's exactly why I should raise her daughter."

"Apparently she cared about her faith more than she cared about me and our father." Cory's words oozed bitterness.

"Only a believer could really understand Ashley's reasoning."

Cory snorted. "Well, at least you got that right. I still don't understand why a white shirt at church is better than a blue one."

"Our church is a whole lot more than shirts," he retorted. Then he saw the determined grin on her face and realized she was trying to lighten the mood. He smiled back. "We're almost to your motel. Let's call it quits until tomorrow. Okay?"

She looked at Emily Jane with a longing in her eyes that was easy to read. "Okay."

Mitch forced himself to ignore her silent plea. He was not going to encourage her until he knew exactly where he stood legally. First thing on Monday, he'd make an appointment with his lawyer.

Meanwhile, it might be better not to let the baby become attached to Cory. She would soon be far away in the jungle, hunting wild animals with her camera. Stifling a sudden flare of envy, he glared at the road ahead.

"Uh, you wouldn't know where I could find a better place to stay, would you?" Cory asked. "I mean for a longer period of time. I think I'll be here a month."

He raised an eyebrow but didn't comment on the length of time. Was a month her lawyer's recommendation? Or was it all the time she had between assignments? Part of him wanted to tell her to forget it, but the part of him who'd once watched *Camelot* five times in a week couldn't deny a lady's request for help.

"I'll call around," he said. "If you want, you can come back with me to my house while I do."

"Good. I can play with EmJay."

Well, there went his plan to prevent them from having too much interaction. Still, one day didn't constitute a relationship. "You could feed her, too." He turned the car around.

"Who are you going to call on a Sunday?"

"The bishop in my neighborhood ward ought to be a good place to start."

"Is that the gray-haired man who was on the stand at the church?"

"No. That's my bishop. The people in my neighborhood belong to a family ward, and they have another bishop."

Cory shook her head. "I guess that sort of makes sense."

"Of course. The Lord always makes sense—even if we don't know what it is at the time."

Her eyes dug into him. "So my sister's death makes sense?"

"God didn't cause her death."

"He allowed it to happen."

"He gives us our agency. Would you rather He didn't?"

Cory blinked hard. "Right now? Truthfully? If it would bring AshDee back—yes."

He drove in silence, not knowing how to refute that claim when it was so close to his own feelings.

"I'll want a place close by," Cory said after several long moments. "I'd like to take EmJay overnight sometimes."

He glanced away from the road and then back again. "She needs me at night. Only this past week has she finally stopped crying at night."

"She won't cry when she knows me better."

He shrugged. "We'll cross that bridge when we come to it."

"You think I might take her and run, don't you?"

"You live in Brazil. Can you honestly tell me the idea hasn't crossed your mind?"

She didn't deny his words.

"You see?" he said softly. "I have to protect both her mother's wishes and Emily Jane herself. This has nothing to do with you."

Cory's jaw clenched. "I'm her aunt. That counts for a lot."

Mitch nodded. "But I'm the guardian of her eternal salvation."

"What on earth is *that* supposed to mean?" She shook her head and turned toward the window.

For some reason he didn't care to explore, her words cut him deeply. How could he have even briefly entertained thoughts of allowing Emily Jane to spend time alone with this woman? She was hard, impossible, and downright antagonistic. He wished he could put her on the next plane to the Amazon. She'd be much better company for those Brazilian jaguars.

Glancing over, he saw a single tear on her left cheek before she quickly brushed it away. His anger left as rapidly as it had come. *She lost her sister, her only family,* he reminded himself. *How would I feel if I lost even one of my sisters?* The thought was incomprehensible.

At his house, Mitch took the still-sleeping Emily Jane from her car seat and settled her in her bed. She stirred when he laid her on her side, and he knelt by her bed to soothe her. "It's okay, sweetie. Mitch is here. Sleep a little bit longer. Sleep, sweetie. It's okay."

At last he withdrew his hand and stood. He froze when he saw Cory watching him from the hall. It bothered him that she was there, spying on his private time with Emily Jane.

"So it's true," she said, her voice low. "You do hold her hand at night."

"It's part of the promise." He started into the hall.

"Aaaah!" came Emily Jane's wail. He turned immediately, but Cory rushed to the bed. The baby pushed at her and shook her head. "Much, Much!" she cried.

Mitch gathered her in his arms. "I'm here, sweetie. Don't cry. Hush now." She was instantly quiet, laying her head on his shoulder.

Cory watched them intently. "She said your name, didn't she?"

"Yeah. She just started last night."

"Can you say Cory?" she said to the baby. "Hmm. Maybe I should teach her to say Aunt Cory."

Mitch hoped she wouldn't be around enough to teach her anything. "Aunt Cory is a mouthful. Don't you have a nickname?"

"Cory is my nickname."

"Oh? What's your real name?"

She made a face. "Corrine."

"Not bad. You should try being Mitchell. Tell you what. If you don't call me Mitchell, I'll promise not to call you Corrine."

Her grin softened her freckled face. "Deal."

"Come on," he said. "I'll show you around. Emily Jane won't let me put her down until she's all the way awake—or back to sleep—so you might as well meet the rest of us."

"I noticed the frogs in the bathroom," she commented.

"I was cleaning their cage last night. Did you see a turtle?"

She laughed. "Nope."

"Well, Tartar's around somewhere. Just got him this week. He usually hangs out in my little alcove near the back door, if you want to take a peek. I have a sort of foot-washing sink built into the floor there."

"Tell me, is it potty trained?"

"The guy I got him from said he was. He would have kept him, but he was being transferred overseas." Mitch snapped his fingers. "Hey, I wonder if he sold his house yet. He might have a week or two leeway if he hasn't."

"I need a month."

"Yeah, so you said. But you never know. This might be the answer." Mitch went to the phone. He ended up calling the bishop, who referred him to the Relief Society president, who told him to call the new owners. The family turned out to be moving in the next day but from down the street, and their previous house hadn't sold yet. They were more than happy to let Cory rent it for a month as long as she was willing to let them show the house to potential buyers. Mitch assured them she would.

"So, it's all settled," he said, hanging up the phone. "They'll try to get everything out by noon tomorrow. The wife said she'd call the Relief Society sisters and see if some of them would be willing to go over and help clean so you can move in right away."

"Just like that?" Cory's expression was a little dazed.

"That's the way it always is," Mitch said. "Our church members help each other."

"I'm not a member of your church."

"So? They help others, too."

"I'll bet," she said, rolling her eyes. "Probably want me to join."

He grinned. "Probably. You'd better not talk to any of them. They might brainwash you." She glared at him, and he laughed. She was pretty with her face flushed like that. "Hey, you asked for it."

She relaxed. "Maybe. I guess I'd better go back to the motel and start getting my stuff together. But I'll need my cell phone back from you."

Mitch shifted Emily Jane's weight so he could reach into his jacket pocket. Instead of the cell phone, he came out with a handful of lizard. "Oops. Forgot about her." He started down the hall to the spare room. "Come along, if you want."

Cory stared in amazement at the many cages, and Mitch felt a little pride in the display. He had all the aquariums on knee-high shelves along two walls, with a space where the windows were so the animals wouldn't feel a breeze. Lizzy Lizard's aquarium was closest to the door, with her special lights hanging down from another shelf he'd built. Each large aquarium had a habitat especially prepared for a specific animal. He'd also built in a ventilation system, which really helped with the smell. In fact, the air in here was probably more healthy to breathe than in the rest of the house.

Cory walked along the cages. "Gerbils, another gerbil, a lizard, hermit crabs, fish, and—hmm, what's this?"

"A chinchilla."

"Very pretty."

"Expensive, too," he said. "And these are guinea pigs—they really are the most calm. See? They don't need a lid. The frogs go over there. I used to have the ferrets inside, but they were kind of stinky, and they made the other animals nervous. They're in the garage now."

Cory stopped in front of the fish tank, staring at the brilliant blues, pinks, yellows, and striped hues. "This reminds me of a place where I swim in the Amazon," she murmured. "The fish are the most vibrant colors. It's really incredible."

"Is the water warm?" Mitch asked. During his mission, he hadn't ever made it much past the borders of the rain forest. Not that he would have gone swimming, of course.

"Very—at least at this particular place."

He could sense the yearning in her voice and again felt envious of the opportunities she enjoyed. What he wouldn't give to be so close to those exotic animals.

"I served a mission to Brazil, you know," he told her. "I spent most of my two years southeast of the Amazon River, more or less near Belém."

"Oh, that's right. That's how you knew AshDee's husband." Her tone made it clear she wished he'd never set foot in the country. "I guess you know the language then?"

"Yeah. It's easy. Not like English that has a hundred exceptions for every rule."

"You can say that again. Every time I try to write something, it comes out all wrong."

"It helps knowing a foreign language. Especially with conditional tenses. I write a lot for my job, and I've never had any complaints."

She turned away from the fish. "I don't even know what conditional tenses are." Her face was angry now, though he sensed the emotion wasn't directed toward him.

"Is something wrong?"

"Not really. I was just thinking of a friend of mine. Or rather, someone I *thought* was a friend. He turned out to be a big jerk."

Obviously, there was much she wasn't saying about this so-called friend. Mitch felt a surge of unreasonable jealousy. This man must have wounded her deeply to cause such bitterness to creep into her voice. Previously, he'd heard that only when she talked about her sister, or during their fights over Emily Jane.

"Why don't we have lunch?" he suggested. "We could have a barbecue."

"You don't have to feed me. There's a restaurant near my motel."

"But it's Sunday. Even lapsed Baptists don't eat out on Sunday. Or do they?"

She shrugged. "A person's got to eat."

"Well, you can do it here. Besides, it looks like Emily Jane is ready to get down and explore. If you don't mind, you can try feeding her a jar of applesauce, while I get the chicken ready."

"Okay. But I don't eat meat. Well, unless it's fish."

"I make a mean grilled trout. I'm sure I have some in the freezer.

It'll thaw fast." He felt pleased Cory had agreed to stay. Not that he was enjoying her company or anything. He simply wanted to get a sense of who she was for Emily Jane's sake.

Stepping over the turtle, who was camped out near the door, Mitch set the high chair outside on the patio. Muffin the Mutt shivered with excitement at their arrival, running up to Cory and giving her a thorough sniffing. "I can't let him inside while I'm gone until he gets used to the turtle," he explained. "He's really good around the animals, but once he almost loved one of my rabbits into shock."

Cory glanced around. "Rabbits?"

"By the shed out there." He motioned to the far side of the yard. "They're too messy for inside, but their waste makes great fertilizer for my sisters' gardens. One of them had babies not too long ago, and in a minute I'll get one for you to see."

While speaking, he had removed Emily Jane's shoes and tights and placed her in the high chair. Now he tied the bib around her neck. After making sure she was secured by the safety belt, he turned toward the house. The last thing he saw before he went inside was Emily Jane giggling as Muffin licked her toes.

Moments later, Mitch was back on the patio, trying to light the charcoal on his ancient barbecue grill. "Looks like I'm going to need a bit of lighter fluid."

Cory shot a pointed glance at his new gas grill that sat against the house. "Isn't your gas one working?"

Mitch groaned. He'd hoped she wouldn't notice that grill. "Well, you see," he began, "I bought that at the end of May because I was planning on having a lot of barbecues this summer. But, well . . ."

"It broke? Take it back." She shook her curls, which glinted fire in the sun.

"Actually, it has occupants."

She arched a brow. "Occupants?"

"A family of robins moved in."

"You've got to be kidding." She practically ran over to the grill, and Mitch was glad he'd wired it shut.

"Sorry, you can't see in," he said. "At least not for another few weeks. The babies should be flying by then."

"There's babies?"

He nodded. "If I time it right, I'll hurry and clean out their nest as soon as these babies are on their own."

"I can't believe it." She came back to the high chair and gave Emily Jane another bite of applesauce. "You buy a new grill, and you can't even use it?"

He sighed. She must think him a total idiot. A pansy. A mama's boy.

"I wonder," she said.

"Wonder what?"

"I bet we could get a tiny camera to hook up to the computer. It'd be really neat to peek at what's going on in there. Might even be able to get some good photographs."

"I've been thinking the same thing for weeks, but I never got around to figuring out how." Mitch was so involved in their conversation that he allowed the match he was holding to burn down too low. "Ouch!" He dropped the match and shook his fingers.

She watched him with an amused smile that made his heart feel . . . well, quite happy and odd all at once. A part of him wondered at how differently he might have felt toward Cory if she and Ashley hadn't been estranged. If maybe she had joined the Church with her sister.

"I'll get some lighter fluid." He gestured in the direction of his garage.

When he returned, Cory was letting Emily Jane out of her chair. The baby immediately toddled to the corner of the patio where Muffin rested in the shade. Babbling a flurry of words, she sat down on the dog and tugged at his fur. Muffin endured the abuse with barely more than a flick of his tail.

A short time later, the grilled fish was on the patio table, accompanied by a fresh green salad with ranch dressing. Emily Jane refused to eat from her own plate or to sit in the high chair but came up often to beg for bites.

When they finished eating, Cory reminded Mitch about the baby rabbits, and after securing Muffin to his chain again, he brought out two white ones for her to see.

"Oh, they're adorable!" Cory exclaimed. "I have to get some pictures of EmJay with the babies." She dug in her purse for a camera, slipped off her sandals, and squatted on the grass.

Emily Jane seemed to know what a camera was and stopped to give Cory a large grin whenever she asked. Cory didn't ask more than a few times, obviously preferring the more natural approach to photography. Mitch was amazed at her patience. She didn't try to pose the rabbits or Emily Jane but simply waited until the perfect shot presented itself. Neither did she seem concerned about her dress getting dirty as she sat in the grass; in fact, Mitch guessed he thought about it more than she did.

Mitch went to get his own cameras. He took pictures of Cory, Emily Jane, and the bunnies, and then he turned on the video recorder, focusing it first on Emily Jane, looking cute with her red-orange curls and freckles, and then on Cory snapping pictures.

After a while, Cory put aside her camera and picked up a bunny, running her hand over its soft fur. Emily Jane walked over to her and babbled something that sounded important. "Oh, yeah?" Cory asked. "I think so, too. They're very soft, a good pet for a young lady like yourself."

Pleased, Emily Jane babbled something that sounded foreign, with rolling letters and soft sibilants. Mitch kept the video recorder on the pair, marveling at how alike they were. He tried not to think about Lane and Ashley, except to wonder if they were feeling as peaceful as he did at that moment. He picked up his 35mm camera to take another shot.

After a while, Cory noticed him and came over. She briefly looked at his camera while Mitch turned off the video recorder. "This reminds me," he said. "Ashley's lawyer sent some boxes with pictures and videos. They were only married a few years, but there seems to be a lot of them. I thought—well, would you like to see them?"

"I would."

"Keep an eye on the rabbits, would you?" He glanced to where Emily Jane sat by the rabbits, who were nibbling grass.

He retrieved the box with the picture albums from the closet where he'd stuffed them, saving the framed pictures and the videos for another day. He planned to keep all these things for Emily Jane, but if Cory wanted copies, she could make them.

The first album out of the box was full of pictures from Ashley's youth. Cory flipped through them eagerly. "I didn't know she'd kept all these. These photos are my first works of art."

"Is that your father?" Mitch pointed to a wiry, stern-looking man reading a newspaper.

She studied the photograph. "Yeah, but he didn't always look that way."

Mitch wondered what that meant, but he didn't feel it was his place to ask.

The next book was more recent, showing Ashley's wedding and the birth of Emily Jane. Mitch was surprised to see his own face staring out at him from more than a few photographs. He remembered in particular the one at the hospital the night Emily Jane was born. He'd sat in the waiting room for hours, pacing until Lane had finally come to take him to see Ashley and the new baby. There he was, holding Emily Jane, not even thirty minutes old—and suddenly he remembered how deeply he'd felt for the baby that day. How terribly he had wanted her to be his own. He blinked his eyes and swallowed hard, hoping Cory wouldn't look over and see his emotion. How could he have known then what would happen? In the picture Ashley was watching him from her hospital bed, a knowing smile on her face. *She knew how I felt,* he thought, *when I didn't even know it myself.*

He looked up to see Emily Jane trailing the bunnies as they hopped across the grass. "I'd better get them back in their pen," he said, grateful for the chance to collect his thoughts.

To his surprise, Cory followed him. "It's funny, you having all these animals."

"My first memory as a child was bringing home a baby bird to my mom that had fallen from its nest."

"Did it live?"

He shrugged. "My dad put it back in the nest, so I believed it did at the time."

"Ah, then that was what was important."

"Exactly." Other baby birds he'd found hadn't been so lucky, but that first successful experience had inspired him to continue trying to make a difference.

"Maybe I should have been a vet instead of a zoologist." He opened the rabbit hutch and returned the babies to their nest. "I'm good at fixing up animals, and at least I would have seen more of them than I do now."

"Yeah, but not many unusual ones." Cory reached in to pet the mother rabbit, who was sniffing Mitch's hand in the hopes of a carrot or other treat.

He sighed. "I know. That's why I ended up in zoology. I may have spent the last year of my life studying the territorial habits of wolves, but at least they're more interesting to me than, well, say, a cow." He picked a few long grass stems from the base of the cage and gave them to Cory for the mother rabbit.

A comfortable silence fell between them as they walked back to the patio. Emily Jane was lagging behind, so Mitch lifted her onto his shoulders. She grasped his hair and hung on. "What pets do you have?" he asked Cory.

"None. Unless you count Meeko. He's this little dwarf cebus who sort of follows me around the jungle. Sleeps in my tent, even."

"A monkey?" he asked.

She grinned. "I considered him more a friend than a pet. I have pictures of him somewhere."

"I'd think a wildlife photographer would have at least a few pets, even in the Amazon. Maybe a dog? A bird? A turtle? I know they have turtles there."

"I guess I'm never in one place long enough. I always thought one day that I'd move near AshDee, but now . . ." She trailed off. She began studying the photo album once more, her fingers occasionally resting on the plastic covering her sister's face.

"You'd need at least a few roots if you were going to raise a baby," Mitch said.

She bristled immediately, and the goodwill between them shattered. "I know. I can do that." Her words were rimmed in iron. "I'm still going to fight you for custody. Whatever happens, I'm going to be a part of EmJay's life."

Chapter Twelve

On Tuesday afternoon, the day after she moved into the rented house on Mitch's street, Cory went to see Mr. Howry, the attorney Vikki had recommended. He was good-looking enough as men went, but his appearance was overshadowed by an arrogance that bordered on bad manners.

He was just the man for the job.

He had utterly ignored her since the moment he sat down, a sandwich in one hand, her papers in the other. The only indication she had that he knew anyone else was in the room was the firm shaking of his head at various intervals.

At last he looked up from the papers. "These are the tightest custody documents I've ever seen. The will, too."

"So there's nothing you can do?" Despair filled her heart.

He gave a little sneer. "Oh, there's plenty I could do, but it would take a lot of money, and unless his attorney is a total idiot or he's unfit—which seems doubtful—we simply couldn't win. Your sister and her husband were direct and thorough in their requests and preparations. The only way . . ." He rubbed his chin, picked up the papers again, and followed a particular passage with his finger.

Cory leapt on his hesitation. "What?"

He leaned back in his brown leather chair. "The will and custody papers reiterate several times that the main reason your sister and her husband felt Mr. Huntington was the right person to raise their daughter is that he's a member of their church. They also state briefly that if Ashley's family became members, she and her husband reserved the right to change the document in the future. The addition is odd because of course they have that right. It leads me to believe that your sister hoped you'd become a member at some point in the future, and if that happened, she might choose you as guardian of her daughter instead. So if you became a member of the Church, we could use this argument to sue for custody."

She gaped at him. "Is this a conspiracy? What kind of a state is this that everyone can refer to a religious organization as The Church"—she lowered her voice to mimic him—"and everyone understands what church it is?"

The first sign of a smile flickered over his well-defined mouth. "A state founded by Mormons. Or more correctly, by The Church of Jesus Christ of Latter-day Saints."

"Good grief." She gripped the armrests on her chair. "You're one of them!"

Mr. Howry shook his head. "Not me. My sister and her husband are. I get to hear about it at family gatherings."

Cory relaxed and took a deep breath. "You're saying if I became a member of this church that I would have a better chance at custody?"

"No, I said it was your *only* chance. However, I must caution you. Mr. Huntington could certainly challenge the reason for your membership."

"You mean he could argue that I did it only to gain custody?"

"Exactly. You would have to convince him—or perhaps a judge." Checking his watch, Mr. Howry leaned forward, gathered her papers, and handed them to her. "Of course, if you could convince

Mr. Huntington to give up his claim voluntarily, you could get custody that way, too—whether or not you joined his church."

Cory flicked a piece of shredded lettuce from her documents. "They wouldn't simply find another member to take care of her?"

"No. The guardian has full rights and can act as he sees fit."

"I see. Well, thank you for your time."

He nodded. "Please contact me if you wish me to pursue further action."

They shook hands, and Cory couldn't help but compare his soft grip to Mitch's firm, slightly callused one. She didn't have to guess which one would be better on a nature hike through the Amazon forest.

Did Mitch ever plan to return to Brazil? Given the longing way he listened to her stories of the Amazon, she was surprised he hadn't gone already. What could be holding him back?

When she climbed into her rented silver Camry, she checked her phone messages and found that her agent had asked her to call back. She dialed the number, and Vikki picked up on the first ring. "Hi, dear," she said. "How'd the visit with the attorney go?"

"Worse than I'd hoped. He says the only real chance I have is to convince Mitch to give up custody—or to join their church."

"Mitch?"

"That's the man who has custody."

"You're on a first-name basis with him?"

"Well, I've been trying to spend as much time as I can with EmJay. Unfortunately, he comes along with the deal."

"Afraid you'll take off with her, I'll bet."

"Something like that."

"So what's he like?"

Cory gave a mirthless laugh. "Nice, actually. Just your average guy. Tall, sort of skinny. You know, active. Has nice blue eyes, but his hair is probably his best feature. It's short in the back, but the front is longer and parted in the middle. Sort of pushed back on each side. He really likes animals—he's a zoologist."

"My, my," Vikki said. "A simple 'he's nice' would have sufficed. What's he like as a guardian?"

"He's good with EmJay," Cory admitted reluctantly, "though I guess it could be an act. She's extremely attached to him."

"In three weeks?"

"Three and a half now. But you'd understand if you saw them together. Never lets her cry. He even has her bed by his so he can hold her hand if she wakes up at night."

Vikki was silent for a moment and then said, "That's hard to beat—for a man."

Cory let out a long sigh. "Maybe, but she belongs with me."

"I know. I know. And you'll win, dear. I'm sure of it. Does he like you? I mean, you're an attractive woman. That could help him decide to give you custody."

"I don't think he's impressed. After all, I'm not a member of the Church."

"Ah. The Church. Do I sense capital letters?"

"Exactly. It's like I'm behind enemy lines or something."

"Well, how about some reinforcements?" Vikki didn't let her respond but forged ahead. "The magazine is pleased with your work, but I think we could use a boost in an area or two, and I'm betting you have some shots from your Nikon that will fit the bill. My mother is much better now, and I'm getting in my father's way more than help-ing at this point. Anyway, it wouldn't be a big deal for me to fly out to Utah and stay for a few days to develop the film with you. I'll bring my equipment. We can scan and e-mail any new choices to the magazine before I head home to California. Or overnight them in a CD if there's too many."

"What a great idea! We'll make the deadline for sure with both of us working. And I could really use some support with this custody mess." Already Cory felt less alone.

"Well, when you told me last night that you'd moved into a house with two bedrooms, I thought, 'Why not? I can deal with my other clients from there just as I have from Ohio this past month.' Honestly, dear, I have a cell phone, e-mail, my darkroom equipment. What else do I need?"

"Thanks, Vikki. Now I know why I picked you as my agent—and as a friend."

"You picked me because we're two of a kind," Vikki said. "Besides, you're my favorite photographer. Look, I'll do my best to fly in tomorrow. That'll give us Thursday and the weekend to get everything finished. Give me your address, and I'll get a rental car at the airport. No, don't offer to pick me up. I bet I can find my way better than you can."

Cory laughed. "You got that right. Give me a jungle any time."

She hung up the phone feeling more positive than she had since learning of her sister's death. Somehow she'd make Mitch see that she would make the better parent. But if worse came to worse, she'd join their stupid church!

She smiled. *EmJay will love the Amazon.*

Mitch stared at his computer in complete frustration. He'd written only two sentences, and his next report was due in the morning. The research and outline were complete, but Emily Jane wouldn't allow him to type the actual document. She was cuddled on his lap, drifting off to sleep, and every time he tried to type, she gave a determined mumble and grabbed one of his hands. She didn't hold it but rather slid her little hand around first one finger and then another, moving up the line until she reached the last one. Then she'd start all over again. He tried making her hold onto just his thumb while he typed, but she refused to stay still. So far she'd hit as many letters on the keyboard as he had.

"Emily Jane," he groaned, as she pulled up yet another menu he didn't need.

She opened one eye as if to say, "Deal with it. I'm more important." She moved her hand to another finger.

Mitch settled back into the padded office chair that squeaked with protest, typing with one hand. His progress was slow and tedious. When he absolutely had to use both hands, his movements would startle Emily Jane fully awake—and the finger-grabbing would begin all over again.

Mixed feelings vied in his heart. He resented the multitude of hours Emily Jane added to his work—yet how could he resent such a precious baby? At least she didn't often cry for her mother anymore, though that made him deeply sad on another level. During the occasional nightmare or sleepless night, he still rocked her through it. He wasn't about to change that routine. But when would she finally feel more secure? With Cory confusing the custody issue, he worried that Emily Jane would be in constant turmoil between them. Was that fair to her? Would it be better to let Cory have her altogether?

No. Never. Not to an unbeliever, a confessed atheist. Besides, Mitch could no longer imagine life without Emily Jane. *But this isn't about me,* he reminded himself.

Finally, he gave it up. "Do you want to hear a story about some gray wolves?" he asked the baby. Her eyes cracked halfway open, and he took that for agreement. "Well, you see there once was a mother wolf who knew she was going to have a baby . . ." Mitch told her the story he'd researched, simplifying it greatly. Emily Jane couldn't understand yet, but in a few years he'd tell it to her again. Meanwhile, it passed the time. Instead of counting down the minutes until she was asleep enough to lay on a blanket, he could enjoy these moments together.

Soon Emily Jane's eyes were tightly closed, and a warm feeling of love spread through him. She was so tiny, so priceless, and he was her only defender against the world. Against Cory Steele and her godless ways. Sighing, he knelt on the carpet to lay the baby down on her blanket.

Returning to the computer, he found himself typing the children's story he'd been telling to Emily Jane instead of his report. *This'll only take a minute,* he thought.

A half hour later, Mitch jerked his hands from the keyboard when his doorbell rang, sounding ominous in the quiet of his small living room. With a soft groan, he hurried to the door, wondering who would bother him in the middle of the day. Perhaps Cory? He couldn't tell if he was more excited or upset at the prospect—and that definitely made him angry. Who did she think she was? What right did she have to come at all hours?

His more practical side told him to take advantage of her presence. Put her to work playing with Emily Jane while he finished his report. Maybe after he finished, they could have dinner together.

Whoa! Wait a minute. What on earth am I thinking? He was acting like Cory was a beautiful woman he found himself attracted to, instead of the woman who was trying to separate him from Emily Jane.

As he reached for the door, the ringing came again. "Cory," he growled, throwing open the door. But it wasn't Cory, it was Tyler. Mitch didn't know which was greater, the surprise of seeing his brother or the surprise at the keen disappointment flooding his body.

"Stop that ringing!" He recovered enough to knock his brother's hand away from the bell. "I have a baby in here."

Tyler removed his backpack. "Of course you do. I came to help out. Amanda said you had a report due tomorrow, and I didn't have any pressing classes, so here I am."

"Where's Savvy?" Usually the two came together.

"At the dentist." Tyler shook his head. "I don't get that girl. She *hates* the dentist. Remember the time she went three months with a toothache before it hurt so much she had to go?"

"Yeah, I remember."

"Well, this is her third dental visit in three weeks."

"Maybe she's overcome her fears." Mitch backed into the house, and his brother followed.

"Maybe." Tyler looked at the sleeping baby. "Oh, I guess you don't need me."

"Well, she could wake up any minute." Mitch was torn between wanting to get Tyler out of the house quickly so he wouldn't wake Emily Jane and keeping him here in case she did wake. "I know," he said to his brother, "you could wait in my room and watch TV. I moved it to my dresser when I set up my computer in here."

"Naw, I've got stuff from school to read. Never anything good on daytime TV anyway. Unless you've got cable." He gazed at Mitch hopefully.

"I don't have time to watch TV, so cable would be a waste of money. And believe me, if I don't get this report in, I'll need to save all the money I can because I'll be fired."

"You'd better get to it then. Hey, you got anything to eat? I forgot lunch."

Mitch stifled a sigh. "Sure. Come on, I'll show you." He led the way to the kitchen. "I have some TV dinners, mac and cheese, of course, and some ramen noodles. Or there's baloney and bread. Cheese."

"All the college staples, I see." Tyler grinned and pushed up his glasses.

"Hey, I've got fruit, too. And lots of baby food—but that's not for you."

"Aw, I like those pureed pears."

Shaking his head, Mitch started to return to the living room. He was in the doorway when Tyler spoke. "Uh, Mitch?"

"Yeah?" Mitch stopped and turned to where his brother was standing in front of the cupboards. The smile was gone from his face.

"Have you noticed anything strange about Savvy lately?"

Mitch rubbed his forehead. He didn't want to break Savvy's confidence, but maybe this would be a chance to set the couple on the right path—if he could find the words. "What do you mean?" he stalled.

"Well, she's not studying nearly as much as she used to. And I don't think she's even registered for school this fall."

"What?" Mitch didn't bother to hide his surprise. "She's supposed to graduate in January."

"Exactly. It doesn't make sense for her to quit now."

Mitch frowned. "Ever since I've known her, she's wanted to be an astronomer. She used to talk about going to California and studying with some bigwigs there."

"She doesn't talk about that now." Tyler leaned back against the counter. "There's more. I think she went to the doctor last week."

"People do that, you know," Mitch said. "Doesn't mean a thing."

Tyler began to pace. "But she tells me everything. Maybe it's serious."

"Maybe it's one of those woman things. She wouldn't tell you that."

"You think?" Tyler looked hopeful.

"What I think is that you're spending way too much time worrying about it. Why don't you just ask her?"

"I tried, but she changes the subject."

"To what?"

"Whatever. What I'm going to do on the weekend. Do I want to catch a show? Something like that."

"Sounds to me like you should ask her out."

Tyler's pacing faltered. "What do you mean? We're just friends."

"Does *she* feel that way?"

"We don't talk about it." Tyler's brow furrowed. "Besides, I'm dating Cheryl—I mean Sharon—right now."

"Another cute girl from school?"

Tyler shrugged. "I can't help it if women find me attractive. It's these new glasses, I tell you. They're in style." He touched the black frames.

"Maybe I should get some." Mitch forced a laugh. He wished he dared say more to his brother about how Savvy was feeling, but his brother didn't have a clue. Maybe it was better to feed his worry. "Well, whatever Savvy is seeing the doctor for, you probably shouldn't worry too much. I'd feel terrible, though, if something happened to her."

Tyler's expression darkened. "I'd feel terrible, too. I guess I'd better try to talk to her again."

"You'd better," Mitch agreed. "You never know how much you care for someone until they're gone. Or so they say." Certainly he felt that way about Lane and Ashley, and if something were to happen to Emily Jane . . . His throat constricting, he pushed the thought aside. "Look, help yourself to whatever you want to eat, but keep it down, okay?"

Tyler pulled his attention back from some far-off place. "Okay. Will do. Holler if you need me." He opened a walnut-finished cupboard. "Let's see. Mayonnaise, mayonnaise."

"Usually mayonnaise is kept in the refrigerator," Mitch said.

"Oh, right." Tyler shut the cupboard and started toward the refrigerator.

Sighing, Mitch went back to his computer. Could it be that Tyler liked Savvy more than he was willing to admit? Hopefully, it should only be a matter of time until some good sense kicked in. Good sense ran in their family. Look how well he was handling Cory.

I wonder what she's doing now?

Yesterday, he'd gone over to Cory's rented house to see if she needed help moving in or if she needed to borrow some cooking utensils. But the women in the ward, who had done wonders cleaning the small house, had already taken care of everything. Cory was set.

But for how long? Mitch sort of enjoyed knowing she was down the street. He could almost imagine little Emily Jane getting off the school bus sometime in the future and staying at her aunt's until he arrived home from work.

What a fantasy! Cory wouldn't be around to see Emily Jane go to school. Before long she'd be chasing animals in the rain forest, while he researched animals on the computer. With a heavy sigh, Mitch put his hands on the keyboard.

From the floor came a long, screeching wail. Emily Jane was awake.

Cory saw them coming down the street, the man bending slightly to hold the hand of the little girl. She heard his laughter, and her heart joyed at the sound. How nice to hear him laugh! And how nice that they were coming her way. She'd wanted to see EmJay but had worried about showing up unannounced and uninvited. Her arms yearned to hold the baby again, to see her sister's features in that small, trusting child. Even if that meant she had to face Mitch Huntington.

Yet as the pair approached, she saw that it wasn't Mitch at all, but his younger brother, who wasn't quite as tall, though perhaps more arresting in looks with his green eyes and rounder facial features. She told herself this was a good opportunity to see EmJay without Mitch around, but that didn't explain the odd surge of disappointment in her chest.

"Hello," she called.

He glanced up at her in surprised recognition. Angling down her walk, he came to a stop before her porch. "I didn't know you lived so close."

"Just renting. Your brother found me this place so I could be near EmJay." She squatted down and held out her arms. "Hi, darling. Come see me. I've missed you." To her delight, EmJay let go of his hand and stepped toward her. Cory swept the baby into her arms, where EmJay immediately buried her fingers in Cory's curls.

"She likes you," he said. "Better than me anyway. She only came with me because I was going outside." He thumbed toward Mitch's house. "My brother has a report due, so I'm watching her."

"He could have asked me."

He shrugged. "No offense, uh—what was your name? I'm Tyler, by the way, in case you forgot."

"Hi, Tyler. I'm Cory."

"Well, Cory, no offense, but given the situation, I don't think I'd call you, either."

She sighed. "I guess you're right." Cory cuddled EmJay, and the baby laid her head on her shoulder, still twisting her hand in Cory's hair. "She seems tired."

"Yeah, she just woke up. Wasn't asleep long."

"Why don't you come in for a drink?" Cory suggested. Anything to keep EmJay with her.

"Okay. I was just going to eat lunch when she woke up."

"I have a casserole if you'd like some. A lady brought it last night. Way too big for one person."

Tyler grinned, and Cory's heart flopped inside her chest. His smile was the same as Mitch's. "That's the Relief Society for you," he said. "Boy, I love those ladies."

Within minutes they were in her kitchen, chatting like old friends. Tyler sat at the square card table left by the previous occupant, perched on one of the two wobbly chairs. He was soon into his second helping of tuna-potato casserole. Cory cradled EmJay, who had fallen asleep, one of her perfect little hands tangled in Cory's hair.

Tyler finally pushed back his plate. "I don't know why Mitch doesn't like you. You're not at all what I expected."

Cory stiffened. "What do you mean?"

"Uh, nothing."

"Tell me." Cory stared at him unblinkingly.

"Well, the other day he—"

"Yes?"

Tyler quailed under her steady gaze. "He said something about you being hard to get along with, that's all."

"He did, huh." Not good news. Seeing the attorney had really opened her eyes to her options. To charm Mitch into giving her custody, she somehow had to change his opinion of her. Fortunately, he was a good conversationalist and attractive, so it wouldn't be too much of a chore, even if he wasn't her type.

Tyler blinked, his eyes looking large and appealing under his glasses. "Look, I can understand why you two don't get along, fighting over Emily Jane and all. But for the record, I don't think you're difficult at all. In fact, I don't see why you guys can't come to an arrangement."

"You're nicer than your brother, that's all," she told him. "He's probably the most infuriating person I've ever met."

"Infuriating? Mitch? I think you got the wrong guy. Mitch wouldn't anger a flea."

"Exactly. He's much better with those animals of his than with people."

"Don't you like his animals?"

"I like his animals just fine. I *love* his animals. But I think he's . . ." She wanted to say arrogant, but that wasn't really it. Arrogant was that stupid Evan. No, Mitch was rather awkward, dramatic, energetic, stubborn, insistent, serene, unruffled, and . . . well, infuriating. Why couldn't he just give her what she wanted?

She knew the answer to that all too well. The answer was in her arms. The stakes they were playing for were simply too high. They both knew she had no intention of staying in Utah, so unless one of them made a significant lifestyle change, custody of EmJay would have to be all or nothing.

"You should at least be able to work something out while you're here. Of course, the family is helping, too." He hesitated briefly before asking, "Do you have a lot of friends in Brazil? I mean, I know you want custody, but if you had it, you'd need someone to watch her while you worked."

"Plenty of natives would be glad to let her play with their children for a little money," she said, trying to keep the ice from her voice. This boy who was barely a man seemed to be on her side for now. "And I could take her into the jungle sometimes. It would be a good education."

"But it's dangerous! What about mosquitos and malaria and alligators and snakes?" He made a face.

She shook her head, angered by his lack of knowledge. "The Amazon is a wonderful place! Sure, there are dangers, but not any more than, say, riding a bike to school here. All kinds of things could happen. The Amazon is no different. Tons of children have great lives there. I would never let anything happen to EmJay. Never. She'd have constant supervision, an education, friends. We even have a doctor in the camp where I'm working." She stopped, feeling flushed with her ire. So much for trying to keep him on her side. She took a deep, calming breath. "Besides, it's not like I'll be there forever. When I'm finished with my next job, I might go somewhere else. Maybe Europe."

Tyler looked around, apparently losing interest in the discussion. "Do you have anything to drink? I mean, besides the wine you offered me before. I don't drink alcohol."

"There's soda in the fridge." She was lucky the owners had bought a new refrigerator for their new house, leaving their ancient one for her use.

While Tyler helped himself, she set out a plate of chocolate chip cookies the neighbor had brought last night with the casserole. When he sat down opposite her again, a can of orange soda in one hand and a cookie in the other, his question surprised her. "Do you believe in God?"

She shook her head. "I did once. But I don't think so now."

"Well, we—Mitch and I and my family, that is—believe in God. We believe that He is the literal Father of our spirits."

Cory listened with amused interest as he explained the characteristics and purpose of the Mormon God. Then he talked about Jesus Christ and His role in the great "Plan of Happiness." It was much like the doctrine Cory had learned growing up but more personal, more loving. Cory began to feel almost sorry that she couldn't believe in such Beings. Then Tyler told her about the Book of Mormon. "You don't have to accept my word for it," he said. "You can know for yourself that it's true."

"Do you always do this?" Cory asked. "I mean, preach to people you meet? If you do, I bet you don't get many repeat dates."

Tyler grinned the smile that so reminded her of Mitch. "The girls I date already know this stuff. But I served a mission awhile back and talking to you . . . well, it's kind of like being on my mission again. I guess I sort of fell back into the habit." The glint in his eyes told her that maybe it hadn't been so accidental.

"So you're telling me what Mormons believe."

He nodded. "Is that okay?"

Cory looked down at the baby in her arms. "I do want to know what my sister believed. Is there more?"

"Yeah. A lot more. But you should probably read a little bit in a book before we go on. I've got one in my truck. It's my personal copy, but I'll lend it to you until I get you another one."

"I can buy it." Cory didn't want to feel obligated to anyone.

"Don't worry about it. They're cheap."

She walked him to the front door and sat down on her porch with the still-sleeping EmJay to wait while he retrieved a book with a worn, brown leather cover. "Why have you crossed out so many paragraphs?" she asked, placing the book on her knees and scanning through the text.

He laughed. "Not crossed out. Highlighted. Those are my favorite verses."

"You have a lot of favorite verses."

"Every time I read it, I find more verses I like. Things that apply at that time in my life."

Cory eyed the small print doubtfully. "You've read it more than once?"

"Yeah. Or at least the part that's the actual Book of Mormon. There are two other books there as well—the Pearl of Great Price and the Doctrine and Covenants. Anyway, each time I finish the Book of Mormon, I write down the date in the back."

Cory flipped to the back and saw that he had seven entries in a three-year span. She shook her head. How weird that a young man had wasted so much time rereading a simple book. Her father had been like that with the Bible.

"When should I come back?" Tyler asked.

She shrugged, not excited at the prospect but knowing that her commitment to EmJay meant she had to hear it all. She owed that much to AshDee and EmJay. Not that listening would make the slightest difference in how she felt. Of course, the most important reason for her to hear Tyler out was so that if Mitch didn't agree to give up custody, the way would be paved for her to join their church. It would be a last resort but one she wouldn't hesitate to use if it became necessary.

"I guess you could come tomorrow," she said. "How long does it take?"

"About an hour each time, give or take. Depending on how many questions you have. Do you mind if I bring some friends?"

Ah, he needs reinforcements, she thought. "Sure, why not?" She'd grown up hearing about the scriptures and the will of God and was confident she could hold her own. Except if the infuriating Mitch were present. She didn't want that, not until she was sure which of her plans she would have to follow—charming Mitch or pretending conversion. More than likely she'd need a combination of the two. "But don't tell Mitch, okay?" she said to Tyler. "He and I have enough to work out as it is. This has nothing to do with him."

"Fine." Tyler glanced at the baby on her lap. "Look who's awake."

She looked down to see EmJay staring up at her. "Momma," she said in a soft, sleepy voice.

Cory hugged her. "No, darling. I'm your mommy's sister, but I'm here for you." *I want to be your momma,* she added silently. But that was too personal to say in front of Tyler.

"Poor little girl. I'd better get her back. It's been an hour. Mitch might worry."

EmJay was struggling now to get down, so Cory let her, though the child didn't seem in a hurry to leave. She was too busy checking out the porch stair railing.

"Come on, Emily Jane. Let's go back to Mitch."

The child looked up and grinned. "Much?"

"Yeah, Mitch."

EmJay grabbed Tyler's outstretched finger and began her descent on the cement stairs. Cory wanted to cry out that she hadn't spent enough time with her. Strange how strongly this little girl had entered her heart. At the bottom of the stairs, she let go of Tyler's finger, turned around, and waved good-bye to Cory. Cory waved back. Then EmJay grabbed Tyler's finger again.

Cory watched until they reached Mitch's house and disappeared inside. She didn't know she was crying until a tear splashed from her chin onto her hands that tightly gripped Tyler's leather book.

Chapter Thirteen

Cory awoke early Wednesday morning, feeling as though she hadn't slept in a week. Not only did she miss the buzzing and cries of the insects and animals in the rain forest, she'd been disturbed by strange dreams that now eluded her grasp. She stretched in the twin bed the owners of the house had kindly lent her. The quilt they'd also left was on the floor in a heap, since she'd been hot during the night.

Utah's heat was nothing like the Amazon's, but the lack of moisture in the air made her skin and hair feel dry. At this rate, she'd have to buy special lotions to keep her skin from shriveling and her hair from frizzing.

Light filtered through the curtained window, making the room cheery despite its relative emptiness. She forced herself to her feet and opened the window, enjoying the cool breeze from outside. The morning sky was cloudy, but she suspected the clouds would burn off before afternoon.

Dragging herself across the carpet, her foot hit the edge of the book Tyler had given her. *That's probably why I had such a lousy night,* she told herself. She'd read for some time in bed and the last thing she remembered was a war where the soldiers all strangely looked like Mitch. Or was that from her dream?

In the kitchen, Cory started to make herself a cup of coffee before she realized that she'd forgotten to buy any. She wondered how the Mormons woke up in the mornings. AshDee had been a big coffee drinker before her baptism, and getting her out of bed in her teenage years had been a challenge. Cory wished she could ask how she'd felt about giving up the coffee.

Grief hit her then, completely and totally, taking her by such surprise that she sank down onto the patterned ceramic tile, holding her gut and trying not to scream aloud. *AshDee! Why? Why did you leave me? Oh, AshDee!*

Refusing to cry, Cory wrapped her arms around herself and gritted her teeth. She tried thinking about EmJay or even Mitch, but the emotions in her heart only intensified. *AshDee, I need you!* The oak cupboards and empty white walls seemed to press down on her until she felt she would smother.

Dear God in Heaven, she prayed—not because she believed, she told herself, but because the words from her childhood might bring comfort.

At that moment, her eyes spotted a discoloration on the wall where a picture had once hung. Focusing on this, she forced herself to breathe through the ever-increasing flow of grief. That spot saved her. She stared at it until the emotions receded, like the tide on a gritty shore.

At last she could stand. Forgetting her growling stomach, she stumbled to the shower to wash off the sheen of sweat clinging to her brow. She emerged feeling better but not ready for battle. Her plan had been to go to Mitch's this morning and begin to work on him, kicking her charm into high gear. But it felt too soon after such an emotional start to her day. She didn't want to show any weakness.

As she dressed in khaki shorts and a T-shirt, still debating what to do, her cell phone rang. She hurried to the kitchen where she had left her purse. "Hello?"

"Cory. It's so good to hear your voice! I got your e-mail and called the first instant I could."

"Evan." She kept her voice purposely cold as anger simmered to the surface of her volatile emotions. "I wondered if I'd ever hear from you. What on earth were you trying to pull? I can't believe you'd try to steal my job!"

"Whoa, calm down."

"Calm? Why should I be calm? Evan, you tried submitting your pictures for the article—and you claimed some of my shots as your own. You're lucky I don't call the police and have you arrested." This was good for her, this call. Already she felt more like battling Mitch.

"What are you talking about? I'm not sure where you got the information, but it's all a mistake. That's why I'm calling. Cory, sweetheart, I thought I was doing you a favor. I knew you weren't quite finished, so I gave them extra photos to choose from. I had absolutely no intention of taking your place and certainly none of stealing your work. I knew your agent would be submitting your photographs."

"Oh? Then why did you send some of mine?"

"Must have been included by accident. Honestly, Cory. I'd never do anything to hurt you."

Cory wasn't sure she believed him, though he sounded sincere. "You shouldn't have done it," she said, sitting down on one of her borrowed folding chairs. "At least until you heard from me or the magazine."

"You didn't leave me your contact information. I had to get your new cell number from your e-mail."

She blinked in surprise, realizing he was right.

"I would have called sooner if I hadn't been on a plane home," he added. "Believe me, I was only trying to help. Yes, I'll admit I was hoping the magazine would like my pictures, but that's only so I'd get another spread with them. You'd have done the same."

"No, I wouldn't." Yet as much as Cory hated to admit it, his explanation made sense. If her pictures had been lacking, his could have made the difference in whether or not the article was actually printed and if they would have a chance at doing future articles.

"Would so. Come on, admit it so we can make up. I'm dying to see you! The week you've been away seems like a month."

Cory felt herself softening. "You're in the States?" She brought a finger to her mouth and tore off a bit of nail.

"Of course I'm in the States. Without you there was nothing left for me in Brazil. Don't worry, though, I packed your things and paid to store them—if you decide to go back."

"I have to," she said, letting a note of pride seep into her voice. "I'm doing the *National Geographic* spread."

"Wonderful! Now we really have to celebrate. When can I see you?"

Cory shook her head, unsure that she even wanted him in her life at this point. Could she trust him? "I can't leave here. There's a problem with custody."

"Where's here? Texas?"

"No, Utah."

"You're in Utah? No way."

"Yes. And they're every bit as strange as you would expect."

He laughed. "Oh, Cory, I've missed you."

Though she wouldn't admit it to Evan, she'd missed him, too. Being alone in Utah wasn't exactly her idea of a fun time.

"Well, there's nothing for it," he continued. "I guess I'll have to hot-foot it to Utah. I've been meaning to visit my cousin, anyway. I have an article to write, but I have a small window of time before I need to get working on it."

"You're coming here?" Cory felt a surge of excitement at the prospect.

"Yes. When I get there, I'll take you jet skiing at a lake my cousin likes to go to. We'll go Friday and make a day of it. It'll be crowded because of the Fourth, but it'll still be fun. Afterward, we'll dump my cousin and go somewhere romantic. What do you say?"

"Sounds fun. Really fun."

"So tell me what's happening with your niece?"

Cory quickly outlined the problem and was rewarded with Evan's sympathy. "I guess I'm in limbo for a while," she concluded. "My plan is to prove to this guy that she needs me more than she needs him."

"You think that's going to work?" Evan sounded doubtful.

"Well, he's a man, isn't he? Tell me, wouldn't it cramp your style suddenly inheriting a child you're not even related to? I can't believe he's in this for the long haul." Even as she said it, Cory somehow felt she was betraying Mitch.

"I don't know. I mean, if this is a religious deal for him, it might not be that easy for him to give her up."

"She's my niece," Cory said stubbornly.

"I know. I'm sure you'll get it all worked out. Meanwhile, I can see I'd better waste no time in making arrangements. You need a break big time."

Cory found herself smiling. She was glad the picture mess had been a misunderstanding. Right now she could do with a little of Evan's pampering. At least she wouldn't be lonely.

"Where're you staying?" he asked.

"In Sandy. I'm renting a small place."

"Is there room for me?"

"Sorry. My agent will be here soon, and we'll be up to our ears in work. You'd better find another place." She wanted it clear from the beginning that they were not a couple. Not yet. She wasn't going to rush their relationship. Besides, what would Mitch think? Now that she was trying to impress him, his opinion meant everything.

"I'll stay at my cousin's, then," he said, obviously disappointed. "He's in Orem. I think that's farther south, if I remember my geography."

"That reminds me. We should probably invite my agent to come with us to the lake."

"Not a problem. My cousin owns several jet skis. An inflatable boat, too, I think."

"Okay. Call me when you get in."

"Will do. Bye, love."

Cory hung up the phone, and once again her kitchen was plunged into silence. Not a comfortable silence, but one that was loud and lonely. With a sigh, she arose and sliced a piece of homemade bread from the loaf the Relief Society president had brought her yesterday evening. With the homemade raspberry jam that had come with the bread, the bread would make more than a halfway decent breakfast.

The doorbell rang as she was cleaning up. Cory smiled. Most likely it was another neighbor bringing her a food gift. So far she'd received two casseroles, the bread and jam, a mound of chocolate chip cookies, a pan of brownies, and a plate of snickerdoodles—most of which had come last night around dinnertime. She'd accepted the storm of food hesitantly, wondering all the while what they expected in return. So far no one had even invited her to church.

Most likely they were waiting until she was really in their debt, then *slam!* they'd ask her to pay tithing, or something, hoping she'd feel obligated. Whatever their plan was didn't really matter. In fact, their kindness might actually help her later if she had to implement her backup plan of joining their church. After all, turnabout was fair play. If they planned to use her, she could use them.

A glance through the peephole showed a woman on her doorstep, her features greatly distorted by the thick glass. What would this one have to offer? No one could claim they made cookies at ten in the morning, could they?

She was startled to open the door and find Mitch's oldest sister standing there, a little boy in her arms and a big diaper bag slung over her narrow shoulder. "Uh, hi," Cory said, her eyes dropping to the two towheaded children at her side. Behind them on the sidewalk was a double jogging stroller.

"Hi. I'm Kerrianne Price, Mitch's sister." The woman gave her a tentative smile.

"Sure, I remember you," Cory said. "I, uh, would you like to come in?" She was suddenly aware that her living room was empty. Clean but empty. She was tempted to keep Kerrianne out on the porch, but the angry-looking clouds gathering over the mountains signaled an impending morning shower.

"Okay. But could you get Emily Jane? She's in the stroller."

Cory paused only a second before rushing down the steps to get the baby. EmJay blinked sleepily as Cory went down on one knee, scraping her skin on the concrete walk. "Hi, darling. How are you?"

The little girl from the steps poked her porcelain-doll face into the stroller. "Hey, Emily Jane, you're finally awake," she said in a baby voice. "Guess what? We're going to visit your aunt."

The baby didn't smile, but she didn't cry, either, and Cory took that as a good sign. EmJay went into her arms freely enough, though she kept searching the front yard with her eyes. "Much?" she asked.

"In a minute, Emily Jane." Kerrianne started up the stairs again. "You'll be back with Mitch soon. Don't worry, sweetie."

"Where is he?" Cory glanced down the street at his house as she went up the stairs past Kerrianne. His obnoxiously colored car wasn't in the driveway.

Before Kerrianne could reply, they were inside, and the middle child, a thin, bright-eyed boy of about four, asked, "Where're we gonna sit, Mommy?"

"Just on the floor, Benjamin." Kerrianne set down her baby, who Cory surmised to be at least several months older than EmJay. "Misty, honey," Kerrianne said to the blonde girl, "help keep an eye on Caleb, okay? You too, Benjamin."

Nodding, Misty stepped up to Cory, proffering a plate she hadn't noticed before. "We made you peanut butter chocolate bars last night. They're yummy."

"Thank you. I'm sure they're wonderful."

EmJay immediately reached for one. Cory stopped her since she didn't know if a baby was allowed to eat such things. "Can she have one, do you think?" she asked, hoping her ineptness wouldn't get back to Mitch. "All the children, I mean," she amended hastily.

Kerrianne studied the plush, off-white carpet doubtfully. "Maybe in the kitchen?"

"Yeah!" the older kids shouted in unison.

Soon the children were happily eating their treats in a circle on the kitchen floor. All but EmJay, who remained in Cory's lap, making what Cory surmised to be the biggest mess in history. The little girl refused to allow Cory to feed her but wanted to hold the bar herself.

"So where is Mitch?" Cory doubted that he was aware Kerrianne was here with EmJay or he'd probably come to make sure Cory didn't run off with her.

"He had a meeting at work." Kerrianne held the bar she'd taken for herself but didn't bring it to her mouth. "He stayed up all night finishing a paper he was supposed to present today. Apparently Emily Jane had another rough night, so when he wasn't at the computer, he was with her. They were both worn out when I arrived this morning. Cranky, too."

Cory's eyes fell to EmJay. "She doesn't look cranky."

"That's because she's been sleeping for the past hour and a half while we've been walking. She doesn't take to me very well yet, so I have to take her on a walk. She doesn't mind staying with us if we do that."

"I would have watched her." The peanut butter bar in Cory's mouth suddenly lost its flavor.

"I know." Kerrianne's eyes dropped to her hands lying on the card table. She took a breath and met Cory's gaze. "Look, Mitch didn't just go to work. Afterward, he was going to talk to my dad's lawyer—his lawyer now."

Cory knew how that would go. "According to my attorney, I need to convince Mitch that I'm the one who should raise EmJay." She'd leave out the possibility of suing for custody if she joined the Church—for now.

Kerrianne appeared surprised at her honesty. "That's pretty much what our lawyer said to my father yesterday on the phone."

"So what's the chance that Mitch will give me custody?" Instinctively, Cory's arms tightened around EmJay.

"I don't know." Kerrianne shook her head and sighed. "If you'd come two weeks ago, or three—you know, right when Mitch was in the thick of adjusting—you'd have had a better chance. But he has bonded with her now—all of us have. She's part of us. It would be difficult to let her go."

Cory felt a surge of jealousy at the words. EmJay was part of them. Part of the busy, friendly, crazy Huntington family. For a moment, she desperately wished she could make such a claim. "She's part of me, too," she said instead.

Kerrianne didn't reply. She glanced at her children, who were playing with toys they had taken from her diaper bag.

Now Cory understood. Mitch's sister was here to fight his battle for him, a battle that according to her attorney he'd already won. "You want me to leave, don't you?"

Kerrianne's face whipped back to her. "It's not that at all. I . . . well, maybe just a little. Look, growing up, Mitch and I weren't the closest. He and Amanda were like twins, doing everything together. I was older and got stuck a lot with the baby, Tyler, so we sort of hung out together by default. I was always close to Amanda because she was my only sister, but Mitch, well, we were just siblings." Tears started to form in Kerrianne's eyes. "But when my husband died, Mitch came over every day. He looked for ways to help me around the house—still does. Without him . . ." She blinked rapidly, trying to stop the tears. "Without him I would have been lost. I wanted you to know what kind of man he is. What kind of family we are. That's all. No one wants to kick you out of Emily Jane's life, but we won't let her go, either. Please try to understand. Not only do we love her, but Mitch made a promise to your sister, and he'll fulfill it if it's the last thing he does."

Cory welcomed the fury that rose in her heart. She *wanted* to be angry at this woman who took so much upon herself. How appalling that Kerrianne would accept an invitation to come into her house when she had only come to intimidate—despite her pretty words to the contrary.

"It's so hard raising children by yourself," Kerrianne went on, oblivious to Cory's internal raging. "I didn't know how hard until my husband died."

"But you're doing it." Cory's words were sharp, bitter.

"Not alone." Kerrianne's eyes willed her to understand. "That's what I'm saying. Without my family, I couldn't do it half as well."

Cory lifted her chin. "So you're saying I couldn't raise EmJay by myself?"

"No, I bet you could. But as well as someone with a support system?" Kerrianne shook her head. "I don't think so. And Mitch will get married soon. If he'd opened his eyes to all the good women around him, he'd already be married by now. When he does marry, Emily Jane will have two parents again."

"I could get married." Cory tried to picture Evan holding EmJay—and failed. Mitch's face kept inserting itself in her mind. She lifted her chin. "I can't just go away. AshDee was my sister. Don't you understand that? How would you feel if your sister died? Wouldn't you want to take care of her baby?"

"You're right. I don't know the answer. All I have to go by is what Emily Jane's parents wanted for their daughter."

Cory felt like crying but refused to show any weakness. "All I know is that EmJay is *my* family. My only family, and I'm not about to give her up. I'll do whatever I have to do in order to keep her. As for Mitch getting married, how will that woman feel about EmJay when she has her own children? What if my niece gets second best? I won't stand by and watch that happen."

"Mitch wouldn't let it. None of us would."

"You wouldn't be able to stop it."

"Well, what about when you have your own children?"

"EmJay's my *sister's* child. I would love her like my own. I love her already, and nothing can change that. AshDee and I have a shared past. Only I can give that past to EmJay." Cory wanted to stand and demand that Kerrianne leave, but her hands were full of a sticky EmJay. Besides, a glance out the window showed her it was raining. She couldn't very well force the woman out in the rain—especially when she'd take EmJay with her.

"Here, let me." Kerrianne took out a container of baby wipes and began washing one of EmJay's hands. Cory started on the other.

EmJay squealed, "Ow, ow! Ow!" though she wasn't in any pain. The other children came to watch. EmJay's pink shirt wouldn't come clean, but the chocolate on her hands and face came off easily. Kerrianne squatted on the floor and began cleaning little Caleb's hands.

"Do you like Uncle Mitch's animals?" Misty asked Cory.

Cory nodded. "Yes, I do. In fact, the other day I took a whole bunch of pictures of EmJay and his baby bunnies. And I've been thinking about getting a camera that will let us peek inside the robin nest in his gas grill."

"Really?" Misty's blue eyes opened wide. "Can I see?"

"Me too," Benjamin said.

"I'm sure he'll let you. I'm going to buy the camera this afternoon." In fact, that would be the perfect excuse for her to confront Mitch or at least to begin bringing him around to her way of thinking.

After the children's excitement died down, Cory felt Kerrianne's eyes on her. "What?" Cory asked, wondering if maybe her wet hair was drying funny or something. Probably. The humidity brought by the rain would help, but it was still likely to be shooting everywhere—just like EmJay's. After living in Utah, no wonder AshDee had worn her hair long.

"You like Mitch's animals?" Kerrianne asked. "You actually *like* them?"

Cory laughed at her incredulity. "Of course I do. I'm a wildlife photographer, remember?"

A smile stole across Kerrianne's thin face. "Exactly. Then maybe we've solved a problem."

"What?"

"You should marry my brother. Then you'd both have EmJay."

Cory's heart skipped a beat. "Well, I'm not sure my boyfriend would approve." *There, that should fix her.*

Kerrianne started laughing. "I'm joking! I'm joking. Of course you and Mitch can't get married. He wouldn't think to marry out of—uh, never mind. I was just joking. But I can't tell you how many times Mitch's relationships have fallen through because of those creatures." Kerrianne bent and began retrieving her toys. "I think the rain is letting up now. I'd better get to Mitch's. If he's back, he'll be wondering where we are."

"So he doesn't know you're here?"

"Of course not." Kerrianne laughed. "From what I hear, he's the only one allowed to fraternize with the enemy." As she talked, Kerrianne expertly herded her children to the front door and out onto the porch. "I'll tell him, though, when I get back."

"So why did you come?" Cory asked, watching her take a thin blanket from her bag and mop up a few raindrops that had blown inside the covered jogging stroller. "Aside from the peanut butter bars." *And trying to scare me away,* she added silently.

Kerrianne snapped Caleb into his seat and then took a reluctant EmJay from Cory's arms. "Because," she said matter-of-factly, "I thought you would like to see Emily Jane." She bent and strapped EmJay into the other stroller seat. "There now. All ready."

Her answer, and the sincerity of it, caught Cory by surprise. "Thank you," she said softly.

Kerrianne smiled. "You're welcome. And for what it's worth, I'm very sorry about the whole situation. I hope you understand that I don't have anything against you personally. I just don't want to see my brother hurt—or Emily Jane, either. They've both been through a lot."

Watching them leave, Cory breathed in the pungent smell of the rain-washed asphalt. She loved the clean feeling that the smell brought to mind. Sometimes when it rained, she'd go outside and stare up into the sky, wishing the drops could wash her clean as well—wash clean the weak and tarnished part of her that had permitted her father to bar AshDee from their lives. But no matter how many times she stood in the rain, she remained stained and broken.

She noticed that Mitch's bright orange-red car was back in his driveway. For the second time that day, Cory felt like crying.

Chapter Fourteen

After her nap, Mitch took Emily Jane to the patio for her snack, glad that the afternoon sun had chased away the clouds. He didn't think he could face cleaning off her high chair tray again.

"No, Muffin," he said to the dog. "Stay inside until I finish feeding her. And leave the turtle alone."

The rare summer storm had left his grass looking green and stiff, and the air felt clean and new. After making sure the concrete wasn't too hot, he set Emily Jane in the shade of the tall walnut tree next to the patio. Between them was a plate of freshly sliced pears and a bowl of cinnamon oatmeal. He'd learned that if he allowed her to hold a pear, he could feed her better. There were, however, some unfortunate side effects. As if reading his thoughts, Emily Jane smashed a pear on her head. Then she gave him one of her mischievous grins.

Cute but messy.

He laughed and handed her another pear. Despite the morning rain, it was warm enough to fill up the little pool he'd bought her, so what was one more overripe pear?

"Open up, sweetie." He gave her a spoonful of milk-thinned oatmeal.

"Oh, there you are," came a voice from the side of the house.

Swivelling, he caught sight of Cory coming through his tall wooden gate. He scrambled to his feet. She was wearing khaki shorts and a baby blue T-shirt that made her eyes stand out. Her red hair appeared less orange, and the tight curls looked windblown, though there wasn't any breeze. Her purse hung over her shoulder, and in her hand she carried a plastic shopping bag.

"I hoped you'd be out here." She fastened the gate behind her. "Your car's in the drive, but when I rang, no one answered."

I should tell her to go away, he thought. But Emily Jane made an expression of gladness and waved at Cory as though excited to see her.

Cory sauntered across the patio, squatting down by the baby. "Hi, darling."

"Hi. Hi," Emily Jane said with a smile.

"You look so pretty," Cory added. "I've heard pears do wonders for the hair."

"Shabahs mash-lama shing gasna ba." Emily Jane brought another piece to her mouth, and juice dribbled down the sides of her mouth. Cory gave her a bite of oatmeal from the bowl Mitch had left on the concrete.

They were getting along far too well in Mitch's view. "We have to talk," he said. "I've been to see my lawyer."

A lost expression replaced the smile on Cory's face, making her look younger than her twenty-six years. She returned the spoon to the oatmeal bowl and stood. "I know. Your sister told me when she brought EmJay over this morning."

Mitch rubbed his jaw as he thought how to reply. Kerrianne had told him about the visit, and he'd given her the same lecture he'd given Tyler the day before. But at least Tyler's visit had been an accidental encounter, not a premeditated one. His sister had shrugged his concerns aside. "She needs to see that baby," she'd told him. "Whatever happens, you can't keep her out of Emily Jane's life."

He knew Emily Jane could use as many people to love her as she could find. He knew that someday Emily Jane would want to learn about her mother's childhood and upbringing. Only Cory could give her that. But until the custody issue was settled to his satisfaction, Mitch wanted to be present during the visits to assure Emily Jane's safety. At least that's what he told himself.

"I saw my attorney, too," Cory said when he didn't speak.

"Then you know the papers will hold up in court unless I'm unfit." He shrugged. "I may be a lot of things, but I'm not unfit."

She didn't rise to the bait. "I know." Hefting her plastic bag, she said, "I bought the camera so we can see the baby birds. It hooks up to the computer, but the cord's not very long. You'll have to move your computer out here."

All the fight seeped from Mitch's body. She remembered the birds! She actually cared enough about them to remember. "Great! Let's see it." Then, in case he'd shown too much excitement, he added, "If you have time."

She smiled a slow smile that made a knot form in his stomach. "That's why I'm here."

Remembering the baby, Mitch turned to where she was sitting, one hand now grasping her spoon, the other patting a handful of oatmeal into her hair. "Ohhh," he said, closing his eyes.

Cory giggled. That started Emily Jane laughing, and Mitch, too. "Well, now we'll really have to fill up the pool."

"Are you kidding?" Cory asked. "The water will be too cold."

"Not if we connect the hose inside. Don't worry, I did it all the time when I was young. My mom must have grounded me a dozen times. I could never make her understand that my dogs liked warm water for their baths."

Cory laughed again. "I'll feed her the rest of the oatmeal while you get the pool ready."

By the time Cory had finished giving the baby her food, Mitch had the tiny pool half filled with warm water. Emily Jane toddled up to the edge and fell into the water, giggling wildly. Her shorts and top were soaked. "Hold on," Mitch said. "You don't want to drown." Emily Jane shrugged off his hand and plunged into the water again. She came up gasping but laughing.

Mitch glanced toward Cory, but the laughter was gone from her face. "AshDee loved the water," she said. "She was always going to the beach or the pool. She'd take a big umbrella and wear this funny straw hat to keep off the sun. Looks like she took EmJay into the water a lot."

"Yeah, she did." Mitch remembered many times that he had gone to the indoor pool with Lane and Ashley. He wanted to share these memories with Cory, but the sadness in her face forbade his intrusion.

After Emily Jane was oatmeal-free and dressed once more, Mitch put away the pool and let Muffin outside to play with Emily Jane. As Cory began sliding the mini camera into a small opening on the side of the barbeque, Mitch brought out his coffee table and set his computer on top, plugging it into the outside electrical outlet. Cory sat on the concrete to install the software.

"I can't get the see-in-the-dark function to turn on," she said after a few minutes. "We'll never see the babies if we can't figure that out. Pass me the instructions."

"Instructions? You don't need those."

She snorted. "Hey, don't give me that machismo. Do I look like a guy? I'm not afraid to read the instructions."

"That's not what I meant. Look." He pointed to where Emily Jane sat contentedly munching on the folded instruction paper. No matter how hard he tried to convince her otherwise, she still adored eating paper. He'd finally decided that as long as he got to her before she swallowed too much, it probably wouldn't hurt her.

Cory gave a little gasp and ran to the baby. "Oh, no. It's ruined!" She looked up at Mitch. "Are you just going to sit there and laugh? Do you know how much these cameras cost? I can't believe it. She actually ate the instructions!" Cory tossed the remains of the page to him while she fished a wad of pulp from Emily Jane's grinning mouth.

163

"Ooooow!" Emily Jane howled when she realized what Cory was doing.

Mitch opened the instructions. "Hey, I think we have a budding artist. It looks like one of those folded paper snowflakes. Sort of."

Cory walked over to him and studied the paper with the large gaping holes. "No way we'll read them now."

"Yeah. I've lost more books that way. And you should see what she did to my last month's *Ensign*."

"Your what?"

Her comment reminded Mitch how far apart they were. "A magazine I get every month," he said, feeling a melancholy he couldn't name. "There's a whole bunch in the magazine rack by the kitchen door."

Cory was staring again at the computer. "Well, nothing for it but to experiment."

An hour passed before they had a live image of the newly hatched baby birds on the screen. But the wait was worth it.

"Oh, look at that!" Cory took a long sip of the lemonade Mitch and EmJay had gone inside to get a few minutes earlier.

"Yeah," Mitch agreed. But he wasn't looking at the screen. Cory was kneeling close to him—so close he could smell an exotic spicy scent that for some reason called to mind an untamed jungle.

She turned and met his gaze, falling immediately silent. Her eyes were large and luminous, her many freckles standing out darkly against the rest of the tanned skin. Mitch had never in his life wanted to kiss anyone as much as he wanted to kiss her right then. No matter that it didn't make sense. No matter that she planned to fight him for custody of Emily Jane.

Only one thing saved him. Emily Jane toddled up behind Cory, an old copy of the *Ensign* in her hands, the corner already wet and tearing. *She must have snagged it from the rack when I got the lemonade,* he thought.

Mitch drew away from Cory but slowly so as not to be obvious. "I bet Emily Jane would like to see." Picking her up, he turned to the screen but not before he saw Cory flush a deeper red than her hair. He hadn't fooled her, not for a moment. Her attractiveness was even more apparent to him at that moment, but he couldn't allow his emotions to rule his choices. Emily Jane was too important—his future was too important. He wasn't going to mess that up no matter how much he was beginning to like Miss Cory Steele.

While showing Emily Jane the birds, they recaptured some of the camaraderie they had felt before the Kiss-That-Never-Happened, but there was an obvious awkwardness between them.

Emily Jane tired of the birds and reached out for Cory, who took her gratefully. The baby wrapped a hand in Cory's curls and laid her head against her shoulder.

"Do you think," Cory said, "that I could take EmJay with me to a lake on Friday? A friend of mine will be in town, two friends actually, and I'd like to spend some time with her. You know, showing her off."

"It's the Fourth. We were going over to my family's for dinner. And then there'll be fireworks. I wanted to—" He broke off. He'd wanted to be the first to show Emily Jane fireworks.

"I won't take off with her. I promise."

But her word wasn't good enough for him.

"Please, Mitch." She didn't look at him as she spoke but looked instead at Emily Jane.

Mitch shook his head. His heart urged him to give her what she asked, but did he know Cory well enough to trust her? Besides, Lane and Ashley had drowned in a lake, and Mitch wasn't about to let Emily Jane go unless he could be sure of her safety. "What if," he began as an idea came to him. "What if I came along? Would that be all right?"

There was a flare of anger in her blue eyes, quickly squelched. "What about your family dinner?"

"I can go later. Surely you won't be at the lake all day. I'll join them for the fireworks."

"Okay."

She gave in so quickly that Mitch felt a thread of suspicion. That was augmented when she reached over and put a hand over his. "I appreciate you letting me spend time with EmJay." Mitch had the distinct impression that she was attracted to him, despite the failed kiss, and wanted to let him know. His desire to kiss her was amplified tenfold.

At that moment, Emily Jane decided she'd had enough of Cory and reached out to Mitch. He cuddled her tenderly, watching while Cory recorded the baby birds on the software that had come with the tiny camera. "I can get some pictures from this later," she explained. "I'll set up some files that you can e-mail to me."

A ringing came from Cory's purse on the picnic table. Jumping to her feet, she sprinted over and answered. "You're what? Already? I'll be right there." She hung up and looked at Mitch. "My agent's here. She's going to be spending a few days with me. Do you mind if I take EmJay to see her? You can come, too," she added hurriedly. "She's at the house."

Mitch had nothing better to do, and he felt he owed it to the people Cory was renting from to see what kind of woman she'd invited. He hoped they wouldn't have any wild parties. Did Cory even have wild parties? She didn't seem the type, but of course he didn't know her well. He had to be prepared for anything she might do. Why was it so hard for him to remember that she didn't share his faith?

Chapter Fifteen

Cory saw Vikki leaning against a white sedan in front of the rented house. As usual, Vikki was attractive in suit pants and tall heels that made her short frame seem taller and leaner than it actually was. Her thick brown hair was swept up with a gold alligator clip. A few hairs had escaped, softening the sharp lines of her cheekbones and long nose.

"Vikki!" Cory smiled widely and embraced her friend. "I'm so glad you're here."

"It's good to see you, dear. Who's this?" Vikki's blue eyes traveled past her to Mitch, who carried EmJay in his arms.

"That's my niece." Cory purposely didn't introduce Mitch. Yes, she was trying to woo him into giving her custody, but that didn't mean she was going to fawn all over him!

"I knew it right away. Looks just like you. She's adorable!"

Cory started for the house. "Come on in."

"What about my equipment?" Vikki asked, turning on her heel and heading for the trunk of her car. She glanced back at Mitch. "Will you help me take it in?"

Cory thought they could have handled the luggage themselves

later. She didn't want Mitch involved. She hoped she wasn't being petty because he hadn't kissed her. Yes, she had to get him to like her, but it didn't have to happen in a day. She could charm him easily in the three weeks she had left—if she could judge by the expression on his face while they'd been at the computer.

"Glad to help." Mitch handed Emily Jane to Cory.

In a few minutes, Mitch had all of Vikki's luggage in the living room and her darkroom equipment lying on the floor of the tiny mudroom off the kitchen that also served as a laundry room. The room wasn't perfect, but with the sink, counter space, and no window, it was the most logical spot to set up. Cory had already strung lines to hang the drying photographs.

"Thanks, Mitch," Cory said.

"Mitch?" Vikki eyed him curiously. "And you are . . . a friend?"

He smiled at her confidently, but the finger he brought to his jaw suggested to Cory that he wasn't as sure of himself as he liked to think. "I'm Emily Jane's guardian."

"Oh." Vikki blinked twice in surprise. She glanced at Cory and then back at Mitch. "I'm Cory's agent, Vikki Moline. I have my card around here somewhere. Here it is." She found one in her purse and passed it to Mitch.

"She's a good friend, too," Cory added.

Vikki smiled. "Nice to meet you." Cory could tell by the gleam in Vikki's eyes that she had a million questions.

Mitch motioned to EmJay. "Looks like she's getting tired again." The baby had her cheek pressed against Cory's neck. He reached for EmJay.

Reluctantly, Cory let him take the baby. She wished she could keep her, that she could sit and stare at her while she slept.

"See you later," he said, as they walked to the front door.

"Don't forget Friday," she said.

"Right. Jet skiing."

Vikki blinked. "You're going jet skiing together?"

"We're all going jet skiing," Cory corrected. "Mitch agreed to come along because I want to take EmJay."

"Oh." Vikki's reply clearly showed that she had no idea what Cory was talking about.

The two women watched Mitch go down the walk and across the street, gently cradling the baby.

Vikki sighed. "There's nothing so attractive as watching a man with a baby."

Cory started to nod and then shook her head. "What are you saying?" She strode back inside the house. "That's my *enemy* you're talking about."

"Oh? Well, dear, you two sure didn't look like enemies. He couldn't keep his eyes off you. And you were just as bad."

"Ha! That's part of the plan," Cory said. "If you remember, you were the one who suggested I use my charms. It's either that or become a member of his church."

"I see," Vikki said dryly. "You seem to be charming him quite well. I only hope you don't get yourself hurt in the meantime."

"Ha! To be hurt, you have to care. I'm only pretending. He doesn't interest me in the least."

Vikki studied her. "Well, he's really good-looking. A little on the thin side, but that's easily cured with a bit of good cooking. And he seems nice. Are you sure you know what you're doing?"

Cory put an arm around Vikki. "I know exactly what I'm doing. Come on now. Let's get that darkroom set up. We can get started on the photographs before dinner."

They went to work, and Cory was able to put both Mitch and EmJay from her mind. At least until she saw Vikki giving her sidelong glances. "What?" she asked, trying to stifle her irritation.

"Nothing." Vikki shook her head. "That I can pinpoint anyway. You seem different. Hey, let's take a break. You got anything to drink around here?"

"Some soda. And a bottle of wine. I have something for dinner, too. Casseroles—two different kinds."

"You made casseroles?"

Cory rolled her eyes. "Don't be so incredulous. I cook. But, no, these casseroles were gifts from the neighbors. They're very friendly." Perhaps leaving the so-called Relief Society out of it was better for the moment.

"Wine sounds good," Vikki said. "Just one glass. But let's eat later. I still want to see your pictures tonight."

Cory got two glasses from the cupboard and opened the wine while Vikki studied the decor—or lack thereof. "I'm lucky the owners left me a table," Cory informed her mildly. "If I were going to be here longer, I'd have to go to California and get my stuff from storage."

"But you're not staying, right?" Vikki sipped the red liquid.

Cory sat down in the wobbly chair opposite her. "There aren't a lot of things I'd give up *National Geographic* for."

"Go, girl!" Vikki made an upward motion with her fist.

Would you give it up for EmJay? asked a voice in Cory's head as she brought the glass of wine to her lips. The liquid tasted bitter. She set the glass down and pushed it away.

"Don't you like it?" Vikki asked.

"I drank like a quart of lemonade at Mitch's earlier. That must be it."

"Oh." Vikki drained her glass and poured herself another quarter of a glass. "Shall we get started on those pictures? I'd like to try to send them to the magazine before the holiday."

"That reminds me. I talked to Evan."

Vikki rolled her eyes. "The writer? I hope you yelled at him good."

"He claims he was trying to help me out."

"And you believed him?" Vikki asked.

Cory sighed and made a sour face. "I know he did it more for himself than for me, but I guess I do believe that he didn't feel it would damage me or my chances at the magazine."

"He still shouldn't have done it."

"No." Cory waited a minute before adding, "He didn't have my contact information, so he couldn't have asked me what I thought. If I'd said no, I'm fairly certain he wouldn't have submitted them. Anyway, you can judge him for yourself. He'll be in Utah by Friday. He's the one who's going to take us jet skiing with his cousin."

"He's staying here?"

Cory shook her head. "I'm not that stupid."

"Good. I don't trust him."

Cory found herself agreeing, which didn't really bode well for her relationship with Evan.

"Well, dear, I'm ready." Vikki pushed back her chair and stood.

They had barely begun to develop the film when the doorbell rang—once, twice, and then several more times. "I'd better get it." Checking to make sure she wouldn't ruin any exposed film, Cory ducked out of the mudroom and shut the door behind her.

At the front door stood Tyler Huntington and two young men wearing black name tags. Too late, Cory remembered her appointment to learn more about her sister's church. "I forgot you were coming," she said, standing back so they could enter. "Now's not really a good time. I have a friend over."

"She can listen," said the missionary with the dark hair. *Elder Rowley*, Cory read on his tag. He was average height and shorter than Tyler but wider in the shoulders. He had a nice, friendly face.

"Or he," added the other missionary. "If your friend is a he, that is." This young man had light brown hair, and his name was Elder Savage. He was taller than the other two by a head and extremely thin. He brought to Cory's mind an image of what Mitch might have looked like on his mission to Brazil.

"Is it a he?" Tyler asked with Mitch's grin.

Cory didn't smile. "No. And she can't come right now anyway. She's in the darkroom. If fact, I guess you might as well stay for a little while since I don't want my pictures to be ruined. But we'll have to make it quick. I'll need to help her in a bit."

"She's a photographer," Tyler explained to the missionaries. "Did I mention that?"

Elder Rowley shook his head. "So, should we talk in here?" His eyes scanned the empty room.

"Yeah. I only have two chairs in the kitchen. I'm renting, and I'm only in town for a short time."

"Because of her niece," Tyler supplied. "Now I'm sure I told you *that*."

Elder Savage sat on the carpet and opened a folder. "This is great. Not a problem."

Cory and the others joined him on the floor. Tyler offered an opening prayer similar to those her father had said—that she'd said as a child. She bowed her head out of respect but kept her eyes open to study the missionaries.

At that moment, Elder Rowley opened his eyes and met hers. Cory flushed and closed her eyes for the rest of the prayer. *Why should I care? I'm only listening to get custody of EmJay.*

The missionaries began discussing Jesus Christ and His role in the redemption process. Cory experienced a feeling of déjà-vu. This could have been her own father talking. Or her pastor. Could Mormons really believe in the same Christ? Not according to her father. But here the missionaries were, sounding just like him. *Except . . . well, maybe their idea of Christ better matches the pastor's than my father's,* she decided. Cory didn't want to follow the thought because the truth for her father was that Christ would forgive only those her father deemed worthy of forgiveness. Too bad AshDee hadn't been on his exclusive list.

Well, AshDee broke his heart. She killed him by leaving. Cory tasted bitterness at the thought. But was that true? Maybe AshDee had been dying by staying. Dying by bits like Cory had been. In a real way, her father's death had freed her.

"Do you believe in Christ?" asked Elder Savage.

Cory hesitated only an instant. "If I were to believe in Christ, I'd believe in your view of Him, that's for sure."

"So you don't believe," Tyler said. The missionaries rewarded his comment with frowns.

"You have to admit, it's all so . . . well . . . unbelievable," Cory said. "But that doesn't necessarily mean it's not true, I suppose." Cory shifted her position so her legs were no longer under her but to the side. "I guess I'd put myself on the fence. I'll wait and see."

"Wait until what?" Tyler asked. "Until He comes again?"

Once again Elder Savage frowned at him, but Elder Rowley kept his gaze on Cory. "I want you to know," he said, "that I believe in Jesus Christ. That not only did He pay for my sins but that He has experienced my fears, my heartbreaks, and all my disappointments. He is there for me whenever I need Him. I know this. I feel it with every part of my being. And He is there for you, too."

Heat began in Cory's belly. Her arms felt odd, too, as though they ached with emptiness, but somehow she knew that all she had to do to change that was to reach out and—

"How do you feel at this moment?" Elder Savage asked.

"Strange," she admitted. "Like I want to believe."

"That's the Spirit testifying to you that what Elder Rowley said is true. Remember when we said the Spirit testifies of all truth?"

She nodded. Is that what had attracted her sister to this church? The promise of a sure knowledge? Cory would be the first to admit how handy that would have been during her father's fire and brimstone lessons. For a sudden, terrible, searing moment, she hated her father more than she'd ever hated anyone. He'd separated her from AshDee, the only person she had loved more than her mother. He had twisted Cory's loyalty to him into blind obedience. He'd cost her many nights of caustic tears. He might have even cost her EmJay, her precious niece, who surely would have been hers if she and AshDee had remained close. His bitterness, his anger, his condemnation had robbed Cory of so much, wounding her more deeply than the worst of his frequent slaps.

"Cory?" asked Tyler.

Startled, Cory glanced at him and realized the missionaries had continued talking. But she wasn't sure she wanted to hear more about Christ or the Book of Mormon. "Tell me what you believe about families," she said. "I've heard your church is big on families."

"The Lord is big on families," Elder Rowley gently corrected, "and He does have a plan so that families can be together forever."

Cory thought of AshDee. This doctrine was what she would have loved—knowing she could be with her baby and her husband forever. Knowing they would see their mother again. *Knowing,* Cory scoffed, *or believing?* The two were *very* different things. Besides, if such a place as heaven existed, and Cory wasn't holding her breath on that one, there was one person Cory wasn't exactly anxious to see. Her father was likely to be as ornery and cantankerous as he always had been. Sometimes at night after AshDee had left, she'd shed tears into her pillow, wishing she could do the same. But she hadn't been able to leave. She'd loved and idolized their father as much as she feared and resented him.

As she listened to the missionaries teach, Cory again felt the burning in her stomach. *It's the wine,* she told herself. *Or maybe I'm hungry. That's it, I'm hungry.*

She listened politely, reserving her questions for another day—after she read the booklets they gave her. When they'd finished, they invited her to pray; she declined. When Elder Rowley didn't press, she changed her mind about making them leave immediately and dug out some of the many cookies she'd been given by the well-meaning Mormons. No sense in letting them go to waste.

"Can we come back tomorrow?" Elder Savage asked, downing half a cookie in one bite. Cory offered him some of Kerrianne's peanut butter bars to take with him. He really needed the calories.

"Not tomorrow," she said, walking them to the door. "Or the Fourth. Look, I'm not really sure I need you to come at all."

"You might have questions," Tyler put in, pointing to the handouts. "And there's still more they have to explain."

Cory knew that. She was curious about the tithing she'd heard about in church on Sunday, but so far they hadn't brought that up. Besides, she might need them if she was to become a Mormon. "Saturday, then," she agreed. "But only you three. Okay?"

"Deal." Tyler grinned and shook her hand.

"See you then," the elders said together. They went down the steps and headed toward Tyler's battered green truck.

"You haven't told your brother, right?" she asked before Tyler could follow them.

He shook his head. "Nope. How's it going between you two any-way?"

"Us?" Cory nearly choked on her last piece of cookie. As far as she was concerned, there was no "us," only a stubborn man standing between her and EmJay. "We're still discussing custody." She glanced down the street. The sun was just beginning to set, and there was still plenty of light for Mitch to see them by if he happened to be out in his front yard. He wasn't.

Tyler nodded. "Maybe you should get a job here and hang out until she's grown."

"I have a good job already. And EmJay would have many unforget-table experiences in the Amazon."

"Maybe Mitch would move down there. He speaks Portuguese, you know. My mother would have a fit, though."

"Mitch wouldn't need to move," Cory said in frustration. "I can take care of EmJay myself. She *belongs* with me."

Tyler shook his head. "Mitch loves that baby like she was his own. They've really connected. I—I—I don't know what to say. He was so close to Emily Jane's parents before—and to her, too, but now . . . boy, I think it would kill him to lose her."

"She's only been here four weeks. Not quite four weeks, even. That's barely any time in his life—or hers, for that matter."

"I don't agree. Four weeks is a long time. Four weeks can change your whole life."

The thought crossed Cory's mind that four weeks was about the time she would be spending in Utah. She didn't plan on changing.

Tyler's seriousness vanished. "Hey, the longest I've ever dated a girl was three weeks. That was tortuously long. If I dated her four weeks, well, that would mean something."

"What about that girl at the memorial service?"

"Oh, we're just friends." A line of worry appeared between his eyes. "At least we were. I think she's been avoiding me."

"I wonder why," Cory said dryly.

Tyler shrugged. "I don't know. But I'll find out." Then he brightened. "Hey, I bet she'd come with me on Saturday if I asked her. Would it be okay if I brought her? Maybe then I could find out what's wrong."

"Might be nice to hear a woman's point of view. For instance, I still don't understand about Mormons and polygamy."

"Oh, that was just a blip in our history," Tyler said, shrugging. "That's what our prophet says. It was needed then, but it isn't now. No one should worry about that anymore." His confidence impressed her. What would it be like to believe in a living prophet?

"Anyway," Tyler continued, "God loves his daughters every bit as much as his sons—probably more, my dad always says." He scrunched his forehead. "I think he's trying to tell Mitch and me something when he says this, but Mitch just agrees."

Cory laughed as he'd intended. "We'll see you Saturday."

"See you." Tyler sprinted down the sidewalk to his truck.

Leaving the pamphlets and the new Book of Mormon the missionaries had given her on the floor in the living room, Cory went into the kitchen. She knocked on the mudroom door.

"Not yet, dear," Vikki called. "Give me another ten minutes. But wow, Cory, these are great! It's amazing what that old camera can do! Or rather the two of you together."

Smiling, Cory began thumbing through one of her sister's photo albums that Mitch had lent her. She'd already looked through all the photographs from her sister's younger years, and this was the first album from AshDee's new life. She'd met Lane and they were together in almost every picture. They weren't alone; Mitch was also in many of the photographs, smiling and laughing. He was at their parties, best man at the wedding, and even at the hospital, smiling as someone took a picture of him holding a newborn EmJay, who looked more like a bundle of receiving blankets than a real baby. In the background of that picture, AshDee smiled at him from her hospital bed with genuine admiration. *She loved him,* Cory thought, reading her sister's expression. *As a friend, at least.* Because there was no doubt in her mind that AshDee loved her husband. Their mutual affection for one another was all too apparent on each page and caused an impossible lump to form in Cory's throat. Would she ever know what it felt like to love a man like that? Or to have a man love her?

Tears stung her eyes. She should have known love by now, shouldn't she? But whenever she'd begin to get close, her father's sermons had come to mind—which had been punctuated more often than not with smart slaps to her arms or face. She'd never been able to give her whole heart.

Closing her eyes, Cory struggled for composure. Her father was dead; he couldn't hurt her again. She didn't have to believe his words anymore. Not about his church or about Jesus. After all, where was Jesus when she and AshDee were crying in the night?

Yet AshDee had risen above their past. She'd freed herself. She had loved.

Taking a last peek at Mitch holding EmJay, Cory closed the picture album and held it to her chest. She loved, too. She loved EmJay. "I won't let you go, EmJay," she whispered. "I won't."

Chapter Sixteen

"What do you mean you might not make it to the barbecue tomorrow?" Amanda demanded when Mitch called her late Thursday morning.

Holding the phone between his ear and his right shoulder, he waved a bowl of baby cereal at Emily Jane, who grinned at him from the high chair. "Emily Jane and I are going jet skiing, and we might not make it back in time."

"But, Mitch, you know how Mother loves having us all together. Why can't you choose another day to go? Wait a minute. Does this have anything to do with Emily Jane's aunt, Cory What's-her-face?"

He spooned a bit of cereal into Emily Jane's mouth. "She's got some friends visiting and wants to show the baby off."

"Oh, I see. You don't trust her enough to let her take Emily Jane by herself."

"Do you think I'm wrong?"

Amanda clicked her tongue. "No, I don't think you're wrong, but I'm wondering what's the point of letting her go at all?"

"The point is that Emily Jane likes Cory, and how can I deny her a chance to know her aunt?"

"Yeah, but Cory's made it pretty clear she's going back to the Amazon."

"That's why I can't leave Emily Jane with her. When I think about how she disowned her sister because she joined the Church, I get nervous about what kind of person she really is. And she keeps talking about Emily Jane and the Amazon, as though they'll end up there together." He couldn't keep the irritation from his voice. "Anyway, I can't trust her."

"With good reason. For a minute there, I thought you were going soft on me."

"No way." Mitch made the words hard. No use letting his sister know how close she was to the truth. "I don't even like the woman."

Amanda was immediately suspicious. "Are you trying to convince me or yourself?"

"I don't need convincing. She's nothing like the women I'm attracted to."

Amanda didn't speak for the space of three heartbeats. "Right. She's pretty, witty, independent, loves Emily Jane, and has a job you envy." She snorted. "Yeah, she's nothing like the women you date."

Ignoring her, Mitch gave Emily Jane another spoonful of cereal. "So, will you tell Mom? Don't wait dinner on us, but we'll be to the fireworks for sure."

"Why don't you call her yourself?"

"And risk another wife lecture? Or answer 'why haven't you brought over all those pretty girls from the singles ward?'" His voice rose to mimic their mother's tone.

Amanda giggled. "You sound just like her."

"I can't deal with that right now. I was up half the night working and the other half with Emily Jane. I'm going to finish feeding her and see if we can both get a bit more shut-eye."

"Okay, okay, I'll tell her. But don't forget your drysuit tomorrow."

"I'm not taking it." Normally he would have because, unlike a wetsuit, the drysuit prevented the cold water from touching his skin and setting off the allergic reaction that could affect his breathing. Only his hands, feet, and face would itch and swell. "But don't worry," he added quickly. "I'm not actually going into the water. I'm only there to make sure Emily Jane's okay."

"You sure? I know how you love jet skiing." Amanda didn't sound happy about his decision, and he knew she was envisioning him alone on the shore while Cory and her friends had a good time in the water.

"I'm just not up for it," he said shortly. Amanda was right that he loved jet skiing—in fact, he loved all water sports, but with his allergy to cold, participating was never easy. Besides, he wasn't about to tell Cory and her friends about his disability.

"You wouldn't have to explain the drysuit. Everyone will be in a swimsuit anyway."

Sometimes Mitch wished his sister didn't know him so well. "Forget it. Please, Manda?"

"Fine," she growled. "But take the toothbrush."

That was their code word for the epinephrine he always carried—just in case. "I never leave home without it," he quipped.

He hung up the phone, feeling rather depressed. He wondered if Cory was sorry that he was coming along.

Cory slept late on Thursday. She and Vikki had been up half the night, but the result was worth it. Vikki had chosen ten stunning photographs, which they would e-mail today to catch the photo specialist before the holiday weekend.

Vikki was waiting for Cory in the kitchen, a mug of steaming coffee in her hands. "I went to the store this morning," she said. Instead of her usual business dress, she wore black knit pants and an embroidered T-shirt, her hair once again pinned up. "I can't believe you didn't have any coffee."

Cory shrugged. "I see you bought some mugs, too. Good thinking."

"Look, I scanned in the photos and was going to e-mail them, but you don't seem to have an Internet connection."

"Oh, that's right," Cory said with a groan. "I've been too busy to even think about it."

"Well, there's only a few, but the resolutions are too high to use anything but high speed Internet. And the CD or hard copies wouldn't make it there until tomorrow. Do you know where an Internet café is?"

Cory shook her head. "Someone gave me an old phone book, though." Then she had an idea. "I bet Mitch has high speed Internet. He works from home so he can stay with EmJay."

Vikki's eyebrows rose. "He gave up work to stay home? Wow, this guy is too good to be true. Too bad there aren't any sparks between you."

Cory blew out a disgusted sigh. "Oh, there are plenty of sparks! Every time we're together we fight."

"Ah," Vikki said, as though discovering something important.

"What do you mean 'ah'? It's been really hard, I'll have you know. Of course, now that I'm trying to be charming, I have to bite my tongue and let him think he's right all the time. That's even worse than fighting." Cory helped herself to one of the blueberry bagels Vikki had also purchased. "Anyway, we might as well go over there. I need to see EmJay."

"Need?"

Cory met Vikki's eyes and looked away. How could she explain what she felt? Vikki and her former husband hadn't had children, and she didn't have any nieces or nephews yet. "I'll get dressed so we can go. But remember that I'm trying to convince him to give me EmJay, so if I act funny, go with it."

Vikki laughed. "Don't worry. I'll take every opportunity to leave you two lovebirds alone."

Cory changed into jeans and a spandex shirt, slipping her feet into sandals. Then in the makeshift darkroom, she grabbed a picture of

Meeko. *EmJay will like to see this,* she told herself, though she knew it was really for Mitch.

They rang at Mitch's numerous times before he finally opened his door, wearing black lounge pants with green dinosaurs and a green T-shirt. His brown hair looked mussed from sleep and his eyes heavy.

"Are you all right?" she asked. "Where's EmJay?"

He raked a hand through his hair, letting the door open wider. "She's, uh . . ." He looked confused. "She was sleeping when I dropped off. We were up most of the night."

A noise behind him caused them all to turn, and there was EmJay munching on a handful of gerbil food. Mitch groaned and ran to her, while Cory exchanged a superior look with Vikki. Cory had suspected Mitch wasn't up to the task of single parenting, and this was clear proof of his negligence.

"Must have forgotten to shut the door to the animal room," Mitch muttered, brushing the seeds from EmJay's hand.

Uninvited, Cory stepped into the house, followed by Vikki. They could see gerbil food scattered down the hall. Mitch tried to fish the seeds from EmJay's mouth; obligingly, she spat a mouthful into his hand. Pocketing the seeds, he sighed and picked her up.

Cory opened her mouth to point out what a rotten guardian he was and how much better she would be. Then she remembered her plan. Quickly, she softened her words. "You might want to put a self-shutting hinge on that door." She really, really hated not rubbing this incident in his face, but she had no choice if she wanted him to like her. She gave him her best smile, holding his gaze until he looked away. The slight blush on his face almost made her laugh aloud. *Plan working perfectly.*

"Don't know why I didn't think of it." He glanced at the baby in his arms, his forehead furrowed tightly. "She looks like she didn't sleep at all." Sure enough, the baby was rubbing her eyes.

Cory held out her arms. "Want to come to me?" EmJay turned her head away.

"Maybe in a bit," Mitch said. "Probably needs to sleep off all that gerbil food. You know, a full stomach and all."

Vikki snickered, and Cory smiled, trying not to show how much the rejection stung—especially after all the times EmJay had been happy to see her. "It won't hurt her, will it?" she asked. "The gerbil food, I mean."

He shrugged. "The gerbils don't keel over when they eat it."

Cory glared at him hotly for a brief second before remembering her plan. She took a measured breath. "We came to use your computer, if you don't mind."

Vikki held up her tiny silver USB mass storage device. "Do you have high speed Internet? If so, we wanted to know if we could use your computer to send something to the magazine we're working for. We wouldn't need your e-mail or anything. We both have online accounts."

"Sure. I had high speed put in when I bought the house."

"We really appreciate this." Vikki's eyes roamed the small living room, and Cory wondered if she was comparing it to her spacious condo in California. *At least he has a place,* Cory thought. Her own home consisted of a tent in Brazil and a storage unit in California.

"My computer's right here," Mitch said unnecessarily. They could all see it in the corner of the living room, the screensaver sending a ball bouncing repeatedly across the monitor. "Looks like I left it on. I worked late last night."

"You really must have been tired," Vikki said, sounding too sympathetic for Cory's liking.

Mitch nodded. Once more he pulled a hand through his hair, which immediately fell back to the sides of his face. Cory had a hard time looking away.

"Go ahead and help yourselves," he said. "I'm going to see what Emily Jane did with the sack of gerbil food and then get something to eat. I haven't eaten yet except for a few bites of baby cereal earlier when I was trying to convince her how good it was."

Cory smiled. "And was it?"

"A little soggy for my taste."

Vikki walked to his computer and reached for the mouse, clicking on the Internet connection. The word processing program that had been open before vanished.

"Well, I'll leave you ladies to it," Mitch said. "Looks like I have to put this baby in bed before I do anything else."

"When you're finished with everything, I'd like to see your animals, if you don't mind," Vikki said. "Cory said you have ferrets?"

"Not for long. Those critters are mean. I found a guy on the Internet who'll give them a good home. I don't want anything around that might hurt Emily Jane, even accidentally."

Then don't go to sleep on the job, Cory retorted silently, sitting down at the computer. "I'll send the files, Vikki," she said sweetly.

"Where are the ferrets?" Vikki glanced around, as if expecting to catch the animals sneaking up on her.

"In the garage. Just a minute while I see if Emily Jane will let me put her into bed." Mitch left the room.

"Can you believe that?" Cory whispered. "Gerbil food! You see now why I have to take her away. She's not safe here."

Vikki blinked at her vehemence. "Honey, I think you're going to need a lot more than that to convince anyone that he's unfit. You should have seen the things some of the kids in my neighborhood used to eat when I was growing up—canned dog food, grasshoppers, dirt. Once someone dared the kid next door to eat a fly—and he did. Yuck!" She shivered. "Next to that, gerbil seeds are a delicacy."

With a sinking feeling, Cory knew Vikki was right. Still, the idea of EmJay awake and alone, chomping on pet food, made all her protective urges kick into high gear.

"By the way, I really think he likes you," Vikki said. "He watches you a lot."

"Sh, he's coming."

Too late Cory realized that she hadn't done a thing on the

computer. Mitch didn't seem to notice. "Would you listen for Emily Jane?" he asked. "She'll probably wake up the minute she senses I'm not within twenty feet of her."

Vikki chuckled, and Cory reluctantly joined in. Yes, he was amusing, but she didn't want his ego to get any bigger. "I'll take care of it," she assured him. As Cory watched them leave, she couldn't help but think how adorable he looked, hair on end, wearing those ridiculous dinosaur lounge pants.

Dismissing the thought, she began downloading the picture files to attach them to an e-mail. His equipment was up to date, and the process went rapidly. She clicked off the Internet with a sigh of satisfaction.

The previous document returned to the screen. Before she thought the better of it, Cory began to read about gray wolves. The words made her wish she could see these wolves, that she could hide outside their den and watch their antics, snapping pictures to forever record their lives.

She looked up as Mitch came into the room alone. "Uh, I'm finished," she said, wondering where Vikki had gone. "This just came up. I—I wasn't snooping. Honest." She grimaced at his face, which carefully showed no expression. "Well, I guess I was a bit," she felt compelled to add. It wouldn't serve her plan if he thought she was totally uninterested, would it? "But I didn't mean to. It was already here when I got off the Internet, and I started reading and couldn't stop."

"Don't worry about it," he said. "Do you know how many people will see it? Well, actually, I guess not too many but enough that I don't make it personal. It's designed to get funding, that's all."

Cory glanced back at the text. "You're really a good writer." She said this without even having to embellish for her plan. "I meant it when I said I couldn't stop reading. Have you ever thought about writing for magazines?" A brief vision of her and Mitch working together in the Amazon came to mind, bringing a flush to her face.

He studied her, as if trying to determine her seriousness. "My brother says I have talent. He's studying journalism and thinks he's an expert. But truthfully, I'm not interested in writing for magazines, at least not magazines for adults. Too much like report writing, and that's basically what I do now. I'd rather be out working with animals."

"Oh." Cory felt deflated, as if she had somehow offended him. "I didn't mean anything other than that I was really intrigued by the style."

"I appreciate that." He paused as if waging an internal debate. "This isn't something I like to broadcast, but sometimes I do write a little bit as a hobby." He took the mouse and went to his list of files. Cory saw many names she recognized: Dizzy, Hiccup and Elvis, Muffin, Lizzy Lizard, and Lady. He clicked on one named Wolf. "This is something I wrote for Emily Jane. You know, for when she's older."

Emily, the gray wolf knew she was going to have a baby. She made a nice bed in her den. Her baby would need somewhere warm to sleep. As Cory continued, she saw essentially the same story she'd already read but on a child's level. "It's wonderful," she told him after the first page.

He grinned, sending a strange tingle to her stomach. "I'd like to add photographs—big, realistic pictures that capture the imagination. Sort of like *National Geographic Kids*. I could do books on animals all over the world. I'd like to do a TV show, too. Or DVDs. On each segment I'd show kids what is so great about a certain animal, what they eat, what they like to do. Things to look out for. I saw a series like that once, and it struck a . . . chord . . . in . . . me." His words trailed off as he finally noticed the change in her expression.

"*National Geographic?*" Cory scowled. Why had he brought that up? Was he trying to use her to get in with the magazine the way Evan had hinted at doing? She couldn't remember if she'd told Mitch about it. "They're my next assignment in the Amazon." She struggled to make her voice matter-of-fact, instead of accusing. *Remember the plan.*

Mitch cocked his head. "They are? Neat. That's pretty prestigious. I can see why you're anxious to get back to Brazil."

Cory could detect no duplicity in his words or demeanor. He really hadn't known about her job. She should have left it at that, but the gutsy part of her took over. "Why don't you do what you want?" she asked bluntly. "I mean, life is too short to work at a job you hate."

"I don't hate my job."

"You'd rather be working with animals—or writing about them for children. So why don't you do it?"

He had no response except his lips forming into a thin, hard line.

"Are you afraid?" she asked. "What's holding you back?"

"Things," he said finally. "Things you know nothing about." With that he turned on his heel. "I'd better see how Vikki's doing. She went out to see the rabbits."

Cory glared at his back, but already she was feeling stupid for nosing about where she didn't belong. Her job was to get EmJay, not to change Mitch's life. But she was right, wasn't she?

Turning back to the computer, she searched for and found the file on Hiccup and Elvis. The story of the gerbils' first meeting and the sub-sequent delivery of their babies made her laugh. It wasn't just the writing; she could tell he knew these animals well and cared for them. The story made her understand him better, made her wonder what might have happened between them if they'd met in another lifetime. What if there had been no EmJay to complicate things?

A sudden vision of Kerrianne came to Cory's mind. She'd implied that there was no possible way Mitch would ever be interested in Cory as a woman. But why? If that was true, she might never gain his approval.

A high, thin wail from the bedroom made her close the file and sprint down the hall. Seated in her toddler bed, EmJay's red-orange hair poked out in every direction exactly like Cory's did each morning. "Hi, darling," Cory said. "How'd you sleep, huh? Come to Aunt Cory. Come on."

EmJay smiled, her face still stiff with sleep. "Moncree," she said.

Moncree? It sounded like a mixture of Mommy and Cory. Or maybe "my Cory." Could it be? Cory smiled wistfully as she swooped EmJay up in her arms. "Oh, I've missed you!" The baby promptly stuck her fingers in Cory's curls.

EmJay laid her head on Cory's shoulder. Suddenly, Cory remembered her sister doing much the same thing after their mother's death. "I love you so much, EmJay," she whispered. "I'm going to do everything I can to make you happy."

"Oh, she's awake," came a voice behind her.

Cory jumped. How long had Mitch been standing there? Had he heard what she said? Not that it mattered. She loved EmJay and didn't care who knew it.

"Much!" EmJay exclaimed with a giggle.

"Yes, Mitch is here," he said, his brow furrowing when the baby didn't hold out her arms.

Ha, she thought. *Take that!*

Mitch led the way back to the living room where Vikki was removing her USB device from his computer. "All done, I assume?" she asked.

"Yes. I told them they'd also get hard copies in the mail by tomorrow."

"Good." Vikki's hand went to her stomach. "I'd say it's time for lunch."

"I'd offer to barbecue," Mitch said, "but I'm out of briquettes, and my gas grill still has its tenants."

"Won't be long, though, before they're out." Cory shifted EmJay to her other hip. "They look almost big enough to fly."

Vikki grimaced. "Okay, this is really scary. Does anyone else in the entire world know what you two are talking about?"

Laughing, Cory explained about the nest in Mitch's barbecue and their method of spying on the babies. "I got an extension last night so you can see it in here, if you want," Mitch offered. "It'll just take a second."

Vikki watched as he called up the program on the computer. "You got some copies of this, didn't you?" she asked Cory. "I know exactly where we can sell them."

"Mitch sent them to my e-mail, but put your USB back in and copy them now. We can get a higher resolution."

As the documents transferred, Vikki rubbed her hands together. "Very well, then. I'm starved. I need food—lots of food."

"We'll go out," Cory said reluctantly. What she really wanted was to stay with EmJay. "Mitch, I don't suppose you'd let me—" She couldn't finish. He wouldn't agree, so what was the point of asking?

Vikki's knowing gaze was compassionate. "Hey, Mitch, in thanks for your help, I'd like to take you and EmJay out to lunch. What do you say?"

Mitch's gaze fell to his dinosaur pants. "Do I get time to shower and change?"

"Why not? Looks like the baby needs some clothes, too." Vikki touched the sleeve of EmJay's pink pajamas.

"I'll get them." Mitch dashed down the hall, returning shortly with a multicolored corduroy jumper and an off-white blouse, complete with suede shoes, off-white tights, a hairbrush, a hair bow, and a new diaper. Cory would have grabbed the jumper and called it good, but she was growing accustomed to his thoroughness.

That he was leaving her alone with EmJay while he showered didn't escape Cory's notice. Was he starting to trust her?

"Thanks, Vikki," she said to her friend.

Vikki shrugged. "Can't charm the guy if you're not around him, right?"

Cory smiled. "Right."

She sat on the couch and began to dress EmJay—not an easy task despite the baby's willingness. EmJay especially loved her shoes and insisted on holding them to her chest until Cory was ready to put them on. The only real trouble began when Cory combed her hair. "Ow! Ow!" she screamed, which made Vikki laugh and call her a pretender. Cory finally gave up on the bow.

By the time she finished with EmJay, Mitch was back. His hair was freshly washed, the long bangs parted down the middle and brushed back. He wore dress slacks and a white, long-sleeved, button-down shirt with the sleeves rolled up twice. In his hand were more diapers for EmJay's baby bag.

Cory never remembered afterward where they ate lunch, but she remembered Mitch opening the doors for them and seating them at the table. She recalled laughing and feeding EmJay halibut from her plate. She remembered EmJay dropping the fish on the floor in favor of eating her napkin. Several times Cory's hand brushed Mitch's across the table as they tended to the baby, and each time she found it more difficult to breathe. Mitch's smile made her feel warm inside as she had when discussing the gospel with the missionaries.

What did it all mean?

At the moment, Cory didn't care. She didn't want to think about her conflict with Mitch. Or the past. For today, at least, she would live one day at a time.

Chapter Seventeen

After their late lunch, Cory, Mitch, and Vikki decided to stop at a park to play with EmJay. The day was hot, but a scattering of puffy clouds saved it from being sweltering, and tall trees shaded much of the play area and the grass. Cory felt oddly content as she carried EmJay to a swing designed for toddlers. Mitch and Vikki trailed behind, discussing Vikki's plans to leave Monday morning.

"Oh, I just remembered," Cory said, stopping under the swing set. She switched EmJay to one hip and took the picture of Meeko from her purse with her free hand. "I brought this to show you and EmJay. It's the little monkey friend I told you about." In the picture, Meeko was stealing something from a bowl on the big camp table.

Mitch laughed. "Is he really such a stinker?"

"Definitely. Once he even managed to drink my shampoo. Good thing it was environmentally friendly!"

Mitch studied the picture. "Boy, wouldn't he make a good children's story? You don't have more pictures of him, do you?"

"Rolls and rolls." She laughed. "Like I said, we're good friends. Would you like to try to—" She broke off, remembering that he'd shared his hobby with her in confidence.

"You should do something with them," he said, handing back the picture pointedly. Cory put it away.

"I think I'll take a rest under that tree." Vikki pulled a novel from her purse. "I see a patch of grass with my name on it."

Cory placed EmJay into the swing and stepped back, letting Mitch take the first push. The silence was broken only by some children playing with a soccer ball on the other side of the park.

"So, I'm curious," Mitch said casually. Almost too casually. "Do you think you'll get married someday?" He didn't look at her as he spoke. Cory froze. She wondered if she should answer honestly, or say what he wanted to hear. Or were they the same thing?

"Why do you ask?" she said, stalling.

He gave EmJay another gentle push. "Well, I know you want Emily Jane to be a part of your life, but who would watch her while you're working?"

The careful way he spoke told her he'd been thinking about the subject for some time. Was he considering the idea of letting EmJay be with her at some point in the future? If so, that was big progress. "I won't always be in the Amazon," she said.

He met her gaze. "So you might stay home and raise a family?"

She leaned back against the metal pole of the swing set. "My job is flexible. I can take her with me anywhere."

"Really?" He stared at her, and she looked away. "Well, what if you were in Brazil and Emily Jane went to visit," he continued. She noticed that he said "visit" and not "live." "What if there was a really long hike you had to take for your work, something she couldn't do?"

"I'd leave her with the natives at the camp. They're good people. They'd look after her."

"What if she didn't want to stay with them? What if she was afraid? You know she's not good with strangers. Or what if she had a fever?" Though he said the words without accusation, it seemed to Cory that they made a mockery of her mothering skills.

"I'd manage," she said, barely hiding her mounting anger. Was he implying if she didn't give up her job and get married that she'd have no chance at custody? Was he saying she couldn't be a good mother? She felt ready to explode.

"I know your intentions are good, Cory." His calmness called her back from the edge of anger, from which there would be no turning back, no carrying out of her plan to win him over. "I just wanted to know if you'd thought about these things. And to point out that where children are involved, there are sacrifices."

She lifted her chin. "I'm willing to make sacrifices."

He nodded. "Anyway, all I'm saying is if you were married and had two incomes, it wouldn't be such a big deal if you couldn't take a certain job at a certain time because of Emily Jane. You could pick and choose. You'd have someone to support you, emotionally as well as temporally."

Emotionally as well as temporally, she thought. *He must have practiced saying that a hundred times to have it come out so smoothly.* What did it even mean? But she knew. Like Tyler and Kerrianne before him, he was pointing out her lack of a family, the absence of someone in her life to share the burden of raising a child. But it didn't matter. She could do it alone.

Couldn't she?

"I'll probably get married someday," she said. What was wrong with her? She wasn't normally so unsure of herself. Of course, being a parent was unexplored territory.

He smiled. "Me too."

"I even have a boyfriend," she added impulsively. "Well, a guy I started dating a few months ago." Would that ease his fears further, or would it make her less attractive in his eyes and therefore less likely to gain custody? Her head hurt from trying to figure it all out. "He's good with kids." She'd seen him toss a battered ball around with the native children at the camp at least twice.

"Oh, yeah?" His hands paused in midair, not pushing EmJay as she swung up to them.

She shrugged, trying to act casual. "Not sure how it'll work out. He's a writer. We've been working on an article together."

"I see." A muscle flexed in his jaw. "That's good, then." His eyes were shuttered, as though a door had closed. Cory hoped she hadn't sabotaged her own plan. *Well, at least he doesn't think I'm completely alone.*

An hour later, Cory said good-bye to Mitch and a sleepy EmJay and returned to her house with Vikki. "Are you all right, dear?" Vikki asked, sinking onto a chair in the kitchen. Her eyes invited confidence, but Cory wasn't sure what to say.

Cory stood by the counter, fingering the pamphlets the missionaries had left. She had put them there so she would remember to read them. "I told Mitch I had a boyfriend. Now I'm worried that will mess up my plan. I mean, he'll meet Evan tomorrow. What if he hates him? That could make things worse."

"Relax, dear." Vikki grinned and stretched her legs under the table. "A little competition is good for men. When Mitch sees how wonderful Evan thinks you are, it can't help but make a good impression."

Cory hoped so.

"Oh, and before I forget again, I brought you a Longaberger basket from Ohio. But if you're going to use the basket to, say, catch fish in the Amazon, you can't have it. Those things are too expensive to actually use."

Cory laughed. "Okay, I'll put it in storage. I'll have a house or apartment someday."

Vikki was silent, but by her thoughtful expression, Cory knew she had something more to say. "What, Vikki?" she urged.

"I don't know." Vikki sighed and shook her head. "Maybe I'm more traditional than I thought I was, because suddenly I find myself wondering how you're going to raise a child alone if you get on permanently with *National Geographic*. I mean, I know their pay scale is phenomenal, but some of their assignments take up to eight months. In the Amazon, you know you have natives to watch EmJay, but what if they send you somewhere dangerous? Where there's an illness epidemic, or political unrest? Could you still take her along? And what about a house or permanent residence? A kid needs stability."

"Not you, too!" Cory dropped the pamphlets and strode to the table, hands on her hips. First Tyler, then Mitch, and now her own friend! "Your dad was in the army. You moved around a lot."

"But we didn't live in a tent. Besides, I always had my mom when he was working. She was my constant."

"That's what I'll be for EmJay! I can take her everywhere. You said yourself that I'd be making a bundle—and that doesn't even take into consideration all the photographs they don't use that I'm permitted to sell elsewhere. I'll take that money and hire a nanny to come along. I'll teach her myself for as long as I can, and after that I'll pay for a tutor. It can work—I know it!" Cory set her jaw, daring her friend to contradict her.

"She'd probably learn a lot," Vikki agreed. "Stuff not in books, I mean."

With a sigh, Cory sank to the other chair. "After a while we could have a place that we'd always go back to between assignments," she added more calmly. There was always the option of leaving her with Mitch, but if she ever managed to get custody, how could she possibly risk doing that?

Vikki nodded. She glanced down at her clothes and flicked something off the leg of her pants. "Not to change the subject or anything, dear, but what are you going to wear at the lake tomorrow?"

"I hadn't thought about it. Do you have a swimsuit?"

Vikki shook her head. "It's back in California. You?"

"Mine's in Brazil."

Vikki grinned and took her purse from the table. "Well, it sounds like a little shopping is in order."

Cory groaned. She had never been big on shopping. She tended to buy anything that looked halfway decent to spare herself the torture of finding something perfect. Still, she wanted to look good tomorrow. Not only for Evan but to further her plan with Mitch.

"Well, you could always use your shorts," Vikki said, standing. "But I for one never underestimate the power of a bathing suit with a good cover-up that really does cover up all my flaws." She looked up and down the length of Cory's body. "Of course, you don't need a cover-up. You should get a really skimpy thing. That'd knock him dead!"

"Wait a minute." Cory held up her hands. "I'm trying to convince Mitch that I'd be a good mother for EmJay, remember? I can't wear a skimpy bathing suit." That wasn't the only reason. Growing up, her father had barely permitted her to own a bathing suit. The one time he'd caught her in a two-piece as a teenager, she'd ended up with a bruise on her back that had lasted for two weeks. Even now, as an adult, she never felt comfortable in anything too revealing.

Vikki's eyes gleamed. "I wasn't talking about Mitch. But you're probably right. He'll want a good role model for EmJay. I guess you'll have to settle for boring."

"In this case, boring is good." Cory reached for her purse.

Vikki dragged her to six department stores before she finally let Cory buy a deep blue suit that set off her eyes. A matching cover-up of slightly sheer fabric to tie around her waist provided exactly the right effect Cory wanted—modest but with unmistakable style. She hoped Mitch would approve.

Vikki bought a black suit with a built-in tummy reducer and a shoulder-to-thigh black-and-white cover-up. Cory admitted the ensemble made her look slimmer. At the last minute, they remembered to buy two beach towels.

As they were leaving the store, Cory's cell phone rang. "Hello?"

"Hi, sweetheart," Evan said. "I'm in Utah!"

"Great! Where are you?"

"At my cousin's in Orem. I was hoping to take you out to dinner, but Gordon's wife has fixed a fabulous spread, and I can't really leave them tonight. You don't mind, do you?"

"Truthfully, I'm exhausted. We've just spent hours searching for the right swimsuit. Neither Vikki nor I brought one. So, no. I don't mind." And she didn't really—except she wondered why it didn't bother *him* more that he couldn't see her tonight after more than a week apart.

"About tomorrow," he added. "Roberta—that's my cousin's wife— has the food all planned and ready. You don't need to worry about anything."

"She shouldn't have gone to all that trouble."

"No trouble. Her youngest child is away at college this summer. Couldn't make it home for the holiday. Roberta says she's glad for visitors."

"I didn't realize there was such a big age difference between you and your cousin."

"Yep, fifteen years."

"Oh, wait. There's been a change since I talked to you," Cory said. For some reason she dreaded what she had to say next. "I decided to bring EmJay, but her guardian won't let her come unless he does too. So add two more to the list."

"Oh." Evan didn't sound bothered. "I'll tell Roberta. If there's a problem, we'll just buy more food."

"Well, I'll bring some things. Just in case. Vikki and I planned to stop at the grocery store on the way home."

"Are you sure it's a good idea, bringing your niece to the lake?" Evan asked.

"I think she'll have fun. She loves the water."

"I'm sure. But what about you? I thought you were going to take a break."

Cory knew he was looking out for her, but she felt annoyed. "Don't worry. Mitch practically doesn't let her out of his sight. I won't be stressed, and I promise you won't have to do anything. I really want to introduce her to you."

"Okay, then. I'll look forward to it."

"Good."

There was a brief, awkward pause, and then Evan's voice fell to a husky whisper. "I can't wait to see you."

Then come over after dinner, she wanted to say. "Tomorrow," she said aloud. "I'll see you then." She hung up the phone feeling oddly unfulfilled and irritated at Evan. He hadn't changed since the Amazon, so what was wrong? Had she?

Vikki was watching her closely. "I'm not sure about him."

"Neither am I."

They bought several bags of groceries at the local supermarket and headed home. After they put away their purchases in the kitchen, packing most of the items to take with them the next day, Cory picked up the missionaries' pamphlets and started for her room. She couldn't help but wonder what Mitch and EmJay were doing at that moment. Oh, how she wished she could give her niece a hug and kiss goodnight!

Instead, she turned to Vikki. "About our conversation earlier. I do worry about taking EmJay with me to the Amazon. I wonder if I'll be enough for her compared to Mitch and his family. But I think I can be."

Vikki came to her and slipped a warm arm around her shoulders. "The fact that you're thinking about it is proof enough to me that you'll find a way to make it work."

"Thanks." Cory gave her a watery smile.

In her bedroom, she looked out the window. The street lights left clear circles of yellow on the ground, while the moon and stars illuminated darkened sky. "Tomorrow is the day," she said aloud. "Tomorrow I'll convince Mitch that she belongs with me."

The warmth she felt at the prediction should have made her happy. Why then did she feel a sense of impending doom?

Chapter Eighteen

Shortly after nine the next morning, Mitch drove toward Orem. Vikki rode next to him in the front passenger seat, and in the back Cory was playing with EmJay. He had volunteered to drive to Cory's friend's cousin's house and follow them up Provo Canyon to Deer Creek Reservoir.

The morning was clear and beautiful, promising a sweltering heat later in the day. Mitch hoped that meant the water in the reservoir would be nearing tepid instead of freezing. Not that he was going in; he hadn't even brought a swimsuit. He wore long jean shorts and a white T-shirt with comfortable brown leather sandals. In the trunk of his car, he'd stashed his backpack and a small cooler filled with special foods for the baby.

Mitch glanced in the backseat at Cory. He'd hardly been able to take his eyes off her since he'd first seen her that morning. Her fiery curls were tamer today, looking glossy and soft, her freckled face smooth and unlined. The blue suit she wore modestly enhanced her curves, and the long, flowing cover-up added to her femininity. Had she always been so beautiful?

For the past few days, she seemed to be going out of her way to be

RACHEL ANN NUNES

nice. Did that mean her attitude was softening toward him as Emily Jane's permanent guardian? Or was she perhaps looking at him as more than just Emily Jane's guardian?

Maybe they weren't as opposite as he had first thought. But then, he shouldn't begin hoping for something romantic between them. He had to remember that she couldn't possibly be interested in his life or his values. She wanted Emily Jane, and that was that.

Strangely, he found himself missing the angry sparks that had flared during their initial days, when they were definitely opponents. At least he'd had no doubts that she was being honest, and he had known exactly where they stood. Now he wasn't so sure.

Unsure what to expect in Orem, Mitch and Vikki waited with EmJay in the Mustang. Cory jumped out to meet two men who were hooking up a truck to a trailer that held two jet skis. One of the men, an average-sized, narrow-chinned blond man, hugged Cory and kissed her firmly on the mouth. The contact didn't last long, but Mitch felt an urge to fly from the car and slam his fist into the other guy's face. The stranger was taller than Cory by a mere few inches and, in Mitch's judgment, would look more fitting in a snooty restaurant than doing anything remotely athletic like jet skiing. But who was he to evaluate Cory's boyfriends?

Then again, everything that affected Cory affected Emily Jane—and that *was* his business. One thing for certain, he was going to check this guy out thoroughly before he let him anywhere near Emily Jane.

The second man was shaking hands with Cory now. Mitch leaned closer to the open window. "Nice to meet you, Gordon," Cory was saying. Gordon was a robust, deeply tanned man with dark, slightly graying hair and only a bit of extra weight around his stomach. His friendly, respectful response to Cory gave Mitch an immediate good impression. A brown-haired woman came from the house and joined them. Like her husband, she was tanned and in good shape, though not slender by any means. Mitch didn't catch her name, but Cory was bringing them all over to the car. He and Vikki got out to meet them.

200

"This is Evan Hammer," Cory said of the blond man, who promptly put a possessive arm around her, his hazel eyes sending an unmistakable message. "And this is his cousin, Gordon Hammer, and Gordon's wife, Roberta."

"Nice to meet you. I'm Mitch Huntington." Mitch shook hands with them all. Evan's grasp was like a limp, moist fish; Gordon's and Roberta's were dry and firm.

"I'm Vikki Moline." Vikki proffered her hand. "Cory's agent." She stared hard at Evan, who didn't appear to notice.

"A pleasure, a pleasure," Gordon said. "We were glad to hear from Evan. Our kids deserted us this holiday, and we really didn't make other plans. But this is working up to be a real party."

"Sure is." Mitch felt a little guilty that he'd abandoned his own family get-together.

Cory shrugged off Evan's arm and opened the car door. "Now for the most important person. Oh, she's fallen asleep again."

"The car does that to her," Mitch put in. "But she'll be rested and ready to go when we get there."

"Oh, she's a doll!" Roberta exclaimed. "Is this your daughter, Cory?"

Mitch didn't miss the pleased flush on Cory's face. "My niece, actually. But thank you. She is adorable."

"I miss babies," Gordon put in. "Our oldest daughter is expecting soon, and we're thrilled." Roberta grinned and nodded vigorously.

"We should get going." Evan clapped his hands together. "Daylight's a wastin'."

Mitch wanted to ask him if he even knew how to jet ski but managed to bite his tongue. *It's none of my business what the pansy boy can or can't do.* He felt guilty almost immediately for the unkind thought and promised himself he'd go out of his way to be civil to Evan. After all, it wasn't his fault Cory had brought him into the middle of their custody battle.

"Why don't you ride with your friends?" Gordon said to Evan. He glanced at Mitch. "You know where Deer Creek Reservoir is?"

"Yeah, but I'll follow you." The last thing Mitch wanted to do was get stuck with Evan all day. At least Gordon and Roberta were friendly and real.

Evan climbed into the backseat with Cory, and Mitch felt a measure of satisfaction, knowing they were separated by Emily Jane's car seat. On the drive, the talk quickly turned to the Amazon, as Cory questioned Evan about her belongings, leaving Mitch to wonder further about their relationship. He found himself growing angry and finally tuned out their words. He even stopped glancing in the rearview mirror to peek at Cory. In the front passenger seat, Vikki was almost as silent.

Mitch breathed a sigh of relief when he finally parked the car and began helping the women unload the trunk.

Cory was eager to take EmJay from her car seat and wake her up so that she could introduce her. Thankfully, Evan seemed to warm to the baby, tickling her stomach and playing peek-a-boo. EmJay endured his attention, but her round eyes followed Mitch.

Around the reservoir, groups of people were beginning to gather, and Cory could hear cars passing on the road behind them. Though the surrounding mountains were green and beautiful, she felt a sudden, raw longing for the isolation of the Amazon and its balmy, lush beauty. For an instant, she could almost feel the spongy, verdant ground; smell the tempting perfume of the flowers and fruit; and hear Meeko's screech of surprise as another dwarf cebus stole his piece of fruit. She missed swimming in clear, cool water and exploring narrow, untouched rivers. She missed the unexpected roar, stomp, or whistle from the jungle and how the occasional storm thundered across the sky, hurtling warm, cleansing rain to the ground. She missed feeling that she belonged.

"Are you all right?" Evan was at her shoulder, his eyes showing concern. People kept asking her that. Couldn't they remember that her sister was dead? Of course she wasn't all right. She might never be all right again.

Or would she? In the pamphlets she'd been given by the missionaries, she'd read that the Savior could heal all wounds, that He had shouldered the burdens of all men. To be free, one had only to give the burden to Him, to the One who had already paid the price. Cory wished it was true.

Evan hugged her from behind, and she let him, enjoying the feel of comforting arms around her and EmJay. His touch reminded her of simpler times before she had learned of AshDee's death. Feeling eyes on her, she glanced up to see Mitch standing by the truck watching them. "I'm fine—really," she said to Evan, making her voice light. "But Gordon looks like he could use a hand."

Evan went to help Gordon unload the jet skis, and Mitch joined them. After placing the food on a portable camp table that Roberta took from her truck, Cory and the other women watched the men put the jet skis into the water. Mitch stopped at the water's edge, arms folded across his chest.

Roberta and Evan took the first rides. "See, it's easy," Gordon said to Vikki.

"What if I fall off?" Vikki put a hand over her eyes to shield her eyes from the shimmering lake that reflected the morning sun like a mirror.

"It'll come back around," Gordon assured her. "Won't have to swim more 'n a stroke or two."

Cory hadn't been on a jet ski for five years, and she was looking forward to the experience. "Who's next?" she asked when Vikki took over the machine Evan had been using. "Mitch?" She smiled at him brightly, mindful that Evan was staring. She would have to explain about Mitch and her plan.

Mitch shook his head. "No, I'm good. I've got work to do. You go ahead."

"You brought work?" Cory held tightly to EmJay when he reached for her. She touched his arm, her smile purposely flirtatious, drawing him away from the others. "Is something wrong?"

He looked down at her hand on his arm. Her fingers stilled. "There's nothing wrong," he said in a low voice. "I'm just remembering why I'm here, that's all. I'm not a friend or a cousin, I'm Emily Jane's guardian, and *you* want to take her away from me. Let's not pretend this is anything else."

Cory felt the anger behind his words, but there was more, something she couldn't pinpoint. He hadn't been angry when they'd left Sandy that morning. Then she had it. He was jealous! Yes! That meant her plan was alive and strong. She might as well take advantage of it. "Mitch," she said, looking at him earnestly. "Can't you try to have fun?"

His eyes searched hers for a long moment. When he spoke again, it was without any trace of anger. "Go and enjoy yourself, okay? You play with Emily Jane as much as you want, and when you'd like to go out on the water, I'll watch her. You can even take her on that inflatable boat Gordon brought, if you'd like—I borrowed a little life jacket from Kerrianne. But don't try to include me. We both know why I'm here."

"Is this because of Evan?"

"You mean, am I jealous?" he asked, arching his brows. "Now that would imply that I had some claim on you, wouldn't it?"

The moment when he had almost kissed her came to mind, and Cory flushed. "You are so impossible!" she hissed, forgetting her flirtatious veneer.

"Look in the mirror," he retorted. "Then you'll see the true meaning of impossible." With that, he took Emily Jane from her arms. "They're calling you. It's your turn."

Cory whirled and stalked down to the water. *Stupid, stupid plan,* she thought. *I can't take being nice to him anymore!* She decided then and there to flirt outrageously with Evan to show Mitch what he was missing.

The rest of the morning and into the afternoon, Cory took turns with the others jet skiing. Only Mitch kept himself apart, though upon closer examination, it was only from her and Evan that he maintained a distance. He and Vikki were getting along well, and he spent a lot of time talking with Gordon and Roberta. He was as loving as ever to EmJay, and for some unexplained reason, Cory found herself jealous of her niece. She'd just decided the group had divided into Mormons and non-Mormons when she remembered that while Gordon and Roberta were members of the Church, Vikki certainly wasn't.

To make matters worse, Evan kept trying to hug or touch her when she least expected it—on her hand, her arm, her shoulder, her waist—until she wanted to scream at him to leave her alone. But how could she when he was only responding to her flirting? His conversation was worse. One magazine said this about his writing, another said that. He was sure *National Geographic* would accept him as a writer if someone recommended him.

Her heart had leapt at seeing Evan that morning, a thing she felt portended good things for their relationship, but now Cory just wanted this day to be over. She knew that somehow she had been the one to ruin everything, but she was angry at Mitch, too. So what if she had flirted with him this week? It didn't mean he owned her. Seeing her with Evan should make it clear that he could not control her life. Maybe it would make him appreciate her more. Yes, make him jealous!

Unless . . . another thought came—an unwelcome one. Her play-acting today might make Mitch believe she wasn't a good guardian for EmJay. *He could give me an F for parenting. He'll think I'm . . . well, fickle, feckless, and flirty,* she thought with despair. *Stupid, stupid, stupid!* She felt like an utter fool, prancing around in her bathing suit, laughing and giggling with Evan, but she didn't know how to stop. She wanted to go home and cry.

In the late afternoon, she stomped up the beach to where Mitch sat on the folding camp chairs with the others. Evan was still out on a jet ski, but she was tired of it. If she giggled one more time, she would throw up.

"Are you doing fireworks tonight?" Mitch was saying to Gordon.

"Wouldn't be the Fourth without fireworks," Gordon answered. "Some of the neighbors meet in the next cul-de-sac and set them off."

"My family has a big thing, too," Mitch said. "Emily Jane and I are going there tonight." He fell silent when Cory arrived and began tying her cover-up around her waist, but his words reminded her that he had given up a day with his family to come here. Right now she would give anything to be at his family party instead. Plopping into an empty chair, Cory brought a finger to her teeth and ripped off a sliver of nail.

"Why don't you take EmJay out on the boat?" Roberta said to Mitch. "She keeps looking at that water with the saddest eyes."

Mitch grinned. "Hey, I've already been down to the water with her a dozen times."

Cory had seen them from the jet ski, though he'd always gone back to the chairs when she'd come in. She had also taken EmJay down to the water, but the baby would stay for only a few minutes before running back to Mitch for another chip or a drink of water.

"No, Emily Jane, keep the hat on." Mitch replaced the pink-and-white checked hat on her head. "You're getting too much sun."

"Yes, let's take Emily Jane on a boat ride," Cory surprised herself by saying. Why did she say that? She didn't want to be anywhere alone with Mitch. Or did she? Maybe if she got him alone, he'd start to act normal instead of this cold, reserved stranger he'd become. Maybe *she* could act normal.

Mitch's eyes rested on her for a long, silent moment. Cory wriggled in her chair. She was deeply embarrassed—and angry, too, at herself. Why couldn't she leave well enough alone? Why did she always have to push things to the limit? If she'd been herself today, he probably wouldn't be so angry and aloof.

"You can't row and watch EmJay at the same time," she said to hide her growing angst. "Neither can I." She arose and picked up the baby. "No, darling, leave the hat on. Come on, we're going on a boat." She strode over the hard dirt and sparse vegetation to the water, hoping that any flush on her face would be attributed to heat exhaustion or sunburn—despite the massive amount of sunscreen she'd been applying all day.

She had placed EmJay in the boat and was pushing it into the water when Mitch came loping down to the shore after them. His feet were bare, so she knew he'd taken time to slip off his sandals. "Get in," he said, tossing in three life jackets he carried. "I'll walk it out for us."

Relieved, Cory held up the edges of her cover-up and hopped in next to EmJay, drying her feet on the towel someone had left earlier. She put a life jacket on EmJay, and then she put on her own.

"Wait!" called Vikki. She ran slowly toward them carrying a life jacket. "I'm coming, too. Someone's got to stop you two from drowning each other." Giving them a smirk, she splashed into the water and climbed aboard.

Would Mitch still come along? Since now he wouldn't be needed to row or tend EmJay, Cory had her doubts. *Not that I really care,* she added silently.

Mitch pushed them out into the water until it was nearly up to his knees before climbing in. Cory tossed him the towel that Vikki had just used, letting out a long breath that she hadn't realized she'd been holding. Whatever his feelings toward her, his devotion to EmJay had apparently forced him to come along.

Mitch rubbed down his lower legs with more vigor than Cory thought necessary. She and Vikki locked eyes and shrugged. On Cory's lap, EmJay was giggling and reaching for the water. Cory held onto her tightly but let her lean over the edge and splash around.

With his legs dry, Mitch donned his life jacket and began rowing in healthy strokes that took them out to the middle of the lake. Cory couldn't help comparing his efforts to the less effective ones Evan had used when they'd gone out earlier.

"Can you show me how?" Vikki asked him after he had rowed them nearly to the far side.

He handed her an oar and explained the process in detail. Vikki was a natural, surprising Cory, who had never thought her friend was athletically inclined. Maybe she should invite Vikki to visit her in the Amazon.

So far Mitch hadn't said a word to Cory, but neither did he appear to be upset with her any longer. In fact, now that Evan and his cousins weren't around, he seemed his old self. *As if I know what his old self is like,* she thought. In the end, she knew only what he let her see. Still, maybe her plan hadn't gone completely awry.

Mitch seemed to have something wrong with his right leg. A large, red, swollen patch was spreading over the front, and he was scratching at it absently. "Mitch, what happened to your leg?" Cory could have sworn the patch of red wasn't there ten minutes ago. She looked at the other leg, but he had the towel draped over it, and she couldn't tell if it was similarly affected.

"Just a rash." He stopped scratching. "Hey, Emily Jane. Look here, sweetie. There's a whole bunch of fish. Hurry!" He reached past Vikki and pulled the baby away from Cory. "Fish," he repeated, holding her so she could peer into the water.

"Psh," she said.

"No, it's fish. F—f—fish."

"Ish!" gurgled EmJay.

"Good girl! Fish!"

Cory watched this exchange with a smile, trying to imagine Evan teaching EmJay how to speak. Her smile faded.

"Look who's coming our way," Vikki said as Evan waved at them. She returned the oars to Mitch and took EmJay onto her lap. Fascinated with the water around her, the baby didn't appear to notice who held her.

With continuous long strokes, Mitch made the inflatable boat skim rapidly over the water. They were in the middle of the lake when Evan passed them again, screaming something they couldn't hear above the noise of the jet ski engine. Cory waved. Evan released his left hand from the jet ski and made a strong arm pose. Throwing back his head, he laughed, and for an instant, Cory thought he looked maniacal. He put his hands back on the jet ski and turned in their direction, bearing down upon them.

Cory knew it was a joke, but she didn't feel comfortable with such a prank in the middle of a lake—especially not with EmJay aboard. She felt more than saw Mitch hand the oars to Vikki and gather EmJay protectively in his arms. For a brief, terrible instant, she wondered if AshDee had known in the few seconds before her accident that she was going to die.

Going onto her knees, she waved at Evan. "Turn away! Turn away!" More thoughts of AshDee flooded her mind. Had someone on another boat been fooling around like Evan was doing now? Was that why her sister was dead?

"What an idiot," Vikki snarled. "Can't he see we have the baby with us?"

Mitch's face was tight with anger. "Get away!" he shouted.

Grinning, Evan kept coming. At the last possible second, he smartly turned the jet ski, spraying them with cold lake water. EmJay sucked in a startled breath before she began to whimper. Immediately, Mitch wiped her off with the towel. "It's okay, sweetie. Don't cry." EmJay quieted, but she looked tiny and sad with her red hair plastered to her head.

Evan was still smiling. He made another strong arm motion, and that was when it happened. The jet ski jerked to the right with his sudden motion, tumbling him into the water with a loud yelp. The whine of the jet ski engine fell idle.

Cory realized that Evan wasn't wearing a life jacket, but she'd fallen off once that morning, and it had been easy to climb back on. She'd been shivering with shock from the cold water and embarrassed under Evan's mocking stare, but it wasn't that big a deal. "Ha!" she screamed at him. "That's what you get!" Vikki and Mitch laughed.

Evan's arms flailed out, splashing water everywhere and making them laugh harder. The jet ski made a lazy circle just beyond his reach. "You'll have to swim a bit!" Cory called.

The smile suddenly left Mitch's face. "I think something's wrong. Doesn't he know how to swim?" Evan was thrashing more furiously now, but the effort didn't seem to be getting him far.

"He knows how." Cory saw that Evan had managed to move into the jet ski's path. "There, he'll get it now."

Evan screamed something Cory couldn't catch, but Mitch thrust EmJay toward her. "He's got a cramp." Even as Mitch spoke, Evan sank below the water. He came up almost immediately—just in time to bang his head on the approaching jet ski. He disappeared under the water again.

Vikki began to man the oars, but Mitch shook his head. "We'll never reach him in time." Taking a breath, he stood awkwardly and dived into the water—but not before Cory saw that his left leg was mottled a puffy red and white, much worse than his right one. Apparently unmindful of his swollen leg and the cold water, Mitch hurtled toward Evan.

"What happened to the jet ski?" Vikki asked. "Sounds like the motor stopped."

"The jerk probably damaged it with his hard head." Despite her callous response, Cory was worried about Evan. "Can you go any faster?" she asked. "Here, give me one of the oars. I can make EmJay sit here and hold her with my legs."

Silently, Vikki passed her an oar. Mitch was a fast swimmer and had reached Evan now. He pulled Evan to the jet ski, but after fiddling with the controls, he gave up and began to swim toward the shore.

"Wait!" Cory shouted. "We can get him in here." Mitch either didn't hear her or didn't think it was a good idea because he kept swimming.

"They might dump us all out," Vikki said. "Mitch looks like a strong swimmer. Let's just follow in case they need us."

Cory had to admit that even dragging Evan along didn't seem to slow Mitch's progress. As they passed the jet ski, she tied the end of the now-soaked towel around a handle and the other end to the rope that surrounded the entire inflatable boat.

With the added weight of the jet ski, they fell farther behind Mitch and Evan. After what seemed an interminable time, Mitch reached the shore, where Gordon and Roberta helped both men from the water. Mitch and Evan collapsed on the ground while Gordon and Roberta hovered over them anxiously.

"I'm leaving this stupid thing," Cory muttered, releasing the jet ski.

At last they were close enough. With EmJay in her arms, Cory splashed up to the shore, leaving Vikki to bring in the boat the rest of the way alone. Already, Evan was sitting up at the edge of the water, moaning and holding his head, but other than his tormented expression, he appeared undamaged. She glanced toward Mitch, eager to thank him, but he was sprawled on the ground with his head back and eyes closed. His breaths came in sharp gasps. Her first thought was that swimming to shore with Evan must have exhausted him, but then she noticed that the rash on his legs now covered them completely. His arms, face, and neck were also a bright red and swelling rapidly.

"Mitch?" she asked, her voice more shrill than she intended. "Are you okay?"

His eyes opened and stared at her dully. His wheezing became worse.

"Mitch?" She was really starting to worry now.

"Looks like he's in shock!" Roberta said. "Did he get stung with something?"

Evan stood up shakily. "Definitely in shock. I've seen it before."

"What should we do?" Cory asked.

"I don't know." Evan limped a few steps until he was next to Cory. "Take him to the hospital?"

"Good idea," Gordon said.

Mitch took another tortured breath. "Backpack," he wheezed. "Toothbrush holder."

What? Cory thought. *He wants to brush his teeth now?*

His eyes held Cory's for another few seconds before he added, "Hurry."

Gordon snapped his fingers. "His medicine must be in the backpack!"

Cory thrust the baby at Roberta and ran back to the chairs, where she'd last seen Mitch's backpack. Grabbing it, she opened the zipper and rifled through the contents as she ran back to the shore. Diapers, wipes, wallet keys, a change of clothes for EmJay, a man's thin jacket. In the bottom was an orange toothbrush holder. She pulled it out and let the backpack fall near Mitch's head.

"Here!" She tore the ends apart, and out popped a smaller tube made of transparent yellow plastic. It fell to the dirt, and Vikki scooped it up.

"EpiPen," she read. "Epinephrine auto-injector." She looked up. "It's a shot of some sort."

"Well, give it to him," Cory said.

"I don't know how." Vikki handed it back to her.

"Neither do I." Cory looked helplessly at the others, but they all shook their heads.

"Ask him," Roberta said.

Gordon bent down near Mitch. "I think he's fainted."

Cold fear fell over Cory, freezing her insides and making her feel like vomiting. Mitch was sounding worse by the second, and it came to her with startling clarity how much she cared for him.

Don't die! she pleaded. *There's more we have to say. There's more . . . I think that I . . . well, EmJay needs you . . . Oh, just please don't die!*

Chapter Nineteen

Hands shaking, Cory tore off the top of the yellow tube and shook the EpiPen into her hands. "There's instructions," she said with a rush of hope. The first line said how to hold the auto-injector. The second directed her to removed the gray cap. The rest described how she was supposed to jab it in to his thigh. She knelt down beside him and took a deep breath.

"Does it work through jeans?" Vikki asked.

Cory hesitated. Should she push up his shorts? His lower legs had large ugly welts all over them and so did his face, neck, and arms.

"Pull them up, I guess," she ordered the men.

Before they could act, Mitch opened his eyes, groaning slightly. With a lunge he grabbed the EpiPen from her, checked with his thumb for the cap, then plunged it onto his jean-covered thigh with aggressive force. Everyone heard a loud click. Mitch fell back and shuddered. "Towels," he said after a minute. Already his breathing was better, though his skin was still swollen with patchy white and red welts. "Need to get warm. Drug won't last . . . fifteen minutes or so."

Roberta returned a whimpering EmJay to Cory and went with the others to get their towels. Vikki was the first one back, bringing

Roberta's picnic blanket that had covered the table. As she tucked it around Mitch, he struggled to sit up. After several failed attempts, he gave up, moaning and holding his stomach.

Cory sat on the ground beside him. "What's wrong, Mitch?"

"Nauseated. And dizzy."

"I mean, why did you have this reaction?"

"It was to the water."

"You're allergic to water?"

He shook his head. "To cold." His eyes met hers. "I need to get to the hospital. I don't have another EpiPen."

Fear trembled up Cory's spine. When Roberta and Gordon arrived with more towels, she made them help Mitch to his car. Evan walked with them but didn't look steady enough to support Mitch. "I'm taking him to the emergency room," she told them.

"I can do it," Vikki responded.

Cory shook her head. "You don't know where it is."

"Neither do you." Gordon bent to fasten his sandals. "I'll go with you. Besides, you might need help with him during the drive." He smiled at his wife. "The rest of you stay here and try not to worry. We'll be back."

Roberta shook her head. "I'll follow in a few minutes with the truck. We don't know how long he'll have to stay, and you'll need a ride back here if Cory can't bring you."

"Right, I didn't think of that." Gordon kissed his wife on the cheek. "Why don't I call you, instead? You have your phone, right?" She nodded.

Cory strapped EmJay into her car seat. "Here's Mitch's backpack," Vikki said. "You might need something from it. And don't forget your purse and sandals."

"Do you want me to go with Gordon?" Evan said to Cory. "You could stay here."

Cory felt a surge of anger at him for his part in the whole fiasco. "*I'm* the reason he's here. I insisted on bringing EmJay."

"I know, but—"

"I'll be back."

"All right, then." Evan leaned in for a kiss as Mitch watched from the passenger seat, his head thrown back between the door and the seat. What was it in his eyes? Anger? Sadness? Indifference? Cory wondered if she would ever know. She started the Mustang's engine.

"I think the closest hospital is in Heber," Gordon said.

By the time they reached Heber, Mitch was having trouble breathing again. He huddled under the blanket and towels, shivering. Cory reached over and put her hand on his arm. She could feel the tenseness of his muscles even through the blanket.

"There's a hospital sign," she said, pointing.

Gordon nodded. "Yeah. Turn here."

Gordon helped Cory get Mitch out of the car and inside, where the hospital personnel took over, whisking him out of sight.

"Do you have the auto-injector you used?" the emergency receptionist asked when they went to check him in with the medical card Cory found in Mitch's wallet.

Cory switched EmJay to the other hip. "I didn't think to bring it."

"We like to dispose of them properly."

"I'll call my wife and have her find it," Gordon promised. "She was going to pick me up anyway if this takes long."

"He'll be here for a good while," the receptionist said.

Gordon looked at Cory. "You should call his family. They'll probably want to give him a blessing. Or I could do it."

Cory had no idea what he was talking about. "I'll call his family," she said. "I'm sure the numbers are on his cell." She turned back to the receptionist. "He's going to be okay, isn't he?"

"Would you like me to ask if you can go back with him?"

Cory nodded. While the woman was gone, she searched through Mitch's backpack. There was no cell phone, but she found a PDA in one of the small pockets.

"Ah, a Palm," Gordon said. "I hope he hasn't locked it with a password." He hadn't, and after some experimentation, Cory was able to find his phone list.

The receptionist returned to the desk. "The doctor says he's going to be fine. They're getting him out of his wet clothes and administering some heat and an IV. Apparently the patient said . . . well, he'd rather you wait out here for a while."

"Then he's all right?"

The woman smiled. "Yes. He's uncomfortable, but his condition is stable."

Cory breathed a sigh of relief. "Thank you. I—I guess I'll call his family now."

"Why don't you sit down?" Gordon suggested. "You're looking a little pale. I'll wait by the doors for Roberta."

Taking his advice, Cory pulled the backpack straps over the shoulder where her purse hung and carried EmJay to the seats in the waiting room. The backpack slid down her arm, making the load seem heavy and unwieldy. Her legs felt wobbly. Dropping into a chair, she set the backpack on the floor. EmJay kicked to get down. "Okay, darling, but stay close."

Four other people were in the waiting room, two women on the opposite side of the room, a man sitting near Cory, and another woman pacing. They all stared at Cory's wet bathing suit, and her face flushed with embarrassment. At least she was wearing her cover-up, though most of it was wet now as well. She shivered with cold in the air-conditioned room. Remembering Mitch's jacket, she fished it from the backpack, along with EmJay's white-and-pink cover-up and matching sandals. After making sure EmJay was warm, Cory slid her arms into Mitch's black jacket, pushing up the long sleeves. Then she dug out her cell phone from her purse.

His Palm had listings for his family, as well as his job and a few friends. Some of the names were female, and Cory felt a surge of unreasoning jealousy. Was he dating any of them seriously? She hadn't heard him mention anyone, but then she really hadn't talked about Evan, either.

The jerk! she thought. This outing had completely changed her opinion of Evan. How could he have thought it amusing to pull such a dangerous joke? She'd been too stunned at the lake to say anything, but when she saw him again, she was going to let him have it.

She passed over the names of Mitch's parents and his sisters, opting instead to call Tyler's cell phone.

Tyler picked up on the second ring. "Hello?"

"Tyler, I'm glad you answered."

"Who is this?"

"Cory."

"Is something wrong? Aren't you supposed to be jet skiing?"

"I was, but there was an accident. Mitch got into the water and—"

"Is he all right?" Tyler's voice was anxious.

"They say he's going to be fine, but he went into some kind of shock."

"Anaphylactic shock."

"That's it."

"Did you use the EpiPen?"

"Yes."

"Good." Tyler let out a breath. "So you took him to the emergency?"

"That was what I was supposed to do, right?"

"Exactly. Thank you."

"No problem. I'm just glad he's okay. Would you call your parents?"

"Yeah. I'll call the family. I'm at Savvy's apartment in Orem right now, but I was headed over to my parents' for a barbeque. I'll call instead and have them meet me there. Which hospital is it?"

"Heber. It seemed to be the closest. EmJay and I will wait till you get here."

"I forgot about the baby. How's she taking this?"

"She cried a bit, but she's all right now. She's too little to understand."

"Good. Thanks, Cory. I really appreciate all you've done."

"It was nothing," she said, though that wasn't quite true. She'd been scared half out of her mind.

"We'll get there as soon as we can," Tyler added.

Feeling relieved, Cory hung up the phone.

When Roberta arrived at the hospital, she came over to Cory. "Are you sure you don't want us to wait with you?"

Cory shook her head. "No, you two go on. Enjoy yourselves. I'll go back later after his family gets here."

"Okay, then. Good luck."

Cory watched them leave, feeling suddenly lost and alone. She spent the next forty minutes following EmJay up and down the halls. Mitch's parents were the first to arrive.

"Cory." Jessica Huntington said in greeting. As in their first meeting, the woman was stylishly dressed, this time in silky navy pants and a festive, red-white-and-blue, short-sleeved sweater, and her elegant blonde hair was in place. Cory felt scraggly and windblown by comparison. "I'm so sorry this had to happen," Jessica added, eyeing her swimsuit. "I hope it didn't ruin your whole day."

Not expecting the sympathy, Cory blinked. "Things were pretty much winding down."

"Tyler told us you administered the epinephrine." Cameron Huntington's round face was smiling. He looked so ordinary in worn jeans and what must be a double extra-large T-shirt that Cory immediately felt less out of place.

"I just got it and took off the cap," Cory admitted. "He's the one who actually jabbed it in. No one else knew how."

"Well, thank you for helping." Cameron pushed up his glasses and held out his arms to EmJay who was in Cory's arms. "Hi, sweetie. Come to Grandpa? Huh? Come on."

EmJay grinned. "Hi, hi." To Cory's surprise, she leaned toward Cameron.

"Watch this," Cameron said, winking.

Jessica touched her husband's arm. "I'm going to ask about Mitch at the desk."

"I'll be right there," he answered.

Once in Cameron's arms, EmJay reached into the pocket of his T-shirt and pulled out a fistful of mini Tootsie Rolls. Then she grinned and reached for Cory.

Cameron let her go. "They learn fast. I started keeping these in my pockets when Amanda married Blake. Had to entice little Mara to come to me. Now she'll come to me over either of them in a heartbeat. The other grandkids too." He laughed. "I'm working the same magic with this cute little grandbaby."

Cory admired his persistence and the love he apparently had for EmJay, but it troubled her to see him taking on the role that should have belonged to Cory's father. "This might seem like a weird question," she began, "but doesn't it bother—worry you . . . I mean, do you feel differently about your natural grandchildren than your adopted ones?" Even as she asked the question, she felt herself cringing inside as she pictured the rage it would have elicited from her own father.

"They're none of them adopted—yet. Though we hope to have it happen some day. For now it's enough that Kevin and Mara's mother has given up custody." His eyes fell to EmJay. "Children are so precious. It doesn't matter to me how they came to us, just that we do our best to teach them and love them. Isn't that what it's all about?"

"Yeah. I guess."

"Well, I'd better get back to my wife." With a smile, he walked to the desk where Jessica was talking to the receptionist.

"Moncree. Uh!" EmJay shoved a soggy Tootsie Roll into her hand. Cory unwrapped the candy, which EmJay popped in her mouth. She reached for the wrapper as well.

"No, no, darling. I know you like papers, but you can't eat this."

Unfazed, EmJay examined her fistful of candies.

"Cory!"

She looked up to see Tyler coming through the door. "Hi, hi," EmJay said around a mouthful of sweets.

"Hi, sweetie." Tyler kissed her proffered fist, and she responded by handing him a Tootsie Roll to open. "How is he?" Tyler asked.

"I don't have any more news, but your parents are at the desk. Or were." Jessica had disappeared, and Cameron was headed their way.

"Well?" Tyler handed EmJay an unwrapped candy, pocketing the wrapper.

Cameron hugged his son, who was taller than he was. "Apparently he hasn't been taking his daily medication, so the episode was worse than it might have been."

"Daily medication?" Cory asked.

Cameron looked her way. "A simple allergy medicine. But he often doesn't take it during the summer because he doesn't run into many cold situations. Anyway, he's fine now, and the rash will be gone soon, but it was severe enough that they want to keep him overnight for observation. Just a precaution."

"He'll miss your fireworks," Cory said.

Tyler shrugged. "Well, it serves him right. He knows better than to go into the water without his drysuit. Well, I'd better call Amanda and Kerrianne to tell them not to come."

"They should be at our place already with the kids," Cameron said. "We told them we'd call if they were needed. Amanda was about to come up here with guns blazing—you know how she gets when he does something like this—but I made her stay put. She doesn't need the stress while she's pregnant. And neither does Mitch."

Tyler laughed. "You can say that again. Well, I'd like to see him for a minute, and then I'll head back."

"Your mother is with him now, but they said they'd let two people inside. Go ahead. I'll go after you're finished."

With a parting tickle in the stomach for EmJay, Tyler went in to see his brother. Cory waited a moment before asking Cameron, "Does Mitch have a lot of these episodes?"

"Oh, no. I mean, not too many. The first was when we went water-skiing when he was fifteen. He's always loved water sports and was the best swimmer in the family. He'd never had any problems before. But that day he had a severe reaction. We were all shocked and didn't know what to do. Fortunately, we were with some people who had some medication with them. Later he was diagnosed with cold urticaria. From that time on, he's carried an EpiPen. He's had a reaction with about every member of our family since, except his mom, but nothing that has seriously scared us. This was probably about the worst."

"I didn't even know he had an allergy. And I've never heard of being allergic to cold."

Cameron chuckled. "Neither had we, but we've met several people with it since. I'm not surprised you didn't know. He's pretty closemouthed about it. It's taken a toll on him. Sometimes I wonder—" He stopped speaking, his face growing wistful.

"Wonder what?"

"Well, as a parent who wants the safety of his son, I'm glad he works at a computer here instead of in the wild with animals, but I also want him to be happy. I worry that he has allowed his allergy to get in the way of what he really wants to do." Cameron sighed. "No, what I really worry about is that my fear for him, and his mother's, has prevented him from following his dreams."

His comment transported Cory back to the time when she had first told her father she wanted to go to the Amazon. He was sick then, and she wouldn't have left him, even if he hadn't been so violently opposed. "You have a duty to me," he'd insisted. She knew that and she'd stayed, but she didn't lie to herself about her relief when he had died.

Died with a broken heart because AshDee had the courage to do what I didn't. Or had she? What took more courage, staying or leaving? Maybe both took equal courage. Cory had never thought of it that way before.

"He could work around his allergy," she said, aware that Cameron was waiting for her to respond. "If he wanted to enough."

Cameron smiled. "You're right. And maybe I should remind him of that. I guess I'm still reluctant to let him go. Oh, look, Tyler's coming this way. I think I'll slip in and scold my son a bit. You know, show my fatherly love."

Cory wondered if Mitch had any idea how lucky he was to have such a father.

In less than fifteen minutes, Mitch's parents came to the waiting room where she sat with EmJay, who was starting to act sleepy. "Oh, there you are," Jessica said. "He'd like to see you and Emily Jane. We'll wait out here for you."

"You don't have to," she said. "You should go to your party."

Jessica looked embarrassed, but Cameron said firmly, "We're supposed to take Emily Jane home with us."

"I see." Cory felt heat boil in her heart. She hadn't considered what Mitch would do with EmJay, but it wasn't fair giving her to his parents when she was willing to take her.

"We'd love for you to come to the house for the barbecue and fireworks," Jessica said.

"I have to go back up to the reservoir to pick up my friend and my things. I'll have to use Mitch's car since he's the one who drove."

"I'm sure that's fine." Jessica shrugged, and Cory thought how odd it was that they didn't seem to give a second thought to the fact that she had Mitch's car, his house keys, and his wallet with his credit cards. All they were worried about—all *he* worried about—was EmJay.

"At least come to the fireworks after." Cameron pulled out a business card from his wallet and jotted down the address before handing it to her. "We put on quite a show on our street. Bring your friend."

Jessica nodded. "Please come. We'd all be happy to have you. Especially Emily Jane."

There the reminder was again. Her niece was part of this family, and Cory was only an invited guest. She wanted to hate these people, but they were just so stinking nice. "I'll see how it goes," she said.

"We'll wait for you, then." Jessica smiled and sat in a chair.

Cory left them, hoping Mitch was fit enough to endure a good scolding. He was lying in a bed with an IV hooked to his right wrist. Several blankets were tucked around his body except on the upper half of his chest where she could see a thin white wire disappearing into the top of his hospital gown. *A heart monitor,* she thought. An automatic blood pressure cuff circled his left arm. The white swollen welts on his face were all but gone, though much of the redness remained.

"Much! Much!" EmJay bounced in Cory's arms.

"How're you feeling?" Cory asked.

"It's not as bad as it looks," he said, lifting both arms slightly. "I feel perfectly fine. I told them that, but they don't want to let me go. Something about my blood pressure, I guess."

"You feel *perfectly* fine?"

"Well, considering." He didn't meet her gaze but looked at EmJay. "Come here, sweetie. Has your Aunt Cory been treating you well?"

EmJay launched herself at Mitch, and Cory had no choice but to settle her carefully between his left arm and his body. EmJay babbled a jumble of incomprehensible words between drools of chocolate candy. Mitch reached to the wheeled tray by his bedside and got a tissue to wipe her mouth. The baby promptly tried to eat it. Cory took the tissue, wiped her mouth, and threw it away.

EmJay laid her head contentedly on Mitch's chest, her mouth still full. Mitch put a hand on her back.

"Why did you jump into the water?" Cory asked. The question had been burning in her since the accident.

"You saw the fool. He was going to drown."

"I could have jumped in after him."

"I wouldn't have asked you to do that."

"Because you're the guy? Honestly, Mitch, I like your old-fashioned gallantry, opening doors and the like, but risking your life is just plain stupid."

"Hey, for all I knew, I might not be allergic anymore. The doctors say it might go away one day."

"Your legs were already red and itching. You knew. At least you could have swum back to the boat. We could have gotten him in."

"Not with how he was thrashing about. We'd have dumped everyone, and I wasn't about to risk Emily Jane."

Cory couldn't dispute that. She'd been worried about the baby herself. "Well, I can't believe you went to the lake without telling someone you're allergic to cold."

"Actually, I'm not allergic to cold per se, just rapid changes to colder temperatures."

She put her hands on her hips. "You should have told me you could possibly die if you got in the water."

"I wasn't even going to get *in* the water. None of this would have been a problem if that idiot boyfriend of yours had any intelligence!"

"He's not my boyfriend!"

"That's not what he says."

"Well, he's an idiot!"

"You were kissing him!"

"He kissed me!"

Mitch grinned. "You know what? Your face matches your hair almost exactly."

Darn the man! She wanted to strangle him.

"You should have told me," she repeated stubbornly.

He shut his eyes and sighed. "You're right. I should have. But if I think your boyfriend is wimpy, where does that leave me? Being allergic to something so utterly idiotic, I mean."

Cory was surprised that he even cared what she thought. He'd always seemed so sure of himself. "An allergy doesn't mean you're weak. You can't help an allergy."

Mitch didn't reply, but she saw his face relax. *At least he has some sense,* she thought. On his chest, EmJay had gone still, signaling that she was finally asleep.

"What about EmJay?" she asked.

"She can stay with my parents. Or one of my sisters will take her home."

"I'll keep her."

His eyes dug into hers, as though searching for the hidden meaning in her words.

"If I was going to take off, I would have by now," she said, lifting her chin in challenge.

"I guess that's true." His gaze drifted to EmJay, asleep on his chest, one hand still clutching an unwrapped candy.

"Well?" she asked. "She'll just cry with your parents—or your sisters. Unless they want to walk outside all night. I promise we'll come back for you in the morning. In your car, I might add." When he didn't speak, she continued. "Come on. She'll be happier with me. *We belong together.*" She hadn't meant to let this last slip out, but it came without her volition.

Mitch regarded her for a long, silent moment and then said quietly, "I know."

From those two little words she knew she had won far more than one battle. It might not mean that he would give her custody, but it meant that he recognized her importance in EmJay's life. "Okay, then." She reached for EmJay before he could change his mind.

"Take her to my house, will you?" he said, raising his head from the pillow. "She'll feel more secure. You still have my keys, don't you?"

Cory most definitely didn't want to go to his house. She wanted to take EmJay home with her to prove to him and to the world that the baby would be happy wherever Cory happened to be. But was that selfish? Probably. She had to admit that staying at Mitch's would mean less change for EmJay. "Okay."

"And hold her hand if she wakes up?" His face scrunched as though he was waiting for her to laugh at him.

"Of course." Couldn't he guess how much she longed to do that for AshDee's baby? Couldn't he possibly understand how much EmJay's presence alleviated her ever-hovering grief for her little sister? Not to mention her guilt for letting AshDee walk out of her life.

His face relaxed. "Thanks."

She held EmJay to her chest. The baby roused enough to curl her fist around a lock of Cory's hair, a few pieces of candy sliding unwanted to the hospital bed. "See you tomorrow," she said softly.

"Oh, and could you take her to the fireworks at my parents'?"

She wanted to say that it was too much to ask—she didn't want to share her time alone with EmJay.

"Just for a while," he amended. "I really wanted to be the one to show her the fireworks, but since I can't, I don't want her to miss it."

"Okay." What else could she say?

Mitch sighed and closed his eyes, as though unable to watch her leave with EmJay. Cory hurried to the curtain that separated Mitch from the other emergency room occupants, thinking to leave without looking back, but at the curtain, she couldn't resist. Mitch had opened his eyes and was staring at her in much the same way as when Evan had kissed her.

Cory wanted to explain how it was between her and Evan, but more than anything she wanted to escape that look, or how the look made her feel inside. She remembered too well the horror she'd experienced during Mitch's reaction and how she'd silently begged him not to die. Well, he hadn't—and now what?

I can't tell him how I'm beginning to feel about him, she thought. *I can't.*

She realized now how utterly her master plan had backfired. She'd wanted to charm Mitch into giving her custody, but she'd never planned to care for him in return.

I don't, she told herself. *I won't set myself up for heartache.*

Silently, she vowed to continue with her plan. When she got custody, she'd escape to the Amazon and forget she'd ever been to Utah and met anyone named Mitch Huntington.

With that thought, Cory turned her back on him and left.

Chapter Twenty

On Saturday morning, Cory buckled EmJay in her car seat for the drive to pick up Mitch from the hospital. Yawning, she wished for a few more hours of sleep. She'd stayed up far too late last night.

Yesterday, when she had gone back to the reservoir for Vikki, she'd broken her date with Evan, who had not been gracious. Cory found herself strangely uncaring of what he thought or said. It was enough to have EmJay with her. Vikki declined to accompany her to the Huntingtons' fireworks, so Cory headed there alone. She worried that she'd be an outcast because of her claim on EmJay. Instead, the family was warm and friendly, and Cory had enjoyed herself more than she expected. For one magical evening, she was a daughter in a large and loving family. EmJay also had a wonderful time running around with her so-called cousins on the front lawn while waiting for the fireworks to begin.

There had been only one awkward moment when Cory had seen Kerrianne staring at the sky. "Are you all right?" she'd asked.

Kerrianne nodded, her smile bright. "My husband loved the Fourth of July. He was like a little kid, rushing to light the fireworks. He brought a lot of joy to the day for us."

"Do you really believe that he's somewhere waiting for you?" She felt stupid even as she asked the question. Surely, if any of Mitch's family believed in the afterlife, it would have to be Kerrianne.

"I don't believe he's somewhere waiting for me," Kerrianne said, her glittering eyes reflecting the light from above.

"You don't?" This surprised Cory to no end.

"No. Belief is something you hope for and that you mostly feel is true. I don't feel that way. I *know* Adam's waiting. I've felt him near me, just as I've felt my Savior." She lifted her face again to the heavens. "Adam's here tonight. I'm sure of it. Loving me and watching over our children."

A lump formed in Cory's throat. She wanted to contest Kerrianne's words, but how could she in the face of such quiet conviction? Cory was glad when EmJay toddled to her and held out her arms, breaking the awkward silence. But an odd feeling remained with her the rest of the evening as she imagined something otherworldly there with the family. Something warm and special—something that made her want to laugh and weep at the same time.

Shaking off the memory, Cory backed Mitch's car down his drive. She preferred his car over her rental—mostly because the car seat was so difficult to move.

At the hospital in Heber, Mitch was pacing outside the front doors. Someone must have brought him a change of clothes the night before because he was dressed in faded jeans and an ugly green sweatshirt that had definitely seen better days. "Can't wait to get out of jail, huh?" she asked as she approached.

"I thought you'd never get here! They brought me out in a wheel-chair. Said it was policy. It was embarrassing." He took EmJay from her arms, giving her a big hug and kiss. "So how'd she do? She sleep well?"

"Like a baby." Cory began walking to the car.

Mitch hurried to keep up. "She didn't wake up?"

"Well . . ."

"She cried, didn't she?"

Cory stopped. "No, she didn't cry. In fact, I held her all night on your couch. Satisfied?"

He threw back his head and laughed. "I did the same thing when I first got her. She wouldn't sleep if I put her down. Besides, it was so fun watching her."

Cory smiled. She had spent far too much of the night doing just that. "She's a miracle, that's for sure," she said softly. "I can't get over how much she reminds me of AshDee."

"She looks like you, too." They started walking again before Mitch said, "When I first saw you in the chapel that day, I thought you were Ashley come to check up on me."

There he went again, talking about her sister as though she were alive somewhere.

"But only for a minute," he added. "You were far too ornery to be Ashley." She scowled at him, but he grinned. "I'm kidding. So how'd the fireworks go?" He bounced EmJay in his arms. "Was she scared?"

"No. What she was, was sleeping. She tired herself out running around with your nieces and nephews and fell asleep before they began lighting them. Didn't see a thing."

"Aw." He looked at the baby. "Don't worry, sweetie. There's always next year."

"You're tickled pink that she fell asleep, aren't you!" Cory accused, her mouth twitching as she struggled against a smile.

He shrugged. "I guess I did want to show her myself. And I was worried she'd be afraid of the noise."

They'd reached the car, and Cory opened the door so Mitch could put EmJay in her seat.

"And my family? Did they throw you to the wolves or try to convert you?"

Cory thought of her conversation with Kerrianne. "They were all sweet. Especially your father." She looked away from him to the majestic mountains that loomed to the south and added, "You don't know how lucky you are to have him as a dad."

Mitch was silent so long that Cory turned to look at him. "I'm sorry," he said softly.

"For what?"

"For whatever makes you look so sad. Is it because of Ashley? Or something else? Ashley said a few things to me once about your family, and I—"

Anger washed over Cory. "There was nothing wrong with my family."

"Then why do you and Ashley seem to hate your father?"

"Do?" she shrilled. "Don't you mean *did?* Ashley doesn't *do* anything anymore."

Cory suddenly felt his arms around her, drawing her close. "I'm sorry," he whispered. "I'm sorry for everything. Please, let's just be friends."

She leaned into him, enjoying the solid, comfortable feel of his chest. "I'm sorry, too," she said softly. "And you're right. My father was a bitter old man who bullied his children. I tried to tell myself that it was because my mother died and he was sad without her, but I think he would have done it anyway. AshDee and I used to imagine that she was alive and that she took us far away from him. I might have left, but I stayed—mostly for AshDee. But not just for her. I loved him, I really did. When AshDee took off and became a Mormon, he had a stroke. Then I couldn't leave, even if I'd wanted to. He had no one else. It was a miserable year before he died. But AshDee never knew. She was too busy being a Mormon."

"That makes it harder for you to believe, doesn't it?"

Cory drew away. "Maybe."

"I'd like to help. I can explain why Ashley joined the Church."

"I'm doing research on my own." She was absolutely finished with this conversation.

Cory went around to the other side of the car. For some reason she was irritated that he hadn't questioned her further about her father. Sometimes she wished she had someone to talk to about him.

By the time they'd driven down the canyon and arrived at their street, they were talking easily again. Cory found her efforts to charm Mitch weren't really efforts at all. She enjoyed being with him.

Mitch dropped her off outside her rented house. "Drop by later, if you want. If those birds are flying, I'll be barbecuing up some trout."

"Won't be until at least next week."

"Maybe."

Cory had the feeling he couldn't take his eyes off her. That for this moment in time, he was perfectly content to drink in her presence. *What foolishness,* she told herself. Stepping back, she waved at him as he drove away.

When Cory opened her door, which was curiously unlocked, she found Vikki, Tyler, Savvy, and the two missionaries sitting on the floor in her living room. Belatedly, Cory noticed two extra vehicles parked in front, one a little red Subaru and the other Tyler's green truck. It was a wonder Mitch hadn't noticed them, either.

She shut the door. "Hi. I forgot you were coming."

"Come and have breakfast," Tyler invited. They'd spread a large picnic cloth over the carpet, atop which were huge cinnamon rolls and cups of orange juice.

"These are out of this world!" Vikki said, taking another bite. "Sit here, Cory."

"I was picking up Mitch," Cory said to no one in particular.

"Yeah, we heard," Tyler said.

Cory sat down between Vikki and Savvy, who smiled and passed her a pitcher of orange juice. "Thanks." Cory had talked to Savvy briefly last night at the fireworks and had found her friendly and lively to be around.

"I can't believe what happened to Mitch," Savvy said. "That man should be slapped silly. What did he think, jumping into the water like that? Hey, he didn't have any of his animals with him, did he?"

"I don't think so." Cory hadn't thought to ask. "Probably knew he'd have his hands full with EmJay."

"EmJay?" Savvy asked.

"That's what she calls Emily Jane," Tyler told her.

"My sister and I planned baby names when we were growing up." Cory didn't want any of them to forget that *she* was the relative here, the person who should be raising EmJay.

Savvy nodded. "My sisters and I used to do that, too."

"Speaking of which," Tyler grumbled, "you and your sisters seem to be doing a lot of stuff together lately."

Savvy grinned at him sweetly. "How kind of you to notice. I would have thought you were too busy with all your girlfriends to pay attention to what I'm doing with my time."

"Hey, I care. We're friends."

Savvy continued smiling, but Cory noticed the happiness didn't quite reach her eyes. "True, and that's why I hope you'll write to me on my mission."

Tyler's mouth gaped open. "Your what? You're not twenty-one."

"I am next month. I've already turned in my papers."

"Congratulations!" said Elder Rowley. "You won't regret it."

Elder Savage nodded. "Best time in my life so far."

Savvy grinned, and this time the elation in her eyes was clear. "Thanks, guys. I'm so excited. I've been thinking about this for a long time."

"You have?" Tyler was staring at her, his sweet roll and juice forgotten. "You didn't tell me. Why didn't you tell me? I tell you everything."

"Everything?" Savvy gazed at him.

He looked down at his hands. "Well, most stuff."

"It was a personal decision. Not easily made. But now that the papers are on their way, I wanted you to be among the first to know."

Tyler didn't look up, and Cory thought she saw a shimmer of something in his eyes, but it might just have been the way the light reflected from his glasses.

232

"I think we should begin," said Elder Rowley. "We can have a prayer, and those of you who aren't done yet can finish while Elder Savage and I talk. Savvy? Would you say the prayer?"

With a last curious glance at Tyler, Savvy bowed her head and asked the Lord to send his Spirit to attend the missionary discussion. Cory envied the way she did this with such confidence, such childlike faith. *The faith of the untried,* Cory thought. But for all she knew, Savvy had suffered terrible hardships that ate at her soul.

"Today, we're going to talk about the restoration of the gospel," Elder Savage began after Savvy finished. "We've talked about God and Jesus, the Book of Mormon, and eternal families, but now we want to discuss the authority by which the Church was restored."

Cory had been curious about the Mormons' claim to authority. *Now I'll find out,* she thought. *I just hope it doesn't involve more angels.*

Mitch was giving Emily Jane a bath when his doorbell rang. "Why does it always do that when I'm busy?"

Emily Jane grinned at him. "Choing lally biya nollola."

"Exactly." He pulled her from the tub and wrapped her in a soft towel. "Grrrr," he growled, unable to pass up the moment.

"Grrrr!" Emily Jane clapped her hands and laughed.

The doorbell rang again, and Mitch hurried down the hall. "All right already," he called. "Sheesh!"

Tyler was standing outside. "Savvy put in her mission papers!" he said, pushing past Mitch.

"Hello to you, too."

Emily Jane waved a hand. "Hi, hi."

Tyler grabbed her hand and kissed it. "Can you believe that?"

"Well, at least you know why she was acting so strange."

"Yeah, but a mission?"

"You went on one."

"That's different. I didn't know her then. She couldn't miss me."

"Ah, so that's what's bothering you. That you'll miss her."

"No! That's not it. But criminy—she didn't even tell me!"

Mitch went down the hall to his bedroom for Emily Jane's clothes. Kneeling beside the foot of his bed, he began diapering and dressing her with an ease born of daily practice. "So are you mad because she didn't tell you or because she's going? Because I think it's really cool."

Tyler slumped to the edge of the bed. "Definitely because she didn't tell me. We're best friends, for Pete's sake."

"So you tell her everything?"

Tyler groaned. "That's what she said."

"Smart woman." Mitch held up a hand at his brother's coming objection. "Look, I told you to talk to her."

"You did?"

Mitch blew out a sigh. "Do you ever listen? Anyway, all of this makes perfect sense. Now you know why she went to the doctor and the dentist—so she could send in her papers. She'll be gone, yeah, but it's not like you won't be busy here with your studies and all those girlfriends you're dating."

Tyler grunted. "It's the principle of the thing."

"The principle? Tyler, Savvy doesn't owe you *anything*. It's not like you're even dating. You said so yourself." Mitch pulled Emily Jane to a sitting position. "Or is that the real problem—that you've decided Savvy is more than just a friend?"

"You're nuts!" Tyler glared at him.

Mitch helped Emily Jane jump off the bed. "Have it your way. But she certainly isn't going to change her mind at this point."

"She prayed about it. I heard her tell Cory."

"Cory? When did Savvy see Cory?"

For an instant his brother's face froze. "Uh, we were together last night, you know. For the fireworks."

"I thought you just found out."

"Savvy and I met somewhere this morning. After she told me, I came here. What kind of brother would I be if I didn't check on you after being in the hospital?" Tyler gave an exasperated sigh and came to his feet. He lifted his arms. "Look, don't bother me with details. I'm upset here."

"You're hiding something."

Tyler shook his head and strode into the hall. "I'm leaving. Maybe Kerrianne will have more sympathy for me."

"I can't think why you came clear over here anyway," Mitch said, following him. "Last I heard, Savvy lived in Orem. Kerrianne's place would have been a lot closer."

"I told you. I came to check on you."

"Try again. You called me at the hospital like five times last night and then again this morning. You knew I was fine."

Tyler stopped short. "Okay, if you must know, I went to see Cory."

"Cory?" Mitch's stomach churned. "Why?" he asked slowly.

"Why not? She's a beautiful woman—which you would know if you'd stop fighting with her long enough to take a good look."

Blood pounded in Mitch's ears. He went from calm to seething anger almost instantly. "I know she's beautiful," he roared. "But she's not a member, and she's off-limits to you!"

"Since when do you tell me what to do?" Tyler challenged. He appeared serious, but there was something else in Tyler's green eyes that didn't add up.

"And you wonder why Savvy's leaving?" Mitch grated. "To get *away* from you, no doubt. Stop playing games, Tyler. Emily Jane's life is at stake. Cory's trying to take her away from me—away from the Church that her parents believed in with all their hearts."

The belligerence seeped from Tyler's face. "I'm not playing games." Turning on his heel, he continued to the front door. Mitch picked up Emily Jane and followed silently. His anger was gone, but he marveled at the intensity of his reaction. So what if Tyler thought Cory was beautiful? He was only twenty-two years old, a mere boy to her twenty-six. Of course, that might just add to her appeal.

Tyler opened the door and paused. "Do you really think she's trying to get away from me?"

Mitch couldn't hurt him by agreeing. "I think," he answered carefully, "that Savvy's doing what she has to do for herself and for her desire to serve. When it gets right down to it, we can't control other people. We make the best choices we can and leave them to make their own decisions. You said Savvy prayed about it, and I'm sure she did. It's between her and the Lord now."

Tyler nodded. "Like being back on a mission, huh? Wanting so much for people to accept but knowing you can't force them."

"Something like that." Mitch smiled and put a hand on his brother's shoulder. "The good news is that Savvy's coming back. Meanwhile, you'll write to her—at least until you get married and your wife makes you stop."

"Yeah, right." Tyler pretended to slug Mitch. "Well, thanks. I'd better get going. Bye, EmJay—I mean, Emily Jane."

The little girl waved her hand. "Bye-bye."

Mitch watched his brother sprint out to his truck. He felt a certain measure of relief when he didn't stop at Cory's down the street. He remembered vividly how she had pranced and flirted with Evan at the reservoir until he felt ready to explode. *I have to protect my little brother,* he thought. *I know exactly how she can make a guy feel.*

Therein, of course, lay the real problem.

"Oh, Emily Jane," Mitch said to the baby in his arms. "What have I gotten myself into?"

Chapter Twenty-One

Cory spent Saturday afternoon developing photographs of EmJay with the rabbits. When they were dry enough, she spread the large proofs on her living room floor and stood back to consider the outcome. They were probably some of the best photographs she'd ever taken of a person. She wished Vikki were there to admire them, but she was out shopping. Should she call Mitch? He'd hinted at barbecuing together that evening, and she was hoping he'd come over to invite her, but she worried about making a fool of herself like she had at the reservoir. The memory of her antics with Evan brought a flush to her face.

When the doorbell rang, she started suddenly. Then her hand went to her hair. *Silly,* she thought.

Opening the door, she was surprised to see Evan. Behind him in the driveway was the blue sports car he'd rented. "Good, you're home," he said. "I've been calling your cell like crazy. Why haven't you called me back? I have to leave town tomorrow."

She opened the door and let him in. "I've been in the darkroom. My phone's off."

His gaze went to the pictures. "Ah, working. That explains

everything. That happens to me when I write." He flashed her a smile that once would have turned her heart inside out.

Not anymore.

He bent down to study the pictures. "These are really good. I like how her face is in the shade, but you can see the bits of sunlight on the grass around her. Very, very nice pictures. I don't know how you do it."

"She's so cute—anyone could take good photos of her."

He straightened. "I don't know about that. I think you're talented."

"Thank you." His words meant a lot to her because she knew how hard he'd been working at his own photographs. She clasped her hands behind her back and smiled.

"Look," he said. "We need to talk."

She remained by the still-open door, uncertain what would come next. "I don't understand. I thought you had another pressing writing assignment." She touched the door but didn't shut it, enjoying the warmth of the sun on her face.

"I have several, but they shouldn't take more than a few weeks. I'd be available to go back with you to Brazil, if that's what we decide. I could hang out, help you with your pictures. Maybe toy with writing some text for them."

Ah, so now it comes down to it, Cory thought. She focused on his handsome face. He apparently hadn't shaved that weekend and was working up some serious dark blond facial hair. That wasn't like him— he was usually more meticulous about such things. Even in the Amazon he'd been clean-shaven. She shook her head slowly. "I wouldn't expect you to do that. I know how much you dislike it down there. We probably should keep in touch over e-mail until I finish my shoot."

"I thought you weren't coming back." He put his hands in the pockets of his dress pants and rocked on his heels. "At least not soon."

"I might. It depends on how things go with my niece." She leaned slightly back against the door frame, her eyes wandering down the street. There was no sign of life at Mitch's place.

"Your niece or her guardian?"

Cory pulled her gaze back to Evan. "What are you talking about?"

Evan's jaw clenched. "To tell you the truth, I don't know. Yesterday you acted like you were glad to see me. I thought we were having a good time. But after a while I began to see that it was all for show. You were performing for him!"

"What?" Cory took a step toward him. "That's ridiculous!"

"Is it?"

"Of course! He has nothing to do with us."

"Nothing?" Evan reached for her, pulling her close. "Oh, yeah? Then how come you aren't as happy to see me today as I am to see you?"

"Evan, don't." Cory pulled away and headed for the kitchen, leaving the door open in case she needed to call for help. At the sink, she filled a glass with water—anything to busy her hands.

Evan followed her into the kitchen. "At the reservoir, you were laughing and joking with me, but all the time you wanted to be with *him*."

"That's not true!" Cory turned. "Look, Evan. I knew you'd think I was acting weird, but you don't get the situation I'm in. Try to understand! Mitch is the only one who can give me custody of EmJay. He decides if I see her or not. I have to convince him that I should be EmJay's guardian!"

"By throwing yourself at him?" Evan grated. "Because anyone could see that's what you were really trying to do. I was just a pawn."

Deep shame filled Cory. Had it really been that obvious? "I'll use whatever means it takes! Don't you see? I have to be with EmJay. She's *my* niece. The only child my sister will ever have. My only family. I'll do anything to get her—anything."

"So you don't care for him?"

"I don't feel a thing for him," she lied. "Not a thing."

"Well, I personally don't like the guy."

239

Sudden anger sliced through Cory. "Why? Because of me? Evan, he saved your life! You owe him."

"I would have been fine." Evan muttered a curse and added, "I was carrying him half the way back to shore. You saw how he was."

"That was *so* not what happened." Cory welcomed the opportunity to confront Evan about what happened at the reservoir. She wanted him to know how irresponsible he had been—even if that meant defending Mitch. "I saw him dragging you. And if you hadn't been such a jerk, none of it would have happened. All of it was your fault! What if you'd hit the boat? Did you ever stop to think that we had a baby on board?"

He made a sour face. "I was just having a little fun."

"Well, grow up already."

He stared sullenly at her for a long moment, but gradually his expression lightened. He took a breath and held up his hands in truce. "Okay, maybe I was a little jealous, but I didn't mean to hurt anyone. And I'm sorry. But that's not really what's at issue here. I'd like to know where we stand."

She shook her head. "I didn't know my life was going to change so drastically. I didn't know I would feel so strongly about EmJay."

"I could help you with her." He looked at her like a little boy asking for permission.

Cory smiled, recalling how kind he'd been to her the night she'd learned about AshDee's death. Despite his mistake at the reservoir, Evan wasn't a bad guy—even if she no longer cared for him. "I'm sorry. I can't. If Mitch even suspects that you're around, he'd never give me custody. Not after what happened."

There was a flash of hurt in Evan's eyes, which he quickly squelched. He nodded. "Okay, you deal with this, and call me when you're ready. But that offer to go back to the Amazon with you is still open."

Even if Cory suspected his reasons for volunteering, it was still a nice offer. After all, she'd acted like a bigger jerk at the reservoir. "Thanks, Evan. I appreciate it."

They walked into the living room, Cory feeling relieved. The front door was ajar only a few inches, not nearly as open as Cory remembered leaving it, and she felt a premonition of unease. As she pulled on the doorknob to let Evan out, he took her in his arms and kissed her firmly on the mouth. "Good-bye," he said. "Let me know."

When he let her go, she turned to see Mitch at the bottom of the stairs, EmJay in his arms. His eyes were angry and accusing.

Evan went down the stairs. "Mitch."

"Evan." Mitch dipped his head slightly, but his eyes didn't leave Cory. Remembering the open door, a chill crawled up her spine. How much had he heard?

"Come on in," she said as Evan drove away. "What brings you here?"

The street was deserted, with only a few children riding bicycles at the end of the block. "The door was open," he said without inflection. "I knocked, but you were obviously too busy to answer. I heard what you said."

Cory swallowed, her throat feeling dry. "And what was that?" She wanted to reach out to him, but he was too far away.

"The bit where you admitted to leading me on to get what you want."

She looked at him pleadingly. "Is that so bad? Is it? Considering what's at stake?"

"I guess not." But his eyes said otherwise. Cory felt she had hurt him far worse than she could ever have hurt Evan.

EmJay struggled to get down, catching sight of some bright rocks in the flowerbed. Mitch let her go.

Tears stung Cory's eyes. "It's not as if it changes anything between us."

He walked up two steps until their eyes were even. "It does change things. You know why? Because lately I find myself wishing we could

241

have met under different circumstances. I keep thinking that if we didn't have to fight over custody, we might have discovered something important." He was leaning forward, too close for comfort, but Cory couldn't seem to back away.

"There'd still be your church," she retorted to stave off the biting pain that had begun in her heart. "Tell me honestly—you wouldn't even consider marrying a nonmember, would you?" She had learned that morning from the missionaries that Mormons were encouraged to marry only Mormons. She should have known; her father had felt the same about Baptists marrying Baptists. At least now she understood what Kerrianne had been talking about when she'd implied that Mitch would never be interested in her. "Well?" Cory prodded.

He sighed. She was right, and they both knew it.

"How utterly egotistical." She shook her head in disgust.

"Not from where I'm standing. I want my family with me forever. I want someone to share my faith. I want someone who will help me pass on that faith to my children."

"And to EmJay." She looked down at the little girl who stood in the flowerbed on a bunch of purple pansies, her hands full of rocks.

"Especially to EmJay. I need to teach her how she can make it to where her parents are waiting. I want to help them become an eternal family."

Cory felt no triumph over his first use of the baby's nickname. She only felt sad, discouraged, and alone. Once more a stranger cut off in the darkness. But she had been alone a lot these past years, and she wasn't going to let that stop her. She lifted her chin slightly. "At the hospital, you agreed with me when I said that EmJay belongs with me. Did you mean that?"

He nodded slowly. "I did, at the time."

"And now?"

The muscles in his jaw worked. "I guess I feel the same—to some extent."

A sliver of hope burgeoned in her heart. "What does that mean?"

"It means I'll let you spend time with Emily Jane."

"But you won't let her live with me?"

His eyes dropped to the baby but not before Cory saw his silent question: *Do you know what you're asking?*

Of course she knew. Of course.

"If you joined the Church," he said, meeting her gaze once again, "then maybe we could share custody."

"And if I don't?"

His eyes didn't waver. "Then you'll have visitation, as much as we can work out, but she'll live with me, and you can't poison her against the Church. And you can't take her out of Utah. I'm sorry, Cory, but I won't bend on any of this. Lane and Ashley are her parents, and they want her to be raised in the Church."

"AshDee and her husband are dead!"

His hands gripped the black cast iron railing. "That doesn't mean they've stopped caring about their daughter."

"Look at you!" she said, her face flushing with angry frustration. "Look at you talking about them as though they're in the next room."

Mitch appeared surprised at her fury. "They are, so to speak," he said, leaning earnestly toward her. "I know I'll see them again. Cory, it's simple: the Church really is true. I know it!"

Her jaw clenched and unclenched. "So that's all it takes? Joining your church? Then you'll share custody?"

"If you really mean it."

Cory made her voice deadly soft. "And who judges that? You? The neighbors? Your attorney?"

"No, no." He shook his head, obviously uncomfortable with that idea. "You judge yourself. You live it, that's all."

"In five years are you going to take EmJay away if I'm not living up to par?"

"Of course not. If you're converted, you're converted. The rest is between you and God." His eyes roamed her face with an intensity that resembled a touch.

Cory shivered.

His voice lowered. "But whatever you decide, do both of us a favor and don't pretend you like me when you don't."

Before she could respond, Mitch looked over to where EmJay had started down the sidewalk. He turned and sprinted after her. Without a backward glance, he scooped up the baby and headed toward home.

Cory knew the hoped-for barbecue was canceled.

He acted so high and mighty, looking down on her for trying to charm him into giving her custody, but hadn't he been trying equally hard to charm her into believing in his religion? Not a day had passed that he hadn't somehow brought it into the conversation.

Well, so be it, she thought, going inside the house. *If he wants it so much, I'll believe.* Her first call was to Tyler.

"Hi," she said, a little breathlessly. Her heart raced at what must be a million beats per second. "I've been thinking a lot about what you and the missionaries have taught me, and I've decided that I want to be baptized."

The second call was to her attorney.

Chapter Twenty-Two

On Sunday morning, Mitch didn't feel like attending his own ward. Instead, he decided to visit his parents' ward in Alpine. At least there would be other children for Emily Jane to watch and interact with.

He was feeling depressed. All his thoughts were overshadowed by what had happened on Saturday afternoon. Maybe he should have turned around and gone home when he'd seen the blue sedan in Cory's driveway. But he'd been too curious. Curious enough to listen to the loud voices that had come through the open door.

Then came the words that had utterly riveted him to the spot: "Mitch is the only one who can give me custody of EmJay . . . have to convince him . . . whatever means it takes . . . do anything to get her—anything . . . don't feel a thing for him. Not a thing."

Not a thing. It had all been a lie.

All the laughter, the good times. Even the Kiss-That-Never-Happened—the moment he'd replayed in his mind a hundred different ways. He knew he shouldn't be surprised, especially after her performance at the lake, but the idea pierced him to the core. He'd tried to leave before they'd come out, but he hadn't been quick enough.

A vision of her smile flashed in Mitch's mind. That smile, those eyes, they did something to him. They had awakened a part of him he hadn't been sure existed. But now here it was, appearing at a most inconvenient time.

One thing was certain: she'd only been in his life a week, but he almost couldn't recall a time when he didn't know her. It sounded ridiculous, even to himself.

What bothered him most was that he didn't know what was real and what wasn't. What about the bird watching? Her love for animals? Her supposed enthusiasm for his children's stories? Was it all a facade to convince him how wonderful she was?

He walked into his parents' chapel and searched out the bench on the far side where they customarily sat. His mouth opened in silent shock as he spied Cory seated next to his father, thumbing through the hymnal and looking beautiful in her finger-painting dress—this time paired with a mauve blouse. Her red-orange hair was full and curling in every direction exactly the way he loved it. Mitch blinked several times, but the image didn't disappear.

Emily Jane spotted Cory and began bouncing with excitement.

At that moment she looked their way, and her face froze as though she hadn't expected him—or hadn't wanted him to discover her here. Then she smiled.

Emily Jane waved. The minute Mitch arrived at the bench, she launched herself toward Cory. Only after several hugs was she enticed over to his father to search for mini Tootsie Rolls. Mitch's mother leaned over and gave her a kiss.

"Hi," Mitch whispered to Cory as he sat beside her at the end of the row, the only spot available without making everyone move.

"Hi."

"I didn't expect to find you here."

"I didn't expect to find you here, either."

Yeah, but I have a right to be here, he wanted to remind her. Yet didn't she also have that right? He looked past her to his parents.

His father smiled. "At the fireworks, we invited Cory to come see what a family ward is like. She was kind enough to accept."

Mitch glanced at Cory, who gave him a ghost of a smile.

"Moncree." Emily Jane had finished with Cameron and was reaching for Cory, her fist full of candy. Mitch sighed. He'd have to talk to his father about limiting it to one. After all, there would soon be dentist bills to worry about.

Emily Jane settled in Cory's lap, but she allowed only Mitch to open her candy. He broke each piece in half and put it in her mouth so she wouldn't soil her dress, pocketing the rest to throw away later.

Mitch loved the animation that imbued family wards, and he settled back, determined to enjoy the fast and testimony meeting, which always made him feel closer to his Heavenly Father. The meeting passed without incident, except near the beginning of the closing hymn—"Now Let Us Rejoice"—when Cory stopped singing abruptly and brought her hand to her right eye as though she had something lodged there.

"Are you okay?" he whispered, compelled to ask, though he almost wished she *did* have something there causing her pain.

She nodded but didn't look at him. She didn't sing the rest of the hymn, either, though she kept her eyes fastened on the page. Remembering how she'd reacted when he'd told her about Ashley's favorite hymn, he wondered if the hymn itself had provoked her reaction. Or maybe she was feeling the Spirit? Mitch could only hope.

Probably just wondering when she can get out of here, he thought dismally. *Or maybe the paint on the ceiling is peeling and fell into her eye. Wouldn't that be a great revelation for her?* He sent up a silent prayer, asking the Lord to touch her heart—and to calm his own apparent lack of faith.

"It's much different than a singles ward," Mitch said to her after the meeting.

She smiled, her eyes not showing the least bit red. "It's nice."

Nice. Mitch had the feeling that was all he was going to get from her.

"You two are coming over to lunch, aren't you?" his mother broke in.

Mitch nodded, but Cory shook her head. "I promised my friend I'd be home right after. She's leaving for California in the morning, so I really should spend the day with her." She smiled apologetically.

"We're just glad you could make sacrament meeting."

"Thanks for inviting me."

Mitch watched his father pat her hand before going on to Sunday School.

"I don't suppose you'd let me take EmJay with me?" Cory asked.

Mitch shook his head. "She needs to be here. We have to start indoctrination young, you know." He'd meant it as a joke, but Cory glared at him icily. She turned on her heel and was gone.

I am never coming back here again! Cory swore to herself, though she knew she would have to. But she would refuse to sing. She didn't need songs that reminded her of how often she had felt she was a stranger on earth. First there was AshDee's favorite hymn, and now came another song promising "no longer as strangers on earth need we roam." She had only to look to her Savior.

Look to her Savior? That's what her father had always said. *Speaking from his mouth but not his heart,* she thought acidly, though she knew that wasn't exactly fair. Her father had been a true believer. Was that why she was so against believing in God herself? Had the slaps, bruises, and terse words forever destroyed the part of her that longed for spiritual release? How had AshDee found it within herself to try religion again?

Because I protected her, that's why. For years I took the brunt of his anger. But she still left me all alone. Cory bit back tears as she slammed her car door shut. It wouldn't do to give in to them here.

A tapping on her car window startled Cory. She looked out to see Mitch, with his ever-present jacket thrown over his arm. She thought she saw a flash of dull green briefly emerge from one pocket, but she couldn't be sure.

With a sigh, she rolled down the window. "Yes?" Her voice came out raw and hoarse as though she had been crying.

"I didn't mean it, back there. I was joking."

He looked so absurd standing there with his head hung contritely and with EmJay clinging to him that she actually smiled. "I know that."

"I'd love for you to see Emily Jane today. She does need to be in church because I feel it's important that good habits start young, but I'll bring her over after lunch. You can keep her all afternoon if you like. I—I won't even stay."

She was stunned into silence.

"Unless you're too busy," he added. "With work, I mean."

"Actually, I was just putting together some of AshDee's photographs that I made from her negatives. Mostly of our time growing up. A little family history, you might say. You Mormons like family history, don't you?"

"So they say. I'm not old enough to worry about that yet." He smiled a slow, lazy smile that made her heart beat a bit more rapidly. Oh, how she wished she hadn't tried to work her first plan, that she hadn't let her guard down enough to actually care for him.

"How old *are* you?" she asked, her mouth dry.

"Twenty-five next month."

"I thought you were older."

He shook his head. "According to my mom, I should be long married by now. She knows how to put on the pressure."

"I can't believe that," Cory said, permitting herself another smile. "She's always so sweet—even when she was telling me she was going to keep EmJay while you were in the hospital." Of course, Cory had good reason to appreciate both his parents. By inviting her to church the other night at the fireworks, they had unwittingly aided her new plan.

"Don't let her fool you. She's tough."

"Well, at least she believed me when I said you'd told told me to take EmJay."

"Mom always knows when people are telling the truth. One of those learned mother things, I guess."

Cory swallowed hard. Could Jessica really know if she was telling the truth?

They fell into an uncomfortable silence. From the corner of her eye, Cory saw his jacket begin swinging, but she couldn't tear her eyes away from his to see what animal might emerge. She considered telling him she was going to join the Church, but in light of their discussion the day before, she couldn't do it. She suspected that he would see right through her bogus faith, and she wasn't eager for the recriminations that were sure to follow. Or could he actually believe in a sudden conversion?

Not that it mattered. She'd convinced Tyler and the missionaries, and that was the most important thing at this point. *Let Tyler tell him,* she thought. Though she had sworn Tyler to temporary secrecy, she didn't expect him to contain his enthusiasm long.

Her entire plan was already in motion. Her attorney hadn't been in the office the day before, but she had reached an assistant. When Cory had stressed how little time she had left in Utah—three weeks if she were to start her assignment on time—the assistant assured her he would call her back on Monday morning. Sometime in the next few weeks, Mitch would learn of her legal action.

Then the real problems would begin.

"So I'll bring her over later?" Mitch said, breaking the silence.

"Okay."

He turned to go.

Guilt consumed her. "Hey, Mitch?"

"Yeah?"

"Thanks."

He winked before sauntering across the parking lot, with EmJay waving over his shoulder. Cory wondered what he'd been like before EmJay had come into his life. She guessed that he really hadn't been much different. Children and a family had always been in his future—unlike hers. Lately, she'd begun to wonder if EmJay was the only chance she would ever have of being a mother.

Chapter Twenty-Three

The next week and a half went quickly for Mitch. He and Cory settled into a routine with Emily Jane that for all its smoothness was never quite free of the underlying knowledge that her time in Utah was growing short and that another confrontation was imminent. Mitch tried not to worry about it because he had legal custody, and it didn't seem likely Cory could change that. She hadn't even mentioned custody of Emily Jane since that fateful Saturday. Still, a black cloud seemed to hover just out of sight.

Cory took care of Emily Jane in the afternoons while Mitch worked at home, bringing her back before dinner. The first day he'd worried constantly and had checked outside to make sure her rental car was still there. It was. Next day the car was gone for a short while, but she brought the baby home on time. He stopped looking for her car. While Cory had Emily Jane, Mitch was able to get in five or six hours of work each day, squeezing in a few more hours at night after he put her to bed. He missed the baby when she wasn't around, but he also marveled at how easy it was to work without her little fingers "helping" on the keyboard.

Plus, Emily Jane was happy. Even so, Mitch felt torn. He knew

Emily Jane loved Cory deeply and looked for her when she wasn't around. Seeing them together made him wonder if he was wrong about not sharing custody, if Ashley had been wrong. Emily Jane no longer had dreams that caused her to awake in the night screaming for her mother. It was as though the longings for her mother, the ones that even Mitch's love hadn't been able to completely satisfy, had been alleviated by her growing attachment to Cory. Mitch was glad for this, though it made him worry more about the future and Cory's imminent departure for Brazil.

Only Mitch's firm testimony of the Church and his deep love for Emily Jane kept him from agreeing to joint custody. Emily Jane deserved a chance to know her Savior, and he worried that Cory's bitterness and unbelief would cause Emily Jane too much confusion and eventual heartbreak. Yes, Cory could give her a mother's love and the past of her family, but she couldn't nurture her testimony or help her find her way back to her celestial home. Only Mitch could do that. Lane and Ashley had been right—they must have been right!

In the end, it really didn't matter because Cory would soon be out of the country, and there was no way he would let her take Emily Jane with her. He hoped Emily Jane wouldn't suffer too much when she left. As for himself, he tried to stay aloof with Cory. Sometimes it worked.

Late on a Thursday afternoon, nearly two weeks after that fateful Saturday, Mitch was waiting for Cory to return with Emily Jane from a picture-taking jaunt to the mountains. Amanda, now eight months pregnant, dropped by to see him. He enthusiastically hugged Kevin and Mara before sending them in to see the animals.

"So what's up?" he asked Amanda, sensing there was a reason for her visit.

Amanda sank onto the couch. "Paula called to say she is coming to visit."

"The children's mother?" Mitch felt his stomach grow tight. "What did you say?"

"What could I say? She's their mother."

"She hasn't come for eighteen months. Why now?"

"Kevin's sixth birthday. I haven't told him because she's not reliable, but this time I think she means to follow through." Amanda rested her hands on her belly. "I just wish it wasn't right now. I'm a little emotional."

He sat beside her. "That's natural." Or so he'd heard.

"Mara won't even know who she is. *I'm* her mother. Kevin's, too. You should see the shy little smile he gives me every time he calls me that."

Mitch had seen that tremulous smile, and it was a joyous thing. "When's she coming, exactly?"

"A little over three weeks. What's that—about mid-August? Anyway, we didn't want her to come to the house. She's never been there, and we've gone to great lengths to make sure we're unlisted so she can't find us."

"Sure, she can come here," Mitch said, guessing what she wanted.

Amanda leaned over to hug him. "I knew you'd let us. I could have asked Kerrianne because she lives closer, but I keep remembering that Paula once threatened to burn down Blake's apartment. So in case it doesn't turn out well, I don't want Kerrianne bugged by her. Or Mom and Dad, either."

Mitch grinned. "But I'm okay to bug?"

"You're able to defend yourself." Amanda's brow furrowed. "You're not worried about Emily Jane, are you? That Paula coming here could somehow be bad for her?"

"Oh, no. If it came to that, I'm not in the least attached to this house. I could always move."

The phone in the kitchen rang, interrupting their conversation. "I'd better get that," he said. "Might be Cory. She's out with Emily Jane."

"I should check on the children anyway."

Mitch went into the kitchen. "Hello?" he said, half-expecting, half-hoping to hear Cory's voice. Instead, it was his boss.

Fifteen minutes later, he hung up the phone, feeling rather

stunned. He walked dazedly into the living room, nearly tripping over Kevin and Mara, who were sprawled on the floor with coloring books that Amanda must have brought for them—his sister was always pulling surprises from her purse.

"Who was it?" Amanda asked, looking up from a jumbled mass of white yarn in her lap.

"My boss."

"Good news? I know you've been worried about being fired."

He dropped to the couch. "Remember that report I had to turn in a few weeks back? The first one I did? Well, he called to say how well received it's been. Because of it, we got the funding he wanted, and then some."

"That's good, then." Amanda turned back to her yarn. Kerrianne was teaching her to knit a baby blanket, but apparently Amanda had no talent for it. The little bit she'd finished looked like a misshapen triangle.

Mitch ran his hand over his jaw. "They want to offer me a promotion."

"That's wonderful! What would you be doing?"

"I'd be working in the field in Montana, living in a tent miles from civilization. He said with all my wildlife studies and my zoology degree, I'm exactly what they need."

"Oh, Mitch!" Amanda dropped her needles and smiled at him. "Exactly what you've always wanted! I'm so happy for you. I mean, I'm going to miss you like crazy, but it's not forever, and Montana's not that far away. We'll visit a lot. More than a lot."

Mitch smiled sadly. "To think after all this time."

Her smile vanished. "Hey, I know that look. What'd you tell them? You didn't turn them down, did you?" Her green eyes were huge in her suddenly flushed face.

"Not yet. But I will."

"Now why on earth would you do that?"

"I couldn't take Emily Jane, and I won't leave her behind."

"Oh!" Amanda put her hand to her mouth. "I forgot. But I could watch her for you."

"For two years?" He shook his head. "It wouldn't be fair to your family or to Emily Jane. She needs at least one steady parent—not a weekend one. The only person I could leave her with is Cory, if things were different."

"You mean, if she were a member."

He sighed and sat back against the couch. "Women give up advancements all the time for the sake of their children. Why should I be any different?"

"I'm sorry, Mitch. Really sorry."

"Me, too, Uncle Mitch." Kevin had come to stand by him and patted him on the arm.

"Thanks, Kevin." Mitch hugged him, trying to squish his own stark disappointment into a remote corner of his mind. "Hey, do you guys want to hold some rabbits out back?"

That was where they were a few minutes later when Cory came through the side gate with Emily Jane in her arms. Mitch went to meet them, and Emily Jane clapped her hands and lunged toward him. "Whoa, girl," he said. "One of these days you might fall!" The baby giggled at his tone, and Mitch found himself grinning. He didn't feel as upset as he had even two minutes ago. Her smile had worked its usual magic. He had this beautiful, precious baby, and that was all that really mattered.

"Take a lot of pictures?" he asked Cory. She smiled up at him, and his chest tightened. She looked wonderful in blue jeans and green top, her hair as bright as ever.

"We had a great time," she said. "Your mountains are incredible."

"You should see them in the winter."

Emily Jane spied the children behind him and kicked to get down. Mitch kissed her cheek before releasing her. "I don't like the cold, but you haven't seen anything until you've seen snow fall among the trees up there." He followed Emily Jane across the lawn, Cory at his side.

"I'll bet it's better than a Christmas card," she said.

Amanda stood awkwardly from a lawn chair. "Hi, Cory," she called as they approached the patio.

"Hi." Cory shifted her weight several times, and Mitch wondered why his sister made her nervous.

"Mitch, dear, I should get going," Amanda said.

Mitch hugged his sister. "Let me know when you'll need the house."

"I will. But I think you ought to talk to your boss more about that job before you turn it down. They may have some accommodations you're not aware of. Promise?"

Mitch wished she hadn't brought it up in front of Cory, but he tried to act casual. "I will. Don't worry about it." He helped Amanda round up the children and get them into her van. When he finished, he returned to the backyard, where Cory and Emily Jane were playing with a white rabbit. He wondered why Cory didn't get up to leave but was glad she didn't.

"What new job were you offered?" she asked as he dropped onto the grass next to her.

"It's nothing."

"Your sister seemed to think it was important."

He picked up the escaping rabbit and held it closer to Emily Jane. "Listen," he said. "She learned a new word. Emily Jane, say *bunny*." Emily Jane grinned but didn't speak. "Oh, come on." Mitch shook his head in mock disgust.

"Is this job going to affect EmJay?"

Mitch sighed. Apparently Cory wasn't going to let it go.

"If so," she added, "I have a right to know."

Mitch wanted to question her right to know anything concerning him or Emily Jane. As far as he knew, she was still planning to leave Utah in little more than a week. He felt a sense of desperation at the thought. *Please stay with me*, he wanted to say. With him, not only with Emily Jane. But he knew he shouldn't even be thinking this way.

257

"It's a job in the field studying wolves," he said aloud.

Cory's face became animated. "That's wonderful, Mitch! When does it start?"

He looked away and plucked at the grass. "I'm not taking the job."

"Why not?"

Mitch was becoming irritated. What was it with these women? He decided what was best for Emily Jane—period. "I'm not going to do that to Emily Jane. I can't be away from her for two years."

Cory's face paled, making her freckles stand out more noticeably on her cheeks and nose. "EmJay could be with me."

"While you're out stomping around in a jungle?" Mitch faced her. "Come on, Cory. Let's be honest. You can take your job because you know you can leave her with me."

"That's not true!" Cory jumped to her feet, her fists clenched at her sides. "I'll do anything I can to have EmJay with me! Anything! But that doesn't mean I have to give up what I've worked so hard for all these years. Do you have any idea how many photographers I had to apprentice with to get where I am? How many overtime hours I worked? How often I risked disapproval from my own fa—" She broke off without finishing.

"I'm happy for you," Mitch retorted, looking up into her flushed face. "I really am. I'm glad you worked hard and got everything you wanted. I'll tell you what, I've worked hard, too. I've stuck it out at this job a whole year because I knew it could turn into something I really wanted, and believe me when I say that I'm still going to check out the options, but I think it's just not going to be right for me right now. That doesn't mean I won't have a chance to do something even better in the future."

She shook her head. "I think you're afraid. You're using Emily Jane as an excuse. And before EmJay, I bet you used something else. Didn't you? Was it your allergy to cold?"

She had come way too close with that blow. Memory came to him of a dozen times that he'd put off an idea for his career because of his allergy. Truthfully, he *had* allowed his illness to color his choices, but had his fear written him into this box? No, it wasn't a box yet. He wouldn't let it be.

"Face it," she continued. "You could have pursued another career, but you *chose* this one, even knowing the chances were that you might have to work behind a desk for most of your life."

His hands balled up in the grass. "Unlike you, I'm just beginning my career. Yes, I could take this job if I was married and had someone I trusted to look after Emily Jane while I was working. Or if I could leave her with you. But I can't. I don't have that luxury. And in the end, it really doesn't matter that much. Don't you see? I'm *willing* to do whatever it takes to give Emily Jane what she needs."

"I think you should take it," she challenged.

He rose slowly to his feet. "Why, because you would if you were me? Tell me, Cory, what comes after this photo shoot? Will you stay in the Amazon, or will you go to the next place *National Geographic* chooses to send you? What if that's in a country with civil unrest? What if you're gone months and months? Will they pay you enough to lose out on Emily Jane's life?"

"This is about religion again, isn't it!" Cory glared at him.

"Not really. It's about what it's all worth. It's one thing to be in the fast lane when it only involves you, but now there's Emily Jane. I'll tell you the truth—I really thought about taking that job. I thought about what it would mean to me and my career. But you know, I find that when it gets right down to it, I don't want the job. Not if it means putting my family at risk. And that's what Emily Jane is to me—family. She's *my* choice. While someday I might regret not having accepted the job for what it could have taught me, I have faith that I will never regret giving it up for Emily Jane. Yes, the gospel teaches us about priorities, but when it boils down to it, we're the only thing standing in the way of being with the ones we love."

Cory shook her head. "You are so infuriating!"

"Well, at least you're being honest now with your feelings," he retorted, "instead of batting your eyes and smiling sweetly at everything I say!" He meant it, too. He preferred arguing to her fake emotions. He preferred screaming from a distance to being close enough to smell her scent.

"Forget it!" With that she turned and started for the gate in the fence. But before she'd taken more than a few steps, Emily Jane stumbled after her. "Moncree! Moncree!"

Cory turned around and bent to hug the baby. Her eyes flitted to him briefly and then away again. Still fuming and not trusting himself to refrain from either yelling at her or taking her into his arms to kiss her, Mitch scooped up Emily Jane in one arm and the white rabbit in the other and started for the pens by the shed.

Cory was gone when he returned, and Mitch went into the house feeling mean and grouchy. What was with that woman, anyway? He tried to make a stable life for her niece, and all she did was challenge him at every turn.

He settled Emily Jane in the high chair and cut up little bits of meat, potatoes, and carrots for her dinner. Then he got out a bottle of pears and a baby spoon. When his doorbell rang, he tensed, unsure that he was ready to talk to anyone at the moment.

Tyler was at the door. "Hey," Mitch said. "Come on in."

"So," Tyler asked casually—too casually—as he followed Mitch back to the kitchen where the baby was making a big mess. "Have you talked to Cory lately?"

Mitch whirled on him. "She's impossible! I tell you, I'm really considering not letting her spend so much time with Emily Jane." He didn't mean it, but it felt good to say.

"You can't do that, not when it's going so well! If you're going to make trouble, can't it wait until after the baptism?"

The spoon Mitch held clattered to the linoleum. "What are you talking about?"

"You don't know?" Tyler's green eyes widened. "I thought . . . I mean, she told me not to tell you at first, but last night when we met with the missionaries, she said she'd tell you today."

"Tell me what!" Mitch growled. He grabbed his brother's T-shirt in his fist and pulled him close.

"She's getting baptized!" Tyler voice rose to a squeal as Mitch's hand tightened the neck on his shirt.

Mitch released him so fast that Tyler stumbled backward. "When? Why didn't you tell me?"

"She didn't want me to! Probably didn't want you to obsess about it. As for when, she decided on that Saturday after the Fourth. I think that whole bit with you being in the hospital and spending time with our family really helped."

Mitch rubbed his jaw, feeling smothered in heat. Perhaps that's why Cory had lingered after dropping Emily Jane off today—because she planned to tell him of her decision.

But what game is she playing? he wondered. It all came rushing back, their argument and his offer to share custody if she became a member. *But not like this. She was supposed to really mean it.*

He looked at Emily Jane in her high chair, so innocent and unaware of his turmoil. Was it lip service Cory planned to give to the Church, or had she really felt the Spirit and been converted? He believed whole-heartedly in miraculous conversions, but the timing indicated otherwise.

He gave a disgusted growl. "She's doing this to share custody."

Tyler shook his head violently. "No, I really think she means it. We had a little trouble with her the first couple times we met, but lately, it's been really smooth."

"Since that Saturday, I bet."

"Well, maybe."

Mitch nodded. "I still don't see how she thinks we can share custody if she's in Brazil." A ripple of fear shuddered up his spine. This was wrong. All wrong. He felt it more strongly than anything he'd ever felt before.

Yet he wanted to believe. If Cory had somehow recognized the truth, maybe there could be something more between them. Maybe he could explore the feelings that threatened to overcome him every time he saw her.

Tyler looked at him askance. "I'm sorry, Mitch. I thought you'd be excited about it. Look, I'd better get to Cory's. Savvy and the missionaries are meeting me there for her last lesson. I was going to ask you to come, but maybe you'd better not this time."

Mitch watched his brother back out of the kitchen and head for the door. He started to follow, but an impatient grunt from Emily Jane in the high chair prevented him. He took a deep breath and bent to pick up the spoon.

Could Cory's conversion be real?

He hoped so. *Oh, please, let it be real.* Maybe he should go to her. Maybe he should take her in his arms and tell her how he felt once and for all. She might have feelings for him, despite what she'd told Evan.

He was pulling Emily Jane from the high chair when the phone rang. He hurried to the counter to pick it up. "Hello?"

"Son, where've you been? I called three times. I left a message."

"Sorry, Dad, I was outside. Amanda was over." The baby in his arms kicked to get down, and Mitch placed her by the toy piano his mother had bought.

"Look, I got a call from our lawyer. He tried to call you several times as well, but there wasn't an answer, and he was leaving for the weekend."

The fear he'd experienced earlier with Tyler turned into a shiver of dread. "What's happened?"

"Late this afternoon, Cory's lawyer filed a petition for a custody change based on some wording in the Grayson's will. Unfortunately, our lawyer thinks she might actually have a shot."

"But those papers are solid! He said so. Cory's lawyer even said so."

"Apparently there was a part that mentioned a possible change in custody if Cory were to become a member of the Church."

Mitch's fear was a lead ball in his stomach. "Tyler was just here," he said without emotion. "Cory has been seeing the missionaries. She told them she wants to be baptized."

There was a brief silence on the phone and then, "I was afraid something like that would happen." His father let out a long sigh. "Our lawyer said that we can argue that the change would have to happen while your friends were alive. Plus, the estrangement between Ashley and Cory gives us a lot of weight. Since the courts are reluctant to change status quo, especially when the child is doing so well and has so much support, we have an excellent case. Still, there is always the possibility you might lose."

Mitch couldn't believe her methods, but at least he was getting what he wanted—Cory was becoming a member.

Even if she doesn't mean it?

He shook the thought away. Aloud, he said, "So you're saying there's a good possibility I might have to share custody." He thought it overkill that she was going through a lawyer when he had already promised to share custody if she joined the Church.

"No, Mitch," his father said. "You don't understand. She isn't asking to share custody. She is suing for full custody."

A moment of shocked disbelief filled Mitch's heart, followed swiftly by burning anger. Fury. How could she do this to him? He'd been so nice to her, allowing her to see Emily Jane, even giving her time alone.

"Son?" came his father's voice.

"I feel so . . . betrayed," Mitch managed to say through the hurt and anger.

"Well, let's look at the good side. She *is* getting baptized. And that means she'll have to listen and learn, to make a good showing for the court. There's always the chance that her heart will be softened."

Mitch didn't bet on it. He knew she'd planned this all along. He picked up Emily Jane and hugged her tight, tears leaking from the orners of his eyes.

Chapter Twenty-Four

Tonight was Cory's last official meeting with the missionaries, though they assured her they would continue to visit after she was baptized on Saturday. Cory didn't really care. EmJay was all the commitment she needed.

Her attorney had advised her to wait to file legal papers until after her baptism, but Cory couldn't wait. She had been able to delay her job with *National Geographic* for a few weeks and could possibly delay it longer, but she was hoping not to do that. If necessary, she'd go to the Amazon and spend some of her exorbitant wages to fly back for any custody hearings. She had conceded to the attorney's wishes by a week so that while the papers were filed when she was not a member, she would be one when she appeared at the initial hearing. The attorney had also expressed a concern that the judge might not like the idea of her taking EmJay out of the country. Cory decided to face that challenge if and when it came.

"Tyler's back," Elder Savage said, coming into the kitchen where she was eating a piece of toast to tide her over until they left and she could have dinner. "Should we begin?"

"Let's wait until Savvy gets here."

He nodded and went back to the living room. She could hear them talking and joking together like the boys they were. Amazing that they considered themselves messengers of God.

Yet sometimes Cory found herself forgetting their inexperience as well. They seemed so sure at times, so forceful. Still, whatever else she must do, she refused to allow them to dictate her internal spirituality. She'd done that with her father for too long.

Not AshDee. No, her sister had managed to get free despite their father, and in a way had freed Cory as well, since her father's death was hastened by her traumatic departure. But that didn't mean AshDee had found the truth.

Still, there was *something* about this gospel. Something about the people—about Mitch and his family. And especially the choice Mitch had made regarding his job with seemingly little consideration.

She wished it was all over. In the past two days, she'd begun having serious misgivings. There were so many things she felt were right, like covenants and eternal families, and when the missionaries weren't throwing around their complete assurances, which often irritated her, she could feel a longing to believe. It was hard to forget her father's derision of the Mormons and her own doubt that God existed. Always clouding the issue was her relationship with Mitch and the eagerness with which she looked forward to seeing him each day. Yet she couldn't allow his belief to sway her. She had to stay focused on her plan: get baptized, get custody, leave for Brazil, and never look back. That way no one could take EmJay from her again.

There was a slight commotion in the living room before someone burst into the kitchen. "There you are!"

She looked up to see Mitch glaring at her, EmJay in his arms. Her heart turned over in her chest. She could almost imagine him striding across the kitchen to sweep her into his arms. But even if he tried something like that, which he wouldn't, she couldn't allow it to happen. There was simply too much at stake.

She stood up from the table to meet him. *He's heard from his lawyer,* she thought. All week she'd been waiting, knowing he would be furious.

"I can't believe it," he gritted. "First you lead them on"—he motioned to the missionaries and Tyler, who framed the door behind him—"about wanting to be baptized, and now you want to take Emily Jane away from me! Why, Cory? Why? I was willing to share, but you apparently don't feel the same." His face was flushed, his eyes furious.

Cory took a deep breath. *Stay calm,* she warned herself. "Uh, could you guys leave us alone for a minute?" she asked the others. "I'm sure my neighbor wouldn't mind if you shot a few baskets."

They nodded and disappeared from the doorway, but Tyler hesitated. "Go, Tyler," Mitch ordered.

"It's okay, Tyler," Cory said. "I didn't get a chance to tell him about the baptism when I was over there earlier. I'll explain now." With a last glance at Mitch, Tyler followed the missionaries.

EmJay pushed against Mitch's chest in an effort to be released. When he set her down, she toddled over to Cory, who gave her a small piece of her toast.

"Well?" he demanded, sounding angry but calmer than before. "And I'm not here about your so-called conversion. I want to know why you're trying to get full custody."

She met his steady gaze. "Since I'm going to be out of the country, it would be hard to share custody, wouldn't it?"

"So you think you'll just take her and leave?" He took several steps toward her. "What about what your sister wanted?"

"I'm joining the Church. That is what you both wanted, isn't it?"

"Not if you don't mean it!"

She folded her arms across her waist. "So you are the judge."

"We both know you're not serious. If you were, you wouldn't have gone behind my back. You would be seriously studying—"

"How do you know I'm not studying?"

"Because I'd feel it!"

"You'd *feel* it! Give me a break, Mitch!"

He shook his head. "See? That's exactly what I mean! You have no respect for our beliefs. You don't understand the seriousness. You're playing with things that should not be mocked. Cory, this is real! It's true! But you're using it to get what you want. Never mind how your sister felt. Never mind what's right for Emily Jane."

"I'm doing what I feel is right for EmJay!"

"Are you?" he demanded. "Or are you too busy feeling guilty at what you did to your sister to even think about what's right for her baby?"

Cory clenched her fists. "What do you mean, what I did to my sister? She left us!"

"You betrayed her! Just like you're doing now."

Resentment filled Cory's entire being. "You don't know anything!"

"Maybe," he allowed, his chin set firmly, "but don't for a minute think I'm going to sit idly by while you waltz off to Brazil with Emily Jane. I'll fight you every step of the way."

"Go ahead and try!"

Mitch looked ready to lash out, but she knew he wouldn't physically hurt her. He wasn't that kind of man. Still, she certainly seemed to bring out the worst in him. *The worst and the best,* she admitted, remembering how kind he had been in days past when comforting her about AshDee—and how he'd recently allowed her to spend one-on-one time with EmJay.

"It's still not too late," Mitch said, almost in a whisper. She could tell the words came at great cost. "You can drop the custody suit. We'll work something out between us. As for the Church, you can take it slow. Give it a real chance. You have to work to gain a testimony. Please, Cory. I have no doubt you'll gain a testimony. The gospel really is true."

His pleas threatened to break down the walls she had struggled to build this past week. She couldn't allow that to happen. She couldn't lose herself. She made her voice icy. "You also once said it was simple which sort of implies that I'm stupid because I don't get it like you do.

Well, guess what, Mitch, I'm not stupid. And the bottom line is, church or no church, EmJay and I *need* each other more than anything else."

He blinked, and for a clear instant Cory could tell that her words hurt him deeply. "Did you ever think for even one minute," he asked, his voice so calm and reasonable that she wanted to hit him, "that Emily Jane may need me, too? That *you* may even need me? Did you ever consider that I'm trying to convert you not for my sake but for yours?"

"That's *exactly* what I'm saying, Mitch. I don't think you're looking at me or EmJay as people. I think you're trying to save us as you have all your little animals. But I'm not a helpless animal, and neither is EmJay. We don't need saving."

"We all need saving," Mitch said, his eyes pleading with her. "Especially me. Please, Cory, don't shut me out this way."

"I know what you're trying to do. You're trying to get me to stay here so you can see EmJay. To get me to give up what I've worked for all my life. Well, I won't do it. And I won't give up EmJay, either. I have nothing more to say to you."

But she did. There was a lot she wanted to say. About her experiences while learning the gospel, and how she felt about him. She wished she could weep and fall into his arms, but that would be giving him too much power over her life—her spirituality—and she couldn't permit that.

"Emily Jane?" Mitch's face grew suddenly pale, his eyes darting around the kitchen. "Emily Jane!" He ran into the living room.

Cory's heart took a sudden dive. "EmJay?"

"Not in here!" Mitch called. "Front door's open."

Cory ran after him. "She might be in one of the bedrooms."

"Look there. I'll check outside."

She ran into each of the bedrooms, her heart pounding. Surely EmJay would be there.

No baby.

Beginning to feel frantic, she ran outside where Mitch was talking to Tyler and the missionaries under the basketball hoop next door. They were shaking their heads.

"I'll check around back." Cory ran. From the corner of her eye, she saw the missionaries, Tyler, and Mitch split and go up the street, calling for EmJay.

Her backyard was empty. Next, she checked each of her neighbors' backyards. Still nothing. With each passing moment, Cory's worry grew. How could she have let this happen? How could she have been so negligent? It was her fault. She knew that. She'd caused the tension and arguments with Mitch. Before she had come, the worst thing that had happened to EmJay was ingesting small amounts of gerbil food and paper—neither of which was likely to cause her permanent harm.

Guilt lay heavy on her shoulders. "Please, AshDee," she said. "Help me find EmJay." Tears slid down her face, making it hard to see. She wiped them away.

The missionaries were coming back down the street, and Mitch was talking to a neighbor. Other neighbors had joined the search. Feeling an odd pull to the house, Cory went back inside. She checked under the beds and in the bathroom. She even peeked inside the closed mudroom where she still had photographs drying on the lines she'd extended.

She went outside again. Minutes ticked by. Nothing.

Mitch returned to her front yard. "She's not at my house. I called the police. They'll be here soon."

"Could someone have taken her?"

Mitch shook his head. "Who? Why?"

Cory ran over a list in her mind. The only person she could think of that might have something against her was Evan, but he was long gone on his writing assignment. Besides, she doubted he was that angry at her.

A small red car came down the street. "Savvy," Cory breathed. "Maybe she's seen her."

They both ran toward the car, but Savvy was shocked when they explained what had happened. "I didn't see her," she said. "But I'll help look."

The entire neighborhood was crawling, as more and more people joined in the search. A police siren signaled the arrival of the authorities. Immediately, they took Cory and Mitch aside for questioning. "How old is Emily Jane? Can she manage stairs? How long has she been missing? Has she ever run away before?"

Cory felt impatient at all the questions. *Why don't they do something?* As Mitch answered them, she drifted away, again feeling drawn toward the house. An officer caught up to her. "I need to check the house."

"I've checked it twice, but I was going to do it again."

The officer went with her, searching in closets, behind her suitcase, in the bathtub, in the cabinets beneath the sinks, and in many other places Cory hadn't thought to look. Wouldn't EmJay answer if she were here?

Yet Cory had felt drawn toward the house.

The officer moved to the mudroom. "The door was closed," she said. "She couldn't have gone in there."

He shrugged. "Can't tell you how many times my toddler keeps shutting himself in the bathroom." The room received little light from the kitchen, so he turned on the wall switch. The first place he looked was inside the ancient dryer the previous occupants had left. Then he turned toward a pile of dirty clothes. "Ah," he said.

Cory craned her neck, wondering what was so interesting in her dirty laundry. Her breath caught in her throat as she saw EmJay curled up in Cory's dress—her finger-painting dress, as Mitch called it—sound asleep. The skin around her eyes was slightly red, as though she'd been crying.

She must have shut herself in while we were arguing. We didn't hear her. Remorse filled Cory's heart as she gathered the sleeping baby into her arms, dress and all. "Thank you," she whispered to the officer. "Thank you so much."

He smiled. "No problem. I wish every missing child report could end so happily. I'll go inform your husband and the others."

Cory nodded, not bothering to correct him. She sat on the floor and rocked EmJay. The weight in her arms felt like a blessing.

Had she really felt drawn to the house? Was it AshDee? Or was it the Spirit the missionaries kept talking about? Tears rolled down her cheeks.

"Cory." Mitch came into the room, followed by Tyler and Savvy. "Could you give us a moment?" he asked them. They nodded, and he shut the door behind him.

"She was here all along," Cory whispered. "She'd been crying." Her eyes rose from EmJay's to his. "I felt she was in the house. All along, I felt her here."

She could see by his solemn expression that he believed her—or at least wanted to. He knelt next to her on the tile floor, close enough so that if she moved a little, their knees would brush. "And what do you think told you?"

"I don't know." Cory suddenly felt weary. "I know what you want me to say, and I admit that all your talk about the gospel sounds so logical, so reasonable. But I've lived long enough to know that something is almost never what it seems in the beginning."

"You'll know the truth in your heart, if you search for it." Mitch's voice was soft and compelling, his eyes intense. "Oh, Cory, I want more than anything for you to know it's true."

"I can't be what you want," she said, feeling strangled. "When I'm with you, I want to believe—and that's not fair to me."

"What are you saying?"

Cory hated the note of hope in his voice. "I'm saying that my feelings for you confuse the issue. How can I know if I believe in your church or in you? Maybe I'm just taking the path of least resistance."

He gave a snort. "Doesn't sound like you." He reached out to her then, and her limbs went weak. His arms closed around her shoulders, and his face came close. Cory put her lips to his and returned his kiss.

There was something so right about his touch. Emotions flooded her senses, and she knew that she loved this man. Loved him completely and totally. More even than she loved EmJay or her job. Enough, in fact, to put aside her concerns about whether or not his church was true and follow him blindly.

"Cory," he murmured against her lips.

No! she agonized. *I won't spend the rest of my life wondering if it's really true, or if I did it because of you and EmJay.* She pulled away. "Leave me alone, Mitch. Just leave me alone." With that, she laid the sleeping baby in his arms, scrambled to her feet, and ran to the door.

"What about Emily Jane?" he called after her.

Cory was asking herself the same question. She didn't know. She didn't know anything right now except that she had suddenly awakened to the stark reality that she wasn't better than Mitch to raise EmJay. All along he'd been willing to put EmJay first, while Cory had thought to make the baby fit into her lifestyle. He had also willingly agreed to share EmJay with Cory because that was what was best for the baby, while Cory had only wanted to free her niece from his grasp and whisk her away to the Amazon where EmJay would forget that he and his family even existed, never mind the bond between them. This last ached the most—knowing that had Cory been given her way, she would have compounded EmJay's loss of her parents with the loss of Mitch. How could she have been so blind and so terribly, terribly cruel?

Cory kept running.

And running.

She didn't stop running until she was back in the Amazon.

Chapter Twenty-Five

Cory didn't show up for her baptism on Saturday. Tyler and the missionaries were discouraged, but Mitch was glad. Maybe this meant she was finally taking the gospel seriously. If so, she might someday be able to accept both him and the gospel in her life.

Maybe.

Savvy received her mission call to San Francisco, California, and after Cory's no-show, Tyler called to ask Mitch if he could bring Savvy over for a celebration barbecue on Monday night. "Sure," Mitch readily agreed. "The birds are gone now. I'll make my best teriyaki chicken." He'd keep some fish handy, too, in case Cory came around to see the baby.

On Sunday night, Mitch went over to her rental house and knocked on the door, but she didn't answer. He hadn't seen her since she ran off in her car the day Emily Jane had disappeared. He felt confident that wherever she'd gone, she would soon come back to see Emily Jane. Whatever her feeling toward him and the gospel, she loved the baby, of that much he was certain.

Mitch's first indication that Cory wasn't coming back was the manila envelope the mailman delivered Monday afternoon, filled with pictures of Cory's little monkey friend, Meeko. Over the past three weeks, she had recounted many of the creature's exploits, and Mitch had already written a story for Emily Jane about a monkey who lived in the Amazon near a wildlife conservation camp. His story was hilarious at times, even to Mitch, though he was sure it would never be heard or appreciated by anyone outside his family.

He thumbed through the pictures with excitement—Meeko looking surprised with an upturned bottle of shampoo, Meeko swinging down from a tree, Meeko wearing a pair of headphones, and many more. His favorite was of Meeko balancing atop some kind of small horse.

His smile faded when he saw the short note, stuck in behind the pictures, as though Cory wanted to offer him an apology before breaking his heart.

Mitch:

I've gone back to work. I need space. Please, please, whatever you think of me, tell EmJay I love her. I do love her more than I can say. That's why I'm leaving. You're right, she's better off with you for now. You have so much support, so much love for EmJay. I grew up feeling alone, except for AshDee, and I don't want EmJay to ever feel that way. You have a wonderful family.

I have to figure things out for myself. I can't believe just because you say so. AshDee's picture albums are at the rental house. I'll be in touch. Sorry. Please tell Tyler I'm sorry, too.

Cory

Stunned, he slumped to sit in the open doorway, one ear listening for Emily Jane, even as he tried to take in the information. How could she leave? After making both him and Emily Jane love her, how could she go without even saying good-bye?

This is good-bye, he thought, hefting the envelope.

He still didn't understand. He felt like running into the middle of the street and screaming out his hurt. Mitch shut his eyes tightly, fighting the pain inside his heart. One tear escaped.

As he heard Emily Jane's voice from the bedroom, he wiped it away and went inside. She'd crawled up onto his bed from her small one and was now eating a tissue from the box he had left on his nightstand. Spying him, she quickly swallowed what was in her mouth and shoved in the rest.

Gently, he fished the soggy tissue from her mouth and picked up her little body, cradling her. "Good morning, sweetie. Why didn't you get out by yourself? I know, you wanted me to come and hold you. Well, here I am. I'm not leaving. I promise."

As he spoke, anger slowly replaced the hurt in his heart. *How dare Cory leave her. How dare she!*

Well, he wasn't going to put up with it. He wanted a better explanation than she'd given in that stupid letter. He wanted to know if she still wanted to share custody, if she was planning on coming back. He wanted to take her in his arms and tell her he loved her.

"Let's get dressed," he said to Emily Jane. "My passport's still valid, but we need to get one for you. I wonder how fast we can have it expedited?"

"Look, Vikki, I just want to know where she is exactly," Mitch said into the phone Monday after visiting the post office for Emily Jane's passport. "Please. The baby really misses her." The return address on the envelope was California, and Mitch suspected that Cory had gone to see Vikki before returning to Brazil.

"For what it's worth," Vikki said, "she should be back within a few months. She has oodles of photographs already. Really incredible ones. In fact, I've an appointment next week to go over the ones she's already taken with the folks at *NG*. I think they'll have more suggestions— especially when their writers start digging their teeth into their articles—but it shouldn't be a long project."

"Two months is a lifetime to a baby." Mitch was glad his emotions had become numb or he might embarrass himself by sobbing.

"I know. But it's a good thing she didn't take her."

"She didn't really have a choice. I still have custody."

"And she really left without saying good-bye?"

"She mailed me a note and some photographs of her pet friend. They're for a story I wrote for the kids."

"Story?"

"Yeah. Nothing much. Just a story about some animals."

"She told me about your stories."

Mitch was surprised. "When?"

"On Saturday morning when she was getting on the plane for Brazil."

Mitch swallowed hard, wondering if he would always taste the bitterness when he heard the name of the country that had been so dear to him on his mission. "Are you going to give me the address or not?"

"Sure, I'll give you the address of the camp where she's staying," Vikki said. "She should be there if she hasn't moved. Might be better to e-mail her, though. She bought equipment to e-mail me from wherever she is, so you can contact her that way."

"What I have to say, I want to say in person." Even then, he wasn't sure it was going to do any good.

"Well, keep the e-mail handy in case you can't find her at the camp. The Amazon is a big place."

"I'll be able to find her."

"What about your, um, allergy? Is it safe for you to travel?"

"Don't worry, I lived in Brazil for two years with only minor problems."

He wrote down the address, thanked her, and was about to hang up when she said, "Hey, about that story. Cory's photographs have gained an excellent reputation, you know, and with them your story could maybe go somewhere. I'm not a literary agent, but I have connections. Could you e-mail me the story?"

Mitch was startled into laughter. "I guess, but my brother tells me curious monkeys have been beaten to death as a children's book subject."

"Well, it depends on the angle. If they actually teach something about animals, as well as entertain, then they can be classified as a sort of nonfiction. There's a good market for that."

Mitch didn't really believe anything would come of it, but Vikki was nice to ask. "I'll think about it. I have your e-mail address on your card."

"Well, good luck, Mitch. If it matters, I liked you a lot better than that wimp Evan."

"Thanks—I guess."

Mitch hung up the phone and stared at the address in his hands.

"I just don't see how she could leave EmJay," Mitch said on Monday night to Tyler and Savvy. He'd wanted to cancel the barbecue when he discovered Cory had gone back to Brazil, knowing he was too wrapped up in his own misery to be good company, but after dealing with the baby's passport, talking with Vikki, and checking on flights to Brazil, there hadn't been time to call Tyler. But it was just as well; he wanted to know what they thought of his plan to go after her.

"EmJay?" Tyler asked from his place at the picnic table. "Since when did you decide to call her that?"

He shrugged. "I didn't. It sort of keeps coming out."

"I like it," Savvy said, tickling EmJay, who was on her lap nibbling on a roll.

"EmJay's been looking for her," Mitch continued, waving a spatula. "She walks all around the house searching like she did when she first came here. I know she's looking for Cory now. And she had a nightmare last night." He sighed. "It was horrible."

"Poor baby." Savvy hugged EmJay, who didn't return her embrace but bore it gravely as though she understood every word.

Mitch placed the last bit of cooked chicken on the serving plate and walked toward the table. "That's why we're going after her. As soon as EmJay's passport arrives."

Tyler blinked. "You're what? Are you crazy?"

Mitch banged the plate of meat on the table with more intensity than he intended. "I'm *not* going to let EmJay lose another mother!"

"Cory's *not* her mother," Tyler retorted, "and doesn't deserve to be if this is how she acts."

"She does too!" Mitch knew he was bordering on shouting, but he didn't care. "You don't know her like I do. It's me who drove her away. Me! She thinks I'm forcing the gospel on her. She says she can't think with me around."

"You?" Tyler arose and glared at Mitch across the short expanse of table. "Is that what this is all about? Obviously, you have a thing for her. Well, I think you're better off without her. She's never going to make you a good wife."

"You're just mad because she lied to you."

Tyler shrugged. "To me, to everyone. The bottom line is, she had all the missionary discussions. She just doesn't *want* to believe. Face it, Mitch, she's gone. She made her choice. Isn't it better she left before you and EmJay were really attached? At least now you can find someone who will stick around."

Mitch didn't want to find someone else. He wanted Cory. He couldn't think of anything but her crazy orange hair and all those freckles. "I should have been at the discussions!" he said, pounding the table. "Maybe I could have helped."

"No, you couldn't." Savvy shook her head. "Now will you two calm down? You're scaring EmJay."

Sure enough, the baby was staring at them with huge eyes, looking ready to burst into tears. Mitch felt immediately chastened. "Hey, sweetie, I'm sorry. Come here. I'm not mad. Come to me." EmJay held out her arms to him, smiling tentatively. Mitch lifted her into his arms and sat down at the table. "Maybe I could have helped Cory learn the truth, if I'd known about the lessons."

Savvy slid a piece of chicken onto her plate. "I think this is something she has to do herself. You should have seen the way she reacted to Tyler and the missionaries when they kept pushing her to admit to her feelings. She'd bite her nails and say nothing, or repeat back exactly what they said."

"Sounded good to me," Tyler said.

Savvy shrugged. "Anyway, she didn't seem to want anyone telling her how to feel. And a good thing, too. She needs to find out how *she* feels."

Tyler propped his chin up on one hand. "I'm sorry, Mitch. I wanted the discussions to be a good surprise for you. Only it didn't work out that way."

"Maybe not." Savvy reached for the bag of potato chips. "Or maybe she just needs a little time. Isn't that what she said in her letter?"

"At least she dropped the custody suit." Mitch smoothed EmJay's hair, thinking of Cory's similar locks. "But it's not like her to leave like that. I know she loves EmJay. You should have seen her that day we thought we lost her. She was frantic."

"Amen," Tyler said.

Savvy nodded. "That's why I think you should give her time. She'll come back. If it's not her choice, she'll always wonder if she did it for you and EmJay."

At her words something fell into place for Mitch. "This is because of her father, isn't it? AshDee never really talked about him, but Cory said a few things that got me wondering what kind of man he was. From what I could gather, he basically ruled her life."

"I don't really know," Savvy answered. "But that could affect her thinking, even now."

Mitch let out a long sigh. "Yeah, I guess so."

What made him angry was that he had been so intent on either fighting with Cory or preaching to her that he hadn't bothered to discover what might be holding her back. Even the few times that she had begun to open up to him about her family, he had taken her statements at face value without delving for the whole story. He wished he could have another chance. He had wasted so much time. He should have acted. He shouldn't have hidden his feelings away in the hopes that she wouldn't trample them. What was a little trampling when he might have lost her forever?

"So you think I shouldn't go to Brazil?"

Savvy gave him a sympathetic smile. "Not unless she wants you to."

"What about EmJay?"

Tyler, who had been silent for the last little while, spoke up. "Maybe it's okay for her to leave EmJay. I mean, Cory knows the baby has you, so maybe it's okay that she goes away for a while to think things over. It might be good for both of you. Maybe everything will work out in the end."

Mitch was about to congratulate his brother for saying one of the most thoughtful things he'd ever said, when he realized Tyler wasn't looking at him but at Savvy.

"Bash da bash. Much ken." EmJay was reaching for the chicken on his plate.

Mitch stifled the longing inside his heart. "Okay," he said, breaking off pieces for EmJay. "I'll wait a little longer. But if I don't hear from her soon, I'll—" He broke off. He didn't know what he'd do. What *could* he do?

Nothing. Nothing but pray.

Oh, Cory! he thought. *Where are you now?*

Chapter Twenty-Six

C ory's legs were beginning to ache. She shifted her position in the
tree slightly, knowing that at any moment the sun would begin
creeping up behind the waterfall in front of her, and she would
take what might be the best photographs of her entire life. This time it
wasn't an animal she awaited, but nature herself: God's creation.

The irony was that before her time in Utah, here in the jungle was
the only place she'd felt she belonged, but now that sense of belonging, that sense of oneness with the land, was completely absent. She
was again a stranger, and that broke her heart more than it had already
been broken. Even Meeko had deserted her today.

In the three weeks she'd been back in the Amazon, she had thrown
herself into her work, rising with the sun and going to bed after dark.
Memory card after memory card filled with pictures for *National
Geographic*. Her best work ever. But to what end?

Maybe she was still running.

She didn't care to examine her motives too closely. All she knew
was that Mitch and EmJay had completely transformed her life, and she
wasn't sure she was ready for such a change.

Was the gospel true?

She wanted it to be. With all her wounded heart she wanted it to be. She wanted to feel that God loved her. That Jesus had died for her sins. That she could be reunited with her sister and her mother again. Moreover, she wanted to love Mitch and EmJay forever.

But she wasn't sure. Did God exist? Did He have a plan for her? Or did loneliness drive her to want to believe a fantasy? Was she only investigating the Church to gain custody of EmJay? Was she becoming serious about it because of her growing feelings for Mitch?

How she missed him now! She wished she could talk with him about her uncertainty toward the gospel, but he would probably tell her how much *he* knew it to be true. Her knees would go weak, and she'd follow him as blindly as she'd followed her father.

Mitch isn't my father. If I didn't agree, he wouldn't force me.

Mitch was everything her father hadn't been, that was true. Was that how her sister had felt about her husband? Cory hoped so.

"Maybe I'm so worried about being taken in that I can't see the truth." Her words drifted through the branches of the trees, unheard by anyone but herself. Herself and maybe God—if He existed.

The missionaries had told her to pray. So had Tyler and Savvy. But only Savvy had understood her reluctance. What if it all *was* true? Did that mean Cory had to give up everything she'd worked for?

Mitch had apparently given up his chance at a new career without second thoughts. *I've come too far for that,* Cory told herself. The empty part of her heart mocked the words.

She shut her eyes as a tear escaped and slid down her cheek. More than anything in the world, she wished at that moment to hold EmJay. To see her grin, to feel her little arms around her neck. But she had given that up. For what? For pictures in a prestigious magazine. To see her name in the credits and be honored by her peers. She had thrown away love for something that would only leave her wanting more.

"This is what Mitch knew," she whispered. "That love was more important than pictures or chasing wild animals. He knew. Oh, what have I done?" She tried to tell herself that her assignment was almost over, that she would be back with EmJay soon. And then what? Mitch had asked the question once. Would she accept the next assignment? What about EmJay? What was Cory willing to do to be in EmJay's life?

Cory felt more confused than ever, especially now that the jungle held no answers. She'd thought coming back here would make things clear, but her confusion was worse. How could something that had once been her only salvation, something that had been the only "right" thing in her life, now be so wrong? How could she no longer belong to her work?

She had been praying. She had prayed about the Book of Mormon. She had prayed about Joseph Smith. All of it made sense to her. She felt warmth in her heart when she prayed. But all that meant to her was that the gospel was a beautiful concept. One thing was certain: her father wouldn't approve. She wasn't sure if that knowledge helped or hindered her quest to know the truth.

"AshDee," Cory whispered. "I need to know if it's true. Will you help me? Please, God, if You really are there, if You really love me, let me know." A part of Cory thought how odd it was for her to be up a tree at a remote jungle site, two cameras around her neck, poised for the picture of a lifetime; yet instead of thinking about the shot, she was praying, her eyes open and searching for an answer. "Oh, God, please."

The sun's rays touched the horizon and slowly inched up the sky, forever changing the world with its light. Cory knew that without the sun, the world wouldn't simply be drab and meaningless but devoid of all life.

Light spread farther into the sky, gently fingering the thin clouds poised in wait above the horizon. The tendrils of light tangled with the cloudy wisps, infusing the entire sky with a myriad of colors that were achingly beautiful to behold. This beauty reflected from the pool of clear, clean water at the base of the waterfall, calling out an invitation to any who would answer.

Cory identified the moment she should have begun snapping

photographs, but she didn't reach for a camera. She sat silently, her soul filled with the same vibrant, life-giving light that colored the sky.

My life was like the dark, she thought. *Before God. Before the gospel.*

Love wrapped around her like a familiar blanket. Of course she no longer belonged alone in the jungle. She belonged to God. She belonged with her family. She wasn't a stranger on earth but a child searching and growing, a woman learning to let go of the past and recognize truth. A woman who needed to trust, and especially to love.

Cory didn't take the picture, though she knew it was probably the most incredible sunrise she would witness in her life. Even if she were to wake early every morning and search the world over, there could never be another one to rival it. God had answered her prayer. This moment was for her and only her. The beauty was forever engraved on both her heart and her soul.

Tears slid down her cheeks, but they were happy tears. God existed and He loved her—and that meant AshDee *was* indeed waiting for her in the "next room" as the Huntingtons had implied. God had devised a plan for them to be reunited!

"Forgive me, AshDee, for being so stubborn," she whispered.

Yes, it was she, Cory, who needed forgiveness. She hadn't cared about the new gospel or the joy her sister had found. She had refused to see anything but betrayal. She understood now. *If only . . .*

But regrets belonged to the past, and Cory had room only for the future. She let herself become lost in the beautiful sunrise, marveling at how easily her mind now grasped the concepts that had been so difficult a short time before. The gospel had altered her; she would never be the same—would never *want* to be the same.

Long after the sun sat high among the clouds, Cory urged her stiff legs to climb down the tree. Her movements frightened a small tree squirrel in the brush below, and the creature moved lightning fast through the greenery. Cory lifted her face to the sun and laughed.

Walking back to camp, she considered her next move. For it was her move—she understood that now as she had so much else. Even at the rate she'd been working, a proper job on the photos might take another month.

Unless she didn't stay.

Suddenly, she discovered that her success here meant little to her. Mitch had been right. The choice wasn't between her niece or her work but rather a choice for love that permitted her more opportunities for joy. It meant finding something she loved and could do while raising EmJay. It also meant being with Mitch, if he could forgive her. Could he? If anyone could, it would be Mitch.

Back at her tent, she sent an e-mail to him. She'd written many others before but hadn't sent even one. After five tries, she finally wrote something that conveyed her message without exposing her heart more than she could bear. Her heart, once broken but newly patched by her Savior, was still fragile.

Hi, Mitch,

I've just had the most incredible experience and realize that I've been such a fool about so many, many things! Will you baptize me when I return? I'm sure there's someone here who could do it, but I don't speak the lingo. Kiss EmJay for me and tell her I love her more than any photographs I could ever, ever take. I can't wait to hold her in my arms.

Love,
Cory

Mitch took the napkin away from EmJay and gave her instead the small album he'd bought to hold the pictures he'd taken of Cory and EmJay. The plastic album had proven tough enough to withstand her enthusiastic loving, which invariably involved chewing.

"I think that went rather well," Amanda said. She stood by his front window, holding a sleepy Mara and watching her husband and foster son walk Paula Simmons to her car.

"Especially since she hasn't seen her children for so long," Mitch agreed.

Amanda sighed. "Mara didn't even know who she was. I thought Paula would get upset for sure when she called me Mommy."

"She did sort of look upset for a minute." Mitch bent to gather the used paper plates from the coffee table. Knowing the situation wouldn't be easy, Amanda had opted for food to facilitate the awkward visit of her husband's cousin. "At least Kevin acted happy to see her, though he did seem nervous."

"I think he was worried that she was going to take him home." Amanda returned her gaze to the window, resting her cheek against Mara's dark head. "Paula looks good, don't you think? Blake whispered to me that he could tell she is still using drugs, but I can't tell. I—I feel torn about her recovery. I don't want to lose Kevin and Mara."

"She didn't say a word about taking them back, did she? And her friend seemed to think you were doing a great job with them."

Amanda sighed. "I know, I'm borrowing trouble." She let go of Mara with one hand and patted her stomach, which to Mitch seemed unbelievably large compared with the rest of her. "At least now I can have this baby without immediate worries."

Mitch shot her a quick glance. "Are you in labor?"

"I wish," she groaned. "I'm so sick of being pregnant. With my luck this little stinker will be late."

Mitch laughed. The new baby hadn't cooperated during the ultrasound, so Amanda wasn't sure if the baby was a boy or a girl, but Kevin had assured everyone it would be a little brother.

"They're coming in," Amanda went to the door, still carrying Mara. Her husband took the two-year-old from her as he entered. "Well?" Amanda asked.

Blake shook his head. "I didn't ask her about the possibility of adoption." He kept his voice low so Kevin didn't hear. "I kept feeling that she wouldn't take the news so well. Maybe we should let it go for a little while longer."

Amanda let out a long sigh. "I was thinking the same thing." She turned to Mitch. "Thanks so much for letting us use your house. We'll help you clean up and get out of your way."

"I distinctly remember you promising Kevin ice cream," Mitch said. "You'd better go before it gets too late. I don't need help cleaning up. Besides, Tyler and Savvy are here somewhere. I could put them to work."

"Okay," Amanda agreed, looking exhausted.

Blake smiled his thanks. "Now that this stress is over, I bet we'll have a baby here soon."

"Right now?" Kevin asked, his eyes growing big.

Blake rumpled his hair. "Not now. In a few days. Shall we get some ice cream?"

"Yes!" Kevin hopped to the door. "Bye, Uncle Mitch. See ya, EmJay!"

After they left, Mitch gathered the cups, napkins, and unused dishes and took them to the kitchen. EmJay toddled after him. The kitchen door was open, and Mitch heard low, intense voices coming from the patio. Avoiding the urge to eavesdrop, Mitch scooped up EmJay, stepped over his turtle, and banged the screen open. "Hi, guys!"

Tyler and Savvy were sitting in lawn chairs, their tense bodies angled to face each other. Both relaxed with his appearance, though it was clear he had interrupted something serious.

"Is she gone?" Savvy asked.

Mitch nodded. "And nothing bad happened. Poor Manda was so worried I thought she might deliver the baby in my living room." He grinned to show he was joking, but neither Savvy nor Tyler responded.

"I guess I'd better get going." Savvy stood and looked at Tyler. "Are you coming to church tomorrow to hear my talk?"

"I'll be there. But what about after? Can I see you?"

Savvy bit her bottom lip. "After church we're having a get-together for friends and relatives. I'd be glad for you to be there." She paused.

"But I'll be set apart as a missionary by then so I won't be able to go anywhere with you. We should say our good-byes now."

Mitch felt his heart ache at his brother's anguished expression. "Well, come here, then," Mitch said to Savvy. "I want a last hug." He hugged her with the arm that wasn't holding EmJay. "I know you'll be a great missionary. Don't forget to write."

"I won't," she said, beginning to tear up. "Just don't send me any animals, okay? I don't think they're allowed."

He chuckled. "I'll let you two say good-bye then. I'll be in the house, Tyler. I could use some help when you're through." Tyler nodded without glancing in his direction.

Mitch went inside, firmly shutting the door behind him. EmJay spied her book of pictures on the floor and struggled to get down. "That's Cory," he said, pointing to a picture.

"Cree," EmJay said, promptly sticking a corner of the plastic cover in her mouth. There were little bite marks on the plastic now as well, Mitch noticed. EmJay was cutting more teeth. He hoped that was why she wasn't sleeping well and not because she still missed Cory.

Where are you now? Mitch wondered. *Do you miss us as much as we miss you?* This reminded him to check his e-mail. Cory hadn't communicated with him yet, but he checked every day to be sure.

His computer had begun downloading e-mail when Tyler entered the room. "I can't believe she's really going." He slumped onto the couch and stared across the room at the wall.

Mitch cast him a sympathetic glance. "Did you at least tell her how you feel?"

"I told her my heart was breaking," he said quietly.

"And what did she say to that?"

He swallowed with apparent difficulty. "She said that I had already broken hers a long time ago." Tyler met Mitch's gaze. "I didn't know she felt like that. I didn't know it at all. I feel like an utter idiot."

"Just remember that when she comes home." Mitch didn't want to rub it in, but Tyler had been rather obtuse.

"I will," Tyler said fervently.

Mitch wondered if he really would wait for Savvy. Tyler was a popular guy, and he wasn't the type to sit home moping. What if he met someone else? It could happen. After all, everyone seemed to expect Mitch to find someone to replace Cory.

Replace her, he thought mockingly. *She was never mine.*

That was when he saw the e-mail, sandwiched so inconspicuously between two pieces of spam that he almost deleted it before he recognized the address. He sucked in a breath.

"What is it?" Tyler asked, coming to stand behind him.

They read the e-mail together. The words he'd hoped to see for so long leapt out at him from the screen. She was coming home! She wanted to be baptized!

"I'm going to Brazil," Mitch said, his heart beating faster at the words he imagined were behind each of Cory's brief sentences. Her job wasn't as important to her as EmJay. Maybe he was important to her, too. After all, she'd signed the e-mail "Love, Cory." That was good enough for him.

"Mom will never let you go alone," Tyler protested.

Mitch snorted. "I wasn't going to ask permission."

"What about work?"

"I was due to take vacation last week, but I couldn't face going anywhere. I'd been planning to go to Texas to see Lane and Ashley. So I think my boss will let me go now. Or I'll quit. Doesn't matter anyway. When I told them I wouldn't be taking the on-site job, they said they'd have to find someone else—someone who would take over my job as well. No matter how I look at it, my time there is limited. While I'm gone, Kerrianne can take care of the animals."

"Well, then, I'm going too." Tyler lifted his chin. "I'm the one who taught her the discussions, and I want to see her baptized."

"What about school?"

"Doesn't start for another week. Will that be enough time?"

"Enough to baptize her at least." Mitch proffered his hand. "Welcome aboard!"

"Thank you." Tyler shook his hand vigorously.

Mitch gave his brother a sheepish grin. "I have to admit that it'll make my life easier with Mom if you come along. I'll be eighty before she admits that I don't need a chaperone."

"When it comes to women, we all need chaperones." Tyler returned his grin before sobering abruptly. "Truthfully, with Savvy leaving, I could really use the distraction." His eyes went past Mitch to the screen. "Hey, there's an e-mail that says 'from Cory's agent' in the subject line. That would be Vikki, right? What are you talking to her about?"

Mitch shrugged. "I sent her my story of Meeko. The one you said was wonderful but would never work because *Curious George* already had cornered the monkey market. She asked for it. Really," he added when he saw his brother's doubt. "I wouldn't have sent it otherwise."

"Well, let's see what she wants." Tyler reached over to the arrow keys and pushed down to Vikki's e-mail.

What Mitch read left him almost as excited and flabbergasted as Cory's message.

With Meeko in his customary place on her shoulder, Cory walked into camp for the last time, feeling weary and yet content with her final pictures—though she hadn't yet finished all of *NG*'s requirements. The silhouette of the ocelot pausing before he drank, the fiery ball of the setting sun hovering behind him as if balanced on the river, would make an awe-inspiring photograph for readers all over the world. The only drawback was, of course, that she didn't have EmJay to share her success with. Or Mitch. Maybe when she went back, she'd tell him all about it.

Would he even care? Maybe he had no desire to hear about her adventures. Maybe he didn't want to share in any future adventures.

He'd let his fear stop him before; how could she be sure that he cared enough for her to overcome it now? Besides, her leaving Utah might have pushed him away forever.

Four days had passed since her experience with the sunrise, days in which she had not been idle. She had informed *National Geographic* of her decision to leave. After reviewing the extensive photographs she'd left with Vikki and the low resolution e-mail versions of her newer ones, they'd agreed to work with what she had. If they needed additional photographs, they would pick from a long list of talented photographers who would be eager to fill her place. Cory felt no bitterness at the thought. She loved wildlife photography, but she understood now that being at the top wouldn't deliver the happiness she craved. Only one thing had done that—a complete surety that she was a daughter of a loving God who had a plan for her happiness.

She was going home to settle things with Mitch and EmJay. Yes, she would come back to the Amazon. The lush jungle was hers again and would always be. Someday she would bring EmJay here, and together they would discover more of its treasures. As for Mitch, her thoughts of him always came to a barrier in her mind. She couldn't see beyond the moment with any clarity.

Hoping to slip by without attracting the attention of the others in camp, Cory angled away from the communal table, illuminated by gas lanterns. What she wanted now was her three-minute shower and a good night's sleep.

At that moment Cory saw him. She stopped short with an inaudible gasp. "Mitch!" Her mouth formed the words, but no sound emerged. Blinking, she pushed aside a lock of messy curls—one of many that had escaped the clip she'd used that morning.

It *was* Mitch. He was speaking Portuguese to several of the natives by the cooking fire, looking good in khakis and black boots, as though he were a part of the jungle. EmJay, wearing a blue jumper, was in his arms. Even from where she stood, Cory could see the blue-checked bow in her hair. Time seemed to freeze as she eagerly took in their beloved faces. Had she been crazy to leave? Yes. She knew that now. They belonged together. The fact that Mitch was here could mean only one thing. Or did it? She wouldn't put it past him to have come all this way for EmJay's sake.

Cory took a dozen steps toward them before letting her backpack fall to the ground, startling Meeko, who jumped from her shoulder and skittered into the jungle.

Mitch looked up and met her gaze. "Hi," he said, giving her that slow, familiar smile. "I heard you needed a translator. You know, to find a ward where you can be baptized."

At the sound of his voice, EmJay turned away from the fire and spied Cory. Her face cracked a wide smile, and her whole body lurched up and down as she struggled to get to Cory, alternately giggling and babbling something no one could begin to understand.

Mitch held onto her more tightly so she wouldn't fall. "I think she missed you."

Cory had drawn close enough to see the tears in his eyes. She reached for EmJay and hugged the baby to her fiercely. EmJay's arms went around her neck, and her head pressed against Cory's shoulder. "I'm sorry, EmJay," she whispered. "I should never have left you. I'll never leave again."

She wished she could explain to her how important it all had been and why she'd had to leave, but EmJay didn't care, and she obviously didn't hold grudges. There would be time for Cory to make it up to her later. *The rest of our lives,* she thought. Her tears rolled down her cheeks, falling into EmJay's hair that gleamed orange in the firelight.

"Thank you for bringing her," she said to Mitch. She could barely see him through her tears.

"I figured you might want to see her while you finish up your photo shoot."

"Today's my last day. I quit. I missed her too much."

"Well, you can finish, if you want. We can stay for a while."

And what about us? she wanted to ask. Now that their beliefs were no longer an obstacle, could he forgive her for everything she'd done? Could he begin to care for her the way she cared about him? Or was this visit only for EmJay?

"I can write anywhere, at least according to my agent." Mitch put his hands in his pockets and rocked back on his heels. "But Tyler has to get back before next week. Although if he misses the first week of school, I think he'll live."

Agent? she thought. *Is he serious?* Cory blinked, trying to clear the tears. Turning her head, she caught sight of Tyler sitting at the far end of the communal table with some of her colleagues. He lifted a hand in greeting. Too stunned to return the gesture, she faced Mitch. "Your agent?"

"Yeah, you're right. I guess I should have said *our* agent. You know, Vikki. She loved my story of Meeko with your pictures and has agreed to represent us. Book publishing is not exactly up her alley, but she assures me she has important contacts. She says my incredible text will sell even with your mediocre pictures. Or was it the other way around?" He grinned. "So what do you say? Partners?" He paused but rushed on again before she could speak. "I mean, after you finish this little gig here, of course. Then we can decide where we'll go next and for how long. Between photo shoots for the books, we'll go back to Utah and spend time in the mountains and with my family. You could even take more pictures for magazines, if you wanted to. And I was thinking, eventually we could try to do that children's video series about animals."

Suddenly Cory couldn't stop smiling. "You're crazy!"

"What?" He feigned surprise. "You don't want to be on TV? Well, I guess I can see why that might be a problem with all that orange hair—which I think is beautiful, by the way. No matter. We'll do something else. I always wanted to go to Africa." He paused briefly before rushing on. "But it could be China, Italy, or Timbuktu." He took a step toward her, his voice becoming husky. "Honestly, I don't care where I am as long as I'm with you and EmJay. I love you, Cory Steele, and I want to be with you forever." His face showed hope—and fear, too. He wasn't as sure of himself as his words indicated.

Cory stepped into his arms, lifting her face to his. "Me, too," she said, her voice soft. "I want that too." Their lips met and love suffused her entire being, reminding her how she'd felt during the sunrise when she'd first realized that God loved her.

Now Mitch did, too.

Oh, AshDee, you were right about everything! Cory thought. *Don't worry, we'll take good care of EmJay. Until you have her in your arms again.*

That was the last coherent thought she had as Meeko swung down from the trees overhead and landed on her head, tangling his tiny feet in her hair. On her hip, EmJay screamed in delight, "Bunny!"